The
TEN THOUSAND MILE THREAD

Her husband was leaving her for five years! How would she bear it?

His hand slid down her silk tunic. "I've thought about that day before I left for Canton. It's been on my mind quite a lot."

"Mine, too." Her stomach fluttered.

"I'm glad now we were interrupted."

"What?" She sat up quickly, her eyes wide with shock.

"It's for the best. I shouldn't have given way to unthinking passion."

Meichen rolled onto her stomach, beating the pillows with her hands. She kicked her feet in a paroxysm of fury and bit the quilt to stifle her screams. Chung put his hand on her shoulder and she angrily shook it off. "But you promised," she gasped out.

He sighed. "Think, Meichen. Is this really a good time?"

"It's not just because I want a son to please your mother," she said as she rolled onto her back. "What you did made me feel wonderful. I want to feel that way again."

Chung's eyebrows rose, then a smile slowly formed on his lips. He stretched out beside her. "It's possible for us to reach the peak without actually joining."

Meichen shivered with pleasure as he unbuttoned her jacket.

"For now," Chung soothed, "we'll have the Clouds without the Rain."

The
TEN THOUSAND
MILE THREAD

A Chinese-American Love Story

LINDA HARVILL STROTHER

HISTORY TO FICTION PUBLISHING

History to Fiction Publishing
308 Timberidge Drive
Augusta, GA 30907

Cover & book design: Robin Vuchninch, mycustombookcover.com
Author Photo: Mark Jenkins , My Studio Augusta, LLC

ISBN: 978-1-7346515-0-8 (paperback)
ISBN: 978-17346515-1-5 (ebook)

To Dr. Ed Cashin, who taught me that Augusta's history provides fascinating ideas for novels

AND

Jane Chow, who introduced me to Augusta's Chinese culture when she invited my family to her wedding banquet.

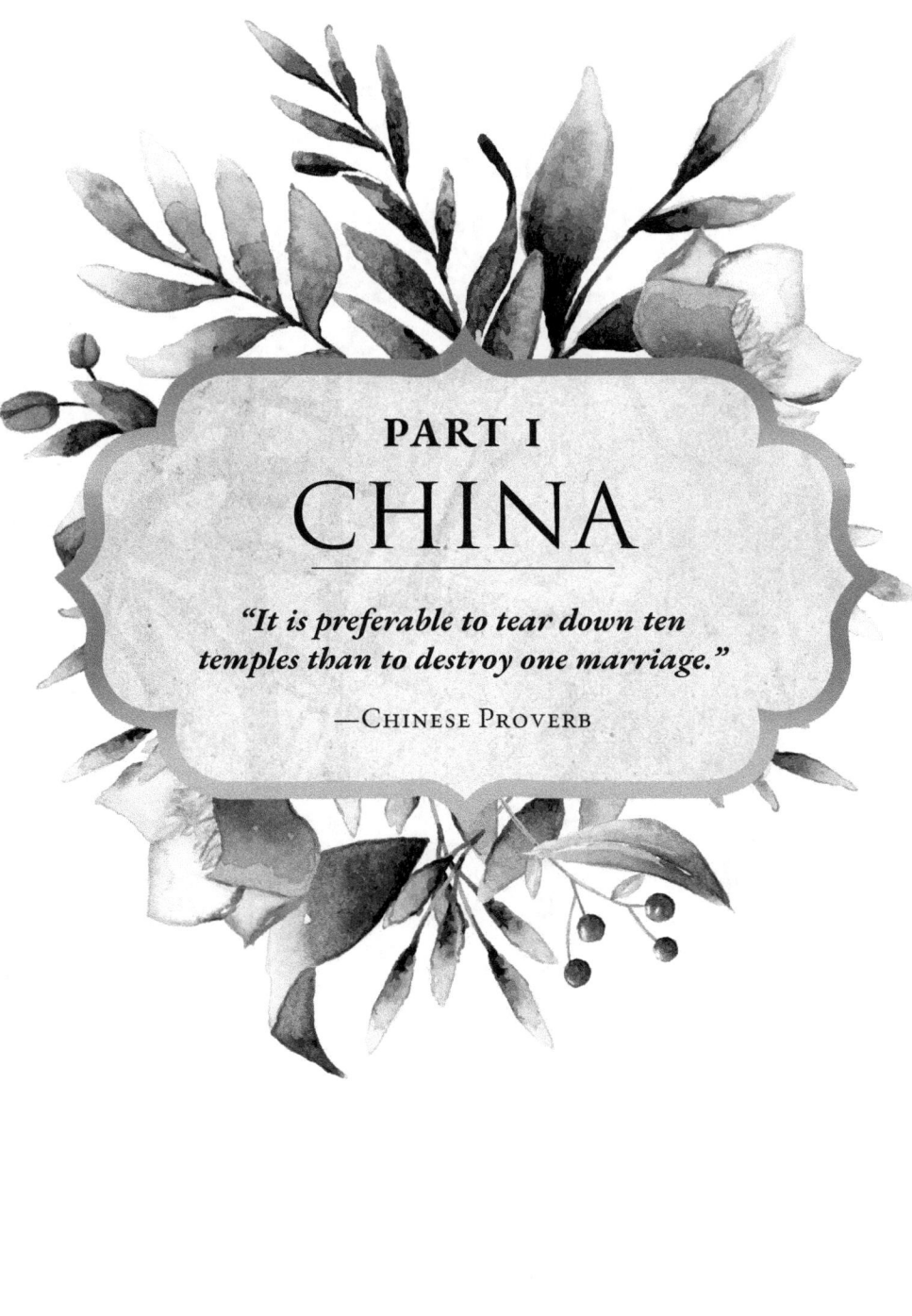

PART I
CHINA

"It is preferable to tear down ten temples than to destroy one marriage."

—CHINESE PROVERB

CHAPTER I

*"Out of ten matchmakers,
nine will lie."*

—CHINESE SAYING

Guangdong Province, Southern China, 1880

WITH HER HEART POUNDING, Wu Meichen crouched beneath the stairs that led to the upper story of the house. Outside, firecrackers and gongs silenced the din of the neighbors who stood at the Wu family's front gate. The bride stealers had come.

Thirteen-year-old Meichen shrank into the narrow space, concealed by her aunt's broad body. Her hand shook as she pulled her red veil over her face.

A stern voice shouted in the courtyard. "Bring out the bride."

"No. You can't have her," the neighborhood girls shrilled back.

"Don't take my niece away from her home." Her uncle blocked the front door.

Meichen heard the girls shriek and laugh, and her uncle's helpless bleats. Feet pounded on wood as the strangers burst into the house. Two of them shouted her name. They searched the ground floor, shoving furniture aside. The stairs over Meichen's head shook as a third man thundered upstairs.

The invaders approached the stairs, ordering her aunt to move aside. Meu Yuk wailed but gave way. Four arms reached into the alcove to seize Meichen. With the game over, she should go with them without protest, but her feet refused to move.

"Come out, Niece." Meu Yuk's cries turned into laughter. "Go to your husband."

The bride stealers led Meichen over the threshold as the crowd laughed and applauded. Mei Yuk smoothed Meichen's red silk tunic and skirt and straightened her veil. Her aunt put her hands on Meichen's shoulder and shoved her forward.

Impatient young women surged behind her, pushing her to the courtyard gate where an enclosed sedan chair waited. Through the veil, she saw the outlines of two servants who stood ready to lift the poles.

Meichen lifted her veil enough to see the eye-catching litter the groom's family had sent to take her to their house. The palanquin glowed red, the lucky color, with silk fringe and red streamers lining the curved roof. Gold symbols for happiness decorated three panels with one side open. Meichen sat and her aunt pulled a red silk curtain shut. The bearers raised the poles and jogged forward followed by the "kidnappers," who included the groom, Chao Chung. Her aunt and uncle boarded a horse-drawn cart hired for the occasion.

Meichen wished she dared open the curtain and look at them. But even a quick peek might bring bad luck, and she needed all the luck the gods would send her.

Fate made Meichen female, an automatic second-class citizen. She never knew her father, her mother died when she was ten, and she became a servant in her Wu uncle's house when he adopted her. Her brother, Ling Mo, who shielded her from her aunt's anger, had run away to America. Her husband was her only prospect for a happy life.

She longed for respect, kindness, maybe even love. Her aunt laughed at her dreams. A wife, she told Meichen, had only one purpose in life, to bear sons. If she did her duty, she would please her husband and his family.

The bridal party passed through the dusty streets of her neighborhood into the village market where the shoppers made a narrow passageway for the parade. They waved and shouted good luck slogans to the couple. The pungent smell of fish and animal manure mingled with the odor of dozens of people. They pushed against the palanquin, rocking it like a cradle.

With the market behind them, Meichen tipped backward. Impatient with the heat trapped behind her heavy veil, Meichen flipped it off her face She opened the curtain just enough to see outside. Her curiosity to see her new home overcame her fear of evil spirits.

The bearers panted as they jogged uphill, passing houses where wealthy people lived. The journey ended as the bearers stopped inside the walls of the Chao compound. She studied her new home as well as she could with her limited view.

The Chao family house formed a large square, the doors decorated with red paint and the green roof ornamented with up-tilted eaves. Meichen saw a stone courtyard lined with plants. Sunlight glinted on goldfish darting in and out of lotus blossoms in a small pond. She counted seven doors that opened onto the courtyard. Her brother had described the Chao family's opulent home. She'd never imagined she would live in such a house.

Meu Yuk fumed when she opened the curtain halfway and saw Meichen's uncovered face. "Why do you invite bad luck?" She snatched the veil back down. "No one should see you until the groom removes the veil."

Meichen fanned herself as she sat in the palanquin waiting for the ceremony to begin. "Why must I wait so long?" She spoke at a low volume so only her aunt could hear.

"The groom has to wash and put on his wedding clothes." Meu Yuk put her mouth against Meichen's ear. "Keep your feet together with the toes pointed when you step from the palanquin. They'll look smaller."

A middle-aged lady came out to help Meichen step from the chair and lead her inside the house. Meichen appreciated the help: the veil hiding her face blocked her vision. She clutched her guide's arm, afraid she'd trip. Inside the house, she heard the muted comments of her husband's family in the main hall.

At last the groom arrived and all the relatives took their places. Chao Chung stepped forward and removed the veil that concealed his bride's face. They studied each other discreetly. Meichen hid her smile behind her fan. *He's tall and well-shaped. Nothing like his father with shoulders hunched from studying. And his face is friendly, not sour, or contemptuous.*

Raising her head, she glanced at her groom's parents. *I'm glad Scholar Chao looks so kind. But Madam Chao's smile looks more like a dog baring its teeth. She's looking at my wedding clothes. Perhaps she thinks there's too much embroidery on them. She thinks I'm vain. Oh, no, she's seen my feet. Surely her husband told her they're not bound.*

She followed Chao Chung to the family altar. Together they chanted a blessing to the sky and earth. They bowed before the altar dedicated to the Chao ancestors and the kitchen god who kept watch over the family. Meichen filled delicate cups with steaming tea which she served first to Scholar and Madam Chao and then to her aunt and uncle. A local official spoke the appropriate words. She and Chung faced each other and bowed. With the wedding rituals concluded, she was officially Chao Chung's wife.

The crowning event of the wedding was a great banquet with nine courses. Many of them were expensive delicacies believed to promote happiness, wealth, and fertility. Meichen gazed with longing at the suckling pig, shark fin soup, sea bass, and whole crackling fried chicken.

She was seated in a chair on a low dais, on display for any guest who wanted to take a close look at the bride. After two hours sitting as still as a mannequin, her back ached. But if she slumped the least little bit, Madam Chao directed a stern look at Meichen.

The men downed wine and more potent beverages. They pressed into a circle around Chung, boomed out bursts of laughter, and slapped each other's shoulders. The women whispered and giggled, speculating what the men were saying.

She tried to ignore the women's jests, humiliated to be the focus of all their ribald comments. Her aunt's description of marital intimacy had done nothing to reassure her. All the teasing convinced her she was facing a night of horror.

She prayed the banquet would end soon before she collapsed. As her endurance gave out, Scholar Chao called the newlyweds to his side. The guests shouted toasts to the bride and groom, wishing the couple long lives and many sons. Chung edged out of the banquet hall and led her to his chamber. A few persistent guests followed, most of them rowdy young men. Chung motioned for Meichen to sit next to him on the bed. She nodded at each visitor as Chung encouraged them to leave.

One young man stopped in front of them, rocking perilously as he balanced himself. He exhaled whiskey fumes as he leaned over the newlyweds. "Chao Chung, I hope you didn't drink too much tonight. You don't want your jade stalk to wilt."

Chung laughed. Meichen pretended not to hear. She studied her hands as she pondered the visitor's words. *I know the stalk is a man part. But can it really wilt like a dead flower?*

Chung's older brother sent the remaining men back to the banquet and closed the door. They were alone. He stared at her and she raised her fan to cover her trembling lips.

"Do you know what we'll do tonight?" he asked.

Meichen's eyes widened. "I thought you would know. Aunt Meu Yuk said all I had to do was lie still, even when it hurts, and let you put your hands and mouth – and that other part – wherever you please. Is that wrong?"

Meichen's heart drummed harder as Chung tapped the knuckles of both fists together and rolled his eyes upward.

"And that's all she told you?" His brow furrowed.

Her stomach tightened as thoughts floundered in her brain. She blurted out Meu Yuk's final advice for the wedding night. "My aunt said men always know what to do because they learn at flower houses. Haven't you been to one?"

He cleared his throat before he answered. "A flower house is not the best place to practice for a wedding night." He stood, turning his back to her. "We should prepare for bed. Do you need my help, or should we ask for a maid?"

"No!" Every nerve inside her shrieked in alarm. "Thank you, Husband, I can manage."

She saw an alcove with a dressing table to the left of the bed. Meichen removed her clothes, jewelry, and the large combs that held her bun in place. Her hair fell down her back and she brushed it smooth. She saw a cloth and a water bowl and debated whether to clean her face or leave on her makeup.

Her aunt had advised her to shed her clothes quickly and hide beneath the covers before Chung saw her nude. Meichen heard him on the opposite side of the room as he doused lanterns. She jerked her breast cover over her head and took advantage of the darkness to leap across the mattress and dive underneath the quilt. Her elbow clunked against the back wall of the enclosed bed.

"Are you all right?" Chung asked. "I don't mind if you sleep on the open side."

"Forgive my clumsiness, Husband. I'm comfortable here beside the wall." She gasped to recover her breath.

"You can move toward the center. I won't occupy the entire mattress."

She slid an inch or two away from the wall.

Chung adjusted the oil lamp beside him until the room was almost dark. Meichen looked away as his night robe dropped to the floor. Then the bed dipped as he settled next to her. She shivered as he turned her face toward him.

"Ling Mo never told me he had such an exquisite sister." He ran his finger along her cheek bone. "I wonder how you look with all that paint off your face."

"I'll take it off." She spoke without thinking, then froze. A bowl of water sat on a table beside Chung. How could she wash her face without exposing her naked body?

"No, let me." Chung took the cloth and water on the bedside table and washed the powder and rouge away. "That's better. Whoever did your makeup has a heavy hand."

"My aunt put it on. I'm sorry you're displeased."

"I didn't say I was displeased. But I like you better like this." His nose skimmed her neck. "Your perfume smells sweet and light. At least in that your aunt chose well."

Meichen recalled her apprehension when her aunt had dabbed perfume between her breasts and her upper thighs. Would he sniff those places, too?

She held her breath as his hand slipped under the quilt. His fingers stroked her shoulders and slid down her arms, continuing past the outline of her hips and thighs. He sat up and balanced on his knees, shoving the lower fourth of the quilt aside. Her upper body remained covered as his smooth hands massaged her ankles. He placed a foot in his palm, stroking the arch with a feathery touch. The other foot received equal attention.

Meichen sighed as her muscles unclenched. *The Matchmaker was right. My large feet don't disgust him.* Chung lifted the quilt and ploughed underneath it, his head emerging beside her shoulders. He pulled her close, and his hand brushed over the small buds on her chest. He stopped, gave a grunt of surprise, and fondled her breasts. Then, without warning, his hand thrust between her thighs.

"What are you doing?" Meichen squeaked, forgetting what she'd been told to do, shocked by the intimate invasion.

"I'm making sure you're a girl, since your chest is as flat as mine."

Meichen cringed as Chung flung the quilt back and stood beside the bed with his back turned to her. He snatched his robe up to cover his body, then turned to pierce her with a furious glare. "How old are you, Ling Mo's sister? You can't be sixteen."

Terror gripped her. Everything was going wrong. She recalled her aunt's final command. "Remember, you are sixteen. Don't admit to anything else."

"Answer me!" He kept his voice low but stern.

What should I say? What will he do if I lie to him? Oh, Aunt, why did you get me in this mess?

She should deny his charge, but she couldn't speak. Her insides shook like congealed pork jelly.

"I'm waiting." He folded his arms across his chest.

"I'll be fourteen this New Year." Her head was bowed so low her words were hardly audible.

"Do you have your monthly visitor yet?"

"Yes, since last year." Her cheeks burned.

"Why did your uncle allow you to marry so young? And why did he lie about your age?"

Meichen spoke in breathy gasps. "My aunt wanted the marriage... because your family is rich. She gave the matchmaker...and the fortune teller... the wrong birth date." Meichen covered her face and sobbed. "Please... don't tell your honorable parents.... If they send me back home...my aunt will sell me to a flower house."

Chung struck his forehead with his hand. "I've told my father he needs spectacles. He saw you when he visited your uncle's house and never noticed you were still a child."

Meichen bristled. "I'm *not* a child" She took a deep breath. "I can do what's required of a wife."

His hands dropped to his sides, but he still frowned at her. His expression made her think he was more puzzled than angry, like a man who held an object and didn't know what to do with it.

"Husband, it's true that I'm young, but you're only eighteen. Our ages aren't so far apart."

Chung glared at her. "But you don't understand. Your brother is my friend. What will he think when he finds out I've taken his thirteen-year-old sister into my bed? I can't do it."

Meichen rose to her knees. "Do you think Ling Mo would want me to be a prostitute? If you send me away, no one will believe I'm still a virgin." She sniffled and a few tears escaped. "I'll have nowhere else to go. And the owner won't care how young I am."

"I must wake my father and ask him what to do." Chung walked toward the door with Meichen sprinting after him.

"No, please!" She grabbed his arm as he touched the knob. "I'll be disgraced, and so will my family."

His eyes flashed as he pulled his arm loose. "And don't you think people will laugh at my parents?"

"That's why we must keep this to ourselves."

Chung turned to face her. "But you can't be my wife. I'm not a jaded Mandarin who seduces young girls. I won't touch you until you're sixteen."

"In two and a half years I'll be sixteen. That's not so long."

"Maybe not for you. I didn't plan to be celibate for the next three years." Chung paced the room. He saw her robe and tossed it to her. "Cover yourself."

Meichen looked down and gasped. She'd forgotten she was naked. She rammed her arms in the sleeves and pulled the sash tight.

Chung slumped into a chair, pursing his lips, lost in his own thoughts. Meichen sat on the edge of the bed waiting for him to speak. Or move. Or go to bed. Or do something. He couldn't ignore her all night. She needed to know what the morning would bring.

He leaned forward, resting his elbows on his thighs as his hands gripped each other. "My father was right. I acted without thought when I gave Ling Mo money to go to America. You needed him to protect you from your aunt. Now it's my duty to take responsibility for you."

Meichen's shoulders drooped. "Your father arranged our marriage to punish you?"

"That's what he said. When he visited your uncle to tell him where Ling Mo had gone, he saw your aunt slap you when you did nothing wrong."

"Then you didn't want me because of my feet?" Meichen's spirit sank even lower.

"Your feet?" Chung's brow wrinkled.

"The matchmaker told my aunt you don't like bound feet. She said that's why your father chose me for your wife."

"Oh, that's true," he said. "I think the custom is ridiculous and cruel. How can China become a modern country if half its citizens are illiterate and crippled?"

Meichen moved to a stool close to his chair. "Chao Chung, my brother will understand if you write a letter to explain what my aunt did. He knows how she is."

"I still can't take you as a wife. It goes against my beliefs. You're far too young."

"I'll get older," Meichen reminded him. "Until then we can pretend we're married."

"And I'll get very frustrated." He exhaled as though he was dragging air up from the soles of his feet. "I'll have to buy you a long nightgown like the missionary ladies wear. It comes up to the top of your neck and covers your arms, and it's white. That should be ugly enough to cool my desire."

"It doesn't sound comfortable." A hint of rebellion flickered over her face.

"I won't be comfortable if you don't wear it." Chung's frown warned her that argument would not help. "Until I find you a gown, we'll sleep in our robes."

They returned to bed and settled under the quilt. Meichen pursed her lips "Husband, how do you know what missionary ladies wear in their beds?"

"Oh ho, I have a jealous wife." He chuckled. "If you must know, I saw them in an English shop in Canton. My professor had to tell me they were night dresses. I thought they were burial shrouds."

They lay side by side in silence until Meichen spoke again, her voice meek. "Do you think we'll have an unlucky marriage because my aunt lied about my birthdate?"

Chung sat up, resting one elbow on the bed to support his weight. "One thing we must have straight between us. I don't believe in those old superstitions. We followed the wedding traditions to please my parents. There's no such thing as an evil spirit so I'm not afraid of them. Neither your birthdate nor mine has anything to do with our future. It's the evil action of your aunt that's caused a problem."

His frown disappeared as Meichen relaxed her muscles and sank into the mattress. He reached over and stroked her hair. "Now go to sleep. We must get up before dawn to visit the ancestors' tombs."

"Husband," she whispered, "thank you for keeping my secret."

He turned on his side with his back toward her. "Let's hope no one else finds out."

CHAPTER 2

"To move a tree might kill it; to move people may give them new life."

—CHINESE PROVERB

CHUNG WOKE MEICHEN before sunrise when his head pressed against her neck. They had fallen asleep with a proper distance between them, but during the night Chung had rolled against her. Her arm was pinned down by his chest. With her free hand, she shoved his head. When he didn't move, she braced her feet against the back wall of the enclosed bed and dug her knees into his kidneys. He snorted and flopped onto his stomach.

Meichen sighed and straightened her cramped limbs. *Is this what married life is like? I want to make my husband happy, but it's unreasonable for me to sleep squashed against a hard wall so he can be comfortable.*

She glared at the back of his head and considered how she could wake him without being blamed. Before she could decide, the maid took the matter out of her hands.

"Master, Missy, are you awake? The sun is almost up," high-pitched words called outside the door.

Chung groaned as he sat up to light the oil lamp. "How I hate that woman's voice."

"Wait," Meichen cried. She jerked the quilt up to her neck and pulled hair across her face. "I don't want her to see me without makeup."

The maid knocked, intruding again. "I brought tea."

"Leave it," Chung snapped. He stood and extended his arms over his head. He froze when he heard Meichen gasp. He watched her fingers cover her parted lips. Her eyes opened wide as she stared at Chung, her eyes focused on the middle of his body. His robe had lost its sash, and his vigorous stretching had pulled the sides apart.

Meichen examined him with avid curiosity. His brown-gold chest was not muscular, but neither was it thin. Her gaze swept past his narrow waist and hips to the organ jutting out from his pelvis. Chung snatched the robe closed and turned his back.

She could not speak as her mind grappled with what she'd seen. The Jade Stalk. It was like what little boys had. And yet it was amazingly different. That's what she'd missed last night.

Chung didn't look at Meichen as he searched underneath the quilt for his sash. When his robe concealed him, he opened the door to get the tea tray. Meichen heard the maid in the hall giggling with another servant about the newlyweds still making the "clouds and rain."

Chung slammed the door shut with his foot and set the tray on a table, rattling the pot and cups. Meichen wondered who'd upset him the most – the gossiping maid or the bride who didn't avert her eyes when she should.

He took a cup of tea to Meichen without speaking. The window to the courtyard showed grey shadows with just a blur of light in the sky. Chung stared through the carved wooden screen as he sipped his tea. Meichen wished she could read his thoughts. If he still brooded over her rudeness, she should apologize. But he could be meditating to soothe his soul and cleanse his mind for the ceremony to come. She should do the same.

He left the window, set down his cup, and took clean clothes from a cabinet. With his back to her, he threw the robe aside and lifted his leg to step into trousers. All spiritual thoughts vanished as Meichen's gaze fastened on his buttocks. Her heart swelled with pride. *My husband is a well-formed man. I'm a lucky woman.* She smiled and looked down into her empty cup, just a second before he turned and caught her staring again.

"Wife, do you need the maid to help you dress?"

"I can dress myself, but I don't know how to make up my face."

"I'll be back shortly," he said. "Then I'll see what I can do."

"Do you know how to paint a lady's face?"

"I haven't tried that," he admitted, "but I've practiced calligraphy for years. I have a steady hand, at least."

He left, and Meichen rushed to the chamber pot. He was kind to leave and give her privacy. She regretted her own lack of consideration for him. Her reaction to his exposed body had been childish, but he already considered her a child and she had proven he was right. She would have to curb her impulsive behavior to win his respect.

She dressed in the long peacock blue jacket and skirt her aunt had picked for this special day – the first she would spend with her new family. Meichen opened the makeup case her aunt had sent with her trousseau. Staring at the different sized brushes, she tried to match them with pots of creams and powders. She managed to apply the rice powder in an even layer, but her hands formed crooked lines on her brows and lips. She wiped off the paint in despair and resigned herself to wait for Chung.

He returned with fruit and more tea. "I thought you might be hungry." He frowned as he looked at her. "Oh, Meichen, you've made a mess of your jacket."

She looked down and saw the fine silk speckled with white powder. Her eyes widened in alarm "What will your honorable mother think of me?"

"'Take it off," Chung said.

Meichen unbuttoned her jacket and gave it to him. She crossed her arms over the thin halter that hid her chest.

Chung searched through a box and removed a horsehair brush. "I bought this in Canton to keep lint off my Western suits," he explained.

He stroked the bright silk gently until the powder disappeared. "I think it works best if you paint and powder before you put on your jacket."

"Oh." Meichen now remembered her aunt had applied the makeup first.

Chung tilted her face up and studied the almond-shaped eyes and delicate cheekbones. Cupping her chin firmly in his left hand, he dipped a brush in a pot and made two graceful arches of her eyebrows. He stroked pale pink in the hollow of her cheekbones and a dark red over her lips. They opened as the brush caressed them.

Meichen smiled when he handed her a mirror. "It's beautiful. You truly are an artist, husband."

He washed the paint from the brushes while she struggled to twist her hair into a proper bun. It escaped before she could pin it in place. She pushed her tongue through her lips as she prepared to start over.

"Stop doing that." Chung took the brush from her hand. "Let me do it before you smear the paint on your lips." He plaited her long hair into a loose braid and wound it in circles, securing it to the back of her head with combs and hairpins.

"You need a maid of your own," he said, "but not that one outside. She's nosy and gossips too much." He frowned. "We need a young girl, loyal to you, who won't carry tales to my mother."

"Will your mother agree to give me my own maid?"

Chung smiled. "Don't worry, I'll find a way." He examined Meichen with a critical eye. "Now you look like a proper matron. We must go. The sun is rising."

...

After Meichen and Chung visited his ancestors' tombs, the couple returned home for the first meal of the day. Meichen stood before the Chao family like a recruit on inspection. Chung hovered near, ready to intervene if Meichen's nerves overcame her. She had met some of the family at the banquet, but all the names escaped her memory. Chung's father was kind enough to introduce her once again.

He smiled, which made up for the stern expression on Madam Chao's face. Meichen's mother-in-law did unbend enough to compliment her on her outfit but then relapsed into silence. Chung's older brother held up his small son to Meichen. She patted the child's round cheeks and exchanged smiles with his mother, who bulged with another pregnancy. Chung's younger brother first scrutinized her, and then Chung. What he looked for she didn't know, but she imagined the adolescent boy wondered if Chung's wedding night was successful.

If he knew what really happened, he would be very disappointed.

Seven-year-old Ching Lan giggled when the scholar lifted her in his arms, so her face was level with Meichen's. The girl's feet had not been bound, a process that normally began when a girl was five or six.

"This is my nephew." Scholar Chao motioned to a chubby young man. "He is the son of my second brother, Cho, who's in America. And this lady is Cho's wife, my sister-in-law, Jiao."

Meichen recognized Jiao as the woman who'd helped her from the palanquin on the previous day. The plump little woman's eyes travelled over the details of Meichen's face and clothes. She nodded her approval of Chung's bride.

"Your maid did an excellent job with your makeup," Jiao said. "I never expected such skill from a country girl."

"My husband did it all," Meichen blurted. Then she realized Chung might want to keep that fact private.

The youngest brother grinned, and Madam Chao gasped. "My son did this?"

Meichen peeked at Chung to see if he was angry. His expression was tranquil except for a glint in his eyes. "Mother, the maid wasn't there when my wife dressed."

"I will speak to her."

"I don't think she could have done makeup properly anyhow. Not like a lady's maid." Chung sniffed. "As Aunt said, that girl is ignorant and clumsy."

"You could give her lessons," his younger brother said.

Chung snorted. "That bumpkin could never approach my skill with a brush. Mother, if it pleases you, I'd like Meichen to have a competent maid. You could buy a young girl for a small price, and your maid could train her."

Madam Chao pursed her lips. "I'll talk to your father about it."

"No, don't get me involved." The scholar held up his hands. "Buy the maid. She can be a gift to our new daughter."

Chung touched Meichen's arm to make her look at him. He raised his eyebrows and flashed her an arrogant smile. "See how easy it was?" he whispered.

Meichen sat between Ching Lan and the eldest brother's wife when the ladies sat to eat. She complimented her mother-in-law's excellent food and delicate porcelain bowls. Madam Chao presented her with a set of lacquered wooden chopsticks in a case painted with butterflies. Meichen accepted them with proper appreciation, but Chung's mother remained aloof.

At first the atmosphere seemed serene and Meichen relaxed, enjoying the food and the quiet conversation. It was so different from the meals at her uncle's house, where Aunt Meu Yuk had ruined everyone's appetite with constant carping and complaints. Her uncle and Ling Mo had escaped as soon as possible, which left Meichen trapped in the kitchen to clean up while her aunt sat and moaned about the pain of her bound feet.

Eventually, Meichen sensed an undercurrent of tension between Madam Chao and Aunt Jiao. Madam Chao was the head woman of the house, but Jiao's voice betrayed scorn as she and Madam Chao discussed the food.

"I see it's not an appropriate time for melon." Jiao punched the fruit with her chopstick. "See how mushy it is."

"I'm sorry it's not to your taste." Madam Chao's eyes focused on her food.

"Tomorrow, let's have pineapple." Jiao spoke in a sugar-sweet tone.

"Perhaps, if it's not too expensive." A tic started at the corner of Madam Chao's mouth.

"Think, Sister, what is money for if not to bring comfort to our lives?" Jiao looked at her nieces, inviting them to agree with her. All three kept their eyes on their bowls.

"It's wrong to spend money if it's unnecessary." A dumpling fell off Madam Chao's chopstick. She impaled it as though it was alive and had to be killed.

"Well, perhaps I'll send my maid to buy some just for me. I can pay for it out of my allowance." Jiao set her chopsticks down. "Do you like pineapple, Meichen?"

"I've never tasted it, Aunt."

"Truly? How odd. Come to my room tomorrow, and I'll give you some."

Meichen hesitated, afraid to offend her mother-in-law if she appeared to side with Jiao. But Madam Chao reassured her.

"Yes, go eat with Aunt Jiao tomorrow, Meichen. You should get acquainted since your husband will join hers to work in his American store."

Meichen froze with her chopsticks midway to her mouth. *No one told me my husband will go overseas. How long will it be until he leaves, and how long will he be gone?*

She forced all expression from her face though inside her heart pounded. The food she'd just eaten sat in her stomach like a stone.

That evening Chung and Meichen retired early. Scholar Chao winked at his son as they left. "Oh, to be a young man again."

Meichen kept her eyes on the floor, followed by the laughter of Chung's brothers. It had been her request to go to bed. She was exhausted after rising at dawn and wrung out by the tension of the day. She'd waited hours for a chance to talk to Chung, to ask him about America, but they'd never been alone. Her body prickled with apprehension.

The minute she reached Chung's room, she sat on the bed and fumbled with the cloisonné buttons on her jacket. In her impatience, she pulled one off and it skidded across the rug. She saw no spot of blue in the elaborate pattern of threads. Meichen sank to her knees and patted the area around her.

Chung watched her crawl across the floor. "What's wrong?"

"I've lost a button. My jacket will be ruined if I can't find it."

Chung knelt beside her and raked his hand across the carpet without success. "Don't worry about it. Tomorrow I'll order the maid to find it." He grinned. "She likes to paw through my things when she cleans the room. This will be the perfect task for her."

Meichen tried to laugh but sniffled instead. He studied her downcast face and helped her off the floor. He sat beside her as she crawled onto the mattress and pressed her hands over her eyes.

"You can't be weeping over a lost button, Meichen. Tell me what's wrong."

She wiped her cheeks with the palm of her hand. "Your mother says you'll go to America."

"Not for a long time yet. I've got five years before I leave."

"I don't want you to go." She twisted her hands together. "What will I do after you leave?"

"It can't be helped. Second Uncle owns this house and he sends money for his family to live well. He's always planned for me to go to America and help run his store. That's why my father sent me to a Christian school, so I could learn to read and write English."

"But why must *you* go? What about your brothers?"

Chung shrugged. "My older brother studies for the Imperial examinations. My uncles chose me to go overseas and support my parents and brothers. No one's decided yet what my younger brother will do. It depends on circumstances in the future."

"I don't want to live here without you." She swallowed past the painful lump in her throat. *Why can't he understand how I feel? Does he care so little for me that it doesn't matter whether I'm with him or not?*

"In five years, you'll be comfortable in this family, and you'll have a child to love you. You'll be busy, and probably glad to have me out of your way." Chung pulled his legs onto the bed and propped his back against a pillow.

"How can I be content when every day takes us closer to the time you leave? And I can't possibly have a baby if you won't touch me for years." Her lower lip stuck out in stubborn defiance.

He laughed at her childish pout. "We'll have time."

She left the bed and went to the dressing table. She removed the combs and pins from her hair with a sigh of relief. For the last few hours of the day they'd been digging into her scalp. The heavy earrings were next to go. She heard Chung leave the bed when she removed her jacket. He was covered by his robe when he returned from his dressing area.

He sat in his chair watching her while she washed off her makeup and brushed her hair. "My father is pleased with you, Meichen. He said we appear to be in perfect harmony. He's proud he chose so well when he picked you for my wife."

"If he only knew the truth, what would he think?"

"I had my chance to tell him when he asked if everything went well last night. But I kept my promise to you. I just said I was satisfied and grateful that he chose you."

She left the dressing table and stood beside the bed with her head bowed. "Thank you, Husband. I don't deserve such kindness."

"I didn't do it just for you. It would upset everyone, and my father prizes tranquillity above all things."

"Your father is a superior person. He had no reason to care about me, yet he went to great trouble to give me a better life and a good husband."

Chung raised his eyebrows. "You've only been here two days. I may be a terrible husband. What if I drink too much wine and beat you?"

"If you were that kind of person, my brother wouldn't be your friend."

"But if you misbehaved, he might agree I should punish you."

Meichen's mouth fell open and she searched her mind for any transgressions she'd committed. At once she remembered one. "I'm sorry I told everyone you painted my face. You must be angry with me."

"No, I'm not. I told you, I'm proud of my painting. Look." He gestured toward the scrolls on the walls. "All these are mine."

22

Meichen admired the elegant calligraphy and pastel sketches. "I like that one with the birds flying over the river. What do the words say?"

"Can't you read? Ling Mo said he would teach you."

"He wanted to, but Aunt said we couldn't afford ink and brushes and paper for me. She said a girl didn't need to read and write."

Chung scowled. "Foolish, ignorant woman."

"Ling Mo did what he could. He brought his papers home from school, and I traced the characters with a wet brush. I learned a little, but there are so many characters and words, and I couldn't stay awake at the end of the day when Aunt finally let me go to my room. I wasn't an attentive student."

"I'll read the scroll for you. The poet Tu Fu wrote it over a thousand years ago.

> A pair of golden orioles sings in the bright green willows.
> A line of white egrets creases the clear blue sky.
> The window frames the western mountains,
> white with the snows of a thousand years.
> Anchored to the pilings are boats from Eastern Wu,
> three thousand miles from home."

They were both silent as Meichen absorbed the words.

"It's exquisite," she said. "I can hear the moving water in my mind."

Chung nodded. "I'm pleased you appreciate a great poet."

"Will you read the other scrolls?"

"Not tonight." He yawned. "We're tired, and poetry must be savored."

"Chung, would you teach me to read and write? I want to send Ling Mo a letter."

"I'll write one tomorrow. I want Ling Mo to know the truth before he hears about the marriage from your uncle and misunderstands our situation."

"I know you can write for me, but I'd like to learn how to do it myself."

"It takes many years to learn calligraphy and all the characters. But I'll teach you how to write your name, so you can add your signature to mine." He quenched the lamp beside their bed. "I think I'll enjoy teaching." He patted her hand. "It will give me something to do for the next one thousand nights."

CHAPTER 3

"When you drink water, don't forget those who dug the well."

—CHINESE PROVERB

IT RAINED THE NEXT MORNING. By the time the sky cleared at noon, Meichen left the house to enjoy the fresh breeze in the courtyard. She heard a high-pitched hum and realized she wasn't alone. Chung's little sister sat on the edge of the lily pond peering into the water.

Ching Lan's round face beamed. "See the tadpoles?" She wiggled her bare feet in the water. "They'll be frogs soon."

"Do you like frogs?" Meichen returned her smile.

"Not really, but I like to watch the tadpoles change into frogs."

The clear water in the pool enticed Meichen to join Ching Lan. She took off her shoes and socks, pulled up her skirt, and settled on the stone verge. She plunged her feet in the water, giving a sigh of contentment as it crept between her toes. Ching Lan slid her foot next to Meichen's and compared them.

The girl frowned. "Do you think my feet will grow large as yours? They look three times the length of my mother's."

"Your mother's feet were broken and wrapped. They couldn't grow to normal size."

"I'm glad she left my feet alone. My friends cry and moan all the time about how much their bindings hurt. It's no fun to visit them. They can't play chase or hide and seek anymore, we just sit and paint or sew." She sighed. "My mother says when I am grown, the other girls will laugh at my big feet, and I won't find a husband."

"Why didn't your mother bind your feet if she felt so strongly about it?"

"I'm not sure, but I know Chung had something to do with it. He argued with my parents until my father agreed with him. My mother yelled and then she cried, but she couldn't go against my father." Ching Lan grinned. "Second Brother is very disobedient, but he always gets away with everything."

"Does he?" Meichen waited, hoping the girl would say more. Ching Lan obliged.

"When he took money from Father's strongbox to help your brother run away, my father shook with terrible anger. I thought Father would beat him. But nothing happened."

Oh, something happened all right. His father saddled him with me.

Ching Lan flipped her feet as the tadpoles darted. "Why are *your* feet unbound?"

"I grew up in a village where people like girls to have natural feet, as the gods intended."

"Your mother was a Hakka," Ching Lan stated. "But your father was Cantonese."

"How do you know that?" Meichen gaped at the girl.

"Oh, I hear things. My parents had a big fight about Chung's marriage. My mother hates Hakkas, and she didn't want you in our family."

"And why are Hakkas so terrible?"

"Mother says they're inferior people who live in round houses and talk a funny language. And the women learn to fight just like men." She looked hopefully at Meichen. "Did you learn to fight? It would be lots more fun than embroidery."

Meichen sighed. "I left my mother's Hakka relatives when she died, and I never saw them again. I wish I could have stayed with them."

"Why would you want to work in the sun all day like a peasant? Mother says Hakka women age early, they wrinkle and turn dark, and they have big muscles because they work so hard. That sounds like a terrible life."

"Hakka women do work hard, but they are brave and determined. And best of all they're free. They aren't kept prisoners in their own homes like Cantonese women."

"My mother said your parents were criminals and traitors."

"Criminals!" Meichen sucked in her breath and pressed her lips together to silence a disrespectful remark about her mother-in-law.

"They fought the emperor," Ching Lan explained. "That's the worst disobedience there is."

"My parents weren't the only *Tai Ping*. Millions of people fought beside them. They wanted the Manchu emperor to fall so they could have a Chinese ruler."

Ching Lan avoided Meichen's eyes, and Meichen realized she'd frightened the girl with her angry outburst. She touched Ching Lan's shoulder, taking a deep breath to calm herself. "What else did your mother say?"

"I don't know. That's when Aunt Jiao sent me out of the house." She splashed her feet to stir up the tadpoles again.

They sat in silence until Ching Lan spoke. "I cried when your brother went away. Why did he have to go? Did Ling Mo break some law?"

"No one in my family is a criminal! Ling Mo wanted to join our father in Hawaii, but Father died and our uncle used his ticket money to bring Father's body home. Ling Mo still wanted to leave China, but my uncle said no. Aunt and Uncle taunted him. They said Father was a fool to join the *Tai Ping* and marry a poor Hakka woman." Meichen closed her eyes, her ears filled again with Meu Yuk's scornful voice. "My brother couldn't stand it, and, when Chung offered to lend him money, he ran away."

"But what about you, Meichen? Did you want to leave, too?"

What should I tell her? Will she understand how much I longed to escape my aunt?

"Ling Mo promised to earn money for my passage. It would have taken a long time, but I agreed to wait. Then the matchmaker came and suggested I marry your brother, and my aunt thought my uncle should accept such a good match."

Ching Lan smiled with satisfaction. "So, you escaped your nasty aunt and uncle after all."

Behind them, a door slammed. Madam Chao's eyes froze both of them. "Why are you two out here? Lazy, disobedient girls! Ching Lan, your father wants you to finish your lessons. And *you*," she said to Meichen, curling her lip as though she saw some species of insect, "should be ready to visit your aunt and uncle, and you aren't even dressed."

Madam Chao glanced down at Meichen's wet, naked feet and gave a sniff. Ching Lan fled and Meichen bowed her head, but Madam Chao had already turned away and hobbled toward the house.

Meichen writhed with unspoken frustration. *I escaped my nasty aunt and uncle, but I exchanged them for a nasty mother-in-law.*

...

The visit to Meichen's aunt and uncle was just long enough to be polite. Chung's face formed an expressionless mask. When her aunt offered him refreshments, he glared at Meu Yuk so fiercely she dropped a plate of sugared almonds. Meichen's uncle, a timid man, looked at his wife in alarm.

Meu Yuk squeezed Meichen's hands. "Here are the happy bride and groom. We've been longing to see you again." She pulled Meichen into the chair beside hers. "Your new family sent us a huge roasted pig. Your uncle has cut the middle portion for us, and I ate a bit. It tasted so delicious, like food for a god. We'll send the head and feet back with you, if you agree to carry it."

"Aunt, I don't think both the pig and I will fit in the sedan chair. We'll send a servant to get it this evening."

Meu Yuk frowned at her husband. "Chao Chung might enjoy the new tobacco you bought. Why don't you ask him if he'd like to try it in your shop?"

Meichen's uncle stared at Chung, his eyes bulging like a fish trapped on the riverbank. He opened his mouth, closed it, opened it again, but no sound emerged. Chung shook his head to decline the offer, and her uncle collapsed back against his chair.

"Meichen, you're so lucky to live in such a beautiful house. Everywhere I looked I saw ivory and jade, fine porcelain vases and jars, silk drapes that shined like jewels. It's so different from our little house."

Meu Yuk's voice injected a note of envy inside her compliments. Meichen could sense Chung bristling. She intervened to ease the tension.

"Aunt, the greatest treasure at my new home is the garden. It's a gift for the senses. Nothing a person makes can compare with nature's creations."

Meu Yuk's mind refused to be turned from money. She grabbed Meichen's hand to examine a gold bracelet circling her wrist. "You got such gorgeous jewelry from the wedding guests. And such a large pile of red envelopes! Scholar Chao has generous friends to give so much cash. Did you get enough to pay for the wedding banquet?"

Chung rose like a rocket, bowed stiffly, and went to the door. Meichen barely had time to say goodbye before he entered the courtyard and she had to leave. He waited at the gate, knocking his fists together. When Meichen reached him, she whooshed in a breath. "I'm glad that's done."

"So am I. It's hard to believe your aunt has lived this long without someone cutting out her tongue."

"I hope you aren't angry I talked with my aunt," she said as he opened the gate. "You and Uncle didn't speak, and it would have been awkward if we'd all sat and said nothing."

"Is your uncle dumb?" Chung asked. "I don't think he spoke to anyone at our wedding."

"Uncle is shy, but he talks when Aunt gives him a chance to say anything."

Chung's face cracked into a smile. "I appreciate your effort to smooth the water. If I'd said a word, I would have shamed myself and my family."

The sedan chair and bearers waited beside the gate. Chung took Meichen's hand to help her inside, and the bearers stood to raise her off the ground.

"Do you think your aunt knows I'm aware of her lie?" He leaned close to the window where only Meichen could hear.

"My aunt is foolish sometimes, but not stupid. I'm sure she knows her plan didn't succeed." Meichen snickered. "I thought Uncle would faint. He warned her your family might take legal action."

"We'll let them worry for a while." Chung closed the curtains over the window and motioned the bearers to go.

Since the visit took so little time, they returned home in mid-afternoon. Meichen hung back as they approached the front entrance. She didn't want to run into her mother-in-law.

"Husband, your aunt said I could visit her. Would now be a suitable time?"

"We'll see." He led her to a side gate that opened into the courtyard.

Jiao resided in a large chamber close to the pond. Red silk drapes with delicate white embroidery framed the windows, and the silk carpet was the largest Meichen had ever seen. Two birds sang in wooden cages as Jiao reclined on plump cushions, her short legs and tiny feet stretched out before her. She helped herself to bits of pineapple and seasoned nuts.

Chung led his bride inside and they bowed to his aunt. Meichen stared in wonder at the exquisite objects crowded on shelves and table tops. Chung nudged her, and she smiled.

"Come, sit here." Jiao's bracelets jingled as she patted the cushion beside her. "I long to know more about my nephew's wife. And you may stay, too, Nephew, if you can."

"I need to talk with my father."

"Ah, yes, the new maid." She smiled at Meichen. "Don't worry about your wife, Nephew. I'll keep her entertained while you're gone."

He left and Meichen took the seat his aunt had offered.

"Please make yourself comfortable. Put your feet up on the ottoman." Jiao seized a gold fringed pillow. "Slide this behind your back."

She beamed as Meichen followed her directions. "I am an informal person and I want my visitors to be comfortable."

"I've never seen such a beautiful room," Meichen said after an awkward pause. She hoped she didn't give the same impression as her aunt.

"My husband is very generous to me. I can't complain in the least." Jiao smiled, yet something in her tone and the empty expression in her eyes contradicted her words.

"How long has your husband been overseas?" Meichen spoke before she realized her question might be painful for her hostess.

Jiao poured two cups of tea with perfect serenity. "I haven't seen my husband since the month after our son was born."

Fifteen years! Meichen almost blurted the words but stopped herself in time. "Your husband must do very well in the Gold Mountain."

"Yes, fortunately for my husband, his eldest brother went before him to California and found him a job. Eldest Brother and my husband worked very hard, and they suffered greatly. But my husband saved enough money to open a laundry, and after that a store, and now he's very rich. And his eldest brother is even richer. He owns five businesses."

"None of Eldest Uncle's family live here?"

"No, he sent for all of them – even his wife." Jiao's singsong voice did not change pitch and Meichen did not ask the obvious question. Why had Jiao not joined *her* husband?

"I have everything I need right here," Jiao said. "My daughters have been married several years now. I found them good husbands with the large dowries their father sent. My son studies for the Imperial examinations along with my oldest nephew. If the gods are generous, surely one of them will pass and receive official rank. Just think, we may have a Mandarin in the family."

"Your son won't go overseas to his father?"

"No, my husband prefers his only son be a scholar. It's good to be rich, he says, but education brings nobility to a family."

Meichen's brother had told her Scholar Chao's history. Her father-in-law had studied Confucian philosophy to prepare for the Imperial government examinations. If Scholar Chao had won a government post, the family's wealth and social position would have been assured.

Unfortunately, Scholar Chao had to settle for a respectable life as a teacher which provided a modest income. The money earned by his merchant brothers in their American stores paid for the large house and handsome furnishings, the servants, and the many luxuries the family in China enjoyed.

Now Meichen understood why her husband must go overseas. Scholar Chao's brothers were aging, and their nephews must replace them to provide money for the family's needs.

Jiao took a square of thick paper from an inlaid mahogany table. "This is a picture my husband sent me last year."

Meichen accepted the photograph, the first she'd ever seen. "How do the Westerners make a perfect image of a man on paper without pen and ink?"

Jiao shrugged. "Who knows? They are devils, so they have powerful magic"

Jiao's husband was an older, plumper version of Scholar Chao, except for his western suit. Then Meichen noticed the person next to him and gasped.

"Why is your husband with a white woman?"

"That woman is my husband's concubine," Jiao explained. "She's not pretty, but there are no Chinese women where he lives. He says she's well behaved and he's teaching her how to cook properly."

"Don't they have a cook?"

"My husband can't afford a cook and still send money to me. Cooks are expensive in the Gold Mountain."

"She doesn't look very young." *Why did my aunt's husband buy an old, ugly concubine?*

Jiao pursed her lips and squinted at the picture. "You may be right, but it's hard to tell with Barbarian women. She should paint her face so she'd look better."

Meichen turned her attention to the woman's costume. "How strange her clothes look! Her jacket is so tight, she looks like she might burst her buttons off."

Jiao sniffed. "She has udders like a cow. Chung told me Barbarian women wrap cloths lined with iron around their waists. It's so tight, they sometimes faint. It's no surprise her bosom thrusts out. It's a wonder her eyes don't pop out." She shook her head. "It's a shame I couldn't choose a proper concubine for my husband. He has to make do with what he can get." She put the photograph away.

Next, she showed Meichen her collection of European music boxes. When Chung returned, he found them giggling as a porcelain lady danced in a ring of flowers.

He smiled at them. "I see Aunt has you well entertained, Wife."

"Nephew, what did you say this music is called?"

"I don't know the name of that song, but the style of music is called a waltz."

"And Western ladies dance to it?" Jiao asked.

"Men and ladies dance together in couples. Here let me show you." He grabbed Meichen's hand and pulled her to her feet. He placed her left hand on his shoulder and his right hand slid around her waist. He took her other hand in his and held it high in the air. "I'm not exactly sure how the feet move, but they turn in circles." He whirled Meichen around. "They go round and round all over the room."

"How very strange!" Jiao exclaimed. "Aren't Barbarian women embarrassed to be held by their husbands in public?"

"They don't dance with just their husbands. A lady can dance with any man who asks her, even a man married to another lady."

"Shocking!" Jiao pointed to the statuette on the music box. "Do Western ladies dance in dresses with the necks cut so low?"

"Oh, yes. Their ball gowns show a lot of their um...shoulders."

"Only a prostitute would show so much of her body to a strange man." Jiao's voice dripped scorn. "Westerners are immoral."

"Aunt, Westerners consider waltzing at balls an innocent amusement."

"Innocent?" Jiao's eyes burned. "How can something be innocent when a man puts his hands on the body of a woman who exposes her bosom? The Barbarians are fools if they think that."

"I suppose they flirt, but the touching is minimal. A man couldn't feel a thing through those hard corsets the ladies wear." Chung redirected the conversation. "My father agrees that I should go to Canton to get a maid for my wife. My mother thinks the village girls won't be suitable."

Jiao nodded. "Very wise of him. Look how badly that last one turned out."

Chung bowed to his aunt and thanked her for receiving Meichen. Jiao invited her to come again.

Meichen followed Chung as he crossed the courtyard and entered their room. "Husband, when do you go to Canton?"

"In two days." He stretched and yawned. "I think I'll visit my teacher. All this talk of Westerners reminded me of him and his daughter."

Meichen gathered her courage and spoke in a meek whisper. "Can I go with you?"

"That wouldn't be safe. The city can be rough." He collapsed across the bed and closed his eyes.

Meichen squeezed in beside him. "Please, take me. I've been nowhere since I came to this town. I want to see more of the world — the Westerners and their shops and the big ships on the river. I'd be so happy, and I'd never ask for anything else."

"You would need a sedan chair and carriers."

"My feet aren't bound. I can walk beside you."

He opened his eyes, frowning. "The streets are dirty."

"I have old shoes to wear." Meichen smiled at him, her eyes hopeful.

He studied the ceiling for a moment and sighed. "All right. I'll ask my father if you may go. But if he says no, you'll have to accept it."

Meichen shrieked and threw her arms around his neck. "You are the best husband in the Celestial Empire." She released him and bounced up and down on the bed. Her matron's bun came loose, spilling her hair over her shoulders.

Laughing, Chung grasped an ebony strand and pulled it gently. Her bouncing stopped. His hand moved down to stroke her soft cheek. She slid her body close to his and pressed her head onto his shoulder. His left arm went behind her neck and he curled his hand around her. His right hand hovered over the buttons at the top of her tunic. Then he sighed, and his hand dropped back down. Meichen's head flopped against the pillow as he pulled his arm from beneath her and left the bed.

He mumbled under his breath. "The first thing I'm buying in Canton is a Western nightgown for you."

Chapter 4

*"Hearing about something a thousand times
cannot compare to seeing it once."*

—Chinese Proverb

Meichen thought her heart would burst with excitement as she floated down the Pearl River. She tapped Chung's hand every few minutes to point out every new attraction. The boatman frowned at her and mumbled about men who couldn't keep their wives under control. She glanced at Chung to see if the comment bothered him. He ignored the boatman and smiled to encourage her curiosity.

"What god does that temple honor?" She pointed to a dumpy brick building visible on a hill.

"I don't know. I've never been to that village."

Meichen's joy faded as they passed a wretched collection of houses where ragged peasants tended nearby rice paddies, up to their knees in muddy water. Intent on their labor, they never looked up. A woman with a baby slung on her back stopped her work to shift the child around and opened her stained jacket so he could nurse.

"It's sad they have to work so hard," Meichen said.

The boatman spat into the water. "Everyone in China has to work hard." He gave Chung a disdainful glance. "Unless they have rich relatives overseas to support them."

Chung glared back. "And some men use their brains to earn a good living without straining their backs."

As they drew near Canton, the river traffic grew heavier until the boat rammed the barges ahead. The air rang with the curses of impatient vendors whose produce wilted in the sun. Meichen held her breath as children leaped from the deck of one sampan to another. But none of them fell into the river where rotten vegetables, food scraps, and human waste floated past them.

Chung laughed as Meichen pinched her nose with her fingers. "When you go out to see the world, you must also smell it," he said.

Meichen noticed a small island in the middle of the river. Trees and large expanses of well-tended grass surrounded magnificent mansions. Each house sat alone in solitary splendor, unlike the Chinese houses on the riverbanks, each one jammed against the next.

Chung followed the direction of her gaze. "That's Shameen Island where the European merchants live."

"Could we see those houses up close. They're so different from ours."

"I can't take you there. Chinese visitors aren't allowed."

Meichen felt as if she'd been slapped. *Why are foreigners allowed to tell Chinese people where they may walk in their own country?* She opened her mouth to question Chung about the injustice, but he no longer listened. He stepped onto the dock and held his hand out for her.

People filled the streets of Canton. Chung shouldered his way through the jam of stalls, carts, and porters who balanced poles on their shoulders carrying huge baskets. She would have liked to stop and examine the goods for sale, but Chung led her steadily onward. Meichen kept her eyes on the street to avoid soiling her embroidered cloth shoes with the filth that lay everywhere.

Canals crisscrossed Canton, and Chung paid a boatman to take a shortcut to his destination. On land again, they walked until they came to a plain stone building topped with an iron cross. Meichen knew it was the symbol of the Christian religion, but it also reminded her that foreigners encroached on the seacoast of China.

Chung pulled a bell, and an enormous man with bright red hair and whiskers opened the door. "Chao Chung, what a pleasure to see you!"

He smiled at Meichen who hid behind Chung's shoulder.

"And who is this? Has there been a wedding?" Chung's teacher winked at her.

"A week ago." Chung guided Meichen forward. "This is my wife, Wu Meichen."

Mr. Lester bowed slightly and welcomed Meichen in Cantonese. "Come inside. Alyssa will be delighted you've come to visit."

Meichen stared at the man's huge shoulders and massive head of fiery hair as they followed the missionary to the parlor. She sat with her eyes downcast, to show proper humility in the home of a revered teacher. While the teacher's eyes fastened on Chung, she couldn't resist a few quick looks around the room. She saw several interesting items, especially a strange table with black and white ivory teeth. Chung whispered to her that it was a musical instrument.

A tall lady joined them. Chung introduced Miss Alyssa Lester, the teacher's daughter, to his wife. Meichen guessed this must be the woman who'd given Chung waltz lessons. Meichen decided Miss Lester was not pretty with her red hair, pasty white face, and peculiar green eyes. *Chung could not want such an ugly woman. I have nothing to fear from her. I wonder if all Westerners look so white like ghosts.*

At Chung's request, Miss Lester played a song so Meichen could hear the piano. They applauded when she finished, but Meichen did not find the music pleasant.

"I will speak to my teacher in English," Chung told Meichen. "I need to practice."

"Why don't I show Meichen the school?" Miss Lester suggested. "I'll practice my Cantonese with her." She stood up immediately, not waiting for either man to speak as she took Meichen's arm.

What a strange woman. She acts like a man herself. She speaks with her eyes on her father's face and never bows her head. Why does he allow his daughter to act improperly? I'm embarrassed for her.

In the next room, girls of all ages sat straight in their desks as they read or practiced calligraphy. To Meichen's surprise, a Chinese woman dressed in a white blouse and black skirt taught three young women at a chalkboard. A gold cross hung from a chain on her neck.

"Who sends their daughters here?" Meichen asked.

Miss Lester stared at Meichen for a moment, then waved the teacher over to join them. The lady listened as Miss Lester spoke in English. She smiled and turned her head toward Meichen.

"I am Li Biyu, teacher of the girls' classes. Miss Lester doesn't understand what you asked. I'll translate for both of you."

Meichen looked directly at Miss Li, though it was impolite. *I've never seen a woman so beautiful, and so serene. Her heart must be filled with peace. Yet she has a strong spirit. She compels me to look at her face.*

Meichen focused her thoughts back on the girls. "What families send their daughters here? I've never heard of a girl educated away from her home."

"They are orphans, or girls abandoned as infants," Miss Li explained.

"Who pays for their lessons if they have no parents?"

"It's free. Missionaries get money from their churches in Europe and America to pay for orphanages and schools in China." Miss Li paused to translate the conversation for Miss Lester.

Meichen blinked. "Why do they do that? Don't they have orphans and poor people in their own country?"

Miss Li nodded. "Of course they do. But the true God told Christians to go to all nations in the world and help the poor and bring lost people to Him."

"I understand our duty to respect our elders and take care of our families. But no one can be responsible for every person in the world. The Western god is a hard taskmaster."

"God helps us with our work." Miss Li put her hand on the shoulder of a small girl who listened to the ladies. "I must get back to my pupils. I hope you'll come back soon so we can talk longer."

Meichen watched Miss Li walk on tiny bound feet to the front of the classroom. *I wonder why Li Biyu chose to be a teacher in this place. A woman so beautiful could be married to a Mandarin.*

Miss Lester tapped Meichen's arm to gain her attention and guided her to another classroom where six boys worked, proctored by an older student.

"Chao Chung learn in this room," she said, pride in her voice. "He good student. Learn English talk and write."

Meichen smiled and nodded as she tried to understand what her hostess said.

They entered the chapel where the orphan children and their teachers worshipped. Meichen smelled no incense and saw no statues. A large wooden cross stood on a table. Beside it lay a huge book opened to a colored picture of a longhaired Western man in a white robe.

"That Jesus," Miss Lester said. "He God's son." She turned to other pages in the book and tried to explain them in her version of Cantonese. Meichen nodded, a polite smile stretching her lips. She listened so the missionary could win favor in heaven, although she understood little of Miss Lester's message.

After Miss Lester closed the Bible, Meichen thanked her for the stories. "I like to learn about the Bible. My parents were God Worshipers and I want to know about their religion."

Miss Lester frowned. "I don't understand."

"My parents were Tai Ping. They worshipped your god and fought for the Heavenly Kingdom." Miss Lester stared at her in confusion, so Meichen spoke slowly. "My mother and father were Tai Ping. Christians, like you."

The lady gave a start as she recognized the word "Tai Ping." Meichen studied the shocked expression on the missionary's face as Miss Lester struggled to make a suitable response.

What is wrong with her? She acts like I said something obscene.

Miss Lester abandoned her quest for words. She opened a door and swept her arm in a graceful motion to invite Meichen into her garden. They shared a mutual admiration for the flowers and spent a pleasant half hour with no need to converse. Vegetables and herbs grew in a smaller garden which led to the kitchen where a cook prepared rice in the largest pot Meichen had ever seen.

Miss Lester spoke to the cook in a jargon of English and Cantonese. The woman bowed to Meichen and grinned, showing gaps where most of her teeth had been.

"My mistress says you are the wife of Chao Chung."

Meichen bowed her head as she introduced herself.

The servant bowed at her in return. "My name is Mai. I've cooked here for many years, and I remember Chao Chung well." Her eyes crinkled. "He's very handsome. You're a lucky girl."

"Thank you, Elder Sister. I'm happy to be his wife."

Mai stirred the rice. "The mistress says your husband wants to find a servant girl for you, and she has one in mind. Her name is Yuan."

Meichen raised her eyebrows. *What is this? Does the missionary sell her orphan girls? What will her god think of that?* To Mai she said, "Tell me about her."

"She lived in a brothel all her life. When her mother died, the madam kept her to wait on the ladies. Ordinarily, when she turned eleven, she'd become a prostitute, too, but she's so plain no customer wanted her. The brothel owner said she'd grown too big to keep, she ate too much, so he turned her out, and our master found her wandering on the street."

"Why doesn't Miss Lester want to keep her?"

"The girls here are very innocent, and Yuan doesn't fit in. My mistress will keep her if no one else wants her, but it would be best if she went some-where else. She'd be all right with a married woman. In fact, her knowledge might come in useful." Mai winked at Meichen. "Sometimes it helps to know a few tricks to keep a husband at home."

Meichen's cheeks grew hot. "Let me meet her."

Mai led Meichen outside where Yuan hung clothes on a rope. She put her mouth close to Meichen's ear and whispered, "She'd be safe from all the young men in the house. No one would bother her." Mai waved to the girl. "Yuan, come talk to this lady."

Yuan stood before Meichen and bowed. Meichen had to agree she was plain with a squint in one eye and large ears that stuck out. But her smile suggested she was good-natured.

"You've been a lady's maid?" Meichen asked. "You look very young."

"I've worked for ladies most of my life," the girl replied, her eyes firmly fixed on the ground. "I'm twelve years old."

Meichen had no idea what to ask the girl, and if she made a bad choice her mother-in-law would be angry. She shrugged and looked at the cook. "I need to consult with Chao Chung."

"I'll ask the mistress to fetch him."

Mai left, and Yuan returned to her work. Meichen watched as wet clothes went up on the rope.

"Does the missionary lady wear all these garments?" she asked as she surveyed the long clothes line.

Yuan grinned. "No, not all at once. This is a week's wash." She pointed to knee-length trousers made of sheer cloth. "These cover her bottom, and the sleeveless vest goes on top. Three of the white skirts go over the trousers. This thing that looks like armor is laced tight to make her waist small. These long black socks go on her legs. Over all that she wears a dress."

Yuan pointed to a long white gown with a high neck and long sleeves. "At night she takes off everything and puts this on."

"Western clothes must be very uncomfortable." Meichen's eyes focused on the nightgown.

Yuan nodded her agreement. "I wouldn't want to wear them."

A flicker of movement in an upstairs window caught Meichen's eye. Two boys watched her and Yuan and the clothes flapping on the line. *Aha. Now I know how my husband learned so much about the underclothing of Western ladies.*

Chao Chung came out of the house accompanied by his teacher, who explained Yuan's history once again for Chung's benefit.

He lifted Yuan's head up and examined her face. Meichen started to protest. She knew Yuan must be embarrassed by her deformed eye. But Chung held up a hand to stop her words.

"I hear you're trained to be a lady's maid, but that's not all we need from you. Are you honest and loyal as well?"

Yuan stood straighter. "I've never stolen from any of my mistresses."

"Have you gossiped about them with other servants?"

"When the owner of the brothel asked me questions, I had to answer. But I tried not to make trouble for anyone."

"What would you do if you were offered presents or less work to do if you told secrets about me and my wife?" he asked.

Yuan's face wrinkled into a frown. "Of course I would keep your business private. But who would want to bribe me to find out such private things?"

"My mother."

Yuan gaped at him but agreed to follow his orders.

Chung grinned at Miss Lester. "We'll take her with us."

Meichen whispered into Chung's ear. "Do you think your mother will approve?"

"I don't see why not. The Lesters will give her to us. My parents will be pleased with the money we've saved them. And if you don't like her, the Lesters will take her back." To Yuan he said, "Go pack your things."

I can't believe it. For the first time in my life I can give orders to someone else. Meichen followed Chung back into the house.

...

They spent the afternoon in shops. Chung agreed to buy the things that caught Meichen's eye, and she set out for home with jade earrings and a bolt of bright red silk to make a New Year's outfit. Yuan plodded patiently behind them, loaded with parcels, one of them a plain white nightgown Meichen hated on sight.

Meichen hardly spoke on the trip home, and her eyelids drifted shut several times. She longed to rest her head on Chung's shoulder, but she knew he'd object.

He smiled at her weary slump. "I hope you had enough excitement to last a while."

Meichen nodded." I've never been so tired, even after a day's work in the fields."

"I'm glad you got along with Miss Lester. And I hope you complimented her on her Cantonese. She's worked very hard to learn it."

"Of course I did, even though I could hardly understand her."

"I'm afraid my English must sound the same to them. But I'm still better off than my uncles. Neither of them knew a word of English when they went to America."

Don't make me think of that. She brushed her hand over his. His arm recoiled instinctively at her touch. The darkness hid her humiliation as she laid her hand back in her lap. *Why does it hurt so much that he rejects me?* They looked away from each other, though they saw nothing on the shore except a few flickering lights in the villages.

She jumped in alarm as Chung's voice broke the silence. "I suppose Miss Lester tried to convert you. She's full of zeal."

"She showed me pictures of her god and told me his story. I tried to tell her my parents were God Worshipers, but she didn't like what I said, so we talked of other things." Meichen sighed. "I understand why some Chinese hate my parents, but I thought the missionaries would be on their side. They should be glad the Tai Ping accepted their God."

"To the missionaries, the Tai Ping weren't Christians," Chung said. "Their beliefs offended Westerners."

"But they worshipped the Christian god. My aunt said so!"

"The man who led the Tai Ping Kingdom said he believed in the Christian god and His son, Jesus. But he also claimed to be the second son of God, the younger brother of Jesus. That's blasphemy to Christians, so they wouldn't support his rebellion against the Emperor."

"Why did the Westerners think he couldn't be the son of their god?" Meichen asked. "A man can have many sons, so why couldn't a god?"

Chung shrugged. "I can't explain why Westerners are so sure God has only one son. I do know the leader didn't understand Christian beliefs. He executed his best generals when they threatened his power. He also kept a harem with thousands of women, and that's a terrible sin to Christians."

"Then my aunt was right. My parents were fools to join the Tai Ping. They lost everything for nothing."

"No, Meichen, in the beginning the Tai Ping had good ideas. They promised reforms to help the peasants, and they wanted men and women to be equal. Many people joined them. No one realized at first the leader was insane. Once the Tai Ping rebelled against the Emperor, they had to keep fighting or surrender and die. That's why your father fled to Hawaii."

Chung stopped talking, and Meichen noticed all the passengers were silent. What if one of them was a spy for the Manchu government? Chung could be arrested for talking about the Tai Ping.

An old man spoke. "Talk more, young scholar. I enjoy hearing stories. It makes the trip go faster."

Other people joined the old man requesting entertainment. Chung began the story of the Monkey King, a popular tale with no political significance. When the boat reached their village, Chung nudged Meichen awake. She and Yuan shuffled after him, and Meichen carried some of the packages to increase the servant's pace.

Once home, Meichen handed Yuan a quilt and told her to sleep in a corner of Chung's room. She'd find Yuan a place in the servants' quarters the next day.

Chung insisted she try on the nightgown and she obeyed, suppressing her desire to collapse into bed. She stood before him with the sleeves drooping below her hands and the excess material at the hem pooled around her feet.

Chung pursed his lips. "Yuan will have to alter it."

Meichen yawned and pulled the voluminous garment back over her head. She crawled into her quilts naked, and Chung did not object. For once, he was too tired to think of sex.

CHAPTER 5

"Learning without thinking is ignorance;
Thinking without learning is dangerous."

—CHINESE SAYING

AT THE END OF EACH DAY, Meichen and Chung sat at the desk in his room while Meichen copied ideographs and read simple stories under Chung's tutelage. The house grew quiet as the rest of the household retired to their beds. They spoke softly when words were necessary.

She enjoyed learning, and, even more, she liked the praise he gave her when she copied his examples perfectly. When he smiled, her heart soared. Her thigh burned where their legs touched, and sometimes his arm brushed her breast as he corrected her mistakes.

The bed behind them never left her consciousness. Sometimes she imagined him lifting her off her feet and placing her on the soft sheets, then parting her robe and pressing his face against her breasts, which had magically grown plumper. His dark eyes would lock into hers, melting her inside with love. He would speak her name and she'd open languid eyelids, ready to surrender. Then the mist would dissolve, and she would see Chung sitting in his chair, puzzled by her facial gyrations.

As far as she could tell, he never sensed her emotions, even when she sat next to him. She ached inside for him to do something – anything – to her with his graceful hands. But all he ever did was pass the brush to her so she could copy what he'd written.

One evening the ache inside her swelled unbearably and she released it with a mournful sigh. Chung stopped his lecture on radicals and studied her trembling lips.

"Are you well, Meichen?" He pressed his palm against her forehead to check for fever.

"It's nothing." Her finger traced the flowers on her tunic to hide her burning face.

"You're lying to me. I can tell." He waited for her to speak, but her lips kept tightly closed.

Chung rubbed his palms together making circles. "Please, tell me what bothers you. Am I moving too fast for you? You learn so quickly, sometimes I forget you're a beginner."

She trembled, too ashamed to explain her feelings. She was sure he would laugh at her,

"Has my mother scolded you today?"

Meichen shook her head, refusing to look at him. His voice was calm, but his palms closed and he tapped them together. "A husband and wife shouldn't keep secrets from each other."

"Since we are husband and wife, would you sometimes stroke my arm? Or say some words of love to me?"

Chung's puzzled expression disappeared, and he smiled like a kind teacher dismissing a minor annoyance. "You're a young girl and I'm a grown man. I don't want to hurt your feelings, but I'm past the point of boyish, innocent flirting. It must be all or nothing with me, and you're too young for all. It would frighten you. What you really want is affection and attention, not sex."

He studied her, a hint of a frown on his face. "You have what the Westerners call *infatuation*. Miss Lester explained it to me. It's common for young ladies to think they're in love with an older man. Miss Lester herself had such feelings for a student of her father, and she longed for him to bring her flowers and dance with her and kiss her hand and send her letters. It was a fairy story in her head. She had no idea what real marriage was like."

Meichen's entire body burned with humiliation. "What I feel for you is not fairy tale love. And I know what a husband and wife are supposed to do."

Chung stroked her hair. "I'll show you what a kiss is like. We can do this." He leaned forward and pressed his lips against her forehead. "That's what Mr. Lester sometimes did to show his daughter affection. And sometimes she kissed his cheek." Chung illustrated again.

"Why did Miss Lester want a man to kiss her hand?"

"European men kiss a woman's hand to show admiration and respect. English and American men are more likely to squeeze her hand."

Meichen held out her right hand. "Kiss me there so I'll know how it feels."

Putting his hand under hers, he leaned forward to brush his lips across the top of her hand. Her heart gave a little flip, but he immediately dropped her hand and turned away.

He straightened the papers on the desk and set the brush in her hand. "Now you are an expert on kissing. Finish your work."

Meichen dipped her brush in ink, pushing her disappointment to the back of her mind. She suspected there was much more to kissing. But it was clear he saw her as a child, and there was nothing she could do to change his mind. Except grow up.

...

Chung read a newspaper while she made meticulous copies of his writing. He suddenly slapped the newspaper against the desk, causing her brush to skitter across the paper. He stood up and paced the room as Meichen watched in alarm.

"This is ridiculous. If we lose wars, China must pay reparations. Now we've won a province back from the Russians, and *they* want us to pay reparations. If Russians were foolish enough to buy land and start farms in disputed territory, they should lose what they paid. But, no, we must compensate those idiots when they are forced to go back to Russia where they belong."

"Is it a large amount of money?" Meichen asked.

"It's nothing compared to the money we paid Britain after the Opium Wars. The problem is the more they take, the more they want. China has become a timid dog kicked by every bully in town."

He paced the room, his hands balled into fists. At last he sat down in his chair.

"We live in dangerous times, Meichen. People in China want to pretend that nothing has changed, that we can go on as we always did. But it's not so. Our government is weak, hanging on to power by a silk thread. We're surrounded by wolves and sharks, all waiting for the right moment to devour us."

"What do you mean?" Her eyes darted around the room searching for enemies.

He took a globe from a shelf. She had never dared to touch this prized possession, given to him by his father when he graduated from the missionary school. He pointed at different areas as he spoke.

"The British have Burma and India, the French took Indochina and Russia waits to move on Manchuria. Even the Japanese plan to occupy Korea."

"The Japanese!"

"The Japanese are as greedy as the others. They were wise enough to copy the Westerners' government and industry. Now they have steel warships and a modern army, and they want colonies of their own. The only thing that saves China from being carved up is the greed of the Western nations. They all want equal shares of the spoils, and if it went to out and out war, one of them might lose all their China trade. So they watch each other, waiting for someone to make the first move."

Meichen shivered. Could China become the vassal of a Barbarian nation or, even worse, the upstart Japanese? "What will happen to us if there's a war?"

"I'll start saving the money my father gives me. If fighting starts, the family can go to Hong Kong or further south."

Meichen suddenly realized how little she knew about the world. She focused on her insulated life inside the Chao house, and the balance of power among the women, and her low status in the household. Now she realized there was more to life than the narrow confines of the house and village.

Chung glanced at her paper and grimaced at the long smear of ink. "I know that's my fault for startling you. We'll stop working now."

Meichen washed her brush and cleaned the ink bowl. She undressed and put on her white nightgown, pulling the covers up to her chin.

Chung doused the light but did not undress. He went back to the window to stare into the courtyard. She was still awake when he finally joined her. She pressed herself against his back, seeking reassurance.

He turned his head to look at her, and, to her surprise, he rolled over and put his arm underneath her, letting her head rest on his shoulder. She knew it was an act of comfort, not love, but she snuggled against him as she drifted to sleep.

CHAPTER 6

*"After too much wine,
there is no virtue."*

—CHINESE SAYING

New Year Celebration, February 1882

IT WAS THE SECOND TIME MEICHEN would celebrate the New Year with the Chao family, not quite two years after her wedding. On this holiday, she would be fifteen. She'd hoped her husband would lose his resolve to delay consummation, but nothing had changed. Meanwhile her mother-in-law grew more impatient every month when Meichen failed to conceive.

Chung came to their room to fetch Meichen, a frown marring his face. "Why are you taking so long? My father wants to start the New Year feast."

Meichen lay curled up on the bed wrapped in her quilt, her red silk tunic and skirt still draped on a chair. Chung came over to her side.

"You aren't even dressed."

Meichen groaned. "I don't want to eat."

Chung leaned down to study her face. "You look ill."

"Your mother made me drink a black, slimy tonic, and now I want to throw up." Meichen gagged.

Chung balled his hands into fists. "This must stop." He paced the room. "I didn't mind the tea and the herb soup. At least they were harmless. But now she's gone too far."

"She says I must drink the potion every day to make me fertile."

Chung's shoulders drooped. "I have to tell my parents the truth about your age. I can't let my mother torture you anymore."

"No!" Meichen sat up. "You can't tell them now. They'll be angry with you for keeping it from them all this time. And your mother will want to get rid of me. She already hates me."

He sighed. "She doesn't hate you. She wants me to have a son."

"There's worse news. She wants to hire a midwife to see if I'm normal inside. Won't the woman be able to tell I'm still virgin?"

Chung made a gesture of impatience. "I don't know. And if my mother insists on doing it, I can't stop her. It's better to tell her now and get it over with."

"There's a better way. You could do what you should have done when we married."

His chin went up. "I won't break my word to Ling Mo. And I won't do something I know is wrong."

Meichen dropped on the bed in despair. "You don't want me. I'm not attractive to you."

"You grow more enticing every day." He pulled a strand of her dishevelled hair.

Meichen rolled onto her stomach, pounding the bed with her fists. He didn't understand what she felt. Along with her blossoming body, her longing for him grew. Her untouchable husband tortured her with frustration. She envied her sister-in-law who'd produced two sons already. She hated her mother-in-law's constant surveillance as she watched Meichen for any sign of pregnancy.

Chung rubbed her back. "Now come on, put your clothes on. And don't worry. I'll find some way to handle my mother." Chung stood up. "Where's Yuan?"

"I asked her to bring me some tea to settle my stomach."

"Then I'll help you dress." Pushing the quilt aside, he pulled her out of the bed, handing her the red tunic and skirt. While Meichen dressed, he found her shoes. Kneeling in front of her, he slid them on her feet, his hand caressing each leg in the process. A wave of fierce desire possessed her.

"You need a new outfit," he said. "This one's too tight in the chest."

Meichen preened, encouraged that he noticed her new curves. Chung lifted her foot in the air and nibbled on her ankle to make her laugh. Her hopes sank again. He played with her, as a man would tease a child. At the sound of fingers scratching at the door, Chung dropped her foot and stood abruptly.

Yuan hurried in with tea.

"Mistress, it's chaos in the kitchen! The cook is running everywhere working on twelve dishes at once. I thought he'd chop me up with his cleaver when I said I needed to make tea."

"Yuan, hurry and fix my wife's hair." Chung paused on his way out of the room. "I'll tell Father you're on the way."

Yuan grabbed a hairbrush and, with deft fingers, wound Meichen's hair in a bun on the nape of her neck. She pushed gold combs into the swirl of hair to match the embroidery on Meichen's tunic. After Meichen finished her tea, Yuan painted her face in a few minutes. The girl stepped back to admire her work. "My mistress is the most beautiful lady in this house."

Meichen shook her head, but she smiled. She found her fan and went to the courtyard where her husband waited. As the aroma of roast pork and spicy sauces came to her nose, she discovered her nausea was gone. At least, she reflected with satisfaction, her mother-in-law wouldn't have the pleasure of ruining Meichen's holiday.

The next day friends visited and exchanged gifts. Chung sat with his brothers and other young men telling stories and exchanging news. Meichen, trapped with the women, endured boring gossip about new betrothals and marriages, expected babies, and unfaithful husbands until her eyes drooped. When everyone was distracted by the arrival of tea and cakes, Meichen slipped away to her room, thinking she might nap. But sleep evaded her.

She flipped the quilt off her legs and immediately wanted to cover them. No position was comfortable. She left the bed and paced around the room, trying to still her twitching nerves.

The door opened as Yuan peeked in. "Come in, please." Meichen brightened at the prospect of company. She invited the girl to sit down.

Yuan balanced on the very edge of the chair with her feet tight together. "Have I done something wrong?"

"No, of course not."

"Are you feeling unwell, Mistress? How can I help you?"

Meichen resumed pacing. "I can't be still. My legs are driving me insane. I wish I could just jump out of my body."

Yuan stood up. "Come lie down on your bed. I'll massage your legs to make them relax."

Meichen returned to the bed and lifted her skirt over her knees. Yuan rubbed scented oil on her hands, then slid them down Meichen's right leg. "Mistress, your body is stiff. Picture yourself on a cloud floating across the sky. The world is far below, out of sight. No one there can bother you."

Meichen took a deep breath as she fell under the spell of Yuan's soft voice and supple hands. Her agitation flowed from her through Yuan, and she felt drowsy. The servant moved to the left leg to repeat the treatment. Meichen was nearly asleep when high-pitched screams jolted her awake. She sat up with a hand over her heart and saw Ching Lan race past the courtyard window, closely followed by a young boy.

Yuan pursed her lips. "That child is out of hand. Someone should teach her how a young girl should behave."

"Doesn't her mother do that?"

"The Honorable Scholar thwarts his wife. He won't allow her to punish their daughter, so she's given up on Ching Lan and focuses on her sons."

"That explains why she has so much time to stick her nose in their business."

Yuan went back to Meichen's left leg. "Mistress, your muscles are tight again. Try to clear your mind once more. Breathe deeply and let the angry spirits out."

In a few minutes, Meichen's mind escaped into peaceful daydreams. Yuan lowered Meichen's leg until it lay flat on the bed beside the other leg. She spoke softly into Meichen's ear.

"If you wish to sleep, I'll close the door and leave."

"Stay here, please. I need your advice." Meichen kept her eyes closed. If she didn't see Yuan's face, it would lessen her embarrassment.

"How could I advise you, Mistress? I have no education, I've never travelled, and I've lived almost my whole life in one house. I know almost nothing."

Meichen opened her eyes and studied the canopy over her head. "There's one thing you know very well. You know how courtesans entice men. I want to know their secrets."

Yuan's mouth fell open. Meichen wondered how much the maid knew about the private lives of her master and mistress. She knew about the long white nightgown, of course, and if she wondered why Meichen wore it, she asked no questions.

"Young Master might not want you to know those things. My mother told me a man likes to experiment at the flower house, but at home he wants his wife to be submissive and innocent, especially if she is young."

"No wife can be more innocent than I am. My jade gate has never been opened."

Yuan pressed her hand over her mouth to hide her amazement. "How can that be? You've lain with your husband every night since I came here, and you're a beautiful woman. Is something wrong with Young Master?"

"Something is wrong with me." Meichen supressed a sob. She began with the day of her wedding, telling Yuan of her aunt's lie and the subsequent problems raised by Chung's scruples.

Meichen twisted her hands. "I'm afraid my mother-in-law will send me away if she finds out."

Yuan considered the problem. "It would be foolish to send you away now. She'd be better off to wait another year rather than pay all the expenses of another wedding." Yuan smiled. "Or she might order Young Master to do his duty."

"She'd never give up the chance to humiliate me and my family." Meichen's chest tightened as she imagined herself exiled, shamed, losing the respect of every family in the village. And, worst of all, losing Chung for the rest of her life. It would be unbearable.

Meichen rubbed her hand over the quilt to smooth it flat. "Old Mai at the missionary school said you might know how to make my husband more interested in me."

Yuan laughed. "Surely the young master doesn't need an aphrodisiac."

"He has too much self-control. I don't know how to tempt him."

"Ah, now I understand. You want to raise his desire and overcome his reason."

"Can you help me, Yuan?" Meichen's eyes filled with tears.

Yuan nodded. "I'll tell you what to do, but I won't promise it will work."

...

Meichen waited for Chung to join her, anticipation mingling with fear. He still celebrated with his brothers and their friends, and Yuan whispered they'd been drinking which would make seducing him easier.

An hour later, he stumbled into their room, grabbing the canopy to keep his balance. He snickered as he tried to pull off his trousers. His foot tangled in the cotton fabric and he kicked vigorously to get loose. Meichen heard the fabric rip, followed by a bumping sound. He laughed louder. Meichen crawled to his side of the bed to investigate. He was pulling himself off the floor using the bed hangings as a rope. Just as he regained his feet, the wooden curtain rod snapped. He swayed a few seconds, then fell backward, pinning her to the mattress.

No, don't let him pass out. She wiggled under his chest until she was free. *I must rouse him. If he lies still for long, he'll sleep.*

There was little light in the room, just a few rays slipping through the window slats where a dying torch stood in the courtyard. Meichen used her fingers to find clothing still on his body. His trousers were gone and one sock and shoe. His jacket was buttoned all the way up to his neck.

She kneeled beside him to pull off the shoe and sock. The challenge was the jacket, which went under his back. *Do I need to remove it? The necessary parts are exposed with the jacket on. On the other hand, he might feel foolish when he wakes up with his top half covered and the rest naked.*

There was no time to waste. He had opened his eyes for a moment, but he closed them and was breathing through his mouth in a regular rhythm. Meichen tore the jacket open and tugged his arm through the armhole at an awkward angle.

His eyes opened again and he muttered a protest. Immediately she attacked the other arm. She had to strain her shoulders to reach across his chest, so she straddled his waist, twisting her bottom backward and forward as she wrestled the jacket sleeve off.

Chung revived from his lethargy with miraculous speed. His hands slid over her breasts and he opened his fingers to trap the nipples. Meichen gasped as he closed the fingers tight enough to pinch them without causing true pain. He slid one hand beneath her bottom and pressed her tight against him. Her eyes opened wide when his jade stalk rubbed against her tailbone. It had increased in length and thickness, and it swelled even more when she bumped against it.

Chung groaned as he rolled them over. Meichen didn't feel crushed this time because he used his arms to bear some of his weight. He sucked the skin on her neck, creating currents that shot down her torso. Shifting his weight onto one arm, Chung grabbed her hand, which rested on his shoulder, and pushed it down to touch his stalk. The organ rose as if it were an independent creature. Chung put her hand on it.

"Take hold and squeeze a little. Move your hand up and down." His whispers blasted hot, moist air on her skin. "Yes, that's it."

Her hips rose off the bed as his hand moved between her thighs. This action, which had terrified and disgusted her on their wedding night, made her moan out her longing. She pressed close against him, her body arched, acting from instinct. She was amazed at her own responses which seemed to come from somewhere beside her conscious thought

Contradictory sensations chilled her naked skin while she burned hot as a stove inside. Chung's fingers slipped into the folds of her most private parts. Every time he moved his fingers, she gasped, expanding her lungs tight with air while providing no opportunity to exhale. He pounded her with new sensations, a tidal wave overwhelming her. A sudden fear of suffocation quenched the fire inside.

In a panic, she braced her hands on his chest, trying to thrust him away. But Chung was ready for consummation. He nudged her thighs wide apart, determined to invade her body. Her hips wriggled as she struggled to escape, causing a reaction she'd never intended. He pushed himself barely inside her and she screamed.

"Stop, you're hurting me." She clawed his shoulders, squeezed them as she pushed herself further up the bed, away from the piercing pain.

As her heels kicked against his thighs, Chung suddenly came out of his trance. His face twisted in horror, then his feet hit the floor with a loud thud.

Meichen rolled herself into a ball with the quilt wrapped around her. She heard Chung dress and leave the room. She waited for him to return, but he did not. She cried a long time before she slept.

...

Meichen woke early and discovered she was still alone. Yuan came in with tea, but Meichen's defeated expression and the absence of the master convinced her to leave the tea and go away. As she reached the door, Chung came in. Yuan took one look at him and hurried away.

Meichen could not raise her eyes, her shame was so great. She had failed in her duty as a wife. If Madam Chao chose to send her away, she would be justified. Meichen expected Chung to tell her he'd spoken to his parents and they had arranged for her to leave.

He sat down beside her and stroked her hair off her face. "I'm sorry, Meichen. I despise myself for what I did. I should never have come in here drunk."

Her lips moved but she made no sound. *Is it possible he's forgotten the part I played in arousing him? He should be furious with me.*

Meichen's lips trembled. "Please, forgive me. It's my failure, Husband.

"You didn't fail. Your body was not ready. I was right to say we should wait."

"Give me another chance," she pleaded. "I will do what I should."

"No!" He pushed her away, his eyes blazing. "I don't want a wife who must force herself to have relations with me."

She sniffled. "I do want to. But it hurts so much."

Chung relented and pulled her close again. "It's all right. When the right time comes, you won't care about that. And I'll be sober and gentler with you."

He traced the line of her lips as he stared into her eyes. "I told my father I want to go to Canton to see a Taoist doctor about our infertility."

"Your mother agreed to that?" Meichen's eyes widened.

"She wasn't given a choice. After we see the doctor, I hope things will be easier. At least my mother will stop nagging for a while."

CHAPTER 7

"Knowing others is wisdom.
Knowing yourself is enlightenment."

—LAO TZU

THE TAOIST DOCTOR BELIEVED IN THE INTERACTION of female yin and male yang, and it fit well with Chung's plan. The old man checked the pulses of the young couple and asked numerous questions, but to Meichen's relief he required no intimate physical examination.

Chung stayed with the doctor in his consulting room while Meichen sat in the medicine store, banished from the conference. A wizened woman smoking a pipe sat on a stool next to the only window. She said nothing and offered Meichen no tea. Meichen tried to make conversation, but the old woman shook her head.

She must be deaf, poor old thing. I suppose she is the doctor's mother and keeps an eye on the medicines while he's busy.

Meichen studied her surroundings. The doctor's shop resembled the one her Uncle Ling Tan owned. Cabinets with many small drawers probably held herbs or leaves or preserved animal parts. She saw ivory tusks and rhinoceros horn on one of the shelves, available for old men who wanted to please young wives. Petrified "dragon bones" waited on a counter to be ground into powder for those who could afford it. Pungent smells drifted from the dark corners of the room, mixed with the sweetness of incense. Several wrapped packages waited underneath a counter, medicines for clients to pick up, she supposed.

Fifteen minutes later, a young maid hurried through the door and bowed to the doctor's mother. "My mistress needs her medicine." She held out several coins. The old woman lifted a brass box from under her chair. A lock held the lid shut. She dropped the coins through a narrow slot in the lid.

The old woman handed the girl a package, and she disappeared into the street. The entire transaction had lasted less than two minutes.

The woman grimaced at Meichen, showing her toothless gums. "Dirt," she said as though that explained everything.

What does she mean? Who would buy dirt for medicine?

Meichen waited to see if the old woman had more to say. Sucking hard on the stem of her pipe, she coughed, then spoke in a raspy voice. "When I was young, women were strong and brave. They didn't wail over every twinge in their bodies. That girl's mistress is no better than a child, demanding dirt for the pain in her feet. My son should not sell it, but he's greedy for her money."

Meichen nodded. She asked no questions, but she was still mystified.

"Nowadays people are fools," the doctor's mother continued. "They smoke white dirt until they have no minds left. You know the saying: one false step can cause life-long regret.

The inside door opened, and Chung followed the doctor into the medicine shop. Meichen lifted her eyebrows. She looked at her husband, but his eyes focused on the doctor who stood with his arms folded and his hands stuffed inside his long sleeves.

"Come back in two hours. I will write my report for your honorable father."

Meichen rose and followed Chung. Once outside, Chung shook with laughter. Meichen's curiosity became unbearable. She grasped his arm and shook it.

"What did he say?"

"He said we should sleep apart for three months."

"What! Why would he say that?"

"I told him I'd been diligently working to father a child since the day we married with no results. Then I said I felt weak, and I gave him some other details I don't want to discuss here in the street. The doctor said that, in my zeal, I've exhausted my yang essence and weakened your yin, which is why you can't conceive."

Meichen frowned. "I don't understand why we can't sleep together."

"We must avoid conjugal relations for several months to get the yang and yin balanced again." Chung beamed at her. "It went just as I hoped."

"That's all he said?"

"Well, almost. He also advised me to use another woman, but not to complete the act with her. I'm just supposed to soak in her yin essence." Chung avoided looking at Meichen's stunned face.

"He wants you to take a concubine?" she gasped.

"I can't afford a concubine. I would use a woman at the flower house."

Meichen's heart pounded. 'Will you follow that advice?"

Chung hesitated. "It would make things easier for me. And with the doctor recommending it, my family wouldn't think it strange."

Meichen suppressed her shock. She had caused this catastrophe by failing in her duty. If she'd satisfied him, he wouldn't need another woman. "You must do as you like," she said, staring at the ground.

They walked a while in silence. "Will it make you too unhappy?" Chung asked.

"It doesn't matter what I think," she said. Inside her body, frustration burned. "You're a man, and you may do whatever pleases you." Her voice came out sharper than she'd intended.

Chung stopped to look into her eyes, but she turned her face away. He sighed. "Oh, Meichen, my father will never know what a punishment he gave me for sending Ling Mo overseas. A fifty-pound *cangue* hanging from my neck would be nothing to this."

He started to walk again, and she glared at his back, offended by his comparison. "I am sorry to be a burden to you. Give me another chance tonight. I won't stop you." Her words were conciliatory, but she couldn't hide the bitterness she felt.

He held up his hand. "No more about that. I forbid you to mention it again."

"I don't want you to go to someone else." She was tired of acting meek and accepting her lot without complaining. She couldn't bear the thought of her husband in the arms of another woman.

"All right, I won't. There, are you satisfied? The problem is solved."

He moved ahead, and she knew he expected her to walk two steps behind like a proper wife. Meichen glared at the back of his head. She increased her pace to walk at his side. He frowned at her but did not order her back.

To lure Chung's thoughts to a less agitating topic, Meichen remembered the transaction at the medicine shop. He could probably explain how the mysterious "dirt" cured the sick.

"Chung, why do people buy white dirt to use as medicine?"

He stopped walking and gripped her wrist. She shrank from the horror in his face.

"Who told you about white dirt? Did that old crone try to sell you some?"

She winced from the pressure of his strong fingers. "No, of course not! If I needed medicine, I would let *you* buy it. But a girl came in the doctor's office to buy a small package for her mistress, and the doctor's mother called it dirt."

Chung's features relaxed and he released her. "I'm sorry I frightened you. I was worried for a moment. I thought someone might have approached you..."

"It's something evil, isn't it? And I'm too ignorant to know better."

Chung led her into a noodle shop where he ordered their lunch and some tea. They sat on a bench, waiting for the food, and Meichen absently rubbed her wrist. *What have I done to make him so angry?*

He took her arm and stroked the red mark. "I can't believe I did such a thing to you." He propped his hands on his knees, slumping his shoulders. "I've hurt you twice, first last night and now again. I try to be a civilized person, but when I'm with you, reason deserts me, and my emotions rule. An enlightened man shouldn't let emotion dictate his actions."

"It's my fault you feel that way. A wife should make her husband tranquil, but I disturb your peace." Meichen felt ashamed of her earlier outburst. Chung was a kind husband, and her only friend in the Chao household. "I cause you problems and ask too many questions. My Aunt Meu Yuk told me every day I annoyed her worse than a fly buzzing in her face."

Chung smiled, and her heart eased. "The Master of Scholars said, 'A man who asks a question is a fool for five minutes. A man who never asks is a fool forever.' So ask me what you want to know, and don't be afraid."

"Why is the white dirt dangerous?"

"It's opium, Meichen. Some people smoke it, and once they start, they want it all the time. They want it more than food, and they let their families starve rather than stop smoking it. When they smoke, they feel no sorrow or pain, only peace. Their bodies waste away until they die. Now you know why I would never let you use it."

"Why does the Emperor permit the sale of opium?"

"He can't stop it. The British won't let him. They bring the opium from India to trade for our tea, and so many Chinese are addicted to the cursed stuff they have plenty of customers. Whenever our emperor tries to outlaw it, the British attack our cities with their gunboats and cannon and take more of our territory."

The shop owner brought their noodles mixed with scallions and bean sprouts and scattered with tiny shrimp. The smell of garlic and ginger wafted in the air. Chung pulled a case from his sash and took out his chopsticks. Cradling his bowl close to his mouth, he began to eat. Meichen sipped her tea, ignoring the food.

"Aren't you hungry?" Chung asked.

She shook her head. "It makes me sad that so many Chinese use opium."

Chung snorted. "Don't be sorry for them. They're fools. If it weren't for them, the British and the other Westerners couldn't loot our country." He pushed her bowl closer to her. "Eat, if you want to make my life tranquil. I don't want a thin, withered wife."

Meichen smiled as she scooped up the noodles. *I'll be silent and let my husband enjoy our day in the city. We'll have trouble enough when we go home.*

...

As Meichen had expected, Madam Chao rejected the doctor's diagnosis. "He is a fraud who imagines my son to be a spent old man. Everyone knows young men are filled with endless vigor, and only a fool would suggest otherwise." She pointed at Meichen. "That girl is the one at fault. If only you'll let me call in the midwife, you'll see I'm right."

Scholar Chao shook his head. "There's no reason not to follow the doctor's advice, however strange it sounds. Three months apart won't harm them. If anything, it should spur their desire for each other, and when they join again, a son is bound to be the result."

Forced to yield, Madam Chao gave Meichen a venomous look. A shiver swept down Meichen's back. *I hope this year will pass quickly, and I'll be pregnant right after the next New Year.*

CHAPTER 8

"The supreme art of war is to subdue the enemy without fighting."

—GENERAL SUN TZU

MEICHEN HADN'T REALIZED how difficult the three months of separation would be. Chung told his father about Meichen's evening lessons, and the scholar allowed Chung to continue teaching her, but only for an hour or so in the afternoon. They weren't allowed to sit in their room with the door closed.

Chung's father made sure the young couple followed the doctor's orders. Every week he gave Chung money to go to the teahouse and hire a prostitute. After a reasonable time, Chung returned and slipped the money into Meichen's hand to add to the cache hidden in their room.

Meichen worked on her calligraphy every week while he was taking his "treatment," and he stopped to examine her work when he returned. He pulled a chair close to hers, and they talked with their heads nearly touching.

She always whispered the same question. "What did you do today, Husband?"

Chung glanced around the room before he spoke, because often his father sat in the room reading while Meichen occupied his writing desk.

Most of the time he walked out to the countryside and sat on the rocks beside a stream enjoying the peaceful scenery while time passed.

By the end of the fourth week, Chung dreaded the two hours he had to spend roaming the back alleys of the village to stay out of sight. He wanted to spice up his routine. When Meichen asked her opening question, he had a different answer.

"I walked around the market and stopped to talk to the man who sells newspapers." As usual, he glanced at his father's face. The scholar showed no interest in his son's comments, but Chung knew he had sharp ears. He lowered his voice. "I got the paper man to talk about the latest news and I learned what's happened without having to buy a paper."

Chung picked up a brush to mark Meichen's paper, pretending to correct an error.

She leaned closer to the desk aiming her mouth toward his ear. "If you save all the money Father gives you, what will you do with it?"

"I don't know yet, but I'm sure it will be useful one day." He set his left hand on her thigh and slid his fingers under her tunic. They stayed there rubbing circles on her soft silk skirt while he wrote words with the brush in his right hand as though he had nothing else on his mind.

Meichen tried to suppress a giggle as she carefully copied his words. It was impossible for her to sit still, and her brush strokes became less and less legible. As his hand approached the apex of her thighs, she jumped, and a squeal escaped from her mouth. The scholar cleared his throat and Chung quickly returned his hand to his own thigh. Meichen froze as Chung's father left his chair and came to stand behind them, examining Meichen's work.

His face showed no expression as he looked at the blobs of ink squiggling across the page. "If the pupil is to succeed, both the master and his student must focus their minds on the work they are doing." Saying no more, he clasped his hands behind his back and walked into the garden.

Meichen hid her face with her hands and bent over the desk, her shoulders shaking. Chung clasped her close against his chest.

"I know you're embarrassed, but there's no reason to cry."

Muffled gasps escaped from the desk. Meichen sat up and let loose her laughter. "What's gotten into you, Husband? When we slept in the same bed, you tried not to touch me. Now you're brushing up against me, and I feel your hands on places they should not be with everyone watching us."

A sly smile spread across his lips. "I'm challenged to see how far I can go without being caught. And I don't have to worry about controlling myself if I get too aroused."

"You are very wicked, Husband. Your father knew exactly what you were doing."

Chung shrugged. "My father is a hard man to fool."

"But won't he wonder why you desire me after just visiting the tea house?"

Chung's face looked like he'd sucked a lemon. "He knows my instructions are to lie joined to a woman for as long as I can stand it, barely moving so I won't expel my seed. He can't believe that would be satisfying or enjoyable for me. In fact, I can't think of a more boring way to spend an hour."

"Perhaps I should go with you and read aloud to help pass the time." Meichen opened her eyes wide, pretending innocence, and Chung looked askance at her until he noticed the twinkle in her eyes.

Laughter overcame him and Meichen joined in. They kept laughing until both were wiping tears from their eyes. "I can picture it," Chung gasped, "me lying naked on top of a naked woman while you sit beside us, completely clothed, reading aloud."

Meichen stopped laughing as Chung's mother appeared in the door, casting a shadow over their sunlit faces. They both stood up, bowing.

"The lesson time is over." Madam Chao's eyes struck Meichen like daggers. "Come with me, Daughter. There's work to do."

"We still have half an hour left." Chung frowned, glancing at his father's foreign clock.

Madam Chao raised her eyebrows. "And what are you studying that made you so merry? I never heard your father's pupils laughing."

"And what if we are enjoying ourselves? There's no requirement for lessons to be dull."

Chung's defiance frightened Meichen. She could see his mother's face stiffen into an angry mask.

"Don't be insolent with me, my son. Remember I am your mother, the woman who labored for hours to bring you into this world. Is this how you show respect?"

"Forgive me, Mother." Chung lowered his head. He did not sound repentant though.

Madam Chao turned back to Meichen. "Come with me, Daughter. We need to sew while there is plenty of light to see." She motioned for Meichen to follow her.

"Mother, I haven't finished Meichen's lesson for today."

Madam Chao whirled around. Her frown evolved into an indulgent smile. "I am sorry to interfere in your business, my son, but we have ten members in this family who need clothes and shoes. Are you volunteering to be the person who goes barefoot wearing rags?"

Chung gave Meichen an apologetic glance as he yielded to his mother. Madam Chao marched through the door with Meichen trailing behind her. Meichen turned her head to give her husband a plaintive look, but he only shrugged.

...

After the women finished their evening meal, Jiao invited Meichen to her room. Meichen looked at Madam Chao, expecting her to mention some chore left undone. Madam Chao frowned and studied Jiao's face. Finally, she nodded. Meichen offered her arm to support Jiao as they left the table. Once they were well down the corridor, Jiao tittered.

"My sister-in-law is a determined person, and her strategies are clever, but she needs time to plan. When I take her by surprise, she has no defence ready." She laughed again when Meichen's arm stiffened and her steps slowed. "Do I sound crazy to you? Maybe I am imagining enemies everywhere."

Meichen's face froze and her eyes darted in different directions. "I'm not sure I understand you, Aunt."

"You are too innocent, Niece. In every household there is a struggle for control. Confucius wrote the correct order of precedence. You know, younger defers to older, women defer to men, and so forth. But people don't always follow rules, which leads to all the suffering and injustice in the world. So, what should I do, Meichen, when my place is usurped by my inferior?"

"I don't know, Aunt. I've always been younger and female, thus subject to everyone else."

"Yes, but you've seen situations where the natural order is perverted."

Meichen hesitated before she spoke. "In my maiden home, my Aunt Meu Yuk made every decision. My uncle did what she told him to."

Jiao nodded. "And were you a happy family under her direction?"

Meichen snorted. "No one was happy, not even my aunt."

"Think about this family. My husband is the second son. Your father-in-law is the third son. I was already living here when the Scholar brought his wife here. I already had children, but they were girls. Then she had two sons. My mother-in-law was inclined to favor her, because of the sons. My husband came back for a visit, and I had my son. His birth was difficult, and I was an invalid for a while. During that time, my mother-in-law died. By the time I recovered, my sister-in-law had taken charge as Head Woman, and she never yielded it back to me."

They had reached the door of her apartment, and she flung it open with a dramatic flourish of her arm. "That is why I take every possible action to thwart her plans."

Meichen glanced into Jiao's large sitting room. Chung stood inside with his portable writing desk clutched under his arm. He grinned, obviously surprised, and she clapped her hands over her mouth and gasped. Jiao gave Meichen a slight push to move her forward, so she could shut the door.

"Chung, I thought you might like some uninterrupted time with your wife to finish the lesson that was cut short this afternoon."

"Does my mother know Meichen is here?"

"Why, Nephew, do you think I would deceive your mother? Of course she knows." Jiao used her sugary sweet voice. "Does she know where *you* are?"

"I'd planned to go out with my brothers." He cleared his throat. "They won't be home for at least two hours."

"Should I send word that you're with me?" Jiao lifted her eyebrows.

Chung took Meichen's arm and led her to a chair beside Jiao's game table. "No, Aunt, that's not necessary." He removed paper, brushes, and ink while Meichen poured water into a cup.

Jiao sat down on a couch and rang a bell to summon her maid. She watched Chung test the ink Meichen had mixed and nod his approval at its consistency.

When she looked away to give orders to the servant, Meichen locked eyes with Chung and began a whispered conversation.

"You can't do what you did this afternoon with her watching us."

"She's expecting some entertainment. We can't disappoint her." He suppressed laughter.

"Nephew, I have candied cherries over here. Do you or your wife want some?" Jiao held up the plate.

Jiao's maid had stuffed pillows behind her back and pushed an ottoman under her feet. She gave the appearance of a person who was comfortably settled to watch a performance. Meichen clenched her hands together as Chung crossed the room and lifted a cherry off the plate. He brought the cherry to his mouth, bit off half, and popped the other half between her lips. She had to push the cherry into her mouth to keep sticky liquid from dripping down her chin. She held up her hand while she looked around for a cloth to wipe her fingers. Before the maid could bring a napkin, Chung took her hand and sucked the sugar off, one finger at a time.

Meichen snatched the napkin from the maid and dipped it in the cup of water she'd poured to mix ink. Very deliberately, she wrapped the napkin around the fingers he had sucked and twisted the cloth until her fingers stung. She dropped the napkin into the maid's hand and stared at the wall.

Jiao laughed and clapped her hands. Then Chung laughed with her, and even the little maid let a giggle escape. Meichen sat up straighter, pretending not to hear them.

"Nephew, I'm surprised at you. You're unkind to tempt your wife when you can't sleep together."

"I apologize, Aunt. I thought she wanted candy, but I was mistaken."

Jiao resumed laughing until she had to gasp for breath. "Next time you should ask what she wants. Meichen, don't be angry. My nephew is a bit wild, but I know you can tame him."

Meichen sat still and silent. She heard Jiao sigh and groan, then call her maid's name. "I think I've caused enough trouble for the day, children. I'm going to my bedchamber and leave you alone so you two can make up."

When Meichen was sure Jiao was gone, she stood up. "Good night, Husband. I'm too tired to finish the lesson. I'll see you tomorrow."

Chung grabbed her arm and yanked her back in the chair. "What's the matter with you? We can spend another hour together."

"I don't want to stay in this room. It disturbs me."

"Is it the room that disturbs you, or is it me?"

"We shouldn't do things that are meant to be private when someone is watching."

"I can't believe you're angry about the cherry. Couldn't you tell I was playing?"

"I knew you were playing, but it wasn't for my pleasure. I'm not your toy, Chung."

"My playing didn't bother you this afternoon when my father was in the room."

"I felt comfortable there. I trusted him to limit what you would do."

"But you didn't trust Aunt Jiao to stop me. What do you think I would have done, removed your clothes and taken your virginity for her entertainment? So far, I haven't done that when we're alone, despite all your efforts to break my will."

"You don't understand. I know you wouldn't do that. But I think she might have enjoyed seeing you do it."

Chung's face twisted as he backed away from her. "You think my aunt is perverted? How do you know about that? When we married, you didn't even know what newlyweds did."

Meichen shook her head, refusing to look at him. He slapped his hand on the table, and she jumped.

"Did Yuan tell you about things she saw in the brothel?"

Meichen hesitated. *I don't want him to know I asked Yuan what courtesans do.*

"Do I need to send Yuan back to the mission?"

"No, please don't. It wasn't Yuan. My brother told me." She pressed her face into her hands.

Chung clucked his tongue in disgust. "You haven't seen Ling Mo in two years. When would he have told you?

"It was before he left. Our uncle took him to a flower house, and he paid for Ling Mo to watch a couple..." Her voice faded away. "He never said what the couple was doing, but I knew from Ling Mo's voice that it was disgusting. He told me never to be alone with Uncle, or to go off with him. That's why I was so afraid my aunt would sell me to the flower house if your mother sent me home. I didn't want to do disgusting things with people watching me."

She propped her arms on the game table and rested her face on her arms. He moved his chair closer to hers and slid his arm across her shoulder.

"What made you think my aunt has the same inclinations as your uncle? Did she ask you something personal that upset you?"

"I was shocked when you licked my fingers and she didn't tell you to stop. Then she laughed when she saw I didn't like it. She was encouraging you to do improper things."

"Meichen, what's so terrible about a man sucking on his wife's fingers?"

A shiver went up her spine. "I've never seen any man do that or heard talk about it. It feels unnatural – not what the gods intended people to do."

He played with the loose strands of her hair lying on her neck. "When you're older, and we've been married several years, you'll find married people do many things you've never seen or heard of. And I'll make sure that you enjoy every one of them."

"And we'll be alone when we do them." She raised her head to look him in the eye.

"I promise. Now, sit up and prepare your brush." He slid a sheet of rice paper over the table and set a small sample page to one side. "Let me see how well you write these."

CHAPTER 9

"To know your enemy, you must become your enemy."

—GENERAL SUN TZU

THE NEXT AFTERNOON, as Jiao took her daily walk around the court-yard, she stopped to talk to Meichen. Meichen rose from her spot on the bench beside the koi pond.

"Sit down, Aunt." She set the jacket she was mending in her lap and prepared to listen with suitable respect.

Jiao groaned as she bent her knees. Her maid held onto her arms as Jiao sank down to the seat. Once her mistress was settled, the maid retreated to the courtyard wall.

"I hope you won't be angry with me, Niece. I've talked to your husband's father about the timing of your lessons. Since your husband's mother needs you so much in the afternoon, I suggest-ed evening lessons instead, and I offered my sitting room for that purpose."

"What did Chung's mother say?"

"I don't know. She wasn't there when I told the Scholar my idea. But Chung was with us, and he said he liked my suggestion." She smiled at Meichen. "My nephew likes to spend time with you. You're a lucky wife to have such a devoted, creative husband."

"Why do you say he is creative? Because he creates beautiful scrolls?"

Jiao patted Meichen's hand. "Poor child, you have a treasure and don't realize it. Chung is an artist, but more than that he works hard to please you. Most husbands are lazy. They do what they prefer and never worry if their wives are happy. No wonder so many wives try to make everyone around them miserable."

"Is that what's wrong with my husband's mother?"

Jiao frowned, but Meichen saw a mischievous gleam in her eyes. "It's hard to say. She had three sons before her sixth year of marriage, so I suppose some people might say he was very attentive to her when he was young. On the other hand, I've never seen them spend time together in pleasant conversation in all the years she's lived here."

"I can't imagine what they would both want to discuss. The scholar is interested in ideas and philosophy – things in a person's head. Chung's mother only cares about the body. She thinks about food, and clothes, and outward appearances. When Grandfather Chao chose the wife of his third son he should have looked for a bride with appreciation for the scholar's brilliance."

"When parents look for their son's bride, they are more interested in fertility than intelligence. Grandfather Chao was not educated, and he chose traditional brides for his sons, but each time he aimed for a woman from a higher social class. His first son married the daughter of a land- owner with a small estate. My family were merchants and artisans with customers in all the coastal provinces. Their connections and money helped my husband and his elder brother, Chao Gang, open businesses and send money to the Chao family."

"What made my mother-in-law a desirable choice?"

"Her sister married a Manchu noble who held a minor government post. We all expected Chung's father to pass the Imperial examinations. Then his Manchu brother-in-law could arrange a prosperous appointment for him with the government. But, of course, the plans fell apart when the Scholar failed."

"I guess Grandfather Chao was tremendously disappointed."

"His disappointment was minor compared to the drama my sister-in-law displayed. She cried and shrieked like a professional mourner. She accused her husband of failing on purpose to deny her elevation to the high rank her sister held. She berated him in front of the family until he could barely hold his head up. I had to fight my urge to slap her face."

"I can't believe Chung's grandparents tolerated her disrespect."

"At first, I think Grandfather Chao was so angry he thought Chung's father deserved scolding and criticism. But eventually he tired of the discord that ruined everyone's tranquillity, and he forbade her to speak if she couldn't govern her words."

Jiao called her maid to help her up. "I must finish my walk before we eat. I enjoyed our short visit. I'll see you this evening."

...

After the evening meal, Meichen's feet tapped under the table. Madam Chao was taking an eon to finish eating. Jiao had already retired to her room, and Chung was probably with her

Chung's mother examined Meichen's face. Her lips formed her unpleasant smile. "Are you anxious to leave, Meichen? Jiao sets a bad example. It's not wise to rush off just after eating. It ruins the digestion if we don't allow our bodies time to process our food."

Ching Lan looked up from her plate. "Is that true for everyone, or just people like our family?"

Madam Chao's eyes flashed at her daughter. "What is that supposed to mean? Of course, it's true for everyone."

"Our servants never sit still after they eat. They don't rest until bedtime."

"Quit wasting my time with foolish questions. Eat your cabbage and fish so you can leave the table."

Meichen shifted in her chair and repressed a sigh. *I've eaten everything on my plate except the bones.* She lifted her eyebrows as she caught Ching Lan's attention. The girl looked back at her with wide, innocent eyes.

"What do you want, Sister?" Her voice was sweetly sarcastic.

Meichen refrained from clenching her teeth. "I can't understand why you don't like those delicious vegetables."

Ching Lan wrinkled her nose. "Cook put too much fish sauce on them. They're too salty."

Meichen shifted her backside again and put her hands on the edge of the table. She twined her fingers together and watched the shadows deepen in the courtyard as the sun set. Ching Lan poked her vegetables with her chopsticks, making a mosaic design with the brown fish and green cabbage, while her mother glared at her.

First Brother's wife, who sat across from Meichen, still as a stuffed doll, broke the silence with a barely audible moan. "Honorable Mother, I need to feed my baby. I'm sorry, but I'm uncomfortable." Her plump hand brushed over her bust where a wet spot was spreading.

"Go," Madame Chao snapped. "Why do you sit here and let my grandson starve?"

First Brother's wife fled, and Madam Chao glared after her. "Stupid girl."

Meichen caught a quick movement from the corner of her eye. Half of the fish and cabbage mosaic was gone from Ching Lan's plate.

Madam Chao returned to her scrutiny of Ching Lan and allowed her lips to turn up slightly. "Just two more bites, and you'll be finished."

Ching Lan rearranged her food into a new design. "I'm too thirsty to eat the rest."

Meichen smiled. *You're a clever girl, Ching Lan. You know better than to empty the whole plate at one time. Your mother would never believe you'd eaten it all so fast. Now I have an idea to set both of us free.*

Meichen grasped the handle of the teapot. "Hold up your cup, Little Sister." Before Madam Chao could protest, Meichen moved the pot over the girl's plate and dropped it. Shattered porcelain floated in hot tea as it covered Ching Lan's food.

Meichen leaped from her chair and wailed. "I'm so sorry! I'll get the maid."

"Just go, both of you." Madam Chao shrieked the maid's name, and Ching Lan raced out the door only seconds before Meichen got there.

She was breathless by the time she crossed the courtyard and tapped on Jiao's door. She tripped over the doorsill and landed in Chung's arms. He held her upright as he closed the door.

"What happened?" Jiao asked. "Did all the demons from hell chase you in the courtyard?"

"Chung's mother is furious. I wanted to get away before she stopped me." Meichen sat on a sofa and gulped air.

Chung looked at her with misgiving. "What did you do?"

"I broke the teapot."

Jiao laughed. "It's just like her to have a tantrum over an accident. I'll buy her a replacement."

"It wasn't an accident. I dropped it on purpose to ruin Ching Lan's food. I didn't want to sit at the table any longer."

Jiao and Chung looked at her with puzzled faces. Meichen sighed and recounted the events that had preceded her action.

"Aunt, do you think my father forgot to tell my mother about the new time for lessons?" Chung's brows drew together until they almost met over his nose.

Jiao shook her head. "Oh, I'm certain he told her. She kept Meichen from leaving to spite me."

Chung sat down next to Meichen. "Perhaps we should forget about the lessons until the three months of separation are over."

"I don't want to stop them." Meichen clutched his arm. "Just because we can't share a bed doesn't mean we can't see each other at all."

"I'm trying to protect you from my mother's temper."

"I don't understand why she's angry just because I want to be educated."

"Chung's mother wants to protect him from you, Niece."

"In what way?" Chung asked.

"Surely you've read what Confucius says about marriage. A man should keep a proper distance from his wife." Jiao's voice had a sarcastic edge. "If he acts too friendly, she'll get the upper hand. If he ignores her, she'll be resentful. He must find a middle ground."

Chung snorted. "My mother wants me to copy my brother. He never notices his wife at all until bedtime. I've never heard him say a word about her, even when his sons were born."

Jiao nodded. "Yes, I know. She's nothing but a vessel for his seed. But who can blame him? She takes no interest in anything but food, and she's become round as a dumpling. When I sit with her in your mother's quarters, the girl has nothing to say that interests even another woman, much less a man." Jiao turned to Meichen. "Don't you agree?"

"I know I don't want to turn into a woman like her."

Chung patted her hand. "I don't think you ever could. I can discuss my favorite poems with you and the articles I read in the newspapers. Talking to you is almost as good as talking to Ling Mo." Chung grinned at the indignant look she gave him.

"I'm sure you don't mind that she's a beautiful girl," Jiao added. She looked her nephew directly in the eye. "I'm glad you realize a woman can be intelligent like a man and still be desirable as a woman."

She called the maid to help her walk to her bedroom. Chung watched her hobble to the door, leaning heavily against the maid. His lips formed a flat line as he turned to his wife.

"My father told me his second brother wanted Aunt Jiao to be his bride because she has such tiny feet. When she walked, the swaying of her hips aroused him to a fever pitch." Chung shook his head. "What a foolish reason to marry a woman."

Meichen took her place at the game table where rice paper, ink, and brushes were set out. She began drawing the characters he'd taught her the previous night. "I wonder what attracted him to his American concubine. There is nothing small about her."

He laughed and joined her at the table. "You're eager to start your lesson tonight."

"Yes. I want to be as interesting as my brother." She raised her chin in a haughty pose.

"Don't worry, Wife." He laid his hand on her thigh. "You have attractions Ling Mo can never match."

CHAPTER 10

*"Being deeply loved by someone gives you strength,
while loving someone deeply gives you courage."*

—LAO TZU

MEICHEN SUCKED ON HER TONGUE as she copied a quotation from the writings of Mencius, in defence of Confucius. She concentrated on forming the characters correctly. Chung had commended her the previous night for her improvement in brush technique. She had toiled over the lengthy passage nearly an hour hoping to win more praise. She began to wish Mencius had summarized his thoughts more succinctly.

The door opened and Meichen looked up, expecting Yuan. But it was her husband who came in. He closed the door and leaned against it as though he had no strength to move farther, covering his face with his hand.

Something is wrong. Someone has died!

"Meichen, my father received a letter from my first uncle in San Francisco. He sends shocking news."

"Ling Mo," she choked. "Have the White Devils harmed my brother?"

"First Uncle didn't mention Ling Mo. The Government in the United States passed a new law. In less than three months, no Chinese may enter their country without special permission. I must join my second uncle now, or I won't get in."

Meichen froze at first. Then devastation knotted her insides, and she clenched folded arms over the pain. "But we have three more years."

She rose to pace the room like a frenzied animal in a cage. "No. No. You can't go yet." When he tried to hold her, she pounded on his chest, shaking her head back and forth, denying the words she didn't want to hear. Her fury spent, she sank to the floor in front of him, sobbing. He knelt beside her and stroked her head.

"I'm sorry, Meichen. I must go. It's my duty to my family." He closed his eyes to avoid the agony in her eyes.

"Take me with you." She grabbed the sleeves of his jacket. "Please."

"I can't. It's dangerous over there. Americans sometimes kill Celestial men. Think what they'd do to you."

"I don't care. I'd rather be dead than live without you." More tears flowed out.

He turned his head away. "You'd be worse than dead. I can't allow that, or even risk it."

"But Eldest Uncle's wife is in San Francisco with him."

"Eldest Uncle's wife is an old woman, safe from anybody. If I said yes, my father would never allow it. I know I've been rebellious in the past, but it's time to put childhood behind me and do what I'm told."

"When will I see you again?" She choked out the words between sobs.

"If Second Uncle consents, I can come home for a visit in five years. My father thinks he will agree since I have no son."

"Five years?" she gasped. "I'll be twenty years old before you come back!"

"You'll be even more beautiful. And we'll make the Clouds and Rain every day." He stood up and reached his hand down to help her back to her feet. Instead she wrapped her arms around his legs with her head bowed.

"Give me a child before you go," she begged.

Chung struggled from her grasp. "I can't. I promised Ling Mo we'd wait."

"But everything is different now. If you must leave me, give me something to tie us together and give me status in this house." She held onto him more tightly.

She felt him press his hands on the top of her head. She didn't move as she waited for him to speak, but inside her mind she prayed to Kwan Yin, the goddess of mercy.

He pried her arms loose from his leg and lifted her onto the bed. "Ling Mo, forgive me," he whispered.

Chung unbuttoned Meichen's tunic and pulled it over her head. Her breast halter and skirt followed, and his clothes joined the pile on the floor. She lay back on the bed, pulling him down next to her.

Without saying anything, he kissed her cheeks, burned raw by salty tears. His lips travelled to hers, and he nibbled lightly on the soft flesh until she opened her mouth in response.

He released her mouth and moved his attention to her ear. His lips slipped from there to the nape of her neck. Her hair fell from its bun as he rolled her onto her stomach. His hands stroked her shoulders, down her back, and over the curve of her hip, all the way to her thighs until he reached the back of her legs. He sat up and bent forward, pressing his lips against the velvety area behind her knee.

Her feet and ankles attracted him next. He turned her on her back to give the arch of her foot a gentle massage. His fingers encircled her slender ankles and pulled her legs slightly apart. He paused for a minute, studying the parts of her body.

"Why are you stopping?" Meichen asked as she lifted her head.

"I'm remembering how the doctor told me to build up your yin essence. Be patient."

"What you've done so far is wonderful. I've never felt so good."

He slid his hands up to the top of her thighs. "I am looking for your jewelled terrace. Do you think it might be here?"

Meichen moaned as his fingers rubbed against her outer female parts. When he paused, she took his hand and pushed it further against the wet inside. She moved in rhythm with his hand as he rocked it back and forth.

"I've reached the terrace," he said. "Shall I linger there?"

"Yes," Meichen breathed. She couldn't lay still. She gave a sudden cry and arched her back convulsively.

Chung smiled. "Our doctor would be pleased with all the yin essence you're making."

Chung's slender fingers probed deeper. "I've reached the jade gate. Will it let me enter this time?"

"Yes," Meichen cried. "My whole body is aching for you."

"You're sure?"

"Do it now," she gasped.

He knelt between her legs, spreading them wide. Her body clamored for release, blocking out all other sensations. She forced herself to breathe deeply as he rested his weight on his elbows, preparing to push inside her.

They almost missed the soft knock on the door.

"Master, Mistress," Yuan called softly.

"Go away," Chung growled.

"Master, your mother is coming. She's been looking for you."

Chung cursed under his breath. "Tell her I'll join her soon."

"I see her coming through the courtyard."

Chung gave up, letting his weight fall on Meichen. "No," he muttered. He moved off her quickly and picked up his clothes, pulling them on haphazardly. "Why, in the name of all the gods, can't she wait?"

Meichen sobbed as her climax came to a sudden end. The fever he'd worked so hard to create ebbed away.

Chung's mother ordered Yuan out of the way, then her voice sweetened as she knocked on the door. "Chung, my son, let me speak to you."

Chung hastily arranged his clothes and pulled the quilt over Meichen. He went to the door, opening it just wide enough to slide outside. "Here I am," he said, his voice as sharp as a knife edge.

"What have you been doing all this time?" His mother sounded petulant.

"My wife felt ill, and I was checking on her."

Madam Chao squeezed past him to enter the room. "Let me see what's wrong with her."

Meichen lay still. Her makeup streaked across her face, distorted by tears and Chung's kisses. Part of her hair spread across the pillow while the rest stayed curled in a bun. She shut her eyes, overcome with humiliation. Madam Chao moved away and turned her back on the dishevelled bed and her daughter-in-law.

Of course, she won't have the grace to apologize for interrupting us.

"My son, I need to talk to you about this terrible news."

"Mother, we all knew I would leave someday."

"But to go so soon," she wailed, "and without children to leave behind."

Chung gazed down at Meichen, and back up to her. "Mother, is there something else you need to say to me?"

"We must see about your clothes for the journey."

"I have clothes, and I can buy more in America."

"But your Western suits may not fit. You'll need new ones. And it's cheaper to have them made in Canton. Your first uncle says everything is expensive in the Gold Mountain. And he says you should wear Western clothes and hide your queue under a hat so the White Devils won't attack you."

"And how will I hide my eyes and skin?" Sarcasm dripped from his voice.

Madam Chao burst into tears. "My son, I'd give my life to keep you here, safe from danger. Ever since I've known you would go overseas, I've prayed to the gods to change your fate."

"I promise, Mother, I'll be very careful not to offend the Americans."

"I'll burn incense for you every day." She sobbed louder. "Oh, why do the Barbarians have all the money? Why can't you stay here and find a respectable job?"

Scholar Chao came into the courtyard. "What is this? Why are you weeping, Wife?"

"My son is leaving," Madam Chao said, raising her handkerchief to her eyes.

"Do you imagine I am happy about it?" The Scholar motioned for Chung to join him. "I've thought of some things we must discuss."

Chung walked away with his father and his mother frowned at Meichen.

Madam Chao's voice became harsh. "Get dressed, Daughter. I want you and Yuan to inventory my son's clothing so we'll know what he needs to buy."

The woman swept from the room, and Meichen gathered her clothes to dress.

May all the gods help me. What will my life be like while Chung is away?

...

Meichen and Chung went to Jiao's room for the nightly lesson. She hoped he'd cut his instruction short so they could escape to their room. Meichen finished mixing the ink just as Madam Chao appeared at Jiao's door. Chung gritted his teeth and Meichen watched his lips move while he counted under his breath.

Jiao leaned close to Meichen's ear. "Patience is a great virtue, but sometimes hard to achieve."

Madam Chao nodded at Jiao and apologized for interrupting them. She turned her back to her sister-in-law and focused on Chung. "Your father says you go to Canton tomorrow. Your wife and her maid sorted all your clothes. Go into your room and put them on so I can be sure they fit. We might need to order more."

"I need to finish my wife's lesson, Mother."

"Oh, don't worry about her." Madam Chao waved her hand as if she brushed away a fly. "Meichen can entertain your aunt by reading to her. That can be her lesson tonight."

"It's a shame my nephew cannot spend more time with his wife. I believe their three months of separation are over." Jiao's voice was achingly sweet like one of her candied cherries.

Madam Chao ignored her. She grasped Chung's arm and led him into the courtyard.

Jiao plied her silk fan. "It's too bad my sister-in-law is so stubborn. I've told her my nephew doesn't need fancy suits to work in my husband's store."

"I know she'll keep him with her as long as she can." Meichen plopped her hands on her thighs in frustration.

"I prefer to choose how I spend my evenings." Jiao snapped her fan shut. "I don't care to hear stories tonight. I want to play Mah Jong."

"Don't we need four people for that?"

"I'll send my maid to fetch Ching Lan and my first nephew's wife. My sister-in-law won't need them tonight."

...

Meichen tiptoed into her room much later than she'd meant to. The game had lifted her spirits. After Ching Lan went off to bed, and her other sister-in-law left to say good night to her children, Jiao had offered Meichen plum wine. They'd reclined on the divans, laughing as Jiao told Meichen risqué stories and skewered her friends and relatives with her acerbic wit.

Chung's bedroom was nearly dark with only one oil lamp burning in the corner. It reminded her of her wedding night, and she smiled, thinking how scared she'd been. Tonight, she remembered the pressure of Chung's naked body against hers and tingled in anticipation. She looked at the bed, expecting to see him waiting for her. The quilt was smooth and flat, just as Yuan had left it that afternoon when she remade the bed.

Meichen muttered an oath she had learned from her brother. *Is Chung's mother determined to keep him all night? That woman is a witch, an ill-tempered sow.* She jerked off her clothes and climbed in the bed, clenching her teeth to hold back a scream.

She rolled back and forth from her side to her back, but no position felt comfortable. She kicked the coverlet off her legs. She needed to lie still, to relax and restore her inner harmony. But every minute that passed increased her fury. Chung came at last, locked the door, and sat on the bed, pressing his hands on the sides of his head.

Meichen didn't ask if his head ached. She already knew the answer.

He undressed and fell onto the bed next to her, quiet and motionless. Meichen wondered if he planned to resume his lovemaking although she was hardly in the mood for it. But Chung lay still, disinterested. She tried to rouse him by sliding her hand down his chest. He gave a deep sigh and Meichen curled her fists in desperation.

"Please, Husband, we have so little time."

He made a half-hearted effort to touch her breast and let his hand fall back on the bed. "What should be a pleasure has become a duty," he said, yawning. "I want to enjoy creating my son."

She slid her head next to his and nipped his ear. It was not a love bite.

"Ow!" He glared at her. "It's not my fault I'm tired. My mother hasn't given me a moment to rest. My ears ache from listening to her all day."

Meichen groaned, and he patted her face. "Give me one night," he said, rolling onto his side with his back to her. "I'm going to Canton tomorrow. When all the arrangements are behind me, I'll feel better."

"All right," she muttered. "Tomorrow night.

...

Chung did not return from Canton the next night. He couldn't find passage on a ship. Word of the new immigration laws had created a panic, and thousands of men planned to leave immediately. The Lesters offered him a bed at their mission until he could buy a ticket. He would send another note by the boatman if he had to stay longer. Scholar Chao read Chung's message to the family and shut himself in his library.

The next day Meichen stayed in her room. It was best to avoid her mother-in-law with her emotions so close to the surface. She paced the room, restless as a caged bird who was never allowed to fly. *Why did the gods make me a woman, at the mercy of a man's whims?* A lifetime of isolation and restrictions lay before her. She couldn't even leave the house without permission. *There's nothing in my future but endless waiting.*

After a while her anger burned out, and reason took over. *Chung has a great adventure before him. I can't blame him for thinking of other things besides me.*

Meichen wondered what adventure she might experience, and the mission school came to her mind. In a sudden burst of activity, she jumped up, straightening her clothes and hair, and she called Yuan in to retouch her makeup. Satisfied with her appearance, she went to look for her father-in-law.

She found him in his room reading. He looked up at Meichen, his eyes wary, waiting in silence for her petition.

Meichen hesitated. Faced with the scholar's implacable gaze, the request that had seemed so logical when she first conceived it now seemed outrageous.

He cleared his throat. "Did you want to ask me something, Daughter?"

"Father of my Husband," she said, forcing the formal greeting through a quavering voice, "the school my husband attended has classes for girls. If you'd allow it, I'd like to study there while my husband is overseas. They don't charge a fee, so it would cost you nothing."

Meichen expected an immediate dismissal, but Scholar Chao closed his book and set it on his side table. He clasped his hands together and leaned his head to one side. He glanced at her once and looked down again before he finally spoke.

"Why do you want to leave your family? Married woman don't go to school."

Meichen bowed her head. "I'm sorry, Father. I shouldn't have asked such a thing." Her voice broke. "I only wanted to write to my husband. He's taught me some of the letters, but not enough to read or write well."

Scholar Chao's expression softened. "I can continue your education."

She bowed to him. "Thank you, Father."

She fled to her room, brushing away tears. *Fool, what else did you expect? I must be going mad to imagine such a thing.*

Two days later, Chung entered their room as the sun blazed high overhead. Meichen ran to him and wrapped her arms around his waist. He staggered backward from the force of her onslaught, then regained his balance and responded with a kiss that took her breath away, very different from the ones he'd given her before.

When he released her, she raced to the bed and sprang on top of the covers, spreading her legs and flinging her arms out to the sides.

"I'm ready, Husband. Take my clothes off."

"It's the middle of the day. Besides, I want to talk to you."

"Talk later. Now is the perfect time to make love. Your father and brothers are busy teaching, Aunt Jiao always naps after her mid-day meal, and, best of all, your mother has gone off to visit her friends and taken Ching Lan with her."

He came to the bed and sat beside her "I really do need to talk to you before we do anything."

She glared up at him. "Not another excuse."

"Be patient. I just spoke to my father, and he told me you asked to go to the mission school."

She pulled her arms close to her body and clenched her fists. "He said I couldn't go."

"If he mentioned it to me, he might still be considering it. I'll speak to him myself. It would be good for you, and I know you'd be happier there while I'm gone." His hand slid down her silk tunic. "I've thought about that day before I left for Canton. In fact, it's been on my mind quite a lot."

"Mine, too." Her stomach fluttered.

"I'm glad now we were interrupted."

"What?" She sat up quickly, her eyes wide with shock.

"It's for the best, Meichen. I shouldn't have given way to unthinking passion."

Meichen rolled onto her stomach, beating the pillows with her hands. She kicked her feet in a paroxysm of fury and bit the quilt to stifle her screams. Chung put his hand on her shoulder and she angrily shook it off.

He grasped her arms and made her sit back up. She tried to pull away, but he held her tight. She gave one last explosive shriek and pressed her face against his chest, shaking with sobs.

"Oh, Meichen," Chung sighed, "you're such a child"

"But you promised," she gasped out.

"Think, Meichen. You can't go to school in Canton if you're pregnant."

"It's not just because I want a baby."

"Then why are you so upset?"

"What you did made me feel wonderful." Her lips quivered. "I want to feel that way again."

Chung's eyebrows rose. Seconds later a smile slowly spread over his face. He gently lowered her back against the pillows and stretched out beside her. "Close your eyes," he whispered. "It is possible for us to reach the peak without actually joining."

Meichen shivered with pleasure as he unbuttoned her tunic.

"For now," Chung soothed, "we'll have the clouds without the rain."

CHAPTER 11

"Without experiencing the cold of winter, one cannot appreciate the warmth of spring."

—Chinese Proverb

MEICHEN SAT IN THE SHADED COURTYARD with her sewing kit, pretending not to hear the debate raging in her father-in-law's chamber. Placid on the surface, she strained to capture every nuance in the voices of the three participants. Madam Chao could be heard throughout the whole courtyard. Chung was harder to hear, and Scholar Chao's comments were barely audible.

The pitch of Madam Chao's voice went higher, a sign of increasing anger. Meichen flinched as her needle jabbed her finger. She tossed the cloth on the bench to prevent a drop of blood from staining it and stood to jerk her handkerchief from her pocket. As she wrapped the wounded digit, she edged closer to the open window.

"Husband, why should we pay good money to send a daughter-in-law to school? If she needs an education, give it to her yourself. You're a teacher."

Chung cut her off. "The missionary school is free. The Lesters are eager to take students."

"That's another good reason she shouldn't go there. Her mind will be poisoned with Christian nonsense," Madam Chao countered.

"I spent three years with them, and they didn't convert me," Chung said.

"They almost did. You talked about going to school overseas and becoming a missionary yourself."

"I only threatened that to keep you from binding Ching Lan's feet. I didn't really want to become a Christian, Father, but I would have done it if you'd crippled Little Sister."

"And your father should have taken you out of the school for such disrespectful behavior."

Scholar Chao raised his voice slightly but responded with his usual patience. "You forget, Mother of My Sons, I'm not free to do as I please. Second Brother expects Chung to come to him able to read and write English to help him with his business. What would he do if Chung ran off to be a missionary and refused to work for him? I couldn't risk that happening over a foolish matter like a girl's feet."

"Foolish matter? I'll never find a husband for her!"

The scholar's tone did not change. "We've wandered away from the subject. We're talking about Meichen going to school."

"And I still say it's ridiculous." Meichen pictured her mother-in-law crossing her arms over her chest.

The voices ceased for several minutes before the scholar spoke again. "I need peace to think. Both of you, go about your business. I'll tell you when I've decided."

Chung came out to join Meichen. who had returned to her bench. She appeared absorbed in her work as she plied her needle.

"You heard?" Chung whispered. He nodded, approving her strategic choice of a bench just three feet from the Scholar's window.

"Yes. Thank you for leaving the window open." She kept her eyes on the cloth, her lips barely moving.

Chung squeezed her hand. "Don't give up hope. If he won't give an answer, that's a good sign." He released her hand and stood up. "I have to go now. It's my turn to help with the students today."

Meichen continued to sew, stopping often to glance around the courtyard to relieve her boredom. A young girl came through the gate, someone new to the household. Painfully thin, she bent under the weight of two heavy buckets. She stopped, setting the buckets down. A querulous voice emerged from the kitchen door and Madam Chao emerged into the courtyard. The girl grabbed the bucket handles, but the mistress had seen her.

Madam Chao's hands jerked to her hips. "Why are you so slow? I told you to wash the entrance to the house an hour ago. It should be done by now."

The girl picked up the buckets and staggered past Madam Chao, who followed her into the kitchen, still scolding. Meichen frowned and called Yuan to her side.

"Who is the new servant girl? She seems very young."

"Your husband's mother bought her for almost nothing. And she's not really a child. She's small because her family's been through a famine. You know how it goes. If there's little to eat, the grandparents get the largest portion, then the father and the sons, then the mother. If anything's left, it goes to the girls."

"She must have had almost nothing." Meichen frowned at the kitchen door. She stood, leaving her work basket on the bench.

Yuan's eyes widened. "Please don't interfere, Young Mistress. You'll only make your husband's mother angrier, and that won't help the girl."

Meichen ignored Yuan's pleading and strode into the kitchen. She heard Madam Chao, still scolding, in the entrance hall. *This is my fault. She's angry with me and she's transferred her wrath onto this poor girl.* Meichen walked toward the piercing voice.

"Mother, may I speak to you?"

Madam Chao looked up from the girl to glare at Meichen. "I have no time for you now." She returned her attention to the cowering servant and resumed ranting.

"Stop!" Meichen startled herself with the volume of her voice. "This girl is too weak to work so hard. She needs plenty of food and time to recover her health."

Madame Chao's eyebrows rose nearly to her hairline. "How dare you presume to give me advice? You are nothing in this house, not even as useful as a lap dog. Shut your mouth and go to my son's room. I'll send him there to beat you for your insolence."

"He won't do it, even to please you." Meichen's disdain drove her mother-in-law to shake with fury.

"We'll see." Madam Chao's shriek penetrated every room in the house. "Help me! My sons and Husband, help me!"

At once a crowd collected. The cook and his assistants came from the kitchen, the gardener from the flower beds, the maids from their stations, even Jiao hobbled to the foyer, clinging to her maid's arm. Chung and his brothers ran from the school room and skidded to a stop, transfixed by Meichen and Madam Chao glaring at each other, both clenching their fists. Scholar Chao came last, with his usual dignity intact. He turned back only once to glance at the few curious students who'd gathered at the classroom door. They promptly disappeared.

All voices fell silent while the scholar surveyed the scene. He stroked his beard, his only indication of curiosity.

Madam Chao did not wait for him to speak. She pointed at Meichen. "My daughter-in-law has the arrogance to criticize the way I run the household. I won't tolerate her interference. She needs to learn her place."

Meichen did not lower her eyes or show any sign of humility. She gestured at the servant girl still cowering on her knees. "This girl is starved and weak. She can't do the task she's been assigned." As anger boiled inside her, she added the unthinkable. "My husband's mother needs to learn compassion."

Except for the scholar and Meichen, everyone's mouth dropped open. Meichen stood tall and proud, daring anyone to contradict her. At that moment she didn't care if Chung's family sent her away or the gods struck her dead or she suffered bad luck the rest of her life.

Madam Chao shrieked at a deafening volume. "Chung, take a rod from the kitchen and beat her until she can't stand. Then we'll send her back to her criminal family."

"Mother, I can't..." His voice stumbled to a halt. He gave Meichen a telling look. "Wife, apologize to my mother."

"I won't." Meichen's eyes were hard as mah-jong tiles.

Madam Chao ground her teeth. Like a snake striking, her hand went up, slapping Meichen. The blow sent her backward over the servant girl and knocked the buckets on their sides. Meichen looked up at her enemy, murder in her eyes.

Madam Chao smirked in triumph. "If you feel so sorry for this girl, do her work for her. As for food, I'll feed her as I please."

Meichen looked through the crowd until she found Yuan. "Make sure she gets my share of the food tonight." She rolled onto her knees, grabbed the scrubbing brush, and swept the bristles across the floor.

The servants went off and Chung's brothers returned to the students. Jiao took her maid and the thin servant girl off with her. Only the scholar and Chung remained with the two women.

Madam Chao tossed her head. "You two were no help at all."

Scholar Chao turned to Chung. "I have made a decision. Your wife may go to the mission school. She can leave with you."

Madam Chao gave a little gasp and started to protest, but the scholar forestalled her. "I think your spirit is out of balance, Wife. Go lie down and meditate until you achieve peace." He touched Chung's shoulder and led him back to the students.

Meichen continued to scrub the floor, but satisfaction spread over her in a warm glow. She would escape out of ignorance and oppression. And she would never return.

CHAPTER 12

"The hardest step
is over a threshold."

—CHINESE SAYING

MEICHEN WAITED FOR HER BREATHING to return to a normal rate as she lay beside Chung on Miss Li's bed. The teacher had kindly offered it for the couple's last night together while she slept in the girls' dormitory.

Meichen's legs entwined with Chung's, and her body throbbed and tingled from his magic touch. Moonlight filtered through the room illuminating their faces just enough for them to see each other.

He touched her nipple. "You remind me of the moon. At first, I see only a sliver of light. Then you plump and swell until you burst into a full glow."

Meichen pressed her face against his shoulder and giggled. "Shall I write a poem of praise for the jade stalk?"

"Wait until you know it better, when you know all it can do."

"I wish I could find out now." Her hand inched its way toward his loins.

"No!" He pushed her hand back up. "The right time will come. Until then we have lots of memories for the time we're apart."

Meichen rolled over his chest, balancing the weight of her upper body on her arms while she sought his lips. He laughed and rolled her back beside him. He turned to his side and wrapped his arms around her.

"Wife, you're insatiable."

She struggled to free herself and he held her tighter. "Lie still and close your eyes. We need to sleep."

"I don't want to sleep. I can sleep after you leave."

"But I must board my ship on time. It's nearly morning now." His arms loosened when her muscles went limp. His mouth brushed her earlobe. "Sleep," he whispered.

Despair flowed through her and leached her strength. The substance of her body seemed to melt into the mattress. She tried to banish the thought of his departure, but when he spoke of it, the moment loomed ahead. She swallowed hard, forcing back tears. Jiao had told her not to cry, that men hated wailing women.

While he slept beside her, all her fears grew into a fog of anxiety. *His ship might sink in a typhoon, or he might be killed by vicious white men. And if he makes it safely to Augusta, he might be unable to leave again if the Americans change their laws. And worst of all, he might become comfortable there and never come home, like his uncles.*

Meichen pressed her face against her husband's chest and listened to the regular beats of his heart. *Do you love me, Chao Chung? Do you feel just a little bit of what I feel for you? If you do, you'll come home as soon as you can.*

...

The lavender and pink colors of dawn painted the room. Already the household stirred. Pots clanged in the distant kitchen and high-pitched chatter floated from the girls' dormitory to shatter the silence. Miss Li's calm voice shushed the students as they passed her room.

Meichen's eyes fluttered open. She reached for Chung, but he was gone. She raised her head and saw him standing at the foot of the bed, naked, with his back to her. He stretched his arms over his head. He bent his elbows and clasped his hands behind his neck, turning his body from side to side.

"You're tempting me, Husband." Her eyes focused on his compact buttocks.

"Oh, no, no more." He wrapped himself in his night robe. "I'm stiff as an old man from everything we did last night."

"I'll do the work. All you have to do is lie still." She gave him a coy smile. "If you can."

He pulled her out of the bed and set her on her feet. "Put on your robe. I want to talk to you before someone interrupts us."

"No more talking," she moaned, sliding down to sit on the bed. She held her arms up to him, her eyes bright with hope.

Chung thrust the robe at her. "I am serious, Meichen."

He walked across the room to look out the window while she covered herself. She shuffled over to a worn but serviceable sofa and Chung sat in a wooden chair facing her.

He clasped both her hands in his. "Mr. Lester has our money hidden in his room. It's not to be used except in special circumstances. Remember how often we've talked about all the troubles facing China? If the worst happens, and there's serious fighting, use the money to leave the country. You can go to Hong Kong, or maybe join me in America. The new American law says merchants and their families can come to America. Once I'm an established merchant, perhaps you can get in, too."

"Chung, I'm afraid."

He sighed. "I didn't mean to frighten you, but it's best to know the truth. Whether China collapses because of revolution, or it's attacked by western armies, you should go to Hong Kong."

"What about your father and the rest of your family? Would they leave China, too?"

"My father doesn't want to believe it could happen, but in his heart he knows the danger is there. Unless China gets a new government and modernizes very soon, it's only a matter of time until someone attacks us."

She looked at her hands, still resting in his. He bent forward to kiss her nose. "I need to dress and eat breakfast."

She watched him don his jacket and trousers, then helped brush his long hair and braid it neatly. He turned and saw her mournful face and the quivering lips she tried to still.

He tickled the end of her nose with his queue. "Perhaps I'll cut this off and leave it with you for as a memento."

"Oh, Chung, you can't cut off your hair."

His eyes twinkled. "It will grow back out in five years. Don't you want something to remember me?"

"Not if it causes you to be arrested."

"All right, I'll mail it to you from America."

Meichen giggled. "Second Uncle will think you're foolish to waste money sending hair back to China."

"Why? People pay to send the bones of dead men back to China."

"But they must lie with the ancestors. I wouldn't want my father's bones to lie abandoned in Hawaii."

"I suppose you're right." He stroked her arm. "It's lucky I picked something else to give you."

"Where is it?" Meichen asked, searching the room with eager eyes.

"Never mind. You can open it after I leave. It's something private, just between us.

...

After breakfast, Meichen watched Chung and Mr. Lester tie two chests onto the mission's small cart. Mr. Lester wiped his brow.

"Are you taking everything you own?" he asked Chung.

"My Aunt Jiao is sending gifts to her husband's American concubine."

Miss Lester's eyebrows rose. "Your uncle has a concubine in America?"

Her father looked at all the students scattered around them and gave her a warning frown. "I'll explain later. We need to leave for the wharf."

Chung bid a general farewell to the mission staff and the children. He paused before he stepped into the cart, meeting Meichen's mournful eyes, silently urging her to smile. She rubbed her fingers across her lips to tell him she still felt the warmth of his final kiss.

Mr. Lester joined Chung and slapped the reins on the ancient pony's rump, urging the animal into the crowded street. Chung looked behind him until the cart rounded a corner and disappeared. Miss Lester shooed their charges inside, leaving Meichen on the steps with Miss Li beside her.

"I know you want to be alone, Meichen. But you can talk to me tonight if you need company."

Meichen nodded. She went inside and trudged up the stairs, her hands covering her face.

Yuan worked in Miss Li's room, changing the bedding. Meichen held herself in check as she went to the sofa and laid a pillow across her eyes. She wished the maid would go so she could grieve in private.

"Mistress, the master said for you to look on Miss Li's desk. He left something for you."

Meichen roused herself to examine the flat rectangle wrapped in yellow silk. Overcome by curiosity, she carefully untied the cord holding the wrapping in place. Joy flooded her soul when she saw Chung in a photograph, dressed in his scholar's robe and cap. His solemn eyes looked directly at her.

She pressed the image to her breast, laughing and brushing away tears at the same time. It was the most precious gift she'd ever received.

After staring at Chung's face again, she remembered the silk wrapping. As she pressed the material flat, her husband's elegant calligraphy unfurled before her eyes. He had copied a poem by Chang Chiu-ling, one he had taught her to read. The words held a new, poignant meaning.

Over the sea the round moon rises bright,
and floods the horizon with its silver light.
In absence lovers grieve that nights should be,
but all the live-long night, I think of thee.
I blow my lamp out to enjoy this rest,

and shake the gathering dewdrop from my breast.
Alas, I cannot share with thee these beams,
so lay me down to seek thee in my dreams.

She remembered an old superstition she'd heard in her childhood. Lovers who were parted could meet each other in dreams. Chung did not believe in old women's tales, but still he sent a message to comfort her. She would hang the scroll on the wall across from her bed where she could read it every night.

PART II

AMERICA

"Even a thousand miles apart, a couple destined for one another are pulled together by an invisible thread."

—CHINESE PROVERB

CHAPTER 13

"It is easier to obtain a thousand pieces of gold than to find one person who really understands you"

—CHINESE PROVERB

Canton, China, 1887 - Five years later

MEICHEN RESTED HER HANDS on the Lesters' large globe. She placed her forefinger on the Chinese coast where Canton sat, then slid it across the vast Pacific Ocean to San Francisco. From there she traced the land from California to the juncture of Georgia and South Carolina. Augusta was too small to show on the globe, but her fingertip must be close.

Li Biyu glanced up from the tiny slipper she embroidered. "You must have done that five hundred times in the last five years."

"It helps me remember Chung's still in the world with me, though we're far apart."

Biyu left her chair, moving to Meichen's side. "I remember the first day you moved here. I showed you the route he would take, and we calculated the distance. It was the first mathematics lesson I taught you."

"Almost ten thousand miles." Meichen put her arm around Biyu's shoulder. "What would I have done without you?"

"You would have run out of handkerchiefs. I never saw a person cry so many tears in such a short time. You were a veritable fountain."

"I hope I've learned better since then. Tears change nothing." Meichen turned away from the globe. The two women sat across from each other, a low table between them. Biyu returned to her work, and Meichen threaded her needle. She picked up a black cotton shoe from the stack on the table and formed the outline of a flower on the toe.

"Action is the cure for sorrow," Biyu said as she plied her needle. "That's why you became my best student. And you've worked hard teaching the other girls at the mission. I'm proud of what you've accomplished, and Chung will be, too."

"He praises me in his letters." Meichen sighed. "But he never writes of love. I'm afraid he's learned to live without me. He says nothing about coming home or longing to see me." She squared her shoulders. "I won't give up, though. I still tell him how I miss him, and I describe how I'll welcome him when he returns."

Biyu cut her eyes toward Meichen, smiling. "A Chinese man seldom speaks of love, but I'm sure he thinks of it. When Chung sees you, his senses will overcome him. He left a pretty girl, but he'll come home to a beautiful woman."

Meichen shook her head. "No one can surpass you."

"I'm old now–nearly thirty." Biyu gave the pink peony on the shoe a critical look. "I gave my life to God, and I try to do what He commands."

"I can't believe He intends you to spend your life hidden in this school."

Biyu shrugged. "If He calls me elsewhere, I'll go."

Footsteps racing up the stairs drew their eyes to the door. A young student came to Meichen, her head properly bowed. Then her face shot up, revealing eyes bright with mischief

"Forgive me for interrupting, Honored Teachers. There's a guest to see the wife of Chao Chung."

For a moment Meichen's heart leapt in expectation, but she calmed herself. Of course, it wasn't her husband. But she couldn't imagine who would visit her.

Meichen went to the parlor where a man waited. Seven years had passed since she'd seen him, but it took only a few minutes for recognition to dawn.

"Brother!" she cried.

His smile showed his amazement. "Little Sister?"

They stood staring at each other. Meichen ran forward and threw her arms around his neck, though she knew it wasn't proper behavior for a married woman.

"You look so different," Ling Mo said. "You were a little girl when I left China."

"I was not a little girl," she protested. "I married that year."

"I couldn't believe Aunt would do such a thing. But it turned out to be good fortune for you. Chao Chung is an excellent person."

Meichen shook her head sadly. "He went away too soon."

"But I've come back. And so will he."

Meichen guided Ling Mo to the largest chair in the parlor and chose a chair nearby for herself.

"Why did the eldest Chao Uncle send you home?" Meichen asked.

"To find a wife. He said I worked so hard, I deserved time to go home for a few months. Since I'm a merchant, I can re-enter California without too much trouble."

"But they could keep you out?"

"I have papers supplied by the United States government." He reached in his bag and pulled out an envelope wrapped in oil cloth.

Meichen examined the seal stamped on the document. "And you trust them to honor what they wrote?" She shook her head.

"If I want to marry, I have to come home. No wives are available in California. The Chinese women there are mostly prostitutes, or very expensive to marry."

"Will you take your wife back with you?" She kept her voice calm though her heart pounded inside. An idea came to her fully formed, as though the gods had sent it.

Ling Mo frowned. "It's too difficult for respectable wives to live in California. The white men persecute us Chinese in every way. They tax us and make us pay fees on everything possible. They pass ordinances to shut down our businesses, and sometimes they're violent, attacking us and setting fires to destroy our homes and businesses. I've seen Celestial men hanging from lampposts."

Meichen nodded. "Miss Lester has read about these things in her newspapers." She sighed. "So, your wife will be a Gold Mountain widow like I am."

"I know it's hard for you."

"And your poor wife will have to live with Aunt and Uncle. I pity her." Meichen sighed even louder to emphasize the terrible fate awaiting Ling Mo's wife.

"Have you seen them since you married Chao Chung?"

Meichen shook her head. "Not since the traditional visit after the wedding. I don't want to see them, even if I could. They shamed me by hiding my real age from the Chaos. If Chao Chung wasn't so kind, I'd have been sent home in disgrace."

"I won't let them choose a wife for me," Ling Mo said. "They can call on the matchmaker and choose some candidates, but *I* will have the final say."

Meichen spirits lifted higher. Ling Mo's thoughts were going down the path she desired. "Will they allow that? You know Aunt Meu Yuk will scheme to have her way."

"If she wants me to send them money, she will keep quiet. I've worked long, hard hours to make money for them, but no one forces me to send it. I can stop at any time."

Meichen gasped. "Would you really do that? What would Eldest Uncle Chao say?"

"It isn't his concern. I'm not under his control, except as an employee."

Meichen wrung her hands. "But he could take away your job."

"I know how to make a living by myself. I could run a laundry. And there's the restaurant business, and cigar factories, sewing shirts, making shoes. If I didn't send money home to Aunt and Uncle, I could save much more."

Meichen smiled at her brother's self-confidence. "You inherited a strong spirit from our parents. I know you'll succeed."

Biyu came into the room and set a tray holding three cups and a teapot on a table. Ling Mo stared at her enchanting face before he noticed her Western clothes. He looked at Meichen for an explanation.

"Li Biyu, this is my brother, Wu Ling Mo. He's just arrived from San Francisco."

They bowed slightly to each other. "I'm sorry," he said, his eyes still riveted on Biyu. "I've never seen a Celestial woman in a white women's clothes."

She laughed. "The missionaries who visit the Lesters are also surprised. I suppose I'm a strange creature straddling both worlds. But I think I'm still more Chinese than Western."

"Miss Li taught me when I first came to this school." Meichen smiled at Biyu. "Now she's my dear friend."

Biyu sat beside Meichen on a chair that faced Ling Mo. He smiled at Biyu and Meichen noticed the expression on his face. He looked at her friend in a different way than a man looked at a new acquaintance, especially a female. Meichen fought to control her glee.

"Do you like San Francisco?" Biyu looked directly at him, not lowering her eyes as a woman should. "Are you glad you went overseas?"

Ling Mo's face grew sober. "I like the money I make, but the Americans are violent men. If I leave Chinatown, there's always the chance I'll be attacked."

"You're brave to live in such a place." Biyu's large eyes expressed genuine admiration. Meichen knew she meant her words. The teacher's spiritual beliefs did not allow her to flirt.

Meichen noticed Ling Mo sat up straighter. *If he was a peacock, he would be spreading his tail feathers.*

Biyu's smile did not waver, nor did the directness of her eye contact. "I would love to see America. Mr. Lester's books describe an amazing country, filled with all nations of people and marvellous inventions. Have you ridden a train?"

Meichen could almost see Ling Mo's interest expanding. *He fancies himself a man of the world. I'm watching a play with the gods writing the lines.*

"One time I rode a train to Sacramento. My boss asked me to carry a box of fine cigars to one of the senators."

"What does that word 'boss' mean?" Meichen asked.

"It means the man you work for. No one in America calls anyone his master. Before their civil war, the word described a man who owned slaves."

"Is San Francisco bigger than Canton?" Biyu crossed her ankles, showing a brief view of her tiny bound feet. Many Chinese girls might have done so to whet his interest, not knowing how Ling Mo hated bound feet. But her brother's gaze never left Biyu's flawless face.

"San Francisco is a village compared to Canton, but very busy. Ships crowd the harbor, and more people come from the eastern states all the time. They build houses and tall buildings."

"Don't they worry that earthquakes will topple their tall buildings?"

"Americans are confident people. The city is hilly, and sometimes the ground trembles a little, but no one pays much attention to it."

"You don't worry about an earthquake?" Biyu asked.

Ling Mo shrugged with manly disdain. "If it comes, there's nothing I can do to stop it."

Once again, the gods lent a hand. Miss Lester came in to offer Ling Mo supper and a bed for the night in the boys' quarters. He protested that he didn't want to put Miss Lester to all that trouble. Miss Lester insisted he would be no bother. Again, he declined graciously. Miss Lester insisted he must stay, and he refused again. They argued back and forth until they both were convinced that proper etiquette had been observed, and then Ling Mo accepted the missionary's hospitality.

Miss Lester went off to the kitchen and Biyu left to make sure a bed was prepared. Assured of privacy, Meichen led her brother to the gist of her plan.

"Brother, why don't you go to the town where the Chaos' second uncle lives? My husband says the people are friendly and it's safe for Chinese. His uncle makes good money. There isn't so much competition."

Ling Mo considered her suggestion. "I've thought about it, but I don't know if the Chao brothers would consent. The second uncle may have no use for me."

"But you said you could open your own business in San Francisco. Couldn't you do the same in Augusta? Just think, you could renew your friendship with my husband."

"Why are you so anxious for me to go to Augusta, Meichen?"

Her eyes sparkled. "You could marry Biyu, and she and I could go with you to America and I could join my husband."

Ling Mo snorted. "That's a preposterous idea. First, the Chaos would never allow it. And second, you would almost certainly end up in the hands of the Tongs. They say slavery is abolished in America, but the Tongs openly kidnap and buy women in China and bring them overseas to sell them to the brothels. Would you want to end your life locked up in a crib, servicing every man who has a few dollars in his pocket?"

"What is a crib?" Meichen asked.

"A little room just large enough for a bed and a chair, with bars on the window. When a customer comes, the door is unlocked just long enough to let him inside, and out when he's finished his business. The women never leave, they're caged like animals." His eyes flashed. "The police know about it, but they do nothing to stop it. They're just like the Mandarins here. A few bribes can fix anything."

Meichen stared at him in horror. "That doesn't happen to every woman who comes over from China. What about First Uncle's family?"

"Only the rich men can bring over women in safety. He had the money to hire guards and bribe the Tongs. I can't pay for that, and neither can Chung. Stop this crazy thinking. Wait patiently until your husband returns."

Meichen refused to give up. "Miss Li is beautiful, isn't she?"

"That's true."

"And she has no husband."

Ling Mo looked sceptical. "Is she a widow? She seems old to be a maiden."

"She's never mentioned a husband."

"And why did she become a Christian?" he asked, frowning.

"She had many misfortunes and almost died. Miss Lester saved her."

"I see." He looked sternly at Meichen. "Don't hope for me to marry Miss Li. I need a young wife who can bear sons. Perhaps I'll look among the Hakka girls for someone like our mother." He smiled at her. "Who knows, I might be as lucky as Chung."

CHAPTER 14

"We should feel sorrow but not sink under its oppression."

—Confucius

MEICHEN CAREFULLY FOLDED HER TUNICS and skirts in her traveling bag. "I think this will be a lucky year. It's the fifth year since my husband left, and he'll come home."

"Meichen, don't set your heart on that," Biyu warned. "No one has said he'll come home."

"Why else would my father-in-law ask me to visit this New Year? He must want to tell me Chung will return." Meichen whirled in a circle, laughing. "I'll have a child at last. Wouldn't it be funny if I had twin boys? That would put my mother-in-law in her place."

"I'm worried you'll be disappointed." Biyu wrapped Meichen's silk shoes in cloth and set them in the bag.

A child's voice came from the top stair. "Wu Ling Mo is waiting for his sister."

Meichen closed her bulging bag and hefted it off the bed. She handed Biyu a sack of copper coins. "These are for the orphans' New Year gifts. I'm sorry I didn't have time to wrap them. Ling Mo gave them to me just last evening."

Biyu balanced the heavy sack in her hand. "Tell him I appreciate his kindness."

"You can tell him yourself."

Biyu shook her head. "It would seem forward of me. I'll stay here."

Meichen gave Biyu's hand one last squeeze. "I wish you a happy New Year, dear friend, ten thousand times."

...

Ling Mo followed Meichen up the river boat's gangplank. "It's a good day for traveling." He looked at the blue sky. "When I looked out the window at dawn, I saw dark clouds and I thought it would rain. I know you would hate to go home with your clothes dripping and your hair in a mess."

"Why are you so happy?" Meichen asked as she opened her parasol. "Are you anxious to see Aunt and Uncle again?"

Ling Mo shrugged. "I must go somewhere for New Year and they're the only relatives I have. But I'll see the Chao brothers when I go out to visit friends."

"Just don't bring Aunt and Uncle with you," Meichen cautioned. "My mother-in-law doesn't like them."

Ling Mo snorted. "I'm not likely to go visiting with them. All we'll do together is find me a wife. And the quicker the better."

"You shouldn't be in such a hurry. It's not proper to have too short an engagement. How will the bride's family have time to prepare?"

"There's nothing I need from them, except their daughter. I'm twenty-three years old, and I have one year before I go back to America. I need to sire a son who'll take care of my spirit needs after I'm dead."

Meichen understood his urgency. The worst thing that could happen to a Chinese man was to have no male descendants.

"Will you let Uncle adopt you? He has no son."

"No. I remember my own father and mother too well."

"And you'd never offer sacrifices to Aunt Meu Yuk." Meichen laughed.

Ling Mo nearly snarled. "Not even to keep the gods from striking me dead."

...

The maids were almost finished cleaning the house for the New Year when Meichen arrived at her home. Madam Chao followed the servants at their duties, checking every corner to make sure no cobwebs remained. Later, the paper Kitchen God went to the flames of the stove after a meal of sweet foods and honey. Meichen worried about her own conduct during this reunion with her mother-in-law. The Kitchen God might report her disrespect to Heaven and bring trouble to the family.

She forced her mouth to stay closed when Madam Chao bragged on her five grandsons, produced by her oldest son's wife, and mourned for Chung who had no son. Meichen burned with anger at the injustice. *How can I have a son when my husband isn't here?*

There were moments of happiness, too. She played with her four older nephews and held the little one in her arms. Youngest Brother had married a girl with a merry smile and a mischievous sense of humor. Jiao had taken the bride under her wing, and the two of them kept Madam Chao in permanent discontent.

The family came together for the New Year dinner at the large round table in the inner hall. The chairs were pushed close together to accommodate all the adults, and there were two empty chairs to represent Second Uncle and Chao Chung. Meichen looked at Chung's chair, imagining him sitting there next year. A thrill of anticipation went through her body.

The next morning, they welcomed the Year of the Dog. The children screamed with delight when Scholar Chao passed out little red envelopes with money inside. Everyone, even the youngest, wore his or her finest clothes and the bright colors of silk outfits made the day more festive.

Meichen kept waiting for Scholar Chao to speak of Chung's return. He showed affection for her and pride for her academic achievement, but there was no announcement about Chung. *Perhaps the scholar doesn't know yet, or maybe he doesn't think it's important to let me know.* Despite the elation of the others, Meichen felt more and more anxious.

In the late afternoon, Jiao invited Meichen into her room to share special sweets with her. "My son has passed the second Imperial Examination," she announced proudly. "He plans to move to his own house, since this one is so crowded. It depends on what post he's given by the government."

Meichen savored a piece of fruit. "Do you want to move?"

"I would prefer for my sister-in-law to move. After all, this is my husband's house. But we really need a larger house. We'll need quarters for my husband and his concubine when he returns. And my son will have children, of course."

"Of course," Meichen agreed politely. "Has your husband decided when he'll come back?" She didn't ask the obvious question. If Second Uncle came home, who would run his store? Would Chung be trapped in America?

"My husband hasn't said yet. He'll work a few more years to make extra money for our old age."

Inwardly, Meichen gave a sigh of relief. She pitied Jiao, but she wanted to see her own husband.

"I received a letter from my husband, just last week. I'll have my brother-in-law write him a letter to tell him the good news about our son. He'll be very proud." She offered the plate of fruit again. "Here, have more."

"Has your husband – Second Uncle, I mean – has he said when my husband might come back to China? My father-in-law said he would come home after he worked five years."

Jiao avoided Meichen's eyes as she chewed her fruit. "My husband is worried about the laws the American Devils are passing. He wants to see if your brother can return to the Gold Mountain without trouble. Then he'll decide what Chung should do."

Meichen sat frozen, calculating in her head. Ling Mo would be in China for a year. That meant another year would pass before she saw Chung. Another long, lonely year.

She tried to stop her tears. It was unseemly to cry in front of Jiao, who hadn't seen her own husband in over twenty years. But she couldn't control her outburst.

"There will always be something." She purged all the bitterness in her heart. "The Americans will pass another law against the Chinese; Second Uncle will need Chung to work with him another year or more before he can leave. Or there will be rebellion here, and he won't come home for fear he can't go back. There's no end to the reasons why I'll always be a Gold Mountain widow. I'll never have a child."

"You forget the most likely reason he won't come home," Jiao said sternly. "He may not want to come back. Don't you think I know why my husband hasn't returned? He's content where he is, living with his concubine. You don't see me crying. I enjoy a good life, and I'm grateful for it. A husband isn't necessary for happiness."

"But you have children. You have a son to take care of you. I'm nothing to this family but a burden, a useless mouth to feed." Meichen clenched her fists.

"You should stay at your school. You're too old for lessons, but I've been told you help teach. Learn to enjoy what you have and be glad you're useful there." Jiao handed Meichen a handkerchief. "Here, wipe your face. You've made a mess of your makeup. My maid will fix you up before the family sees you. New Year's Day is no time for weeping. It's bad luck."

Meichen took deep breaths to calm her nerves. While the maid worked on her face, her mind formed a plan, and it did not include spending the rest of her life at the mission.

...

Ling Mo brought his wife, Shuang, to the Lantern Festival so Meichen could meet her. The girl spoke very little, and Meichen learned almost nothing about her. She expressed no curiosity about Meichen, either. She was short, with a flat, broad face and narrow eyes that looked like dark slits in her face. There was nothing unattractive about her; millions of Chinese had the same features. But Meichen was appalled that her brother had chosen an ordinary peasant girl when he might have married Miss Li.

"How did you find a wife so quickly?" she asked.

"She comes from an impoverished family. I sent a pig and plenty of money, and they were glad to give her to me without the formalities. Look how husky she is from working in the fields. She has strong legs and normal feet, thank the gods. She'll give me a healthy son."

Ling Mo's wife watched her husband and his sister in stolid silence, showing no reaction to Ling Mo's comments about her and her family. She might have been a dumb beast, Meichen concluded.

The New Year parade started and Shuang was captivated by the colorful dancers. Meichen drew her brother aside. "Ling Mo, why did you marry this ignorant girl? You're a scholar."

Bitterness colored his voice. "No, I'm not a scholar anymore. I'm one of many Chinese who wash the clothes of white men. I'm only slightly above a peasant myself."

"What will you talk about with her? She will bore you."

"I have the Chao brothers and my other friends to talk to. I didn't marry her for talking. And I won't spend much time with her. I'll be overseas more than I'll be home."

"My husband may never come home." Meichen's face twisted in pain.

"Quit being so gloomy," Ling Mo chided. "Look, the dragon dancers are coming. Let's enjoy the end of the holiday."

He pulled Meichen to the edge of the street with his silent wife following behind. As Meichen moved away from the girl, she glimpsed sad resignation on her face. An uncomfortable wave of shame washed over her. *Why am I rejecting my sister-in-law? Is it because she's not the kind of woman I wanted for Ling Mo? I'm acting like Chung's mother, who hates me because my mother was Hakka. My brother's wife can't be blamed for her lack of education, or the poverty of her family.*

Meichen moved to Shuang's side and put her fingers on the girl's arm. Shuang would not look at her at first, but Meichen soon had her laughing when she described the misdeeds Ling Mo had committed years before, and the punishments he'd suffered for his rash behavior. In return, Shuang talked about the troubles she and her siblings had with uncooperative farm animals, especially their cantankerous water buffalo.

The parade was over by then, and Ling Mo finally paid attention to their conversation. He frowned at his sister.

"Stop telling my wife about my youth. She'll lose respect for me."

"She needs to know in case your sons take after you," Meichen retorted.

Shuang smiled at Ling Mo, then bowed her head. "I will always respect you, Husband."

He touched her cheek lightly. "I'm sure you'll be an excellent wife." He turned away from her. "Come with us, Meichen. We'll walk you to your house."

"Wait." Meichen pulled a gold bracelet over her hand and gave it to Shuang. "This is my wedding gift to you." She locked eyes with Ling Mo. "Tell our aunt, if she takes that bracelet away from your wife, I'll send a man from Canton to chop both her arms off. Then she won't need bracelets anymore."

CHAPTER 15

*"A journey of a thousand miles must begin
with a single step."*

—LAO TZU

Canton, February, 1887

MEICHEN AND YUAN HAD JUST UNPACKED Meichen's clothes when a
young girl tapped on the bedroom door, popping into the entrance before
Meichen gave her permission to enter.

"Miss Li says come downstairs. We have guests." She disappeared with
pigtails flying behind her.

Meichen straightened her hair and clothes, moving slowly. Social small
talk did not suit her mood, but she forced herself to smile as she stepped on
the bottom stair.

"Meichen, come and meet Mr. and Mrs. Cartwright," Miss Lester called.
A dark-haired white man and his blonde wife sat on the sofa with Miss Li
beside them. "Meichen was one of our best students," Miss Lester told her
guests. "She helps teach now."

Mr. and Mrs. Cartwright nodded to Meichen when she greeted them
in English. "You speak so well!" the lady exclaimed. "I wish we'd had someone like you at our mission. It would have been most helpful."

"The Cartwrights were working at a village further up the river." Miss Lester waved Meichen to a chair beside her. "They're going home for a visit." She looked at them wistfully. "I wish I could go home, just for a while, but Papa says the school might close if we leave."

Meichen's vague nods stilled and she directed all her attention to the conversation. *The Cartwrights are going to America!*

Meichen scrutinized the family. Mrs. Cartwright wore a dress long out of fashion compared with the new styles worn by the white ladies of Canton. Her faded felt hat with one drooping feather looked as sad as its owner. Her husband's black suit was grey in places, betraying its age. Missionaries received small salaries, Meichen remembered, and they subsisted on donations from their churches.

Two little girls wearing too-small dresses came in from the garden. The smaller went to sit by Mrs. Cartwright, while the older girl sat down on a footstool.

"Your children behave very well," Meichen said.

Mrs. Cartwright smiled. "They are good girls"

Miss Lester beamed at the children. "How excited their grandparents will be to see them for the first time! You're so lucky to go home after only ten years in the field. I hope you'll stop here when you return to tell me what's going on in Kentucky."

"Indeed, we will," said Mr. Cartwright. "You're so kind to let us stay with you for the night. The inns are so expensive." He shook his head in disbelief.

Miss Lester turned to Meichen. "I hope you won't mind if the girls sleep with you in your room tonight. I can put pallets on the floor for them. Miss Li has volunteered to sleep in the girls' dormitory so Mr. and Mrs. Cartwright can use her room."

"I can't tell you how much we appreciate your generosity," Mrs. Cartwright said, dabbing at her eyes. "It's so hard to travel when we have no money. All four of us will stay in the same cabin on the trip home. It will be crowded, I'm sure, but we'll manage."

Miss Lester squeezed Mrs. Cartwright's arm. "I understand. My father and I must be incredibly frugal to keep this school and orphanage open."

"When must you leave?" Meichen asked as wheels turned in her mind.

"We catch a boat to Hong Kong early in the morning," Mr. Cartwright said. "Then we board a ship going to San Francisco."

Meichen clutched the edge of her chair, suppressing her excitement. The gods had provided a way for her to travel safely to America. She would soon see Chung again.

...

Meichen crept through the dormitory, quiet as a tiger hunting its prey. She saw Biyu sleeping in a corner away from the students. Biyu gasped as Meichen shook her shoulder none too gently. "I'm going to see my husband," Meichen whispered.

Biyu blinked, a frown of drowsy confusion on her face. "Has Scholar Chao sent you a message? When will Chao Chung arrive?"

"Chung's not coming here. I'm going to him. Mr. Cartwright said I can join his family on their ship if I pay for my cabin. I volunteered to help watch their girls. He and his wife will be my companions, so I won't be traveling alone."

Biyu's mouth fell open. "I've never heard of such a thing! How can you even think of leaving China? Have you discussed this with Scholar Chao?"

"He'd forbid me to go."

A child sighed in her sleep and rolled over. Biyu sat up, waiting until the girl settled into sound sleep. She left her bed and motioned for Meichen to follow her to the hall.

Biyu's face radiated disapproval "This is a foolish idea. It's dangerous to go off on your own to a place as wild as America."

"I told them about my situation with Chung, and they agreed to let me stay with them all the way to Kentucky. Georgia is just a little further. I can get there by myself."

Biyu blinked in confusion. "But will the Americans let you enter the country?

"My brother says the laws allow wives of Chinese merchants to join their husbands." Meichen grabbed Biyu's hands. "And I want you to go with me. The gods are telling me to go. It's my fate. And they tell me *you* should go, too. You can work for the mission board to prepare American missionaries for their work in China."

"I don't want to get involved in your mad plans. I don't believe in Chinese gods or fate."

"Maybe Jesus is talking to you through me. You said He sometimes speaks through other people."

"Meichen, I'm ashamed of you." Biyu crossed her arms and held them tight against her chest like a shield. "You're trying to use my beliefs to manipulate me. If I left here, what would the Lesters say? And who would teach the children?"

"There are girls who've been going to school here for years and years. One of them could take your place. Or Miss Lester could do it. She's close to mastering Cantonese."

Biyu still frowned. "But I don't hear the call from God."

Meichen marshalled the most powerful arguments she could think of. "Biyu, there's work you can do in America. The missionaries have schools where they prepare to come to China. You could teach them our language and writing. Mrs. Cartwright said how helpful that would be. You could reach thousands of Chinese with these trained missionaries. They could open schools like this one."

Biyu pressed her lips together, and Meichen threw her arms wide open. "Aren't you tired of this little school? You are meant for greater things."

Biyu gave Meichen a suspicious look. "You're not a Christian. Why are you so anxious for me to do the work you suggested?"

"There's a need for schools in China. I don't need to be a Christian to want education for girls."

"The Lesters will need time to replace me. I can't just run off and leave them." Biyu unclasped her arms and rested her chin on fisted hands.

"They can't be selfish with your talents when you could do so much good. Come with me. You've lived in this refuge long enough. It's time to go back out into the world."

"Meichen, I can't leave without thinking this over and asking Mr. Lester and other pastors for advice. And I must pray a lot before I make such a serious decision. And you should do the same."

Meichen sighed. "In the years I've lived here you've often read the Bible to me. I'm sorry I haven't become a Christian after all that reading, but sometimes I think I understand your god better than you do. He told Abraham to move to a place he'd never seen. Did Abraham say he'd have to think about it, and ask other men's advice? No. He packed his family up and left. Did Noah wait until his feet were underwater before he built the ark? No, he started building it the day your god told him to. Moses..."

"All right, I understand what you're saying. I'm going to the chapel to pray and listen for God's advice."

"When I wake in the morning, I'll wake you, too. You'll have to pack quickly if you're coming with us."

Biyu slipped a robe over her nightgown. Her feet were already encased in bed slippers that covered her bindings but gave no support for walking. Meichen took her arm and helped her descend the stairs in case she lost her balance.

Biyu sat on a pew close to the alter, and Meichen settled a few pews behind her. Biyu twisted around to look her friend in the eye.

"I can't meditate with you watching me. Go back to your room. One of the Cartwright children might wake and be frightened if you're not there."

As Meichen settled into her bed, she had the sudden conviction that Biyu would go with her. She smiled as sleep overcame her. *Biyu, you and I are about to start the greatest adventure of our lives.*

CHAPTER 16

*"A wise man does not argue
with a woman."*

—CHINESE PROVERB

San Francisco, April, 1887

MEICHEN'S HEART POUNDED with excitement as she watched the shoreline of California forming in the mist in front of them. "Biyu," she cried, grabbing her friend's arm, "there it is! America! The Gold Mountain. The Beautiful Country."

Biyu hugged her impulsively. "Only a few weeks and you'll be with Chao Chung. I'm so happy for you."

"And you'll be in Kentucky with the Cartwrights."

"And from there I go to the Missionary Board and start my task."

Mr. Cartwright stood beside them with his arms around his daughters. "Don't forget you must get through the immigrants' checkpoint. That may be difficult."

"But you'll speak for us, won't you, Pastor?" Biyu asked.

"I'll do the best I can. It helps that you came in second-class accommodations."

The ship drew closer to the shore, and the passengers prepared to disembark. The Chinese seamen called to each other as they maneuvered the ship into the harbor. People on the dock gathered to greet the passengers. And a group of men assembled to pass judgment on the Chinese in steerage. A few would be allowed to enter California. Most would be sent back to China.

The inspectors did not know what to make of the two Chinese women. Mr. Cartwright explained that Miss Li would be working with future Chinese missionaries, and after rigorous questioning the men allowed her to go with the Cartwright family.

Meichen declared herself the wife of a merchant. Merchants and their wives were supposed to enter the country without trouble, but Meichen couldn't prove her husband was a merchant who'd sent for her. The officials divided over how to handle her case. One suspected she was an expensive prostitute who'd been brought over for a rich Tong leader and said she should go back to China. Another gave her a speculative look, as though he might sell her to the highest bidder. The other officials were willing to wait for Chao Chung to send a letter and documents from Augusta.

They took the money in her baggage for safekeeping, so they said. But the silver coins sewn inside the hems of her skirt and jacket went undiscovered.

Meichen asked if she could stay with Eldest Uncle Chao in his house, but the authorities would not let her leave the port for fear she'd disappear in Chinatown. She yelled to the Chinese merchants going into San Francisco to tell Chao Gang she needed help. One man waved to her, and she hoped that meant he knew Chung's uncle. A muscular woman in a dark uniform seized her arm and pulled her away to the quarters for female immigrants.

The next day, as Meichen stared through the window of her dreary prison, a Chinese man emerged from an elegant leather-topped phaeton. He struggled to reach the ground because of his short legs and round girth. He hitched the carriage horse to a post and approached the closest guard with an arrogant nod. Although he wore Chinese clothes and sported a long queue, the guard greeted him politely.

Meichen wiped her eyes and looked again. The two men talked and laughed like old friends. It was the first time she'd seen any guard treat a Chinese man with respect. Eventually the visitor slipped a thick envelope to the guard. Meichen pressed her lips together. In America, as in China, bribery was the most efficient way to get around the laws.

Meichen's chest tightened when the guard unlocked her door. He grasped her arm and led her to the dock where the visitor waited, refusing to answer her frantic questions. She shrank back as the Chinese man grasped her elbow.

"Who are you? Where are you taking me?" Her eyes darted around the dock seeking a path to escape. She was a head taller than her new captor, and her slender legs could outrun him. His weight would make him clumsy.

Her leg shot out to trip him. She ran toward the road before the little man regained his balance. She sprinted uphill. She gasped for breath and pushed her tired legs harder. Just twenty feet ahead she saw a crowded road. But a large hand fell on her shoulder and pushed her down.

"Stupid slut." A meaty arm circled her waist and the guard jerked her to her feet. She recoiled from the red face twisted with rage. The guard lifted his fist and Meichen turned her face away. The clatter of hooves accompanied by loud curses stopped the blow as the small Chinese man halted the carriage horse practically on top of the guard.

"No, no, no!" He stood up, waving his arms. He frowned at the guard. "Don't hit!" He looked at Meichen speaking in rapid Cantonese. "I am Wang Jinsong, assistant to Chao Gang. He sent me to get you."

The guard let her up, and Meichen hurried to join Wang Jinsong in the carriage. He tossed a small leather bag to the guard and flicked the reins over the horse's back. The carriage jerked forward.

"Why did you run off like a wild colt?" Wang Jinsong didn't sound enraged, only mildly annoyed. "I had to give that stinking pig extra money for the trouble you caused him."

Meichen bowed her head. "I'm sorry. I thought you bought me for a flower house."

"You sent a message to Chao Gang. Didn't you expect someone to come for you?" He brushed dust off his trousers. "I see you will be troublesome, but since you are the sister of my friend, Ling Mo, I'll do my best to help you."

...

Arriving at Chao Gang's home, Wang Jinsong handed her over to a female servant who led her to a private chamber where she ate and bathed. She wore her best clothing from her trunk and prepared her face and hair with great care for the meeting with Chao Gang and his family.

No one spoke to her until a male servant escorted her to Eldest Uncle. She'd not been greeted by his wife and daughter, and Chao Gang didn't look at all welcoming. No tea or cakes were offered to her.

"Tell me why you're in San Francisco," he commanded. He folded his arms over his chest where they rested atop his large paunch.

Meichen repressed an uneasy stirring in her stomach. "I'm on the way to join my husband in Augusta, Eldest Uncle."

Chao Gang puffed up like a toad. "Did your husband have the temerity to send for you without consulting me?"

"No, Uncle, he doesn't know I'm coming."

"Did my youngest brother send you to him?"

Meichen trembled. "My father-in-law didn't know I planned to leave China. I sent him a letter to explain."

"What explanation can there be?" Chao Gung shook his finger at her. "You are a wicked, selfish girl who has defied her family. I am head of the family, and I decide who goes and stays. You broke one of the Three Rules of Obedience, coming here without my approval."

Meichen knelt and bowed her head. "I'm sorry for my presumption, Eldest Uncle. Please forgive me."

"I will not forgive you," he snapped. "You set a terrible example for all the women in the family. I told Youngest Brother sending you to a missionary school would lead to trouble. You've absorbed the ideas of those ugly, big-footed foreign women traveling around the world, sticking their noses where they don't belong. I suppose they gave you this idea?"

"No, Uncle, I found a way to come here by myself. I want to be with my husband."

Chao Gung eyes burned with fury. "What does it matter what a wife wants? You should want what your elders and your husband say is best for you." He hit his open palm with his fist. "Did Ling Mo give you money to travel?"

Now Meichen felt nauseated. Had she cost Ling Mo his job and his re-entry to America? "No, Uncle, my brother had no idea I planned this. He told me not to come."

"Well, at least one member of your family has good sense. I am waiting. Who gave you the money?"

Meichen kept her eyes on her hands. "My husband gave it to me when he left China, in case of war or some other catastrophe in China."

"Again, you disobeyed your husband. There is no war, and the only catastrophe is his father's choice of bride for him. He has a love-sick, headstrong wife." Chao Gang's eyes speared her. "I cannot stand to see your face. I am going to the temple to ask the gods what to do with you. You stay here in this room and speak to no one until I return."

Meichen's tears turned into sobs as she sat alone in the room. She heard feminine voices in the other parts of the house, but no women appeared. Sometime later, the servant brought a teapot and cup. The woman's furtive manner suggested she had not been told to give Meichen refreshments and would be in trouble if anyone saw her. Meichen drank the tea and thanked her with a watery smile. The woman whisked the pot and cup away just as Chao Gang's feet stomped up the stairs.

Meichen looked anxiously at Chao Gang. He didn't seem any friendlier. "I burned incense and talked with some learned men. They said to offer you three choices."

He held up his fingers as he explained the options. "My nephew must divorce you because disobedience makes you an unsuitable wife. You can go back to China to your birth family at my expense. Or you can stay here, and I will find you a new husband, if anyone will marry such a wilful woman. If you reject these generous proposals, I will send you home in a steerage compartment filled with men and you'll learn what happens to women with no family to protect them. You may find independence is not so pleasant."

"No!" Meichen cried. "I want to go to Augusta."

Chao Gang snorted. "I've already told you your wishes don't matter to me. Which is your choice?"

"I refuse to be divorced until Chung tells me so himself. I don't want to go back to China, and I don't want another husband. Let me go on my own." Her eyes flashed.

"A fool to the end, I see." He turned to a male servant who stood behind him. "Find Wang Jinsong and bring him to me. And fetch this woman's trunk and take it to the front door."

Wang Jinsong came in and bowed to Chao Gang. His eyes brushed over Meichen. His face showed no emotion when he saw her tears.

"Jinsong, remove Wu Meichen from my house. Escort her to my warehouse. She will stay there in seclusion while I arrange her voyage home. I will send someone to keep an eye on her until it's time for her to board a ship. She should be there only a few days."

...

Meichen followed Wang Jinsong, and she was tailed by a young man who carried her trunk. She fought rising panic, commanding herself to think. If she had an idea where to hide, she could escape Wang Jinsong again. She could melt into the street packed with people.

She couldn't go back to the docks, even though the Cartwrights might be looking for her. The police would arrest her, and the immigration officials would ship her back to China. She knew no one in Chinatown who'd give her sanctuary. Wang Jinsong claimed to be her brother's friend, but so far he was following all Chao Gang's instructions. She had to act soon. Once she was locked in a building, escaping would be more difficult.

They passed a temple, and her brain woke. She tapped her escort on the shoulder. "Is there a Christian church nearby?"

"What kind? There are many. The Americans are anxious to save our souls before they ship our disgusting bodies back to China." Wang Jinsong laughed. "Even if you join one of their churches, you'll soon be deported."

"I don't care what kind. Any kind."

"I can't remember where one is right this minute. I'll have to think about it."

He said nothing else as they plodded down a street. She fretted silently. *Will he help me or not? Biyu says to trust Jesus. I hope he directs me soon.*

"If you tell me how to reach a church, I'll give you money." She spoke in English, hoping he understood most of the words and the boy behind her did not.

Wang Jinsong stopped walking so abruptly she nearly ran into his back. He turned and tilted his head up to look into her eyes. His moon-shaped face drooped like a child who didn't know why he'd been slapped.

"Why do you insult me, Ling Mo's sister? Didn't I say your brother is my friend?" Some of his words were English and some Cantonese. "I don't need money to help you."

Meichen calmed as a crushing lump of fear rose off her chest. "What must I do?"

"For now, we walk on this road. At the next crossroad, a careless man will bump me and I'll fall. While I struggle to get up, you run to the right, straight up the hill. I go after you, but I won't find you in such a large crowd."

"Where will I go?"

They slowed their pace as they talked, and Meichen moved close to his side, much too close. Men were staring at them, straining to hear Jinsong's jumble of words, confusion on their faces.

"Stop smiling!"

Meichen jumped as Wang Jinsong shouted. His cheeks puffed out and he glared at her. Meichen tried to interpret his sudden anger. Wang Jinsong continued to frown, but he winked so fast she almost missed it.

"You think you can trick me and escape? You think if you run up the hill to the third street, you'll find help, but I know what you plan, and I'll find you. You'll be sorry when I catch you. Stupid, stubborn woman! How dare you think I desire *you.*"

Meichen dropped back, head bowed, her eyes on the ground as she shuffled behind him. He shouted at a man approaching him, and she almost missed her cue to flee.

Wang Jinsong's victim balanced a long pole on his shoulders with large baskets suspended from the pole. Jinsong bounced against a basket, grabbed it, and pulled the man and his pole down on top of himself. Both baskets emptied folded white shirts on the road, which set the laundry man screaming.

Meichen followed Jinsong's directions, sprinting up the hill of the cross street, dodging men, food carts, booths, wheelbarrows, and the occasional horse and cart. Her body forced her to stop halfway to the second street to catch her breath. The muscles in her calves burned, her sides throbbed from muscle spasms. A cup of water for her dry mouth would have been a gift from heaven.

She moved off the road and crouched behind a bush. She didn't see the young man who'd carried her chest. She expected him to run after her, but he didn't go by. In all the confusion at the crossroads he must have missed her escape. She said a quick prayer for Wang Jinsong's safety. Even if he avoided the wrath of the laundry man with the baskets, he still had to face Chao Gang.

Meichen left the bush and resumed her journey, moving at a slower pace. She reached the third street at the top of the hill and studied her surroundings. There were many buildings, but she soon identified her destination. Across the road stood a large brick house. The words on a sign next to the front entrance were written in English and Chinese: "Occidental Mission Home for Girls."

CHAPTER 17

"It does not matter how slowly you go, as long as you do not stop."

—CONFUCIUS

MEICHEN WATCHED THE MISSION HOUSE for nearly an hour, standing in the shadow cast by the building across the street. Two ladies with wide feathered hats entered the front door. Soon three more women arrived. The only men she saw followed the women and carried heavy boxes on their shoulders. Meichen knew at once these men weren't companions to the ladies. Their scruffy hair and faded clothes marked them as hired laborers.

If women run this mission, I'll most likely get help. They have more sympathy than men.

She wished she knew more about the purpose of the organization. She had to trust that Wang Jinsong had sent her to an appropriate place. With no way to find out more, she walked around the building and knocked on the back door. It took a while for a Chinese woman to release the multiple bolts securing the heavy metal door.

An armed policeman scrutinized her. Meichen froze, afraid she'd come to the wrong place. The Chinese woman pulled a rope, and a loud bell sounded further into the house. Minutes later, a lady appeared, smoothing loose tendrils of hair back and offering Meichen a reassuring smile.

"Welcome. I am the matron of this mission house. How may we help you?

"I am Wu Meichen. I beg you, help me escape from San Francisco." Meichen's soft voice didn't conceal her desperation.

The matron's smile faded, replaced by a grimace. "Are you in danger? Is someone after you? The police or the Tong?"

The matron's voice stayed calm. Her assistant handed her a notebook and pencil. "Don't be afraid to tell me. I've helped many Chinese girls and women escape bad situations."

"I came from China to join my husband, but his uncle wants to send me home. He planned to lock me up until he found a ship bound for China, but my brother's friend helped me escape. I must find a train going east at once."

The matron and the policeman exchanged looks of amazement. They'd never heard clear, grammatically correct English spoken by a Chinese person, male or female. She urged Meichen to sit at a battered kitchen table across from her.

"Where is your husband? Perhaps he could come for you. We could write to him today. Or send a telegraph."

"My husband doesn't know I came to America." Meichen's cheeks burned as she confessed her disobedience. "It would take him a long time to come here from Georgia."

Unlike Chao Gang, the lady accepted Meichen's desire to join Chung as perfectly natural. The word "disobedience" never fell from her lips. She aimed her energy toward solving Meichen's problem.

"Georgia! That's an unusual place for a Chinese man to settle. You still have quite a distance to go." She pursed her lips. "The ticket will be expensive. Do you have money to pay for such a long trip?"

"The men at the dock took my British money. All I have is some silver sewn in my clothes."

"That's typical of our corrupt public officials." She stood up abruptly. "Ah Kum will give you food and tea while I find a bed for you. After you're settled, we'll discuss the ticket price."

Another volunteer came for Meichen. She sat at the table while Meichen finished her tea. Her name was Mrs. Snow. "You can stay here for as long as necessary. We can always use someone to interpret for us." She was eager to offer Meichen information.

"The head of the mission will find a job for you to increase your funds. Do you know how to sew?"

Meichen nodded. "I sewed the clothes for my family before and after I married."

"We'll teach you how to use a sewing machine. Now let me show you where you'll live."

The top floor provided beds for the girls and women staying in the mission house. Some were young girls who'd been brought from China to be servants. Other women, from the age of fourteen up to their late twenties, had escaped from the Tong brothels.

Settling on her cot, Meichen wrote a letter to Chung to explain why she ran away from Chao Gang. She reminded Chung that she loved him with all her heart and promised to give him more satisfaction than he could imagine. It was the only way she could think of to counter Chao Gang's demand for a divorce. *It's been five years since he last saw me. Will he remember the pleasure we shared?*

Meichen's story drew the interest of her dormitory mates. One woman heard Meichen's situation and had her own advice. A former prostitute, she'd been spirited away from her owner by a client who fell in love with her. "If your husband divorces you, my lover can help you find a new husband."

"I don't want a new husband," Meichen said firmly.

The woman shrugged. "We must take what fate sends us. Maybe you are meant to marry another man. But be cautious. Some men claim to want a wife, but when the wedding is over they sell you to the Tongs. A beauty like you sells for lots of money, and the temptation to make a fortune is hard for some men to resist."

"But the Christians would prevent that, wouldn't they?" Meichen asked, horrified.

"They try to find out if a suitor is honorable. But men will lie. You know that. And some girls insist on marrying a man despite any warning."

"Why didn't your lover marry you when he helped you escape?"

"He must pay off my contract. Otherwise, when I leave here, the Tong will claim me again."

"Isn't that illegal? It's slavery."

The woman shrugged. "The police look the other way. If I make trouble, they might send me back to China."

Meichen learned most of the girls and women had been kidnapped or purchased in China. Some of them had run away from their captors and some had been rescued when the Mission directors, backed by public outrage, convinced the police to raid a brothel. On occasion the Tongs retaliated, setting the mission ablaze or forcing their way inside to find women who'd escaped from them.

The next day the matron called Meichen to the parlor. "I've found a job for you. One of our converts makes shirts for white men. You can work for his company sewing." She sighed, and her face grew somber. "I'm afraid my other news isn't so encouraging. Our director inquired about the cost of a train ticket to Georgia. It will be nearly two hundred dollars."

"Two hundred dollars! How will I raise so much money? What if my husband can't pay my fare?" Meichen paced around the room.

"Now, don't give up hope. It will take a while, but eventually you'll get there. You should hear from your husband soon. The director can take your silver to the bank and determine how much it's worth, if you don't mind him taking that liberty."

"I don't mind. I need to know how much more money I must earn.

...

The next day Meichen went to the shirt factory and Chu Donghai, the owner, hired her. She learned the shirts were sewn together by machine and the buttonholes were worked by hand. With no training on the sewing machine, she was assigned to make buttonholes. Meichen sewed until her fingers were raw. By the end of the day, she'd made sixty cents for finishing two dozen shirts.

"You're too slow," Chu Donghai told her. "But you'll get faster with practice."

Once she reached the mission, Meichen collapsed on her bed in the deserted dormitory. She stared at the wall. Even If she worked faster, it would take her months to earn the money for the train ticket. *How will I get to Chung soon enough to talk him out of the divorce? He might be sent back to China to marry another woman before I reach him. I am a fool. I should have stayed in China and waited patiently for Chung to come back.*

Every day Meichen waited anxiously for a letter. but no reply came from Chung. She wrote again, in case her first letter had been lost. Again, she heard nothing. Three months spent making button- holes passed, and every week Meichen added a little money to her savings, but the total went up slowly. Every week she wrote and heard nothing.

Wang Jinsong came by several times to check on Meichen. He considered it his duty as Ling Mo's closest friend. He also wrote to Chung but received no answer.

After a particularly discouraging day early in July, Meichen came home with her head drooping. As usual, she saw no envelope and despair rolled over her. The matron emerged from her office and called Meichen to get her attention. With a wide smile, she waved a letter in her hand. Meichen shrieked and seized the matron's arms, whirling her around in a dance of joy.

When they stopped dancing and caught their breath, Meichen took the envelope from the matron's hand. She clutched the letter to her breast, suddenly afraid to open it.

The lady gave her a light push. "Go read it! The chapel is empty right now, so no one will bother you."

Meichen walked into the chapel. As she entered the room, a ray of evening sunlight focused on the cross atop the altar. Was that a lucky sign? She sat on a bench, worried the letter's message might not match her expectations. She stared at the envelope, her heart pounding.

She forced herself to tear the flap open and slide the contents out. Her hands trembled as she unfolded the paper which was wrapped around a bank draft for three hundred dollars. She exhaled in relief and closed her eyes. Her husband wanted her to come to him.

But Chung had not sent the letter. She glanced at the signature and saw a name she didn't recognize. Her eyes zoomed back up the page to the salutation.

Dear Meichen,

I am sorry we haven't answered your letters, but I just recently found them. My husband hid the letters you wrote, and I discovered them in his account book and gave them to Tom. To keep Tom out of trouble with my husband and Chao Gang, I am sending you train fare with money I've been saving. Come to Augusta as soon as you can. I gave you some extra money to send a telegram each time you change trains, so we'll know when to expect you.

And don't worry about the divorce. I'll put a stop to that in a hurry. I'm anxious to meet you, and I know Tom can hardly wait to see you again.

Sincerely,

Mildred Chow

Meichen studied the mysterious signature. In his letters to her, Chung often mentioned his uncle's second wife. She amused him because she ignored his uncle's wishes and did exactly as she pleased. She had given him the American name Tom, although he had no idea why.

I wonder why Chung didn't send a letter with second uncle's wife. Is he angry with me?

The matron peeked inside the chapel. She clapped her hands in excitement when Meichen held up the bank draft.

"We'll get you packed right away. I expect you're anxious to leave."

A volunteer stood at the door. "I've been looking everywhere for you, Meichen. Wang Jinsong is waiting at the back door. He insists he must see you now."

Meichen handed her bank draft and letter to the matron as she hurried to the kitchen. Wang Jinsong sat on the steps below the back door watching the vibrant sunset. Meichen greeted him with joy.

"My husband's American aunt sent money for my train ticket.

"I hope you are leaving tomorrow." His normally jolly face showed worry.

"Is something wrong?"

"I'm afraid so. Your husband's second uncle told Chao Gang that your husband refuses to divorce you, and he's not used to opposition when he wants something done. I believe Chao Gang intends to seize you and send you back to China. You must leave at once."

"Does he know I live here?"

"Yes, and that's my fault. He distrusted me after you escaped from me twice, and he had me followed for two weeks. I overheard him giving the mission address to the leader of a Tong gang. On my way here, I checked the train schedules. I hoped you could go tonight, but the train you take will not leave until morning. I bought your ticket using a false name, so remember when you ask for the ticket, say you are Wang Ying. Go to the first ticket booth when you enter the station."

Meichen clasped her shaking hands together. "What if Chao Gang's spy sees me leaving with my bags?"

"I've figured out the best way to conceal you. I can't come here myself without being followed, but I've bribed the laundry man who comes early tomorrow to carry you out with the soiled sheets. A few streets away, he'll put you in a Hanson cab. The driver will deliver you to the train station, and from there you ride to Omaha. You'll change to another train to go south. The ticket agent will tell you which train to board."

"What about my trunk?"

"The laundry man will hide it in his cart until you reach the cab, and the driver will carry it into the station. Be sure it goes with you when you change trains."

Meichen smiled at Wang Jinsong. "Thank you for all you've done. Without your help I'd be back in China."

He bowed his head. "I was honored to help Ling Mo's sister. I wish happiness to you and your husband. Tell Chao Chung to write me after you arrive."

He walked away without looking back. She watched his short, round body and bandy legs until he turned a corner and was hidden by a tall hedge. She'd known him just a few weeks, but fate had given him a major role in her life.

Chapter 18

"It is the beautiful bird that gets caged."

—Chinese Saying

San Francisco, August, 1887

Meichen's exit in a large basket passed without incident. A sheet wadded over her head concealed her from anyone watching. The laundry man's wooden cart bumped down the road, picking up speed as it rolled downhill. He held the cart's handle and leaned backward, using his weight to counteract gravity before he lost control of the cart.

The cab was waiting at the bottom of the hill. Meichen stepped out of the basket and climbed into the cab with relief. The driver, a burly white man, pushed her trunk across the floor.

"Pull the curtains shut." He spoke at a low volume, but his harsh voice raised an alarm inside her.

With the windows covered, she could barely see the interior of the cab.

Her uneasiness increased as the cab crawled down a noisy street. Sudden comprehension struck her. The people on the streets spoke Chinese dialects, not English. She snatched a curtain open.

They were in Chinatown, but nowhere she'd been before. She tried to open the door and jump out, but then she remembered her trunk would be left behind. While she hesitated, the carriage came to a stop and a Chinese man reached in and pulled her out.

Meichen screamed, but no one passing in the street seemed concerned for her. The men who walked by averted their eyes or watched with interest as she wrestled her abductor, who forced her into a building. She looked up long enough to read the sign beside the door. She had entered the Palace of Infinite Joy.

She twisted in panic, and the man slapped her hard on the face. She no longer screamed, but still tried to break his grip on her arm as he pulled her up a flight of stairs. Reaching the landing, the Chinese man slung her over his shoulder like a sack of rice. He turned into a room and threw her onto a bare mattress.

A Chinese woman came in. Her broad shoulders and pudgy waist resembled those of a man, and her hands were man size. Meichen wondered if she was some strange combination of male and female parts. She pressed Meichen against the mattress with a determined look on her face. She waved the Chinese man out of the room.

Another woman entered, this one dressed in a silk robe embroidered with exotic birds. Echoes of youthful beauty lingered on her stern face. Meichen had no doubt that this woman ran the establishment.

Meichen closed her eyes, her mind rejecting the evidence of her senses. Just as Ling Mo had warned, she'd fallen into the horror of prostitution.

"We must check you for disease. You won't be hurt if you cooperate." The madam moved behind Meichen's head and dug her fingers into Meichen's hair. "This woman is my healer."

The large woman pulled at the waist of Meichen's skirt, and Meichen kicked her. The healer gave a grunt and doubled over.

The Madam's soothing murmurs turned instantly into a snarl. "Stop that or I'll call my men servants back in here to hold your legs. Do you want me to do that?" She smiled as Meichen shook her head, terrified. "Now, behave yourself. I see you'll need lots of training, and maybe a beating or two to make you useful."

Meichen's stomach churned as the healer spread her thighs. She imagined herself somewhere else, in a beautiful courtyard with peacocks and flowers. She tried to summon Chung's face, but the thought of her fate in a brothel took him away from her. He would never want her again, even if she managed to escape somehow.

The peacocks in her vision screamed, and suddenly the old woman left and the madam followed her. Meichen opened her eyes and realized the scream came from another room in the house. The sharp voice of the madam cut through the walls.

Meichen quickly pulled her skirt down and ran to the door, but its knob would not turn. Apparently, the madam took no chances, even during an emergency. Meichen looked at the one window in the room and saw bars over the opening. She shook the bars and discovered they were firmly attached.

She laid her head against the window sill and wept. "Kuan Yin, goddess of mercy, please help me," she prayed. She also prayed to the Christians' Jesus. Surely, one of them would hear her.

...

The screaming finally subsided into muffled sobs and the madam returned, the large woman trailing behind her. Meichen plastered herself against the wall, looking at the riding crop in the madam's hand. Anger marred the woman's delicate features.

"That idiot," she breathed to the healer beside her. "I'm going to send him back to China if he puts marks on a girl again. He can't understand it takes time for them to heal, and meanwhile I'm losing money." She glared at Meichen, shaking the small whip. "But don't think I won't use this if I have to." She turned to the healer. "Did you finish checking her?"

"I saw enough. She has no pox." The woman gave Meichen a dismissive look.

"Good. Take her to the private room and give her something decent to wear. I'll talk to her later. I'm going downstairs to give the White Devil his money." She stopped to glare at Meichen. "I am paying two thousand dollars for you. You'd better be worth it."

The healer led Meichen to a room on the back side of the house. Meichen still hoped she could escape, but her illusions were shattered. The room was as secure as a prison.

A diminutive servant girl entered the room with clothing for Meichen. The tunic and skirt were not elegant, but they were made of good material. Meichen wondered what had happened to her own trunk with her silk outfits and her scrolls and picture of Chung. She doubted she would see the trunk again. The madam wouldn't want Chung's photograph to remind her of her husband.

She cried until she had no tears left and her eyes burned from salt. She scolded herself for giving up. She should be thinking of who might rescue her. Perhaps someone would carry a note to the Mission House. They would write Chung, and maybe he'd come to San Francisco to free her.

And what good will that do? Chung can never afford the price to buy me back from the madam. And if he tries to take me without paying, the Tong will kill him.

She had only one choice. She would kill herself to avoid disgrace. She searched the room for sharp objects to cut open her wrists and found only a loose nail in the doorframe. She frowned at the nail, doubting its ability to kill. No, hanging herself would be better. She looked for any sort of cord, but there were none. Apparently, the madam was wise enough to anticipate such a plan. Or maybe she'd learned from experience.

Meichen's stomach grumbled when the little servant girl returned with food and tea. She noticed a man unlocked the door when the girl entered and locked it back after she was inside. He stayed outside, leaving the young servant to watch Meichen while she ate.

Meichen eyed the girl, who seemed about ten years old. "How did you come to be in here?" she asked. "Were you kidnapped?"

The girl shook her head. "My father sold me to a ship captain. There were too many girls in my family, and we were poor."

"How long have you been here?"

"Only a year. The madam says I must stay five years to work out my contract."

"How many women work here?" Meichen mechanically shoved rice into her mouth.

"There are fifteen, all of them beautiful and talented. The richest merchants come here, no coolies." The girl gave a sniff of disdain for working men of the lower classes. "You'll have to learn how to dance. If you have a good voice, the madam will favor you. You'll get the best food and sweets, and you have some say-so in what men you entertain."

"Do you ever leave the house?"

The girl gave Meichen a suspicious look. "I never get to leave. Just like you."

"Don't you want a better life?" Meichen asked. "There are ladies from the churches who will help you. They helped me when I had nowhere to go. If we can send a message to them, they'll help both of us."

"I never said I was unhappy. I don't trust the Christian ladies. The girls they take in have to work very hard for the factory owners."

"That's not true," Meichen protested. "They're kind to Chinese girls."

The servant shook her head firmly. "I won't help you run away. I've seen what happens to anyone who crosses the madam. She sends you to the cribs, and no one wants to be there."

The guard let the girl out with her tray of soiled dishes. Meichen collapsed on the bed, too tired to fight the fear devouring her faith. She was past the point of crying. She was falling into a pit of despair with no hope of escape. Her dreams died, and she craved only oblivion.

...

Meichen pretended she'd never sung or danced well. She tried to act clumsy so the madam would take more time to train her, but she could only pretend for a while before the madam lost patience. Meichen wanted to endure the abuse rather than cooperate with her captors. Ling Mo had kept his pride despite their aunt's abuse, and she wanted to stay true to Chung.

But one session with the madam's whip convinced her she lacked Ling Mo's courage. She would have to perform or face more punishment.

"Why are you acting so stubborn?" the healer asked as she tended Meichen's wounds. "You're a married woman. You know it's not so terrible to lie with a man. It's much better than this. If you keep resisting, you'll have scars and the madam will get rid of you. She's already angry that she paid so much for you and she's gotten no return on her money. And each beating she gives you will be worse."

Meichen gritted her teeth as the woman patted oil on her back. "I can't betray my husband."

"Fool, what do you think your husband can do for you? No one will tell him where you are. No one knows but the white man who brought you here."

By the next week, Meichen drifted gracefully around the room with a fan, silk ribbons, or a parasol, in step with the other women. She even smiled on cue, although her smile meant nothing. Most of the dancers were younger than Meichen, some only fourteen or fifteen.

Several women played the pipa, a Chinese lute. These female musicians were highly prized by the madam. They were exempted from prostituting themselves.

The night came when Meichen was forced to perform for an audience of men, all of them watching the dancers with the eyes of carnivores. She whirled with her parasol and nearly forgot her next steps as she recognized one of the clients. Wang Jinsong sat in the room, smiling as he inclined his head to her. It suddenly occurred to Meichen that he might have collaborated with her kidnappers.

After food and entertainment, the men chose bed partners. Wang Jinsong asked for Meichen. She went with him, seething with indignation, hoping he wouldn't dare touch her.

She closed the door to her room, and her eyes flashed. "Who decided to imprison me in this brothel?"

"Come close and talk softly," he whispered. "Someone may watch through a peephole."

Meichen turned her head, looking for evidence. Wang Jinsong grabbed the sides of her face and pulled her head close to his. "I am not responsible, and neither is Chao Gang, though I suspected him at first. The cab driver, the white man, decided on his own he could make a fortune by selling you to the Tong. They sent him to this house."

He led her at a leisurely pace to a bench and sat with his back turned to the bed. "I don't think they can see us here. The peephole is hidden in the painting behind me." His whisper turned into a loud command in case they had an audience. "Come kneel on the floor in front of me."

Meichen followed directions. As she opened her mouth, he touched her lips, reminding her to whisper.

"How did you find me?"

"I checked to see if you picked up your ticket at the train station, and the agent said you'd never arrived. I found the cab driver and threatened to cut off his fingers with a hatchet if he didn't tell me where you were."

He groaned like a man in mortal pain. Alarmed, Meichen's eyes shot to his face.

"Keep your head down! I'm just acting." He grinned at her. "Now give a little scream."

She followed his directions, though she felt silly. He moaned several times and panted heavily. "I'll come back tomorrow with rope, so we can go out the window."

"All the windows have bars."

He nodded toward a window nearby. "Not in the client rooms." He put his hands on her shoulders while he panted like a dog on a hot day. "I have to go."

"Not yet! If you leave so early, the madam will send up another man."

Wang Jinsong reflected on the situation, his eyes uneasy. "I should not be alone with you. It's unseemly, and your husband and your brother will disapprove."

"Would they rather have me used against my will?" Her hands formed tight fists. "This is no time to worry about propriety."

He stood up, pulling her with him. He used his loud client voice. "My muscles are tight. Come massage my shoulders."

He guided Meichen to the left side of the bed, farthest away from the painting. She looked down at the covers as he unbuttoned his jacket and placed it on a chair. He stretched out on his stomach with his head turned toward her. "Take the oil from the table. I like the feel of it." He whispered again. "Remove your outer robe. It will look more natural."

"But the robe underneath is thin silk."

"You just said this is no time for propriety. I'll close my eyes."

Meichen removed the robe reluctantly and moved close enough to dig her fingers into his shoulders. He winced.

"Ah, that's good. You press my muscles just right." He spoke so loudly Meichen wondered if the couple in the next room heard him.

"Thank you, sir. I'm glad to make you happy." Meichen forced a smile to her face.

"Don't worry if I fall asleep a few minutes. I must gather my strength for the ultimate pleasure."

Meichen massaged his back for fifteen minutes. "My arms are breaking," she said between gritted teeth.

"Just a little longer. Then I'll pretend to sleep."

He rolled onto his side, facing her, and produced a light snore. Meichen lay beside him, pulling the silk sheet over her robe. With nothing else to do, she sank down on her side of the bed, smoothing her face into a serene mask while her mind went over the escape plan and she considered all the things that could, and probably would, go wrong.

Time crept at an agonizing pace. She glanced at Wang Jinsong and saw that he slept. A light knock at the door startled the breath from her lungs. She rose and saw the madam looking through a slit at the door's edge.

"Is he still asleep?"

"Yes, Mistress." Meichen fastened her eyes on her feet.

"Wake him gently and encourage him to finish what he plans to do. All the other clients are gone, and the girls have gone to bed. I'll give him twenty more minutes and then he'll have to leave. This isn't an inn."

Meichen leaned over the bed to shake Wang Jinsong. "You can leave now."

He sat up and grinned at her, refreshed by his nap. "Don't worry, Wu Meichen." He studied her face and shook his head. "Anyone can tell just looking at you that you're afraid. You will attract suspicion. The madam will watch you tomorrow night." He patted her shoulder. "I promise I'll come back tomorrow with the rope. I'll ask for you and this room before anyone else has a chance. Meditate often tomorrow to calm your nerves."

"Please be careful, Wang Jinsong. If the Tong learns what you're up to, they'll kill you. I'm not a relative of yours, and you owe me nothing."

"You're the sister of Ling Mo, and since he's not here I'm acting for him. How could I face him again if I left his sister in a brothel?"

He donned his jacket and bowed slightly. "May the gods send us good fortune."

His cloth shoes made no sound when he left the room. Meichen pressed her hands together as she waited for the madam to come back and escort her to the women's quarters. There was nothing left to do but pray. She summoned the image of Kuan Yin and begged her protection. Then, just to be safe, she added a prayer to Jesus.

CHAPTER 19

"Heaven creates no paths that are completely impassable."

—CHINESE PROVERB

"I KNEW YOU WOULD COOPERATE when the time came," the madam said to Meichen. "Wang Jinsong liked you. He'll recommend you to his friends. The better you are, the more you make. You'll pay off your contract in record time."

One of the girls sitting behind the madam gave Meichen a warning look and shook her head. After the madam left, Meichen went over to the girl, remembering her name easily. Lijuan meant beautiful and graceful, and the name suited her well.

"Don't believe what the Old Dragon says. It will take years and years to pay off your contract."

"I know," Meichen sighed, concealing her joy at the thought of leaving. "I cost her two thousand dollars."

"It's not just that," Lijuan explained. "You earn nothing for any days you don't work, even if you're sick or having your monthly time. It's charged against your earnings. And if you're pregnant, you lose all your money for months. The men who come here want slender, supple women, not fat cows."

Meichen's stomach clenched. A prostitute could have a child and not even know the identity of the father. It must occur sometime if a woman joined with so many men.

"What happens to the babies?" she asked.

Lijuan shrugged. "If they're girls, they stay and become servants while they're little and prostitutes when they're old enough. The boys are usually sold to men who want a son, or sometimes they go to houses for men who desire boys."

Ljuan crossed her arms below her breasts and shoved her hands into the sleeves of her robe. "Or, a pregnant girl can ask the healer for medicine to get rid of the baby. Sometimes it works, sometimes not, and sometimes the girl dies. I think it's best to get rid of it, though. Having the child takes too much off a girl's pay. And even better, do what the healer tells you to prevent the problem. I suppose she talked to you?"

Meichen nodded as a sour taste rose from her stomach to her throat. Her skin crawled as she remembered the conversation.

"Did she make you demonstrate it for her?" Lijuan's lip curled.

Meichen lowered the focus of her eyes. "I refused."

"That's a foolish attitude. It's only a little water and vinegar. You'll get over the embarrassment. It's not as bad as being used by dozens of men." Her eyes became even harder. "It's not just to prevent a child. It helps to prevent disease. That's the worst thing that can happen, because you can't work here anymore. The Dragon either sells you to some other brothel, or you go to the cribs where the customers aren't so particular, or she lets some ignorant man pay your contract off and marry you. And you know when he finds out, he won't be happy with his bargain and you will be the one he punishes."

Meichen backed away and Lijuan leaned closer to her. "Have you ever seen someone with syphilis? It causes a horrible death."

Meichen felt nausea sicken her, and she fled back upstairs. She wondered at Lijuan and the other prostitutes who seemed to accept their situation stoically. Some even seemed to enjoy it. Perhaps prostitution was better than the lives they'd left behind in China.

She had known real pleasure with a husband. She grabbed onto the bars over the window and prayed to every god she'd ever heard of. She made a final plea to Jesus. Her bed offered refuge, and she lay down to calm her jangling nerves. Her muscles relaxed, and she cleared her mind of worry. She trusted Wang Jinsong to keep his promise. All she had left to do was rest.

...

The evening came, and the madam invited her customers into the house. She kept her voice soft and melodious as she talked to them, ordering food and wine for their pleasure. The dancing girls came in, ribbons on sticks floating around them as they twirled to the music of the pipa. The men ate and drank and laughed as the girls came to sit around them, telling jokes that were funny but not too ribald.

The girls let the men feed them, opening their mouths like baby birds. Their painted faces resembled delicate porcelain dolls, their eyebrows arched, their lips shaped in cherry red pouts. Intricate latticed screens and silk scrolls decorated the walls. They lived out a warped fairy tale.

Meichen wondered if the men really believed the madam's perversion of a mythical scene. Did they think the girls admired them and longed to be in their arms? Or did they even care about the cruel reality of the girls' lives, as long as they enjoyed their evening?

Meichen looked around the room. An elderly man pulled her onto the cushion beside him and stroked her cheek. She looked into his eyes and smiled pertly, but her insides were roiling with panic. She hadn't seen Wang Jinsong.

What's happened to him? Did the Tong seize him? Kwan Yin, Jesus, help me!

A frail, white-haired elder with a long beard sat beside Meichen. He laid his hand on her shoulder, and the madam nodded, smiling at him.

Meichen scanned the room once more before her mistress gave her a warning glance.

Meichen swallowed and led the man to the room she and Wang Jinsong had chosen the previous night. A regular visitor, he knew where they were going. He seemed unsteady on his feet and clung to her arm to support himself. His weight was surprisingly heavy, given the thinness of his body. Meichen glared into his bleary eyes.

So, this is the man who'll have me first, an old man too drunk to realize the treasure he is taking from me, the gift that should go to my husband. In an instant, she hated him with such fierceness she wanted to kill him.

He sat down on the side of the bed, and she stood in front of him, unsure of what he wanted her to do. He motioned at the loops on his jacket and she began to unbutton them. She worked slowly, dragging out the time. The man began to rock back and forth, and suddenly he fell backward with his mouth open.

Meichen gasped, afraid he'd died because of her curse. Then a snore issued from his mouth, and she laughed softly. She sat beside him on the bed, waiting to see if he would wake, but he didn't stir at all. She ran to the window and looked out, despairing at the long drop to the ground. She tied the sheets together and pushed them out the window. They barely reached the first story. If she jumped from there, she would most likely break something. She hauled the sheets back inside and started over.

With the sheets torn in half, and the four pieces knotted, she pushed a heavy bench over to the window and secured her makeshift rope to a mahogany leg. Taking a deep breath, she climbed out the window.

A clattering cart startled Meichen. She held onto the lowest sheet and looked down. She watched in terror as a guard approached the man pulling the cart, who stopped below her dangling feet. A burst of adrenaline gave her strength to pull her knees up to her chest. She clenched her teeth, her arms aching. Would they come loose from her shoulders? She looked up to heaven and prayed fervently.

The guard challenged the plump driver, who insisted he was bringing wine and whisky to the back door, according to the madam's instructions.

Still suspicious, the guard argued with the driver. As their volume increased, Meichen drew in a deep breath. She knew that voice. Wang Jinsong stood below her.

The guard ordered Wang Jinsong to wait while he went inside to verify the stranger's story. He turned to walk away and Wang Jinsong leaped forward, slamming a wine bottle on the back of his head. The guard crumpled to the dirt, and Meichen screamed.

Wang Jinsong's eyes shifted upward. "What are you doing?"

"I'm going to fall," she wailed.

"Hold on." He pushed the cart close to the wall and jumped on the back. "Now, let go and I'll catch you."

"It's too far."

"Go ahead. We don't have time to waste."

Meichen closed her eyes and let go of her lifeline. She landed on top of Wang Jinsong, who sat forcefully on the floor of the cart with a loud "Oof." She scrambled to the ground, and he followed her when he could breathe again.

Taking her hand, he ran, pulling her through several back alleys until she pulled loose from him and bent over, clutching her side. Wang Jinsong bounced up and down, impatient to leave.

"We have further to go," he said. "You can rest a minute, then we move again."

"Don't you think we'd attract less attention if we walk?" Meichen gasped.

"Not with you dressed like that."

Wang Jinsong started running again, but he reduced his pace as the alleys narrowed and grew darker, and Meichen managed to keep up with him. He ducked inside a rickety shed and lit an oil lamp to illuminate the stygian darkness.

"What happened to you?" Meichen puffed. "I nearly died of fright when I didn't see you tonight."

"I couldn't help it. Your husband's uncle wanted me to run errands." He walked around the small room, making certain the window and slits between boards were covered. To be sure that no light escaped, he checked outside as well.

"Where are we?" Meichen looked around expecting to see evidence of vermin, but the little house was clean and neat.

Wang Jinsong removed a band of cloth wrapped around his waist. "Some friends live here. They work until late at night." Opening the sack, he shook a jacket, a cap, trousers, socks, and cloth shoes onto the bed. The clothes were wrinkled and damp from the sweat on his body.

Wang Jinsong turned around. "Undress and put those things on."

Meichen shed her silk robes like a prisoner tossing off chains. She donned the plain black suit of a coolie, her heart soaring now that she'd escaped. She would go to Chung when she'd thought never to see him again.

"Now to finish." Wang Jinsong removed a brush and a razor from the inside pocket of his jacket.

Meichen pressed her hands over her head. "Do you mean to shave off the front of my hair?"

"I have to if you're pretending to be a Chinese boy."

"I'll keep my hat on all the time." She eyed the razor with horror. "No one will know."

Wang Jinsong snorted. "How do you plan to keep a hat on every minute of a three-week journey? It's bound to fall off, not to mention you'll look suspicious sleeping in a hat."

Tears overflowed her eyes. "I don't want my husband to see me with a shaved head. I'll look ridiculous."

"After all you've been through to reach him, your husband should be glad to see you in any condition. He'll realize this had to be done." Wang Jinsong gave her a stern look. "Sit down so I can finish your disguise. My friends will be home soon."

Meichen stared at the wall and tried to think of her future happiness with Chung while Wang Jinsong's razor deftly slid over the top of her head. He braided the long hair hanging at the back into a queue. Stepping back, he studied her appearance.

"You'll pass, though you're too pretty for a boy. You'll have to stay in groups. Some men, Chinese or otherwise, desire boys." He swept up the hair on the floor and poured out the water he'd used to clean her face.

"Do you want the robes you wore tonight?" he asked.

Meichen shook her head. "Leave them for the men who live here. They can sell them for a good price. Just tell them not to take those robes to The House of Infinite Joy."

CHAPTER 20

"Courage is not the absence of fear, but the triumph over it."

—CHINESE PROVERB

WANG JINSONG WAITED with Meichen until her train let passengers board. They had spent hours in the station's waiting room creating a male identity and family history for Meichen. He quizzed her until she could answer questions about herself naturally. She would pretend to be barely literate in Cantonese with little understanding of spoken English, and she should say she came from the city, since she knew very little of rice cultivation.

They walked to the door that opened to the platform and bowed their heads to each other. Meichen's head bobbed slighter lower, correct behavior for a young boy bidding farewell to an older man. Wang Jinsong turned and walked away as Meichen boarded the train. He had given her a knapsack containing food, a change of clothes, and articles women needed but men did not. Meichen clasped the knapsack with both hands, hoping no one would examine the contents. She had a few gold coins sewn inside the sole of each shoe.

On the platform, white families hugged relatives and women wept. Husbands pulled their wives close to kiss them. Meichen turned her eyes away. *What disgusting behavior. Chinese would never humiliate themselves that way.*

She found a seat in a car where a Chinese man sat alone. He said nothing, merely nodding at Meichen in greeting. Two other Chinese sat behind them. The car they occupied soon filled with rowdy men and the lowest kind of women. A man in ragged clothes pushed to the back of the car near the Chinese passengers. He claimed nine seats clustered together, closely followed by his wife and seven children. The mother carried a howling infant.

More families squeezed through until the car swarmed with people. A conductor opened the door and eyed the car, ordering the occupants to keep the aisle clear so people could get to the toilet in the back of the car. He checked tickets and left as fast as possible. Meichen didn't blame him. She wished she could escape the noxious odors of cheap cigars, unwashed bodies, and the toilet across the aisle from the four Chinese passengers.

The train moved at last and fresh air blew through the windows, making the smell bearable. The Chinese men behind her had met before and began a quiet exchange of polite questions. After a while, they introduced themselves to Meichen's neighbor and he joined in their conversation with occasional comments. Meichen kept her lips closed, pretending she didn't hear what they said, though that was impossible. A younger man never spoke to his elders until they spoke first.

Her countrymen noticed her when the two behind asked if Meichen was related to their new acquaintance. He shook his head, and the three of them looked Meichen over, but they still didn't speak to her.

Meichen closed her eyes, enjoying the sway of the train as the wheels clacked against the rails. The train hurtled forward at unbelievable speed. She smiled, remembering Chung once told her when trains were first invented some sceptics declared people's hearts would stop from traveling so fast. She thought the speed was invigorating.

A hard punch on her shoulder brought her out of her reverie and she cried out in pain. One of the rowdies from the front seats yanked the toilet door open and sat down. He left the door open and expelled wind with a satisfied "ah."

A white man seated near the back of the car stood up. "Close that door, you oaf. There are women and children in this car. No one wants to see your damn behind."

The ruffian laughed and turned his head toward the Chinese men. "Hey, one of you coolies, close the door." They ignored him, staring out the windows. The man growled. "Get over here, one of you. Chop, chop!"

A huge man stood up and curled his hands into fists. "Shut that door before I kick you through the wall."

The door crashed shut, foul oaths issuing through the walls. Meichen expelled the breath she'd been holding, rubbing the ache in her shoulder. Meichen's companion stood up and pushed past her legs to stand in the aisle.

"Younger brother, change places with me."

She complied with gratitude and huddled against the window. He sat in her seat next to the aisle without looking at her. When the ruffian left the toilet and started down the aisle, he stumbled as he passed the seat Meichen had yielded. He flew forward, grabbing the back of a seat two rows ahead. The woman in the seat screamed and her husband jumped to his feet.

"Take your hands off my wife!"

"That Chinaman back there tripped me." The man glared behind him.

The giant rose once again and joined the angry husband. With amazing speed, he jerked a bottle of whiskey from the man's jacket. "No one tripped you. You're just too drunk to walk straight." He gripped the ruffian's arm until the man screamed.

"You're breaking my arm!"

The giant curled his lip. "No, I'm not, but I'd like to, so be sure not to struggle." He turned to the outraged husband. "If you wouldn't mind, sir, please step back there and check the condition of the toilet before I release this man."

The husband stalked to the rear seats and opened the toilet door. All the passengers nearby grabbed their handkerchiefs or pinched their noses. Meichen feared she might faint from the stench.

The husband looked back at the giant. "It's a stinking mess in here."

The giant jerked his prisoner backward to let the husband pass by and return to his seat. This elicited another howl from the ruffian. He shouted toward the front of the car where his friends sat in drunken lassitude. "Get off your asses and help me!"

The soberest of the group struggled from his seat and drew a pistol from his holster. He waved the gun, staggering several feet toward the giant. Screams erupted from every woman in the car, and nearly everyone slumped down behind the seat ahead of them. Mothers and fathers bent over their children.

"Get down!" Meichen's seatmate shouted, grabbing her arm to force her to the floor. She kneeled slightly but kept her eyes above the seat in front. Her eyes were glued to the drama unfolding in the aisle.

"Let him go," the gunman growled.

The giant stared at the man's trembling hand. "Do you love this scum enough to hang for him? There're plenty of witnesses here to testify against you."

The gunman looked around the crowded car, his red-rimmed eyes struggling to stay open as he clasped the seat beside him to stay upright. On his other side, directly behind him, a large woman stood and smacked his gun from his hand with her umbrella. He stared in disbelief as his weapon slid down the aisle. Another passenger seized it and passed it to the giant. The gunman's eyes rolled back, and he hit the floor like a sawn tree.

Meichen bounced into her seat, watching the giant march the ruffian back to the toilet. He used the gun as a prod, still gripping the man's arm. Meichen wondered how strong the giant's hand must be to maintain so much pressure so long.

"Open that door. You're going to clean the bench and wipe the edge of the hole, and wipe everything off the floor. When you're finished, I'll ask that brave lady up front to decide if you've cleaned well enough. If she says no, I'll let her beat you with her parasol."

The passengers burst into raucous cheers and laughter.

"There's no soap or water to clean with, and no rags," the ruffian whined.

"You take off your shirt and neck cloth." The giant raised his voice. "Ladies, please avert your eyes so you'll not be offended by this sight."

Every eye remained glued to the back. The ruffian removed his shirt when the gun pulled slightly away from his back.

"What about soap?" he muttered.

"I think we have an acceptable disinfectant right here." The giant slapped the bottle of whiskey into the ruffian's hand.

The man cursed, and the giant pushed him inside the toilet, bracing his heavy body against the closed door. "Ladies and gentlemen, I have a suggestion." He spoke loudly over the din of conversation, and the passengers became quiet. "I see no reason the law-abiding people back here should be forced to suffer this miasma. With your consent, we can move that man's companions back here to enjoy the aroma, and the rest of us can move two seats forward. And in the interest of keeping the peace should any of them rouse from their stupor, I suggest the Chinese move up to the front row."

While some of the passengers weren't happy about giving preference to the Chinese travellers, the majority agreed with the wisdom of heading off trouble. Meichen and her three countrymen went forward, while twelve male passengers shifted the drunk gang to the back, carrying those who were unconscious by their hands and feet. Their bodies formed hammocks that dragged over the tobacco spit coating the floor. The painted ladies elected to join them in the back.

Meichen couldn't keep her eyes off the giant. She had thought Mr. Lester must be the largest man in the world, but the giant topped the missionary by several inches. His middle was not thick, unlike Mr. Lester. His broad shoulders bulged with muscles. He looked middle-aged, his hair still brown but streaked with grey on the sides. A slight bald spot showed on top of his head.

"Stop looking at that white man," her seatmate ordered. "They don't like that."

"But he's friendly. He stood up for us." Meichen slapped her hand over her mouth. She'd stepped out of her role and contradicted an older man.

He gave her a stern look. "Younger Brother, if you don't listen to your elders and learn how to act in this country, you'll soon be dead. That white man doesn't care about us. He just wanted to punish those bullies. Listen to me if you don't want a bullet in your empty brain."

CHAPTER 21

"To know the road ahead, ask those coming back."

—CHINESE SAYING

MEICHEN PRESSED HER FACE against the train window, captivated by soaring mountains stretching into the distance. Even though it was August, snow coated the highest peaks. She imagined the train surging upward until it reached the clouds. In the distance she saw a long trestle bridge spanning a deep gorge between two mountains. Hundreds of wooden beams latticed together furnished support underneath the bridge.

She turned her face away from the window and clasped her hands under her chin. Her seat mate was still beside her and he jabbed her arm with his elbow.

"What's the matter, Little Brother? Are you scared of heights?" He chuckled. "We are only seven thousand feet above the ground."

"There is a bridge ahead of us, made from wood. How will this heavy steel train cross without breaking the beams?"

"All the wooden beams work together. The weight of the train spreads out across the bridge, and each beam takes part of the weight. Also, the trestle has been reinforced with iron bars over the years."

"It still seems impossible." Meichen's brow wrinkled as she digested his explanation.

"And yet trains have been crossing that bridge for twenty years and the bridge hasn't fallen. There are forces in the world that people don't understand. If experience proves something works, we can use it without understanding why it works."

"But don't you want to know why?"

He shrugged. "I'll let the philosophers and inventors explain the laws of nature. When they learn the answers, they can explain it to me."

"I've never understood how steel ships stay afloat in the ocean. If I throw a horseshoe in the duck pond, it sinks to the bottom, and a ship is thousands of times heavier than a horseshoe."

"But the ocean is thousands of times bigger than a duck pond, and it contains more water than we can imagine. All that water weighs much more than the steel ship."

"It also weighs much more than a horseshoe, but a horseshoe will still sink even if I drop it in the deepest part of the ocean. There's more involved than just weight."

Her companion put his hands over his ears and grimaced. "You tire me out with all your questions. Be quiet awhile so I can rest."

Meichen sighed as her companion closed his eyes and turned his head away from her, resting his neck against the back of the seat. The other two Chinese men had left the train at the previous stop, so there was no one she could talk to. She listened to the conversations of the American passengers and was dismayed that she couldn't understand all their words. In fact, some of the conversation was incomprehensible.

She shifted in her seat, suddenly afraid. The Lesters and Biyu had told her she spoke English well, and she'd thought she'd have no language barrier to overcome. She'd understood the missionaries in China and the ladies in San Francisco. No one had told her Americans spoke many different dialects like the Chinese. Her stomach muscles clenched tightly. After she reached Omaha, she'd have to change trains several times. What would she do if she needed help and no one could understand her?

She glanced uneasily around the rail car. Wang Jinsong had bought her a ticket for the cheapest seat available. He said she would look out of place in a more expensive class because Chinese hated to spend more money than necessary on travel, and it was safer for them to cause as little disturbance as possible. The wooden seats and sawdust covered floors were intended for brand new immigrants, poor farmers, and people of color.

Meichen noticed a wadded newspaper under the seat ahead of hers. She pried it loose and shook off the dirt and sawdust. She skimmed the pages, pretending to study the pictures as she quickly scanned the articles. There was a campaign poster for an upcoming election. Above a beefy man's glowering face large letters proclaimed, "The Chinese must go!"

An article above the election poster reported anti-Chinese riots in five western states. She put the paper back under the seat and clasped her arms around her body. Chills crept up her spine as she imagined what might happen in the days ahead.

The train stopped for the night next to a small inn where the wealthier passengers could get food and spend the night. Meichen didn't want to leave the carriage, but the conductor insisted. She caught up with her companion as he headed for a creek below the railroad bed. He handed Meichen a small iron pot and sent her for water while he started a fire and constructed a tripod.

Meichen balanced carefully on the rocky ledge where icy water plunged over rocks and whirled in circles. She was certain if she fell into the water, she'd be pulled under. She squatted and held her arms over the water to fill the pot.

"What did you bring to eat?" her companion asked as he hung the pot from the tripod.

"I didn't have time to shop in San Francisco. I have money to buy food as I go."

He shook his head and spat. "Did you think there are noodle shops at every stop?"

"The inn has food."

"The owner won't sell it to you. And you'd be risking your life to eat it. White travellers eat nothing but beef and beans and potatoes, and most of their food is rotten. I'll share my rice and dried roots with you. But first I'll make tea."

Meichen lowered her head to hide her humiliation. "Where will we sleep, Older Brother?"

"Here on the ground." He took the pot off the fire and threw in tea leaves to steep. "We should take turns sleeping. One of us should keep watch."

A sudden rustling in the grass above and a few rolling rocks warned them that several men approached their fire. Meichen jumped up, ready to run. But she was reassured when one of the newcomers greeted them in Cantonese. Another round pot and more rice and vegetables came from their packs, supplying plenty of food for seven people.

Meichen was glad more men had joined them. They planned to board the train the next morning and travel to Denver, providing her protection and advice. She listened to their accounts of life in the small towns of South Dakota and Wyoming, mining in competition with Americans and other immigrant groups. A riot in Rock Springs, Wyoming had left them homeless and impoverished, and they were looking for a safe place to resume their work.

The next morning, as she knelt beside the creek to fill a pot with water, one of the men knelt beside her to wash his face. He turned to look at her, and she jerked backward as her stomach contracted. Thick red scars streaked across his cheeks and twisted his mouth up on one side. He rose from a crouch and stalked back up the hill.

Meichen pushed the pot under the water and lifted it with shaking hands. As she rested on the bank, waiting to recover her breath, another man approached her.

"Little Brother, don't be frightened by my cousin's face. During the riot, his store was set on fire and he was trapped inside. He was lucky to survive."

Meichen bowed her head. "I'll beg his forgiveness for my rude behavior."

"It will be better if you say nothing. He's ashamed of his disfigurement. Pretend you don't notice it."

She nodded. She grasped the pot handle and followed him up the incline.

...

The whistle shrieked as the train approached Denver, and Meichen's companions gathered their packs. She easily fell into the evening routine after three days of traveling. Her eyes swept the terrain as they left their car. The engine would take on water and firewood, so there must be a creek or river nearby. She pointed to a spot sheltered by trees, and the group followed her.

The sky grew darker as they sipped their tea and waited for the rice to cook. The wind picked up, swirling cold air over them. Meichen collected extra wood to feed the small fire. When her stomach was full she hunched over and wrapped her arms around her bent knees, wishing for a blanket. San Francisco's late summer temperature had been warm and in her hurry to leave she and Wang Jinsong had not worried about protection from cold weather.

Now, a mile above sea level, the nights were unpleasantly cold. She wondered how cold the mountains must get before she froze to death. Her shivering kept her awake even though she pressed close to the fire, and she thought she might be warmer if she walked.

She was less than two hundred yards from the clearing when she heard voices. Small lights bobbed in the distance. The lights moved steadily toward her and grew larger and grey shapes took substance. She ran toward the campfire, screaming a warning.

"Wake up! We're being attacked!"

The invaders ran after her. The Chinese men were on their feet, arming themselves with whatever sticks or branches they could find. Meichen gasped for air and increased her speed. Suddenly she hit the ground as a burly man tackled her. Air whooshed from her lungs and her forehead struck a sharp stone. Her eyes blurred and the shouts and screams around her faded away.

When Meichen woke hours later, the sun was bright. There was a wooden beamed roof above and painted plank walls surrounding her. The sun pierced through a window shielded with thin gingham curtains. Her boy's clothes were gone, replaced by a nightgown. She sat up, then fell back on the pillow with a moan. Her head ached worse than it ever had before. The skin on her forehead was tight and stretched. She touched the skin with her hand and felt a row of stitches.

She heard footsteps on the stairs. She closed her eyes and breathed quietly as someone entered the room. Another person followed and stopped beside the door.

A woman spoke. "I brought up some oatmeal. Should I wake her?"

A man replied in a gruff voice. "She needs rest more than food."

"Do you really think so? She's so thin."

"The Chinese are small people." The man came closer. Meichen smelled a strong whiff of tobacco as he leaned over her. "The stitches look good. She won't have much of a scar."

"What will happen to her? Do you think she has family to take her?"

"She might have been related to the men she travelled with, but no one has seen them since the fight. There were only three left alive, and they took off through the woods."

The woman stroked the fuzz growing on the top of Meichen's head. "I wonder what happened to her hair."

"She was disguised as a boy. I got quite a surprise when I pulled off her clothes." He laughed. "I'm going downstairs to see my patients. Let me know when she wakes. The sheriff wants her if she's well enough to walk and talk."

"She won't be put in jail?" The woman's voice was worried.

"I expect she'll be sent back to San Francisco and deported to China."

The man and woman left the room. As their shoes tapped down the stairs, Meichen ripped the covers off the bed. She had to hurry before the woman returned. She moved slowly to keep her balance as she scanned the room looking for her clothes. They were not there. She sat on the foot of the bed holding her throbbing head. She had to leave before the sheriff came, and she had no clothes.

"Oh, you're up." The woman's voice made Meichen jump. "Would you like some food or drink?" She'd brought up a teapot and cups

Meichen studied her, wondering if she should speak English or pretend she couldn't. She accepted the oatmeal and a cup of tea. She decided since time was short, she would do better to speak directly to her nurse.

"Where are my clothes?"

The woman's eyes widened. "Oh, my goodness, you speak English!"

Meichen smiled and nodded. "Where are my clothes?"

"They were filthy. The doctor gave them to me to wash. They'll be dry this afternoon."

Meichen introduced herself and learned the woman's name. She was Mrs. Carey, the doctor's wife. She was full of sympathy for Meichen, and anxious to save her from further suffering.

"I'm so sorry you can't stay here a few days, at least until the doctor is sure you're well," she said.

"Do you think the sheriff would wait one more day? My head hurts so bad, and I felt dizzy when I got up."

Mrs. Carey wrung out a rag in cold water and draped it over Meichen's brow. "I'll convince the doctor to keep you here."

Meichen closed her eyes. "I'm so tired."

The woman patted her hand. "Go back to sleep. I won't let anyone take you today."

...

After hours of thinking, Meichen decided she had a workable plan to escape from Denver. She hated to take advantage of Mrs. Carey's kindness, but she saw no other choice. She was halfway to Chung, and she wasn't going back.

When Mrs. Carey arrived with her supper, Meichen was wiping tears off her face. The woman came to her at once and pressed Meichen's face against her soft, fragrant breast. "You poor girl, tell me how I can help you."

Meichen sobbed. "Please help me get to my husband. I've struggled so hard to join him. If I'm sent back to China, my heart will break."

Mrs. Carey listened to Meichen's story while her own eyes overflowed. "I'll tell the doctor and we'll see what we can do."

"Please don't tell him! Men don't understand these things. Just give me my clothes back, and I'll sneak away. No one will know where I've gone."

Mrs. Carey bowed her head. "I just don't know. The doctor will be furious if I help you get away. And it's very likely that someone will see you. You might end up in even more trouble."

"Don't you have a coat and hat to disguise me? I'll be very careful."

Mrs. Carey sat in silence for a while and suddenly smiled. "I know what you can wear."

She went down the hall and Meichen heard her rummage through the closet in another room. She hurried back with a faded black dress draped over her arm. She left again and returned with a black petticoat and camisole.

The dress was too large. She draped a black shawl over the gaping bodice, then added a black hat with a veil and black lace gloves. Meichen looked in the mirror. Her whole body was draped in a black cocoon. No one could see her hands and face. Mrs. Carey helped force Meichen's feet into tight black, high-heeled shoes that laced up to her calves.

"This was my mother's mourning dress when my father died. My aunts and cousins wore it, too, when they lost someone."

Meichen lifted the veil to kiss Mrs. Carey's cheek. "I'll mail it back to you when I reach my husband's home."

"No, don't bother. I was going to throw it away." She lifted a battered carpet bag off the floor. " I put your Chinese clothes in here. You'll need luggage to pass as an American traveller." She blew her nose and gave Meichen a little shove. "Go on before the doctor comes home. Good luck to you and your husband. I'll be praying for you."

Chapter 22

Marriage is three parts love, and seven parts forgiveness.

—Lao Tzu

Augusta, Georgia, September 1887

As the train stopped at the Augusta depot, Meichen stepped onto the platform to search for her husband. The heavy black dress and veiled hat were stuffed in her carpet bag. Her Chinese jacket and pants were cooler than the mourning clothes as she passed through the warm weather of the southern states.

Her heart pounded as Chung approached her. Without a word he grabbed her battered carpet bag and guided her down the street. He led her to a bench away from the platform and wiped sweat off his brow. He told her to sit down, then sat over a foot away from her, placing the bag between them. Her stomach clenched when the stern expression on his face did not change.

I don't understand why he looks so troubled. I thought he'd be happy to see me.

"Before we reach Uncle's house, I want to tell you how to get along with my uncle and his wife. We don't have a lot of time, so listen carefully. Copy the way I address my aunt and uncle, and don't speak Cantonese unless we're alone. Aunt Mildred gets insulted if she can't understand what you're saying. She's strict about some things, but she's a good woman and she's amazed you came so far to live with me."

Meichen feasted her eyes on his face. They were no longer in China and she indulged her desire to study him as much as she liked. She opened her mouth to speak, but Chung put a finger over her lips.

"Uncle wants me to divorce you, and he'll be angry you've come here. He hid all the letters you wrote me, and I wouldn't have known what happened to you if Aunt Mildred hadn't found them."

"I know. She sent me a letter along with money for the train." Meichen looked down at her clasped hands. "I was surprised you didn't write, too."

"After we read the letters, I had to stay at the store and distract my uncle while my aunt went to the bank to arrange to send you money." He spoke in a tense voice that made her uneasy. "Be careful what you say about the family in China. Aunt Mildred doesn't understand our customs, so Uncle hasn't told her too much about the way my family lives. And please, whatever you do, don't tell Aunt Mildred that Aunt Jiao is Uncle's first wife. She thinks she's the only one, and Jiao is an elderly relative that Uncle helps support."

"But what about his son? Does she know about him?"

"She thinks his mother is dead. Just be cautious when you answer any questions about our family. And if she says something insulting, overlook it. She expects everyone to act the way Americans do."

"Why does she call you Tom? When I first read her letter, I wasn't sure who she was talking about."

"I don't know. When I moved here, she decided Tom would be my new name. It doesn't matter to me. One American name is as good as another."

Her hands fluttered as she reached inside her bag, seeking the damp handkerchief she'd used to blot her face just a short time ago. It slipped from her fingers and landed at her feet.

Chung bent over to grasp the stained rag, and his hat fell to the ground. Meichen gaped, unable to speak. She pressed both hands to her face, covering her open mouth.

"Chung, what have you done to your hair?"

"I stopped shaving the front of my head and cut off my queue. My aunt wants my uncle and me to cut our hair and dress like Americans."

"But how will you get back into China? It's against the law to cut your queue."

"I still have my queue. It's hidden in a box under my bed." He laughed at her expression of horror. "Do I look so terrible to you? Are you ashamed to be seen with a strange-looking husband?"

A smile crept over Meichen's face. "I can learn to love it. And I've changed, too." She removed her round cap that covered the stubble of hair on the top of her head.

His lips trembled for a few seconds and he burst into laughter. Meichen's face burned She turned away to hide her humiliation. "It couldn't be helped. It was necessary for me to pass as a boy on the train."

His gaze swept over her. "It will grow back, and your head isn't your only attraction. I'm looking forward to seeing what's beneath that dirty suit. After five years, I expect there are interesting changes."

"I'm sorry I had to come to you looking so ugly. Everything I brought with me was stolen."

"The important thing is that you got here." He squeezed her arm lightly as he pulled her to her feet, and she began to hope the love they'd shared in China was still in his heart.

Longing engulfed her, and she blinked away tears. "I wish you would hold me. I want to be close to you again."

"As much as I'd like to oblige you, two men making love in the street would go straight to jail. We'll have to do that later."

They began the three-block journey to Joe Chow's store, walking side by side without touching. But she felt the invisible thread between them. Five years apart hadn't broken that bond.

Chung studied her face, his smile gone. "Among the letters my uncle hid, I found one from a man in San Francisco. He said he worked for Eldest Uncle along with your brother. He promised me he was protecting you because of his friendship with Ling Mo. What did he mean?

"The gods should bless Wang Jinsong a thousand, thousand times." She clasped her hands together in homage to her absent friend. "He told me about the mission house where I could live until I heard from you, and your uncle couldn't catch me. When your aunt sent the money for my train ticket, he arranged for me to leave San Francisco, but he was betrayed and I was kidnapped. He risked his life to rescue me."

Chung stopped walking. "Who kidnapped you? Did Eldest Uncle arrange it?"

"No, it wasn't him. A white man did it, the cab driver Wang Jinsong hired to drive me to the train station."

"But why..." His voice faded away. There was only one reason Chinese woman were abducted in Chinatown.

Meichen sighed. She had considered keeping her time in the brothel to herself, but she knew Chao Gang knew about it and he would pass the news to his brother in Augusta. It made one more black mark against her.

"The Tong locked me in a brothel. But Wang Jinsong found me and helped me escape and get to the train station. Without him I'd have been trapped in that terrible place forever."

When he said nothing, she struggled to control her overwhelming shame , but she couldn't hold back the tears spilling down her cheeks. "I didn't mean for it to happen. I tried to resist, even when the madam beat me." The silence expanded, creating a huge divide between them.

She sobbed as desperation seized her. "I know you'll never feel the same love you did before. But I swear to you, Husband, I was not dishonored. I escaped before that could happen."

"This Wang Jinsong must be a miracle man. I wonder you didn't stay with him in San Francisco." Chung's lips pressed tightly together.

Meichen winced at the bitterness in Chung's voice. She said softly. "I couldn't stay with him. *You* are the only man I'll ever want for my husband."

"Wipe your face with your sleeve. You don't want people to see you crying." His anger was gone, replaced with worry.

...

Chow's Grocery occupied a two-story wooden house that badly needed a new coat of paint. Only a narrow sidewalk separated the building from the dirt street. A large clay pot filled with pink peonies provided a dab of color next to the door. Chung explained the store occupied the bottom story while the family lived upstairs. Meichen eyed the narrow structure with misgiving, wondering how four people could fit into the upstairs apartment.

She reverted to traditional Chinese meekness as she entered Chow's Grocery behind Chung. His aunt and uncle stood behind the counter. Mildred's mouth dropped open and she nudged Joe in the ribs with her elbow.

"I see your former wife has found her way here all by herself." Joe scowled as he scrutinized Meichen's dirty face and rumpled clothes.

"Uncle, Aunt, this is my wife, Meichen." Chung tugged her closer to the counter.

Mildred came around and enfolded Meichen in her arms. "Thank God you're safe. We thought you might be lost for good. Poor girl, what you must have been through! The Lord surely sent angels to watch over you."

"Thank you, Aunt, for your welcome," Meichen said, struggling to free her face from Mildred's substantial bosom.

"How did you know she was coming?" asked Joe, hands on his hips.

"You aren't as smart as you think, Joe Chow," Mildred snapped. "I found those letters you'd been hiding. Shame on you for doing such a thing. I sent Meichen money to come here on the train." She turned her back to her husband and wrapped one arm around Meichen's waist. "You must be worn out. Come upstairs and I'll help you freshen up and settle in." She opened a door that revealed a narrow staircase. "Tom, bring up two pails of water, please," she said, glancing over her shoulder at the men.

As she followed Mildred up the steep steps, Meichen rejoiced at the thought of being clean again. "Is there enough water for a bath, Aunt? I'll fetch it myself, and it doesn't have to be hot."

"Of course, you'll have a hot bath. Tom will be up here directly with water from the well."

"No, please don't interrupt our husbands while they're talking. I'm sure it will displease my husband's uncle. I can carry up the water myself."

"You have a lot to learn about life in this country." Mildred opened the door at the top of the stairs. Inside, Meichen saw a kitchen and a round dining table with four chairs. "When Joe and I married, he appointed himself my lord and master, but I put a stop to that in a hurry. We all have work to do. It's Tom's job to fetch water from the well when I need it, and Joe should be closing the store.

Half a pail of water sat on the cast iron stove, left from the morning. Mildred filled a kettle to heat and invited her niece to sit at the table while she buttered a slice of bread and spread blackberry jam on top. "Would you like tea?"

Meichen nodded and attacked the bread with enthusiasm. She drank two cups of tea while Mildred looked out a window that faced the well. She tapped one foot and folded her arms across her chest.

"Tom should have brought the water by now," she said. "Pass through the kitchen porch and go down the stairs to the yard. See what's keeping him while I get out the washtub."

Meichen descended the stairs. Half way down she stopped, hearing angry voices outside. She was hidden from Chung and his uncle by a wall that formed a lean-to against the back of the store, but she had no trouble identifying their voices.

Joe snarled at Chung. "It will be crowded in your room with a wife."

"We'll manage," Chung said. His tone of voice was not as respectful as it should have been.

"I'll have to write Elder Brother and your father and tell them your wife is here."

Chung sighed. "Why do you have to spread the news right away? Couldn't we have some time without discord?"

"It's my duty to tell them."

"How do you know my father will side with Eldest Uncle? I'll write him and explain why I don't want to divorce Meichen. Maybe he'll forgive me."

"Of course, your father will agree with his oldest brother, because he is right. Why do you want such a disobedient wife? I admit she's beautiful, but your parents can find you another wife in China just as pretty, a well-trained wife who can give you children right away. Remember, your current wife didn't conceive in two years of marriage."

Huddled on the stairs, Meichen waited to hear if her husband would confess the fault was his. But he left the accusation hanging and ignored the comment.

"Uncle, I can't desert her. She put herself in incredible danger to come to me." He sighed. "She loves me."

"Love," Joe snorted. "That's a silly Western idea. You've both spent too much time learning nonsense from Christian missionaries. What does it matter what wife you have? In the dark, they're all the same, and in the daytime, you can avoid them. I bet you wouldn't remember this one's face if you didn't have a photograph of her."

Meichen fumed. How dare Chung's uncle insult her? She waited for her husband to set him straight.

"It makes no sense for me to waste more time going back to China to marry again when I have a wife right here. Five years without a woman is long enough."

"Pah!" Joe sneered. "You're thinking with your jade stalk, not your brain."

Meichen's pride deflated. *Why doesn't he say he wants only me and no one else?*

"Can you afford to support your wife and your family by yourself?" Joe asked, triumph in his voice. "Eldest brother may insist I turn you out since you refuse to follow his advice."

"I can find somewhere else to work."

"Aren't you ashamed of your wife, Nephew? Especially now, after the Tong had her? You know what they did with her."

"Eldest Uncle wasted no time destroying my wife's honor. She wasn't in their hands for long."

"One day would have been enough," Joe muttered.

"I trust her to tell me everything." Chung sounded confident, and Meichen hoped he was telling the truth.

"And you'll believe whatever she says?"

"Why wouldn't I?"

"Fool!" his uncle muttered under his breath.

Meichen crouched on the stairs as the two men separated, her hands clenched. She would outwit Chung's uncle. Her husband would want her body often, she was sure. She was confident she'd conceive right away and disprove the charge that she was barren. And Chung would never send her away once she was the mother of his son.

...

Meichen crowded into the small bedroom with Chung. There was hardly room for either of them to move in the space around the bed. He stood outside the room to let her undress. Mildred donated a nightgown that was much too large. Meichen accepted it politely, having no intention of wearing it. She wanted Chung to see her adult body.

She settled herself in bed, thinking of their first night together. How different things had been in Chung's striking room with its carpet and silk hangings. The only things left of those days were the few scrolls hanging on the raw pine walls.

Meichen watched him undress. *He's grown more muscles in the last five years.* He'd described the heavy boxes he lifted as part of his work. It had certainly made a difference in his physique.

He settled into the bed, forced to snuggle against her by the lack of space. She lay still wondering what she should do. She longed to lock her arms around his neck and rest her head on his chest. But she was still disturbed by the conversation she'd overheard.

"This is our real wedding night," she whispered.

He stiffened beside her. "Meichen, I know you couldn't help what happened to you in the brothel. I don't condemn you for doing what you had to. But there's one thing I must ask. Let's wait until we're sure you haven't conceived while you were locked up there. Of course, we'll raise the baby, if there is one, but I want to know for certain if it's not my child."

Meichen laughed. "I know it's hard to believe, but I'm still a virgin. I told you no man touched me."

"How is that possible? I know they didn't waste any time making money off you."

"The madam wanted to train me first. She spent two days trying to teach me to dance. I kept pretending I couldn't learn, and she beat me. Then she had to wait three days for my back to heal. The customers wouldn't have liked to see it."

Chung rubbed her back. "You were very brave."

Meichen gave a sigh. "No, I wasn't. I meant to resist longer, but the pain was too bad. I couldn't stand to be beaten again."

"I'm sorry I wasn't there to rescue you."

"The first night I was presented to the clients, Wang Jinsong came to the brothel. He went upstairs with me, and we planned my escape. But he came late the next night, and I was already claimed by a rich old man. By some miracle, he had too much to drink and he passed out as soon as he sat on the bed."

Chung frowned. "You were incredibly lucky."

"While the old man slept, I tied sheets into a rope and went out the window. Then Wang Jinsong showed up and led me to safety. He showed me how to disguise myself as a young man and took me to the train station to make sure I got away."

Chung pursed his lips and said nothing.

"You do believe me, don't you?" Meichen asked. She set a tentative hand on his chest. "Please say you trust me."

He hesitated only a second, but it was a second too long. Meichen pulled away from him as far as she could in the narrow bed.

"Meichen, I'm sorry." He rubbed her shoulder. "It seems impossible you could be so lucky."

Her voice was husky with tears. "I wish I had found a way to kill myself in that brothel. It would have been better than this mistrust."

Chung gathered his breath in a deep sigh. "I didn't say I don't believe you."

"There is doubt in your heart. I can tell. If you distrust what I say, there was no point in my coming here." She sat up on the side of the bed with her feet on the floor and reached for Mildred's nightgown.

"Don't put that on," he ordered. "I saw enough of ugly nightgowns in China."

"No! You're right. I had my bleeding time on the train, but I know I can't prove it to you. Next time I'll show you the evidence. I wouldn't want you to spend the rest of your life wondering about your own child."

Chung groaned. "I was a fool to say that. I can't believe I was so donkey-headed."

"When you stop listening to your uncle we can be true husband and wife. I don't know if you'll be able to tell I'm virgin." Her body hardened with anger, and the words of her mother-in-law came back to mock her. "Perhaps we should call in a midwife to certify it."

"Meichen, please forgive me. I want you tonight."

She stiffened when he placed his hand on her shoulder. "I'll let you know when the time is right," she sniffed. "It shouldn't be more than a week." She lay silently on her side of the bed, her back steadfastly turned toward him.

CHAPTER 23

"Married couples tell each other one thousand things without speech."

—CHINESE PROVERB

MEICHEN ROSE EARLY THE NEXT MORNING. She wore the black cotton tunic and trousers she had washed the previous night. They were still damp, and she huddled close to the stove to stay warm. Yesterday, the weather had been sunny and almost hot. Overnight the temperature had dropped, and the arly morning air chilled her.

When Mildred came in to make coffee, she was surprised to see Meichen. "I expected you and Tom to sleep late this morning."

Meichen had left off her hat though she was embarrassed by the stubble coating the top of her head. She thought Mildred might be shocked, but her new aunt only smiled.

"I see you went all out to look like a boy. Well, don't worry about it. We'll tie a scarf over your bald spot. so no one will know it's there."-

"Thank you, Aunt. And if you don't mind, I'd like to buy some cloth to make more clothes. All the things I brought from China were stolen. I have nothing to wear but this suit and a dress that doesn't fit." Meichen explained how she'd acquired the mourning outfit.

"Do you intend to make Chinese clothes?" Mildred asked as she set a pot of water on the hot stove.

"Will it embarrass you if I do?" Meichen asked. "They are more comfortable for me. I'm used to loose jackets that don't cling to my body. And wearing stiff corsets would be a form of torture."

Mildred grimaced. "I can understand why you think that. When I'm working at home, I tie my laces loose. But, of course, when I wear a nice dress to church, I must lace my corset tight to fit into my clothes. After a while I feel like I'm being cut in half."

"While I was dressed as a boy, I found out trousers made my movements much more flexible than a skirt."

Mildred's eyebrows shot up. "It would be much too shocking for a woman to wear trousers."

"I was thinking I could make an extra-long jacket, going down to my knees, and I could wear trousers under that. It's a style some Chinese women wear."

"Well, I suppose that would be acceptable. But I still want you to have some nice dresses, just in case we go somewhere. I mean to a concert, or a church social, or such." She snapped her fingers and smiled. "There's some beautiful silk cloth that Tom brought here from China when he came over. You could use it to make something nice."

Meichen shook her head. "The silk was a bride gift for you. I helped pack it."

"Then we'll both have dresses made, just for special occasions. And we'll make you some cotton work clothes. You can't go around in that boy's suit you're wearing now."

She tied an apron over her calico dress. "I'll be ready to go shopping in about two hours." She hummed a tune as she assembled food for breakfast.

I've made her happy. She must not get many chances to shop.

They heard Joe stirring in his bedroom, and Mildred dropped a handful of grits in the boiling water. She took out the iron skillet to fry thick slices of ham. Meichen watched her carefully, thinking she could cook breakfast so Mildred would have less to do. And maybe she could teach Mildred to appreciate rice congee for breakfast. The men would like that.

Joe came into the kitchen, his hair wet and combed flat. He looked around the room, frowning. "Where is that lazy nephew of mine?"

"He's still sleeping," Mildred said as she mixed biscuit dough in a wooden trough. "He must have gone to sleep late." She winked at Joe, who looked even crosser.

"He better not make a habit of it."

Meichen went to wake Chung. He blinked at her as though he'd forgotten how she came to be in his room. She knew the second he remembered. He smiled at her and held out his hand to draw her into the bed. But Meichen still smoldered. She didn't linger. She left without giving him a smile.

Chung joined the family in the kitchen. It was crowded at the table and he couldn't help touching Meichen's arm as they ate. She avoided his eyes through the meal, focusing her attention on Mildred. She gave elaborate compliments to her for serving such tasty food, as people did in China. Mildred did not know a Chinese cook would decline compliments until they'd been pressed on her several times, so she beamed her appreciation.

"I've been thinking, Joe," Mildred said. "The old storeroom you built over the back porch is nearly empty since you built the new one downstairs. Couldn't we clean it up and make it a room for Meichen and Tom?"

Joe scowled. "What if I need it again?"

"Don't be silly. You haven't put anything in it for months."

"There's only one little window. It would be too hot in the summer."

"Tom doesn't have a window in the room he's in now. Besides, there's a carpenter who owes us money. He could enlarge the window for us to pay off his debt."

"I'd rather have the money," Joe said as he stuffed pieces of ham in a biscuit. "We'll cut off his credit until he pays."

Mildred huffed. "Joe Chow, I'm ashamed of you. You're supposed to be a Christian and look how you're acting. That man has little children who need food. It would be a kindness to let him work off his debt."

"Then he'll expect to do work for us every time he gets in debt, and you know he will again."

"Well, there's plenty to do around the store. The clapboards are loose on the west side. And we can use a new fence around the back yard."

Joe made a rude sound, and Chung interrupted. "There's no need to make changes for me and my wife. We'll be leaving as soon as I save enough money to start my own store."

"Oh, Tom, don't be foolish," Mildred said. "It could take months or even a year before you can leave. You and Meichen can't live in your little room stuffed together like corn kernels on a cob."

"He has so much money, let him pay for his own window," Joe snapped. He stood up and went downstairs, calling for Chung to join him. Mildred hesitated only a moment before she tore off her apron and went after them. Meichen could hear Joe and Mildred shouting at each other at the bottom of the stairs.

Left by herself, Meichen began to clean the kitchen to show her new aunt she was willing to work as hard as the rest of them. There was no ham left, but she wondered what to do with the grits that formed a sticky mass in the bottom of the pan. Should she throw them away, or could they be used again for another meal? She wondered how to clean the cast iron pan. She decided to treat it as a wok, and wiped out the excess food, then washed and rinsed the pan and polished the inside with a dry cloth.

Mildred returned, smiling. She held up a handful of paper money she'd wrested from her husband. "When I finish straightening our rooms, we can walk to Broad Street and shop for fabric."

"May I look at the storeroom?"

"That's a good idea. I want you to decide if you'd be willing to sleep in there. When Joe and I moved here, there was a balcony outside the kitchen. It was built on the roof of a big open shed behind the store where people parked wagons to load them. We got more customers over the years and needed a place to store extra inventory, so Joe closed in one side of the balcony to make a storeroom. I told him he would get tired of dragging crates upstairs and bringing cans downstairs, but he was afraid someone would break into a storeroom built on the ground floor while we were upstairs sleeping.

"I'm sure he worried about that," Meichen agreed. "Second Uncle grew up during a terrible time in China, when there were rebellions and wars. Millions of people had no homes, and their crops and fields were ruined. People were desperate for food and bandits were all over the country. In those days, if a family owned anything, they had to guard their possessions night and day."

Mildred twisted the dust cloth in her hands. "My goodness, Joe never told me all that. I've always thought he was just a worrywart, always expecting the worst to happen. No wonder he laughs when I complain about the way my folks suffered during the Civil War and Reconstruction."

"My mother's Hakka village was built in a huge circle with high walls facing the outside and well-guarded gates. When I was a child, there were lookouts watching the countryside in case bandits attacked us."

"I need to apologize to Joe. He was raised to be cautious." Mildred smoothed her apron over her dress. "I finally persuaded him to pay for a sturdy storeroom with expensive locks on the door underneath the kitchen porch. He even had iron bars put over the windows. As far as we can tell, no one's ever gotten in it."

"Are you sure you want Chung and me to have this room? You could use it yourself. I would still help clean it."

Mildred blushed. "Ten years ago, I had hopes that I might have children who could play in that room. I planned to put in a stove and carpet and two or three windows, so I could sew in there while I watched the children. But no children ever came, so I lost interest in fixing it up." She smiled at Meichen. "Now that you've come, I want you and Tom to have a place you can enjoy together and be private when you feel like it. And who knows, maybe a little one will come along." She put her hands on Meichen's shoulders and pushed her out on the porch. "The door's over on the left. You look while I wash out the chamber pots. We can discuss what you want to buy on the way downtown."

The storeroom door was warped and hard to open. A cloud of dust rose as Meichen pushed her way inside. Sunlight exposed the carcasses of dozens of insects on the floor. The room was four times the size of Chung's bedroom. She walked over to the small window and realized it was higher than her head. She began to cough and backed out on the porch. Cleaning the room would be a harder job than anything her Aunt Meu Yuk had ever given her. But she would do it, as soon as she sewed her new clothes.

...

Two days later, Meichen stepped into the storeroom, pushing a wide broom Chung had brought upstairs from the store. By the time Mildred checked on her, Meichen's black suit was grey with dust and a mound of dirt sat in the middle of the floor. Mildred seized her kitchen broom and thin rags to cover their mouths and noses. The two of them worked side by side for hours until the dust and dirt was under control. Next, they washed the walls and floor with strong lye soap.

Joe came in and looked at their work. He made no comment, but Meichen could tell by his expression that he was impressed. Chung was amazed and told Meichen and his aunt they had performed a miracle.

In Chung's room that night, Meichen chattered about the plans she was making to decorate the room. "Aunt Mildred says we can color the walls with milk paint and she'll show me how to decorate with stencils. She's so clever, Chung. We talked today about the farm where she grew up and how poor her family was when her father came home from the war with a leg missing. That's when she learned to make pretty things with just a little to work with."

"Hm," Chung murmured. Meichen imagined he gave her words minimal attention. His muscles were tense as her body pressed close to his in the narrow bed. Meichen was still rejecting his sexual advances.

"I told her about my life with my aunt and uncle," she continued, "and how hard I worked for them."

Chung's attention snapped back. "Be careful you don't tell her about my family's house and all the servants. She won't understand, and she'll be angry."

Meichen frowned. "I think it's unfair that Aunt Mildred works so hard for your family to live in luxury. She feels sorry for them, because your uncle told her they live in a hut with just a little food. Meanwhile she cooks, she sews her own clothes and household linens, she does the laundry, she cooks the meals, and she cleans the house and the store. Your mother has servants to do all those things, and she and your other female relatives sit around all day embroidering things."

Chung's jaw tightened. "You want my family to live in a hut and go hungry?"

"No, of course not," Meichen said, surprised by his attitude. "But there should be a more even disposition of money. Aunt Mildred deserves a servant and some luxuries in life. Second Uncle should spend more money on her and this house."

"She's satisfied the way things are. Don't go making trouble."

"How do you know she's satisfied? Just because she doesn't complain doesn't mean she's happy,"

"She does complain every now and then," Chung admitted. "She was angry when I brought all the bride presents Aunt Jiao sent from China. Uncle had to think fast to explain it all, especially the bolts of silk."

"She's going to make me a dress with some of that silk. See how generous she is?"

"I would talk to Uncle about it, but he's cross with me. We hardly spoke today." He sighed. "I must find a way to get out of his house."

"But I don't want to leave," Meichen protested. "I like Aunt Mildred. I'll be lonely without her."

"You'll stay busy working in our store. You won't have time to be lonely."

He wrapped his arm around her shoulder as they lay in the bed. She did not object, and he risked nuzzling the side of her neck.

"I have something to tell you." She took a deep breath before she spoke, embarrassed by the subject. "I have proof I'm not pregnant. Do you want to see?"

"No!" His voice betrayed his revulsion. "I'm sorry I ever suggested the possibility that you would deceive me. Please forgive me."

"So you do believe everything I told you?" she asked. "No matter how unlikely it sounds?"

"If you say it's true, it is." He stroked her cheek. "I'll be happy when we can finally join together."

"I want our first time to be perfect," she said with a sigh of content-ment. "We should wait until our new room is ready."

"That could take a month," he protested.

Meichen giggled. "All the years we've waited, you can't wait another month?"

"No! Right now, I can hardly stand to wait another hour."

"But you will," she said, patting his cheek.

"Be quiet, both of you." Joe's voice came from the other side of the wooden wall. "I need my sleep."

Meichen hid her face in Chung's chest. "Do you think he understood what we said?" she whispered, her face burning.

"Probably not everything," Chung whispered back. "I don't always understand what he and his wife say at night. But I can tell when they're making the clouds and rain."

Meichen was shocked. "And they could hear *us*. Oh, I can't do it if I know they're listening."

Chung sighed loudly and gently slid her head and arm off his chest. "We'll talk about it later." His lips brushed her brow. "Let's go to sleep now."

...

Meichen was surprised when Joe gave Chung free time to work on the new bedroom. Meichen wondered at his sudden cooperation. But with just a little thought, she realized why. If Mildred heard Chung making love to Meichen, she would correctly conclude that the young couple could also hear her and her husband. And Mildred would, no doubt, refrain from participating until there was more distance between the two couples. Chung had told her his uncle always put practical considerations before his personal prejudice.

The room was painted a pale yellow color, and the small window covered with a muslin curtain. Meichen and Chung insisted the enlargement of the window could wait until the weather was warmer. Chung's narrow bed and one chair looked odd in the empty room, but Mildred promised to find them some extra furniture as soon as she could locate used pieces.

At last they were alone, the old bedroom between them and Chung's uncle and aunt. The lights were out except for a small oil lantern in the new bedroom, and Chung's eyes locked on Meichen as he removed her tunic and the halter top that flattened her breasts. She unbuttoned his shirt and the top of his pants.

"It seems strange we're dressed so different," he said. "I am the West and you are the East."

"There's no east or west with us," she murmured, pressing her bare breasts against his naked chest, "now that we're in the same country. I'm so happy to be here with you. My soul has longed for this moment all those years I waited."

"I've been lonely without you. I looked at your picture every night, but it was nothing to the real thing." He cupped her face with his hands. "I want you now as I've never wanted anything in my life."

He slowly removed his pants and she pulled off the skirt she wore beneath her tunic. They'd done this every night in the small room, but now they took their time, examining each other.

Meichen looked at the evidence of his arousal. "The jade stalk is eager."

"Oh, yes, it's obvious with me." He pressed her close to his body. "But how can I tell about the jade gate?"

She guided his hand between her legs. "You'll have to open it."

He lifted her onto the bed. "I'd like to learn about every part of you," he said with a groan, "but I don't have the patience to wait for long."

"There will be many nights for us, Husband. We won't be parted again."

His touch was gentle on her belly and thighs, and the more intimate parts of her body. She responded with greater passion as the pressure of his hands increased the friction between his skin and hers. Heat rose inside her as he slid on top of her. His mouth nuzzled and sucked her neck, then moved to her breasts as he lifted his upper body a few inches above her by resting his weight on his arms.

His hips aligned with hers and his thighs nudged hers apart. She bent her knees and rested her feet on the back of his thighs. The muscles of her inner chamber contracted in a steady throb that brought both pleasure and an ache for more stimulation. She moaned as her body demanded deliverance from its frustration.

"Will you open for me?" Chung asked, his stalk pressed against the opening between her legs.

"Yes," she sighed. Her legs gripped his thighs to tilt her hips up.

When the jade stalk pierced her, her face wrinkled slightly at the pain, and then her muscles relaxed as he slid into her body. The muscles deep inside began to contract as he moved back and forth. She felt like her womb was drawing him deeper inside. She began to anticipate some great sensation building inside her that would explode into pleasure she'd never felt before.

Chung increased the pace of his thrusts and her inner tension wound tighter until it was verging on pain. He groaned, and the sound increased in pitch and volume as he gave a final push. Meichen heard a second voice with a higher pitch. Just as she realized it was hers, rational thought ceased as synapses all over her body crackled at the same time.

When she came back from the brief coma, she floated in a sea of bliss. Chung held her tight against him, and they were on their sides.

"Was it what you imagined?" His palm rested on her waist.

"More. I felt like we melted into one person."

His fingers trailed down her side. "Just touching you makes me long for you again."

Her hand slid from his stomach to his pelvic bone. "Does the jade stalk wake up so quickly?"

"It's been asleep a long time, like a hibernating bear. It needs sustenance. In a little while, it will be ready again to absorb your woman's essence."

Meichen laughed. "You're still following the advice of the Taoist doctor."

"Maybe he was right. A woman's essence might make a man stronger."

"As hard as you worked, I would think it makes you tired."

"It made me happy. Just let me rest a little."

He rolled over onto his back and she curled on her side, her head resting on his shoulder. He closed his eyes and she studied his face in the dim light of the lamp. *How have I been so lucky to get this man for my husband?*

Her hand stroked his smooth chest and she explored all the new muscles he'd developed in the five years he'd worked for his uncle. He'd been a thin scholar with a soft body when he left China. Now he had the strength of a grown man.

He stirred as her hands wandered over his flesh, and his eyes opened. He smiled at her in the final, sputtering light of the lamp.

"How did I live so long without you?" he asked in wonder. He touched her breast. "It's strange to me that Chinese women keep their breasts bound flat, while Western women make theirs stick out like a ship's prow."

Meichen touched her other breast. "Are mine too small?"

He slid his hand around the soft flesh. "Your breasts are the size and firmness of ripe peaches. They are perfect." To emphasize his point, he bent over her and touched his tongue to her nipple and then sucked it with his mouth

She gave a little gasp of surprise. The sensation was pleasurable, but it seemed unnatural for a man to suckle the part of a woman that was meant to feed babies.

Chung positioned himself over her again and nudged her legs apart with his knees. Now she knew what to expect, and she welcomed him eagerly. As his thrusts became more rapid, her muscles tensed and she gripped his arms.

He heard her wince and he stopped. "What's the matter?"

"It's nothing, Husband."

He studied her lips which no longer smiled. "I'm sorry." He kissed her neck. "I'm being selfish. I know it was your first time tonight." He rolled back beside her. "As you said, there are many nights to come. I can wait."

CHAPTER 24

"To forget one's ancestors is to be a brook without a source, a tree without roots."

—CHINESE PROVERB

THE LETTER MEICHEN DREADED finally arrived from China. Scholar Chao had read the missives his brothers sent and made his own deliberations. Nobody was surprised that Scholar Chao had advised Chung to follow Chao Gang's orders. He must send Meichen away, and, in a year or so, he could return to China and marry a woman approved by his parents and his uncles. Chao Gang had promised to provide a settlement for Meichen and arrange another marriage for her with a wealthy Chinese man, if only she would leave the family and make no more trouble.

Mildred had taken over collecting the mail at the post office and handing it out since she'd discovered her husband could not be trusted with other people's mail. She had given Chung his letter, and she stood beside Meichen while he read it. He handed Meichen the letter without speaking and sat silently at the dining table while Meichen translated her father-in-law's words for Mildred.

Meichen's lips trembled as she read. The paper fluttered from her fingers as she reached the last word. She pressed her hands over her eyes and wept quietly. Chung retrieved the letter, refolded it, and set it on the table. Neither of them spoke.

As Mildred watched them, her face turned red and her brows drew together in a tight line. She blew a puff of air through her lips. "I can't believe this! What is wrong with you two? Tom, Meichen risked her life and her freedom and travelled halfway around the world to come to you. Meichen, Tom is happier now than I've ever seen him. He'll be miserable without you. Don't tell me you're going to separate and never see each other again because three old men don't like what Meichen did."

Chung put his elbows on the table and cradled his head in his hands. "If I don't do what they want, I'll lose my family. When I go back to China, my parents will refuse to speak to me. I'll be cut off from my brothers and sister and their children, and all my cousins."

Mildred sniffed. "My mama and daddy died before I met Joe, but my uncles and aunts and cousins stopped speaking to me when I married him and I haven't missed them a bit."

Chung sighed. "I need to go back to work. Uncle will complain that I'm lazy."

"You go back downstairs, Tom, but don't mention this letter to your uncle. After he closes the store and we eat, the four of us are going to talk this over, and we'll find a way to fix this mess."

When he was gone, Mildred hugged Meichen "Don't worry. I'm not letting you leave here. I think Tom will follow his heart, and I know he loves you."

"But that might not be the best decision, Aunt. Now he's young and desires me, but as time passes he'll regret defying his uncles and parents and he will blame me."

"That's ridiculous. A man's first loyalty should always be to his wife," Mildred insisted. "Joe is happy with me. He hasn't said anything about going back to China in the ten years we've been married."

"But it's not that way in China. When a woman marries, she becomes part of her husband's family, not more important than anyone else. It's the husband's parents who are important. A husband never puts anyone above his parents, not even his children."

"I see." Mildred pursed her lips. "Don't forget, you live in America now, and people in this country have a different way of thinking about life."

Neither Meichen nor Chung ate much. Mildred consumed her supper stoically, and Joe ate heartily as usual until he noticed the grim mood at the table.

"What's the matter with all of you?" he asked, his voice cross. "You'll ruin my digestion with your sour faces."

Mildred stood up and began to clear away the dirty dishes. Joe rose to leave, but she ordered him to sit back down. He glared at her in outrage.

"You see?" he said in Cantonese. "It's not right for a woman to step over the boundaries of her role in life." He glared at Meichen, who looked down at her hands.

"We need to discuss a family matter." Mildred sat down again, daring her husband to leave. "And we'll have no talk in your language. I refuse to be left out of the conversation."

Joe tapped his fingers on the table. "What's so important that we must discuss it like a government council?"

"Tom, tell him about the letter," Mildred said.

"My father orders me to divorce Meichen or leave the family."

"I told you he would back his older brothers." Joe's voice was smug. "Chao Gang and I have given money to his family for years."

Mildred glared at him. "Well, I have something to say about that. We can apply blackmail just like they can. If Tom's father insists on the divorce, not a penny of our money goes to them again. *I* don't approve of divorce, and I'll not support people who do."

Joe grunted. "It's not for you to decide what I do with my money."

"It's my money, too," Mildred snapped. "I've worked right along beside you all these years. I've sacrificed for your family along with you, but I won't do it anymore. You can run the store by yourself. And you can sleep by yourself, too."

Joe stared at her, dumbfounded. Chung intervened quickly. "Aunt, it's not just the money. It's a matter of obedience to the family. Eldest Uncle made the decision that I should divorce Meichen, and my father agrees with him. And I'm supposed to obey him."

"I know your customs are different from mine, but I still say Chao Gang isn't thinking about the consequences of his decree, especially the financial part." She turned to Chung with a satisfied smile. "It all revolves around money. If your father says you're out of the family, you no longer have an obligation to support him. He has no authority over you now. You're the head of your own family."

Meichen's head whirled with this new idea. It was a startling concept, alluring and frightening at the same time. Could she and Chung plan their own lives without elders making the decisions? They had little experience to guide them. On the other hand, the uncles could not foresee the future, especially in America. She wondered if Chung had the same rebellious thoughts about abandoning the old ways.

Chung straightened his shoulders. "Why does Eldest Uncle insist I cast Meichen away? He knows nothing about her or even about me. We don't live near him, and no one in San Francisco will ever know what happened, so no one will doubt his authority over our family."

Joe fixed a stern eye on his nephew. "Don't forget all my brother and I have done for you. Without the money from us, your parents would live in poverty. Your father and you and your brothers would never have gone to school. Right this minute, you'd be looking at the backside of a water buffalo all day while you waded through the mud, just like your grandfather."

Chung's expression turned from anger to guilt. "I'm sorry, Uncle. I can never thank you enough for what you and Eldest Uncle have done for me."

Joe was mollified and began to stand up. Mildred glared at him and renewed her attack. "Someone needs to reason with your brother. If he'd just accept the fact that Meichen is not like other women, there would be no problem."

"My brother is set in his ways." Joe crossed his arms over his chest. "I don't think we can influence him."

Mildred snorted. "You must make him understand the results of his decision. You told me your son is ready to set up his own household now that he's passed his exams and he'll get a government job. It seems plain to me that he'll need money so he can marry and have children. And he'll need a suitable house for a man of his status. You and I should send money to *him* and stop supporting Tom's parents. If Tom is disowned, he won't support them either. That would shift the entire support of Tom's family to Chao Gang's shoulders. I bet he won't like that."

Chung shook his head. "He'll just order my younger brother to come here and take my place."

"But what if your brother can't enter this country? The newspapers say very few Chinese men are even allowed off the ships. The captains have to take them right back to China."

Joe laughed. "Chao Gang knows every important person in San Francisco. He'll know who to bribe."

"And your brother will go to all this trouble and expense just to punish Meichen for coming here and Tom for keeping her?"

"He's furious." Joe shrugged his shoulders. "And he's stubborn, too."

Mildred looked at the three Chinese faces in front of her. "At least give it a try!" She threw up her hands. "I won't give up, even if you three do." She snapped out orders like a general. "Tom, go get some paper and ink and a brush for your uncle."

Chung prepared the ink, and his uncle sat down to write. Then he stood up again and motioned for Chung to sit in his place. "You write faster than I do, and your characters look almost perfect. You do the writing."

"Be sure to tell Chao Gang that Joe and I are opposed to divorce, and he'll get no help from us."

"Now wait a minute!" Joe protested.

"And tell him that Joe is doing this because if he doesn't, I will leave him for good."

"My brother won't care about that."

"And, I'll expect to get back the money I invested in this store. Immediately."

"I don't have that much cash in the bank."

Mildred gave him an unpleasant smile. "Oh, that's too bad. I guess you'll have to borrow it from your wealthy brother."

Joe snarled and slammed his hand on the table. He struggled to speak, but no words were formed. He stomped off to his bedroom and slammed the door.

...

The letter was completed and prepared for mailing, and everyone went to bed. In their room, Chung held Meichen close to him as though someone would tear her from his arms. She relaxed at last, glad the conflict she'd caused was over for the night.

Chung gave a sigh. "I don't feel right if I don't support my family. But I would have more money to save for our store."

"I'll work," Meichen volunteered. "I'll take care of children or do housework."

Chung frowned. "I don't want you working in a strange house."

"Chung, this isn't China or even San Francisco. It's just a little city, and the people here are nice to us. I'll be safe."

"If I say no, you'll find a way to make money anyhow."

She lifted his hand to her mouth and kissed it. "I'm glad you are coming to understand me." She snuggled against him. "Mm," she murmured. "It feels so good to know when I wake in the morning you'll still be here."

He slid his arm around her. "You sound like a purring cat who just stole a fish from the market." He shifted so her face was close to his and trailed soft kisses from her eyebrow to her mouth.

"Mm," she whispered as her fingers caressed his chest.

"You want to continue?" he asked, tickling her ear with his tongue.

At moments like this she missed his queue, but she grasped the clipped hair on the back of his head to shift his mouth to her neck. She shivered with delight as he gently sucked and nibbled the delicate skin.

Chung laughed. "That must be your favorite place."

"No. Further down."

His mouth shifted to her breast and he traced a circle around the nipple with his tongue. "Here?"

She giggled. "Farther."

He ducked under the sheet, slithering down until his mouth rested on her navel. Meichen giggled louder and twisted her body.

"You're tickling me, Husband."

"Then this isn't the right place." He moved down her abdomen, shifting over her with his knees between her legs. His voice sounded muffled as his chin rested on her thighs. "Surely this is it." His tongue touched the entrance to her body.

"The place is right, but I prefer a different instrument. Something harder and longer."

"I wonder what that could be." He paused a moment, shaking with silent laughter, then emerged from the sheet and hovered over her, resting his weight on his elbows.

He thrust inside her. She gave little gasps as he moved faster and pushed deeper. When he cried out his release she held him close as her heart rate returned to normal. They lay quietly until Meichen realized he was asleep. She gently eased out from under him and made herself as comfortable as she could in the small space allotted to her.

She stroked his hair as he slept beside her. "The next thing we need," she whispered to his unresponsive ear, "is a bigger bed."

CHAPTER 25

*"We live not as we wish to,
but as we can."*

—MENCIUS

MILDRED WAS NOT HAPPY to lose Meichen's company during the day, but she agreed the young couple would need more income to implement their plans. She consulted the ladies from the First Baptist Church who had started a Sunday School for the Chinese in Augusta. The ladies made inquiries, and Meichen was hired by an older lady who'd been widowed for several years.

Mrs. Hall had no children living with her, and she was hungry for companionship. Her favorite relative was a grandson named Jim, who visited her infrequently. She did not get along well with her son and daughter-in-law.

She followed Meichen around the house as Meichen did her work, and a great deal of her conversation detailed the life and accomplishments of Jim. "I expect remarkable things from that boy. He just graduated from law school near the top of his class. I see a brilliant career ahead of Jim. He might even be elected to the legislature after he distinguishes himself in the practice of law."

When Meichen met Jim for the first time, he was shy and soft-spoken. She wondered if he really had a future in a courtroom. On his part, Jim was elated to meet her.

"I'm fascinated by China," he told Meichen. "You must tell me all about your life there."

Meichen shrugged. "There's not much to tell. I grew up with my uncle and aunt who owned a medicine shop. Then I married and joined my husband's family. I went to a missionary school when he left China."

"Is it usual for married women to go to school? I've never seen it done here."

"My husband is an unusual man. He has a western education, and he wanted me to read and write. It gave me a goal to work toward while he was away, and I didn't have to live with his parents."

She wondered if Jim Hall had caught the undertones beneath the bare words. *Can he tell how miserable I was without Chung, like part of a matched set whose mate has been lost?*

"How many people are in your husband's family? I've heard Chinese families are very large."

Meichen rolled her eyes upward as she struggled to remember. "There were my husband's parents, his aunt, his two brothers, his sister-in-law, his sister, his cousin, two nephews, and me and my husband. And ten servants."

"Good Lord!" Jim exclaimed. "How crowded it must have been. Unless you lived in an enormous house."

"It was hard to find much time alone," Meichen admitted. "We had to share common rooms and the courtyard. But we had private bedrooms, except the servants. They had rooms in the attic above the kitchen, one for men and one for women."

"Was the family rich?"

"I suppose so, compared to most people in China."

"Why did you come here to work as a maid when you had servants of your own?" Mrs. Hall asked.

"I followed my husband. He came here to work with his uncle, so they can send money to the family in China. And I'm helping my husband save money to start his own business."

Jim came to visit his grandmother often after Meichen went to work for Mrs. Hall. At first, she thought he was too shy to approach ladies in his own social circle and just enjoyed having a female friend. Then he revealed his true motive.

"I'm going to write a book about China," he told Meichen, his blue eyes glowing. "Everyone is curious about it now because so many missionaries go there, and the politicians complain about so many Chinese coming over here. If they knew more about China, they might be more tolerant, don't you think?"

"Yes, I suppose so." Meichen noted that Mrs. Hall didn't seem enthusiastic about Jim's project.

"What about your law practice?" Jim's grandmother asked.

"I don't have many clients yet. I have time to write, and I can talk to all the Chinese people in town during the evening hours." He smiled at Meichen. "I've wanted to meet our Chinese residents. Now Mrs. Chow can help me. She can translate, and she can review what I write for correctness."

"My husband would be more helpful," Meichen suggested. "He reads and writes English much better than I do."

"When can I speak to him?" Jim was as impatient as a small boy waiting to go out and play.

"Come by tonight," Meichen suggested. "I'll tell you how to get to my uncle's store."

...

Meichen was excited about the book Jim planned to write, and she urged her husband to help him with his research. Chung agreed to introduce Jim to his friends that evening, but he refused to let her go with them. She watched them leave, pouting because she was excluded. She scolded herself for being unreasonable. She understood a man didn't want his wife tagging along when he visited other men.

It was after dark when Chung came back, without Jim Hall. Meichen met him as he came up the stairs, eager to know who they'd talked to.

"We visited Uncle's friend, Sun Fu." Chung put his coat away. "You know how much he likes to talk. Mr. Hall filled a whole notebook with the things he heard tonight."

Meichen laughed. "No wonder you were gone so long."

Joe sat at the kitchen table making notes in his account book while Mildred sat across from him, sewing. He looked up at Chung and grinned. "Sun Fu gossips like a woman

"Uncle, Sun Fu told Mr. Hall an opium seller has come to town."

Joe cursed under his breath. "That was something we need to keep a secret. So far, the people of this town have been tolerant toward us. But I know they won't appreciate an opium den in Augusta."

"Can't you and your friends make him leave town?" Mildred asked.

Joe frowned at her. "Opium sellers have connections with the Tongs. If we interfere with their business, they'll send hatchet men here. Do you want to find me lying in the yard with an axe through my head?"

"You could tell the police about it. They'd shut it down." Mildred looked at Chung. "You're not afraid to tell them, are you?"

"That won't be the end of it, Aunt. If the police close it, it will spring up again in another place. There are addicts here. And not just Chinese men."

Meichen listened in alarm. "What will the Americans think of us if Mr. Hall writes about opium rooms? I'll ask him not to."

"I doubt he'll listen. He wanted to know all about the opium rooms in San Francisco."

"You don't think he'd go to the one here, do you?" Meichen laced her fingers together. "What will his grandmother say?"

"Grandmothers don't know everything young men do." Joe snickered. "He's not likely to mention it to her, and you had better keep quiet about it, too. You don't want to attract the Tong's attention."

Meichen shivered and Chung put his arm around her. She leaned against his chest, taking comfort from his strength.

Mildred gave a sniff. "I don't believe he'd go there except to make observations. A man in his position wouldn't use opium." She put her sewing basket aside. "What else does Mr. Hall find interesting?"

"He should talk to me." Joe pointed to his own chest. "I've been in this country a long time, and I worked on the railroad in California and the head gates of the canal here in Augusta."

"Meichen can suggest it next time they talk," Chung said. He gave Meichen a meaningful look. "I'm tired. Let's go to bed."

"Get some sleep tonight," Joe called after Chung. "You've been slacking off at work."

Chung followed Meichen into their room. He closed the door with more force than usual. "Slacking off, he says."

Chung unbuttoned the top of his shirt and pulled it roughly over his head, flinging it on the chair instead of carefully folding it as he usually did. He jerked his feet from his boots and kicked them aside. His other clothes followed, and he sat on the side of the bed with his head resting in his hands.

"Chung, what's the matter?" Meichen touched his shoulder, her fingers barely brushing his skin.

"I can't speak of it right now. I'm too angry."

He pulled himself upright and walked to the washstand. He turned his back to Meichen as he rubbed his body with a soapy cloth. After rinsing off, he poured the water he'd used into the slop bucket and returned to the bed. Flipping the linens over himself, he stared at the ceiling, breathing heavily.

Meichen said nothing as she undressed and washed. She knew better than to bedevil him with questions no matter how curious she was. She went behind a screen she and Mildred had constructed to provide privacy. She donned one of Mildred's nightgowns altered to fit her slender frame. It was her signal to Chung that she was menstruating.

Chung glanced at her without comment and resumed his examination of the ceiling. She slid beneath the covers, trying not to press against him, but it was impossible in the narrow bed. She shifted to several different positions but could not relax while she wondered what her husband was keeping from her.

"Are you in pain?" he asked. Sometimes she suffered cramps.

"No. But I'm sorry I haven't conceived a son for you."

He snorted. "A son is the last thing on my mind right now. We need our own home before we have children."

"But it's my duty."

"I've told you before I don't believe in old superstitions. I don't need a son to care for my spirit needs after I die. It's that belief that's made life so hard for Chinese women. A son is no better than a daughter. You don't need to make it the main goal of your life. Right now, we need money to start our own business."

"Is your uncle still insulting you?"

"You heard him. I am slacking off at work." Chung clenched his teeth. "If he hadn't given me twice as much work to do, it wouldn't seem like I'm slacking."

"It's because of me that he's so critical of you." Meichen hung her head.

"Stop blaming yourself for everything that happens. And don't let uncle intimidate you. Show some pride in yourself." He turned over and pulled her close. "You're not an ordinary woman, you know. You have courage and intelligence. That bothers Uncle more than anything."

"But Aunt Mildred is a woman with a strong will. She defies him all the time."

"He expects her to act that way. She's an American woman. And he depends on her to help him run the store."

Chung shifted his weight, trying not to roll too far and knock Meichen off the bed. He gave a grunt of annoyance.

"Chung, I have something good to tell you. Everything isn't as bad as it may seem."

"What can be so good?"

"Aunt Mildred found us a wider bed, as big as the one she sleeps in with your uncle. It will arrive tomorrow."

"Praise all the gods!" He hugged her.

"I thought you didn't believe in the gods," Meichen chided.

"For this blessing I'll make an exception."

...

When Meichen came home the next day, Chung showed her their new bed. The oak headboard looked heavy. Meichen hoped it was well attached and wouldn't fall on her head or Chung's. There were crisscrossed ropes tied to the side rails to support the mattress, which looked lumpy and sagging. Meichen was sure when she and Chung were both on the bed, they would roll to the center. But at least it was large.

Chung was in a happy mood that night, and his uncle watched him with a jaundiced eye. "Don't get too rambunctious," Joe warned. "We don't know how old those bed ropes are. You may end up on the floor."

Mildred chuckled and winked at Meichen. "I suppose you'll be retiring early tonight."

Meichen looked down at her hands to hide her embarrassment. Chung left the table and went to stand by Meichen, resting his hand on her shoulder.

"We can't thank you enough for your gift," he said to Mildred. "We'll enjoy a good night's sleep, I'm sure."

"And other things, too," Joe muttered.

Chung sat down to wait for Meichen as she removed dishes and silverware from the table. Mildred took them from her, shaking her head.

"I can clean up by myself tonight. You two go try out your bed."

The couple went through their bedroom door and Chung closed it, shutting out the sound of Mildred's laughter. They sprinted to the bed, and Chung picked Meichen up and tossed her on the mattress. Her body rolled to the center while the sides of the ticking rose up as though enclosing her in a cocoon.

"I see we have some problems with our bed." He laughed as she struggled to escape from the mattress. "I'll have to tighten the ropes. Otherwise we'll be plastered together like two shrimp in a dumpling."

"Can you do it now? I can't stand another night in that narrow bed." She frowned at Chung's old bed which he'd pushed in the corner.

Chung twisted his lips. "I'll have to ask Uncle if there's any rope downstairs, and he'll probably want me to pay for it. On the other hand, there's no way we can sleep in comfort without reinforcing the ropes."

She could see he was reluctant to go to his uncle and endure more jibes. She sighed in resignation.

"I have an idea," Chung said. "I'll sleep in the new bed and you can have the old one all to yourself."

Meichen was too depressed to argue. She washed her body and slipped her nightgown over her head. Meanwhile, she heard squeaks and groans emitted by the bedframe and recalcitrant mattress. When she emerged from the corner blocked by the screen, she saw her husband stretched diagonally across the bed. It was almost flat. He grinned at her, and she laughed.

"Chung, can you really sleep that way?"

"Of course, I can. No one can say we Chinese aren't ingenious."

CHAPTER 26

*"He who is content
is rich."*

—CHINESE PROVERB

MRS. HALL WAS SEVERELY AGITATED the next morning when
Meichen arrived. "Thank goodness you're here," she said, her voice quak-
ing. She grasped Meichen's arms and squeezed tightly.

"Are you well? What's happened?" Meichen winced as she twisted her
arms to loosen the lady's grip.

"A man broke into my house last night. I was never so terrified in my
life." Her hands fluttered like the wings of a captured bird. "It's a wonder
my heart didn't stop."

Meichen led her to a chair and encouraged her to sit. "Did you see
him? Did he threaten you?"

"No, I heard him. He was walking around my house, but he didn't
come into my bedroom."

Meichen looked around the room. "Did he take anything?"

"Nothing that I can tell. He broke a vase, and I suppose that scared
him off." Her voice broke as she held back tears.

Meichen kneeled in front of her chair and grasped her hands. They were ice cold. "Have you sent for the police?"

"I'll let my son take care of that. I sent a boy over to fetch him."

There was a knock on the door, and Meichen admitted Mrs. Hall's son, who had obviously hastened into his clothes. His hair was barely combed, and the top of his shirt was unbuttoned. He went immediately to his mother and sat in the chair closest to her.

Leaving them alone, Meichen went into the kitchen to make coffee. She returned to the parlor to find Mrs. Hall sobbing into her handkerchief while her son watched helplessly.

"But, Mama," he said. "It could have been the cat."

Mrs. Hall glared at him. "Cats don't make noise when they walk."

"Perhaps you should come home with me and stay a few days." He pushed his chair closer to hers and patted her arm.

"You know Victoria and I don't get along." She sniffled and gave him a reproachful look.

"It's only for a few days, while I think what can be done."

"I'd rather stay here," the old lady insisted. She looked at Meichen. "Could you spend a few nights with me?"

Meichen's eyes widened. "I don't know what my husband would say."

"We would pay you extra," Mr. Hall said, grasping at this easy solution.

"Go home and ask him." Mrs. Hall mopped more tears from her face.

As Meichen had expected, Chung was opposed to the plan. "She should go stay with her son. She should be living with him anyway. This is a strange country where men allow their mothers to live alone."

"But she doesn't like her daughter-in-law."

"That doesn't matter. She is the older woman. She should command her son's wife to show her respect and obey her. Her son is weak to allow his wife to drive out his mother."

"I can't tell Mr. Hall what to do. Think, Chung, I'll make extra money. We need it to start our store."

Chung relented. "It can only be for a few days."

"I'll tell them." She found her traveling bag and threw clothes inside.

She hurried back to Mrs. Hall and her son. He sighed with relief and reassured his mother he'd come up with a permanent solution soon.

Mrs. Hall was calmer by the time Meichen brought her breakfast to the table. "I've already decided what I need to feel safe. I'm not going to leave my house and all my belongings and live as an unwelcome guest somewhere else. What I need is a man to stay here at night."

"You will marry another husband?" Meichen asked, shocked.

Mrs. Hall laughed. "No, not at my age. But I have a grandson. There's no reason he couldn't move over here. Charles and Victoria don't need him at home."

Meichen wondered how Jim Hall would feel about his grandmother's plan. And she wondered if it would work. If Mrs. Hall expected Jim to be home by dark, he would suffer a severe crimp in his social life, not to mention his research.

Meichen stayed three nights with Mrs. Hall, while Jim arranged to move in. He acted cheerful as he brought in his books and clothing and a whole box of journals where he kept his notes about all the subjects he was studying. Meichen was impressed with his wide variety of interests.

She set his books on shelves as he unpacked his clothes and filled the chest of drawers and the closet. She noticed a sketchbook on a stack of notes. He gave her permission to look, and she exclaimed in delight as she examined the birds and landscapes he'd drawn.

He smiled at her praise. "When I can, I go to the river and enjoy the scenery. Watching the water flow over rocks is almost hypnotic." He studied her as she admired each page. "You should go there sometime. I could show you and Tom the best view."

Meichen wisely ignored the offer. Chung would resent it.

"I wish I could draw. My husband does calligraphy and draws very well. In China, calligraphy is an art, and he's practiced it for years."

"What does he write about?" Jim stopped unpacking and watched Meichen.

"He copies the poems of our great poets and illustrates them."

Jim grew more animated. "Maybe he'd be willing to draw some illustrations for my book."

"How is your research coming?" She closed the sketchbook.

"Fairly well. I look forward to talking to your husband's uncle. And I'd like to know more about your life, Meichen. I need the woman's point of view."

Meichen lowered her eyes. "My life has been unusual for a Chinese woman."

"But you can tell me your story." He looked at his pocket watch and gasped. "Gosh, I'm late for work. Thanks for the help with the books. I'll sort the notebooks later."

He rushed out the door, stopping just long enough to give Mrs. Hall a kiss on her forehead. She laughed.

"He's a scamp."

...

"You're home early," Mildred said as Meichen returned with her carpet bag. She tossed the bag on her bedroom floor and returned to the kitchen to help prepare supper.

"Mrs. Hall wanted to fix a special meal for her grandson's supper, so she sent me home." Meichen took some carrots and chopped them. "I'm glad to be back."

"I'm glad to see you, too. Tom has been grouchy since you left."

"But I was only gone three days. He managed to live without me for five years."

"He's used to having you around now," Mildred told her. "Men don't like a change in their routines."

Chung and Joe came in together, and Chung smiled to see her. He didn't kiss her in front of his aunt and uncle, but he squeezed her shoulders. Joe grunted a greeting and lifted a pot lid to see what was cooking.

"Supper will be ready soon." Mildred wrinkled her nose at Joe. "What have you two been doing? You're covered with dust."

"We were moving canned goods from the back of the storeroom into the store." Joe glanced at his dusty shirt and trousers.

"That storeroom needs to be swept and dusted," Mildred said, concentrating on the potatoes she was mashing. "I'll get to it first thing tomorrow."

"No." Joe directed a smug smile at Chung. "Tom can do it."

Chung looked down at his dirty hands, pretending he hadn't heard his uncle.

Mildred shoved a spoon into the bowl and turned to frown at Joe. "Both of you are too dirty to wash in the basins up here. Go wash off under the pump."

"It's cold outside!" Joe yelped. "The water will be freezing."

"It'll only take a few minutes. You won't catch cold." Mildred took a pot of peas off the stove. "Go on. And put on some clean clothes when you come back in. I don't want dust on my food."

"Put on clean clothes! Are you crazy, woman? It's almost time for bed."

"You can wear them tomorrow." Mildred ignored her husband's murderous look.

Chung followed his uncle, turning back to grin at Meichen as he reached the door. Meichen knew he loved to see his uncle cowed by his aunt. Mildred slid the biscuits out of the oven as Joe and Chung returned, and they all sat down to eat.

"I thought you'd be gone until tomorrow," Chung said to Meichen.

"Mrs. Hall convinced her grandson to move into her house. He'll sleep there tonight." Meichen paused to eat a mouthful of potatoes and drink some water. "He's an artist. He let me look at his book of sketches."

"What does he draw?" asked Mildred.

"Pictures of birds and other animals, and the river. He goes there to relax." She turned to Chung. "I told him about your scrolls, and he wants to see them. He said he'd like you to draw pictures for his book."

"How exciting," Mildred exclaimed. "Imagine, Tom's work might be published."

Joe sniffed. "Yes, my nephew paints pretty pictures."

Chung continued to eat without comment, but Meichen saw the cold look in his eyes. She wondered why his uncle was goading Chung.

Mildred glared at Joe. "There's nothing wrong with drawing and painting. You should be proud he's so talented."

Joe glared back. "There is nothing wrong with owning a business, either. At least my work makes us a living."

Chung stood up abruptly. "Thank you for supper, Aunt Mildred." He disappeared into the bedroom.

Meichen tried to finish her meal, but her stomach tightened, leaving the food nowhere to go. Mildred scowled at Joe between bites. Joe ignored her as he consumed everything on his plate. He left the table at last, and Meichen helped clean up the kitchen then hurried to her bedroom.

Chung sprawled across the new bed, his eyes closed. Meichen sat beside him. She stroked the side of his face. She didn't speak when he turned his face away. "I haven't practiced my calligraphy since I came here. There seemed no point in it."

His sudden outburst startled her after the long silence. "But you can start again."

"When would I have time to do it? I used to spend hours working on one scroll."

"Do a little each evening. Or on Sundays."

He shook his head. "Who will care about it? Or even see it?"

"I would see it," Meichen said. "And Mr. Hall."

"My father was so proud of my scrolls." The pain in his voice twisted her heart.

"I am proud of them, too. I know my opinion isn't important, but I love them because they are part of you. I wish the ones I brought with me hadn't been stolen. They're probably in the house of some rich merchant in San Francisco."

"Or on the wall of some brothel."

Meichen hung her head. "I'm sorry."

Chung gave her a wry smile. "Mourning is useless. We can't change what's done."

He got up and went to the washstand to prepare for bed. He removed his clothes and dipped the washcloth in the bowl and applied soap. Meichen sprang from the bed and joined him. She took the cloth from his hand and rubbed it down his chest. He put his hands over hers.

"I washed the top part of me at the pump," he reminded her.

She slid the rag down his body. His hands, still on top of hers helped her move the washcloth in circles around his loins.

"You're waking the jade stalk," he warned.

"I want him awake," she said. She went behind him and washed his buttocks and his thighs. She sank down on her knees to wash his legs and feet. He handed her the towel and she dried him slowly. He closed his eyes and sighed with pleasure.

He raised her to her feet and unbuttoned her tunic. "Now it's my turn to wash you."

She slid her skirt down her legs and stepped out of it. Kneeling, he washed her feet and worked his way up to her breasts where he paused for kisses that made her shiver in delight. The cloth went back down to her firm bottom and he slid the cloth between her thighs, causing her tremors of anticipation. He rinsed off the soap, threw the rag in the bowl, and wrapped a towel around her.

Meichen tried to stand still as his hand moved across her bare flesh. She felt her inner muscles tighten.

"Do you want me?" he asked. His eyes were dark pools as his eyes captured hers

She pressed against him and he carried her to the bed. "Tell me what you want," he murmured into her ear. He nibbled gently on her earlobes, and then his lips wandered to her neck.

"Fill me with your love" she whispered.

She gave a sigh of pleasure and his body covered her. He entered her and began to move back and forth. She locked her legs around him to draw him deeper into her body.

His movements quickened and she tried to keep her voice quiet, but she couldn't hold back the noises that came from her throat. She was in another state of consciousness, aware only of the tension inside of her. It was almost painful, and yet she wanted it to go on and on. Her heart raced and her whole body burned hot as an oven. She felt her womb clench, and a sudden release of energy left her floating in a cloud of contentment.

Chung was hurtling toward his own climax. He cried out and collapsed on her as he sucked air into his lungs. His heart pounded so hard the beats penetrated her chest. He rolled off her and pulled her close against him. She settled comfortably in the circle of his arms.

After a silent interlude, he left the bed and brought a clean washcloth and towel to the bed. He wiped the sweat from her face and body and dried the dampness between her legs. "It does no good to wash before we make love," he teased. "We should wait to bathe until afterward."

Meichen pressed his hand against her cheek. "I missed you, even though I was gone only three nights."

"I won't let you go away again." He sat next to her prone body and bounced on the mattress. "Did you feel the difference since I fixed the bed?"

"There's no valley in the middle. I just noticed."

"Uncle says I used enough rope underneath to support an elephant."

She laughed. "I hope we won't get that heavy."

He lay down beside her, smoothing her hair with his hand. "I'm sorry Uncle was so difficult tonight. It wasn't a good homecoming for you."

"I just hate for him to make you angry." She sighed. "How long will it be before we can move?"

He nibbled the back of her neck. "At least a year."

"I could ask Mrs. Hall for a raise."

"It's all right. We can manage for a year. It's not so hard now, with you here to make the wait bearable. And I have a bedroom bigger than a closet and a fine new bed with plenty of room. I'm content."

Meichen smiled as she snuggled against him. They were lucky to be so happy.

CHAPTER 27

*"Wisdom is attained by learning when to hold
one's tongue."*

—CHINESE PROVERB

THE NEXT EVENING, JIM HALL WALKED HOME with Meichen,
prepared to interview Joe Chow. Mildred offered him supper, but he
declined.

"Meichen cooked for my grandmother and me," he explained. "It's
the first time I ate Chinese food."

"He liked it," Meichen beamed.

Mildred took his coat and set a place for him between Meichen and
herself. She insisted he could still have coffee and a piece of apple pie. "I
like Chinese food, too, but I just don't feel like I've had enough supper
without dessert."

Jim greeted Chung and his uncle with an eager smile. The men
nodded and stood behind the chairs next to their wives. Joe was cheerful
for a change, but Chung did not change his guarded expression. Meichen
hid her annoyance at Chung's failure to greet their guest.

"I'd like to try eating with chopsticks, Meichen." Jim pulled out her
chair for her to sit and pushed it toward the table.

"I have some in my room," Meichen told him. "I'll bring them over tomorrow."

Jim seated Mildred, then took his place. Chung and Joe raised their eyebrows at each other and sat.

Mildred smirked at her husband. "Mr. Hall has the manners of a real Southern gentleman."

"I'm not surprised, since he grew up here." Joe refused to be intimidated. He picked up his fork, waiting for her to pass a serving platter.

"Joe, would you be kind enough to say a blessing, please?"

Meichen and Chung watched in amazement as Joe calmly folded his hands and bowed his head. Mildred cleared her throat, and they hastily bowed their heads, too. He prayed with the confidence of a preacher invited to Sunday dinner by a fawning church member. He smirked back at Mildred as he retrieved his fork and took a platter of pork chops from her.

After the meal was finished, they all went into the parlor, where Mildred offered the guest the best chair, which Joe usually occupied. Jim preferred a hard chair next to a table. He said he could write more easily there.

Meichen had heard bits and pieces of Joe's story before, but Jim Hall pried details out of him that made the tale much more dramatic. Chung's uncle described the snow-covered Sierra Mountains where men in rope harnesses hugged rocky slopes to drill holes for explosives.

"My brother and I worked with a gang of twenty-four men from our village. When we first started, we did simple work shovelling dirt and rocks out of the way. My brother had come to California once before to mine gold, and he knew how to use gunpowder. He taught the rest of us, and our gang was given more skilled work that paid better. We drilled and chipped stone hour after hour, day after day, six days a week for months. Working in the tunnels was worse. We were choked by dust and gunpowder after the blasts."

Meichen looked at Joe with new respect. He was one of the lucky ones who made it all the way to Utah after months of back-breaking work.

"I came to Augusta to work on the head gates of the canal. It was easy work after the railroads," he told Jim.

"And why did you stay here?" Jim asked.

"I was getting older, and I wanted to make a living that didn't involve hard labor. And I didn't want to go back to California, although my brother stayed there. The white men in the West are always ready to kill Chinese or beat them up. The people here are friendly. So, I opened my store, and I married."

Meichen guessed Jim would have liked to ask Mildred why she'd married a Chinese man, but he was too polite.

"Gosh, it's late," he said, looking at his pocket watch. "I'd better leave or Granny will be upset with me."

Joe and Mildred saw him out the door, and Meichen turned to Chung with a smile. "That will make a good chapter for his book," she said.

"Yes, I'm sure," Chung muttered. He went off to their bedroom and Meichen followed.

"What's wrong?" she asked as Chung removed his shirt.

"You are too friendly with him," Chung said. There was accusation in his voice.

"What do you mean by that?"

"You act like you're his equal. Like you're a close family friend."

"He makes me feel like we're equal. He asks me questions about life in China, and he tells me ideas he wants to use in his book. He values my opinion, and he appreciates my interest in his work."

"How do you manage to talk so often?" There was an edge in Chung's voice that alarmed Meichen.

"We talk in the evening when he comes home, while I make supper for him and his grandmother. And sometimes he goes to work late, and we talk for a few minutes while I make his bed and straighten his room. It's not that often."

"You are in his bedroom with him?" Chung's eyes narrowed.

"I have to make up his bed. It's my job."

"But you don't have to do it when he's in the room." Chung clenched his fists.

"I have a schedule to follow," Meichen said, her voice cold. "There is nothing going on. Mr. Hall is a gentleman, and Mrs. Hall is always close by."

"What if he wants to do more than talk? Have you thought of that?"

Tears stung Meichen's eyes. "Do you believe I would be unfaithful? I've never wanted any man except you."

"He might believe you want more than friendship when you talk to him in such a familiar way. He is the grandson of your employer. Keep a proper distance between you."

Meichen sat on the bed, her back turned to him, her head bowed. He washed himself and went to his side of the bed. She heard him settle under the sheets. He didn't turn to look at her when she joined him. He reached up and turned down the lamp.

She stared into the darkness. "Chung, remember how you used to read to me when we were first married? And we would talk about so many things. Why don't we do that anymore?"

"Because I'm tired," he snapped. "When we first married, I had nothing to do all day but help my father and brothers with students and practice my calligraphy. We couldn't do anything at night but talk. I was passing the time."

"But didn't you enjoy it?" Her voice quavered.

"I work hard all day. When I come to bed, I'm ready to sleep. You must choose. Do you want me to make love to you, or to talk?"

"There are days when we can't make love. Couldn't we read to each other and talk then?"

"I'll think on it." He said nothing else and pretended to go to sleep.

She knew he was awake because she felt tension radiating from his body. Ordinarily, she would have stroked his back and teased him to turn over. But tonight, she was angry with him and didn't want to touch him. She rolled as close to the edge of the bed as she could get without falling out.

She woke the next morning still tired and miserable. She'd thought she understood her husband well, but now she saw sides of him she'd never imagined. He'd been kind and considerate in China, and now he often seemed impatient and cynical. Life in America had changed him into a man she didn't much like.

When she woke, Chung was gone, even though it was still dark outside. She dressed quickly and left, telling Mildred she would eat with Mrs. Hall. She didn't want Mildred to look at her face. Her aunt would know something was wrong.

She arrived at work before Mrs. Hall had risen, and Jim opened the door for her. He was wearing a robe and slippers and hadn't shaved.

"Are our clocks running slow?" he asked Meichen. "I didn't expect you for another hour."

Meichen looked at the hall clock. "I didn't realize I came so early. Please forgive me." Her face burned with embarrassment.

Jim smiled and let her into the house. "That's all right. I guess you woke early and couldn't go back to sleep. I do that sometimes."

Meichen went off to the kitchen, and he returned to his room. She sat at the kitchen table. Outside the window, she saw men walking, on their way to their jobs, and horses pulling carts filled with firewood or milk jugs or winter vegetables. She should have noticed the streets were empty. She had been so anxious to avoid her husband, everything else was blotted from her mind.

She wandered around the kitchen straightening containers and wiping the clean table. It was too early to cook breakfast. She heated water to make herself some tea and let Mrs. Hall's cat inside and gave her milk. She paced the kitchen until the water boiled.

She was sitting at the table with her tea when Jim joined her, fully dressed and ready to go to work. She jumped up quickly and reached for the coffee pot. "What do you want for breakfast?"

"Sit down and finish your tea," he said. She hesitated, and he waved her to her chair. "Since you're here early, I can ask you some questions for my book. You said you'd tell me about the life of a Chinese woman, remember?"

She sat, avoiding his eyes. "There's not much to tell. Women there are like women here. They marry, they clean the house, they raise children, they sew. If they're very poor, they work in the fields with their husbands. If they're rich, they supervise the servants."

"I've heard Chinese families don't want girl children. Is that true?"

Meichen shrugged. "It depends on the family, but most want boys. Boys can stay home and help their parents all their lives. A girl marries and goes to her husband's family. Girls cost money to raise, just like boys, and some other family gets the benefit of their labor."

Jim looked at her glum face. "Is there something wrong today? You're not your cheerful self."

Meichen looked down at her hands. "I'm all right."

She waited for him to speak, but he was quiet. "I don't mean to pry," he said at last. "But I want to help you if I can."

She did the unthinkable and looked directly into his eyes. He smiled at her, his earnest eyes encouraging her. With a lurch of her heart, she smiled back at him. He was her friend, whether Chung liked it or not.

"That's better," Jim said. "Let's talk about something that makes you happy. What did you like best about China?"

"The holidays. Especially New Year celebrations."

"And what do you miss the least?"

Meichen grinned mischievously. "My mother-in-law."

Jim shook his head, laughing. "Why do women always dislike their mother-in-law? Granny and my mother have fought like cats as long as I can remember."

"My mother-in-law hated me," Meichen said, "because I didn't have a son."

Jim's cheeks grew pink. "I see." He cleared his throat. "How did you meet your husband?"

"I met him at our wedding. Our marriage was arranged by his parents and my aunt and uncle."

"You'd never seen him before?"

"No. His father was my brother's teacher, and I'd heard of Chao Chung, but we'd never met."

"What would have happened if you didn't want to marry him?"

Meichen gave Jim a puzzled look. "It didn't matter what I thought, or what he thought. Our families wanted the match."

"What did you think when you finally met him? Were you satisfied with the arrangement?"

"He was very handsome and kind. I was happy to have him."

"And I'm sure he thanked his lucky stars for you." Jim said, giving her a look of admiration.

Meichen hesitated, not wanting to tell Jim her secret. "I was very young. I didn't look like I do now."

Jim tapped his fingers on the table absently. "I'm trying to imagine how I'd react if my parents found me a bride and I just met her at the church on the wedding day. And that night..." His voice trailed off and he blushed. "I shouldn't be talking about such things with you."

Meichen stood up abruptly. "I should start breakfast."

"There's one more thing I want to know. I thought all Chinese women had bound feet, but you don't."

Meichen flexed her toes thankfully. "It depends on the family. My mother was a Hakka. They're different from other Chinese, and they don't bind girls' feet."

"I'm glad for your sake. It sounds like a horrible process."

"It is," Meichen agreed. "I hope one day it's outlawed in China."

She went to the stove and took out two pans. She looked at him expectantly.

"I'll have eggs and toast. And a little bit of ham." He was silent while she cooked, but several times she caught him watching her. His face revealed fondness for her, but there was no hint of desire. Chung's jealousy was ridiculous.

Mrs. Hall joined them still in her robe with curling paper in her hair. "You're up early today." She yawned as she sat down beside Jim.

"It's my fault," Meichen confessed. "I came too early."

"Do you see clients this morning?" Mrs. Hall asked her grandson.

"No, Granny. I just have some research to do for Mr. Grayson. He takes most of the cases."

Mrs. Hall patted his hand. "Well, I expect before long he'll pass more of the burden to you."

Jim looked doubtful. "He treats me more like a clerk than a lawyer. He doesn't have a lot of confidence in me."

"But it's early on. I have no doubt your career will take off soon." Jim said nothing, and she continued with a twinkle in her eye. "Who were you out with last night? A young lady, I hope."

"I was talking to Meichen's uncle. He gave me a fascinating story for my book."

"Oh, that book." Mrs. Hall looked annoyed. "I'm proud of you for taking on such an ambitious project, but you shouldn't neglect your social life."

"When I have a larger salary, I'll think about courting," he said. Meichen laid his food in front of him, and he began to eat.

"I'll just have hot chocolate and some toast," Mrs. Hall told Meichen. "Since we're up early, we ought to work on cleaning out the closets. And I need to start making decorations. It's getting close to Christmas."

Jim went to his bedroom and came back ready for work, his hat in his hand. He bent down to kiss his grandmother. "I'm off now. Maybe it will make a good impression on Mr. Grayson if I show up early." He turned to Meichen. "Could your husband introduce me to some more of his friends if I come by tonight?"

Meichen hesitated. "He'll be tired tonight after getting up so early. Perhaps you should visit Sun Fu instead. He knows the same men that my husband knows."

Jim seemed disappointed, but he agreed. Meichen gave a sigh of relief. She needed time to mend her relationship with Chung and bringing Jim Hall home with her would make things much worse.

CHAPTER 28

"The wise adapt themselves to circumstances as water molds itself to a pitcher."

—CHINESE PROVERB

AS MEICHEN ENTERED THE STORE that evening, she heard the babble of men speaking Cantonese. She recognized her husband's voice, but there had to be at least two others. She saw Joe in the dim light of the store as he locked the door behind her. So, he wasn't part of the group upstairs. Rowdy laughter exploded overhead, and she sprinted upstairs, overcome with curiosity.

Chung sat at the kitchen table clutching a cup of tea, his usual habit while he waited for supper. Her mouth fell open as she recognized his companions.

"Ling Mo, what are you doing here? You're supposed to be in China."

"I came back early. Chao Gang took away my job and made sure I can't find another in San Francisco. If I don't get another job with a merchant, the Americans will say I'm a coolie and I'll be sent back to China for good."

Meichen turned to the second visitor. "Surely, First Uncle didn't fire *you*, Wang Jinsong! You're his right-hand man."

Jinsong puffed his cheeks out as his brows drew together. "Some low-class swine told the Tong that I was involved in your disappearance. They sent an assassin after me. I can never go back to San Francisco again. Or any big city. The Tong is like a giant octopus with tentacles everywhere. Chao Gang said it's possible they could find me here."

Meichen sank down on a chair and covered her face with splayed fingers. "Please, forgive me, Wang Jinsong. I never meant to put you in danger."

Jinsong's frown melted into his plump cheeks and re-emerged as a smile. "I'm glad I helped you. I could never have left you in a brothel."

Ling Mo's eyes raked over her. "You shouldn't have come to America. Look at all the trouble you caused. I've lost my job. And Jinsong has lost even more. Chao Gang has no living sons. He trusted Jinsong. He might have made him his heir."

Meichen bowed her head until her chin almost touched her neck. She hoped Chung would say something in her defence, but he sat beside her, silent, with his arms crossed over his chest.

Jinsong bristled. "Don't make me an object of pity. For several years, I've hated being subject to Chao Gang's every whim. Your sister inspired me to abandon the safe path and reach out for a greater life."

"I didn't realize roaming the country without work or food was the start of a great destiny." Ling Mo glared at his friend before resuming his stern glare to his sister. "Do you know how hard and long I worked for permission to visit China? I was expecting a rest from constant work and a chance to wake every morning with a wife ready to make me happy. Next thing I hear, you've run away, you've butted heads with my boss, and turned my life into a shambles, so I had to rush back to America. Thanks to all the gods, my wife conceived before I left. Otherwise, my trip home would have been a total waste of money."

Meichen sniffled. Under the table Chung's hand patted hers, but he let Ling Mo continue his scold.

"The person you injured most is your own husband. You've come between him and his family. You should volunteer to step aside so he can make peace with them."

"No!" Her body shook as she held back sobs.

Chung pulled her tight against him. "That's enough, Ling Mo. You have no say about my marriage. Meichen and I will find an answer without your advice.

Chung's uncle came upstairs following Mildred, who carried a paper-wrapped package of bacon. Joe's lip curled as he held up a finger for each slice of bacon Mildred spread in her cast iron skillet. He gave the visitors a look of distaste as he spoke to Meichen . "How many more of your relatives may show up?"

"I have no other relatives except my aunt and uncle, and they are too old to travel."

Chung spoke quickly to head off more complaints. "Don't worry, Uncle, I'll repay what my friends cost you, and tomorrow they'll find rooms to rent. Tonight, they'll stay with me. Meichen can make a pallet in our old room."

"Absolutely not." Mildred glared at the three men. "Tom, move your small bed back to your old room for Meichen. One of you men can make a pallet on the floor in the new room."

"No." Joe slapped his hands on the table. "If they get too comfortable, they won't leave."

"Yes, they will. My friends don't want your charity." Chung retorted.

"This is all her fault," Joe snapped, glaring at Meichen. "If she had stayed in China, Ling Mo and Wang Jinsong would still have jobs and homes."

"It's your brother's fault," Mildred snapped back. "It wasn't enough for him to reject *her*, he's vindictive enough to ruin her brother, too, and anyone who helped her."

"My brother fired Ling Mo to have a job available for Tom's younger brother when he comes from China."

"Nonsense. Your brother has his fingers in so many pies, he could find a dozen jobs for Tom's brother." Mildred turned her back on her husband and stirred the ingredients for cornbread in a pan. The men avoided each other's eyes and stayed quiet, cowed by Mildred's anger.

Joe snickered as Ling Mo and Jinsong examined the forks beside their plates. Ling Mo took out his chopsticks case, but Chung shook his head. He sat between them to illustrate the use of the fork. Meichen nodded to encourage Jinsong when he delivered turnip greens to his mouth without spilling them. The fried potatoes were easy to spear, and everyone picked up cornbread squares and bacon with their fingers. Meichen was relieved when the meal ended, and she could remove the plates.

"I'm going downstairs to work on my accounts." Joe shoved his chair under the table.

Another blessing. If Uncle stayed, we would argue.

Meichen stayed in the kitchen to help Mildred when Chung, Jinsong, and Ling Mo went to the parlor. "Aunt, you know they won't speak English since my brother and his friend know just a few words. I hope you don't mind."

"I know." She untied Meichen's apron. "That's why I'm sending you to join them. You can tell me later what they said."

Meichen slipped into the parlor, hoping she wouldn't draw attention to herself. She dreaded another scolding. When they saw her, Chung beckoned her to join them. Their faces glowed as they laughed and talked, electrified with excitement.

Chung pulled her beside him on the sofa. "Ling Mo has been saving money to start a business, and Jinsong invested money in stocks. If we add our savings together, we can start a store now!"

"We'll look for a place tomorrow," Ling Mo added.

Meichen looked at Chung. "Will I still work at Mrs. Hall's?"

"I hope so. We need the money from your job until the store makes a profit."

"The property you choose must be close enough for me to walk to her house."

"I'll make sure of that."

Later, Ling Mo and Chung returned the narrow bed to Chung's old room. As Meichen spread the covers, Chung's arms encircled her, and his lips touched the nape of her neck. "I never dreamed we'd leave Uncle's house so soon."

"I'm glad *something* good came from my foolishness."

"Don't listen to Ling Mo's complaints. I'm happy you came to me. Whatever else happens, don't forget that."

Meichen slid her arms around his neck and he lifted her off the floor, pressing his lips to hers as her mouth opened to accept his tongue. His arms slipped under her hips, and she wrapped her legs around his waist.

He moaned. "Right now, I wish we had our room to ourselves."

Meichen pressed her head against his chest. "I hope my brother and Jinsong find new quarters tomorrow."

...

The month went by slowly as Meichen waited for Chung and his partners to find the right location for their store. When she told Jim Hall about their plans, he joined in the hunt as well, finding them an old building that belonged to one of his clients.

"It hasn't been kept up," he warned as he showed them the property. "Mr. Miller will probably sell, if you can afford to buy it. Otherwise, he'll rent it cheap. It's not bringing in any money the way it looks now."

They entered the unpainted building with Jim leading the way. The front porch sagged, and several windows were broken. As they made their way inside, years' worth of dust flew into their eyes and mouths. Meichen held a kerchief to her face and listened as her husband and brother and Wang Jinsong discussed the pros and cons of the site in Cantonese.

"Is this building likely to fall down?" she asked Jim.

"I don't believe so. I had a carpenter look at it."

"That was nice of you. It must have cost you money."

Jim shrugged. "Not so much. It's worth it to find you a place close to Granny. She'd be heartbroken if you left her."

The store, two thousand square feet, was one large room with eight narrow columns to help support the weight of the second floor. They went up narrow steps to see the upper story. The door opened into a large area that took up half the floor space. The other side had been split into two square rooms of equal size that could serve as bedrooms. The large space would provide places for dining and a Chinese kitchen.

"The kitchen used to be a separate building, but it burnt down years ago." Jim said. "At one time this was a house. There's a well in the back."

Chung studied the scarred pine floors. "It looks like there was a wall here." He stood in the center of the large room.

Jim examined the boards underneath Chung. The middle section was lighter colored and the boards narrower than surrounding planks. "Granny said the last folks who lived here were a widowed woman with a married son. The son turned the bottom floor into a general store right after the war, and his mother and her daughter-in-law started a seamstress shop upstairs. I guess they knocked out the wall to make a bigger room."

"Did your grandmother have dresses made here?" Meichen tried to picture her fastidious employer visiting this dilapidated room.

"Only once." Jim grinned. "She said the widow had no concept of fashion."

Meichen looked at Chung hopefully. "We could replace the wall and have a parlor."

"We don't need a parlor. Anyone who visits us won't be too grand to sit in a chair from the dining table. Besides, we have no sofas or fancy chairs."

"We have no dining table and kitchen chairs, either," Ling Mo reminded them.

"Husband, will your uncle give us the bed you mended?"

"After I used so much effort to make it useful for sleeping, I'm taking it." Chung's mouth formed a firm line. "Aunt Mildred will let me have it if I visit her when my uncle isn't home."

Jim took a small notebook from his inside coat pocket. "I'll write down all the things you need. If you don't care what it looks like, we could buy used furniture. But I don't know what you'll do about the stoves you need."

"Why do we need more than one stove?" Wang Jinsong joined his partners ringed around Jim.

"You need one for each story to stay warm in winter." Jim was surprised by the question.

Chung sniffed. "I've lived here for five years and the winters never get very cold. The warmth from a downstairs stove will rise to the second floor if I put a few grates in the ceiling."

"We all come from the very south of China," Wang Jinsong added with Meichen interpreting. "In the winter, people wear heavier clothes, one suit on top of another. And we pile on quilts at night. We don't need to be coddled like flowers grown out of season."

Jim shrugged. "I'll leave that decision up to you."

The partners followed Jim around the bottom floor, discussing where to put counters and shelves and storage. Meichen guessed they would agree to rent the store.

She wandered to the back yard and saw a carpet of weeds. The remains of a fence lay scattered on the ground. *I wish I could have a garden like we did in China. It was so pleasant to sit under the trees and smell all the fragrances. If the store does well, perhaps we can make one.*

Jinsong, Ling Mo and Chung chose a price range to offer for rent, and Jim negotiated with the owner. In just a few days a contract was signed, and Chung prepared to tell his uncle he was moving to his own store.

Joe was not happy when he heard the news. "What kind of way is this to treat me? You know I need help to run my store."

Chung sighed. "Uncle, you've known for months I was saving money to start my own business."

"Yes, but I never thought you could do it so soon. I thought you would be with me another year at least."

Chung gave him an incredulous look. "You wanted to throw me out of your house just three months ago, when I refused to divorce Meichen."

"I was talking out of anger. I never meant I would actually do it."

"I don't wish to be disrespectful, Uncle, but you've treated me with great disdain since Meichen arrived. You've given me the worst jobs to do and you've made jokes at my expense. You haven't acted like you wanted me around. So, I am going."

"This is the thanks I get after paying for your education, so you could be useful to me," Joe fumed.

"Ask Eldest Uncle to send my younger brother to you instead of keeping him in San Francisco. He can be your helper."

"He can only read and write Chinese. He can't even speak English!"

"He can learn English. And he doesn't need an education to carry heavy boxes and stock shelves and sweep up dirt." In a spirit of reconciliation he added, "Meichen and I will tutor him in English."

Joe stood staring at Chung, trembling in anger. "Go on, Nephew," he said. "I don't want to see you again." He stomped down the stairs.

Mildred did not scold them for speaking Cantonese. She had ignored the argument between her husband and nephew and stood beside Meichen, weeping into her apron.

"I'm going to miss you so much," she wailed.

Meichen put her arms around Mildred's shoulders and tried to comfort her. "I'm sorry to leave you. You've been more like a mother to me than my aunt or my mother-in-law ever were."

"This is all Joe's fault," Mildred said between sniffles. "He's been so unreasonable about everything."

"You can come to visit us any time you want," Meichen said and Chung echoed her invitation.

Mildred grabbed her hand. "And you come visit me."

"We will if Uncle allows it," Chung said.

Mildred's eyes flashed. "I'd like to see the day when Joe Chow tells me who can and cannot come into my house."

CHAPTER 29

"To open a shop is easy.
To keep it open is an art."

—CHINESE PROVERB

MEICHEN WAS AMAZED by the transformation in Chung's outlook. He was no longer grumpy and discouraged. Although he worked more hours on the new store than he ever had at his uncle's, he laughed and joked with the others at their evening meal and he never ran out of energy.

After years of separation, he easily renewed his bond with Ling Mo. Jinsong was not an interloper for long. No one could resist his cheerful desire to please, and Ling Mo and Meichen already accepted Jinsong as a dearly loved friend.

Chung even curbed his hostility toward Jim Hall when Ling Mo and Jinsong overruled him and accepted Jim's offer to find day laborers to spruce up the yard and building. Chung reluctantly joined them in granting the white lawyer a small share in the ownership of the store to reimburse him for the money he had spent helping them with legal services and providing workmen.

After a month, they were ready to open. Shelves had been built, cans and barrels were waiting for the shoppers, the grass had been cut with a scythe to clear the yard of weeds, the fence stood upright again, and a coat of whitewash brightened the outside of the building. It was time to make the most important decision – a lucky name for the new establishment. The sign was already prepared with a bright yellow background rimmed in red with hardware attached to hang it. Chung only needed to paint on the correct letters.

Meichen proudly set out a five-course dinner prepared in her new kitchen to celebrate the launch of the venture. She stood behind Chung with her linked hands resting against her waist, ready to serve the four partners sitting around the table. Jim offered her his seat, as any American gentleman would, but Meichen shook her head firmly. Chung had allowed her to stay and listen, otherwise she was there to serve food at a meeting of men.

The main dish was a large steamed bass complete with head and tail. Meichen went to Jim first, prying an eyeball from the fish and setting it on his plate. Jim jammed himself against the back of his chair and pressed his hand over his mouth.

"It's a special delicacy for you as our honored guest," Meichen explained.

"I'm not the most important person here." He struggled to speak, averting his eyes from his plate as he looked around the table. "Your husband should have it as president of our firm. And your brother should have the other eye as vice-president."

Chung and Ling Mo urged Jim several times to accept the eye, but he remained firm in his refusal.

"Take the head," Jinsong suggested. "Fish cheeks are delicious."

"No, you must have it. Your investment greatly exceeds mine." Jim looked up at Meichen, and she recognized his plea for help.

Meichen was puzzled by Jim's behavior, but she reacted as a thoughtful hostess should. She sliced the main body of the fish down its backbone and carefully lifted a section off the skeleton. Jim accepted the fillet with a smile and thanked Meichen.

Nodding his head respectfully at Jim, Jinsong broke the tension by praising the fourth partner for his great humility and respect for the others. Meichen sighed with relief as she presented her other dishes. They were all made with American vegetables and the few spices she could buy in Augusta. And, of course there was rice, which was eaten on both sides of the world.

With the food distributed, Chung opened the discussion. At first, they considered a combination of their last names, excluding Jim, who politely declined to be included. Meichen suspected Jim's family would be appalled to see their name hanging over a Chinese grocery. Ling Mo wrote down every possible combination of the three names remaining, but none of the results sparked any excitement.

"Have you considered using a descriptive word or phrase instead of your names?" Jim asked.

The other three wrinkled their brows and pursed their mouths. Any man who started his own business would prefer to see his name on it. Almost every business in Augusta had the owner's name on its sign.

Jim cleared his throat. "And I don't want to offend you, but many Chinese names sound alike to American customers. You don't want your store to be confused with another."

Meichen abandoned her role as spectator and pulled a stool beside Chung's chair. "I've seen ladies' stores with unusual names. Mrs. Hall took me to a store called Elegant Tables to replace the vase the burglar broke."

"I still say it was the cat," Jim muttered.

Ling Mo sniffed at Meichen's suggestion. "So, shall we call ourselves Supreme Groceries Without Compare?

Jinsong looked down at the table, but Meichen knew he was smiling. Chung gave her a stern glance that warned her to keep her mouth shut. Meichen swivelled on her stool and turned her back to him. She'd worked alongside the men to make the store presentable and she'd provided money to support them while Chung had no income. She considered herself a partner, too.

"We're from the Celestial Empire," she said. "If we used 'Celestial' in our name, it would stand for all of us except Jim. I don't think he'll mind."

Jim nodded his agreement. "Try some possibilities. Think of words that go with 'celestial.'"

Jinsong whispered to himself and Ling Mo closed his eyes, steepling his fingers. Meichen glanced at her husband. He sat still enough to be carved from stone. She looked away from him and concentrated on her task. After a long discussion, Celestial Sons' Grocery was adopted. Meichen served wine to everyone except Chung, who refused a drink.

Ling Mo gave Chung a reproving look. "You don't like the name? You should have spoken up."

Chung shrugged his stiff shoulders. "It doesn't really matter to me. The important thing is to get the sign up and open the store." He excused himself from the meeting, claiming he had some last-minute orders to make. Ling Mo and Jinsong frowned at his retreating back. They returned their attention to the table as Meichen sat out cakes and sweetened fruit.

Jim Hall finished his dessert and insisted he had to leave. Meichen sighed as she looked at Jinsong and her brother after he closed the door. "One of us must talk to Chung."

Jinsong stood up and grabbed two serving dishes. "He barely knows me. I'll stay here and clear the dishes."

Meichen's eye swivelled to Ling Mo. "You've known him since you were just past childhood."

Ling Mo pursed his lips. "We've had some disagreements lately. Chung is worried about the store's success, and it makes him short tempered. It will be best if I stay here and help Jinsong. You're closer to Chung than we are."

"Cowards." Meichen turned her back to them and walked down the stairs. The partners had transformed a storage closet at the rear of the store into a tiny office, and there she found Chung. His ledger book was open, but he held no pen. He had propped his elbows on the desk and his head rested in his hands. He sat up when Meichen opened the door.

She composed her face to hide the irritation seething inside and kept her voice pleasant. Nothing would be gained by nagging. "Husband, I'm sorry you missed the desserts. I made your favorites."

She waited for him to speak, but no sound came from his lips. She studied the floorboards as he remained silent. She heard pages turning.

She raised her eyes and saw him reading the ledger, ignoring her. Her Hakka temper emerged through the thin glaze of Confucian rules for women. She forgot all about speaking in a soft voice.

"Chung, I'm humiliated by your rudeness at dinner. I never imagined you could act so inhospitable to a guest. You didn't even come back to say goodbye. I know you don't like Mr. Hall, but he's a partner and he's helped us when most white men wouldn't have."

He answered without taking his eyes off the page. "Why do you assume I left because I was angry with Mr. Hall? He's not the one who promised to stay quiet and unobtrusive, then broke his word and jumped into the middle of the conversation."

"I was trying to help." Meichen felt a nudge of guilt, then suppressed it. "You men were stumped."

"I was *not* stumped. There was nothing wrong with using our names."

"As long as yours came first."

Chung slammed the account book shut. "And why shouldn't it? It was my idea to start the business."

"Husband, you are acting like a child who didn't get his way. No one is slighting you. Your partners made a smart business decision to choose a memorable name. I think it's excellent."

"Of course you do. You're the one who suggested it. And Jim Hall went right along with you, convincing Ling Mo and Jinsong to follow like sheep. Why do you all accept every suggestion he makes? Do you think a white man's ideas are superior to ours?"

"Jim understands this community in a way we can't. If you were a stranger in China who wanted to start a business, wouldn't you take advice from local people? Jim has knowledge and connections, and he's smoothed the way for us."

Chung's lip curled. "He's done it for you, not for us. He's obsessed with you."

"You're wrong. We're just friends." She pressed her right hand against her forehead as pain throbbed above her eye. *Why must we keep having this same argument?*

"Don't tell me you haven't noticed the way he looks at you. He does everything possible to be part of your life. He's wormed himself into our family and the Chinese community so he can spend time with you. Then he moved into his grandmother's house so he can talk to you every day."

"I am helping him with his book."

Chung snorted. "How do you know he's writing a book? Has he showed you pages he's finished or asked you to read them? Had he started the project before the day he met you?"

"He's never touched me or suggested anything improper." Meichen huffed. "You're suspicious over nothing."

Chung grabbed her arm. "Meichen, I am a man, and I can tell when another man is slinking around my wife. And I can tell when my wife responds to his overtures."

Meichen jerked her arm away. Her lips struggled to form words. "Do you think, after I travelled ten thousand miles to be with you, I would fall in love with another man a few weeks after I got here?"

"I think *you* don't understand why you left China. I'm sure you were lonely and wanted to be with me. If you'd been a bit more patient, I would have come home. But there's something else you wanted that you could never have at home."

"And what is that?" She put her hands on her hips and tilted her head up.

"Freedom to do and say whatever you want. You're barely twenty years old, but you act like you're wiser than the oldest people in our family. You don't respect me, your own husband, or your brother. After only a month with me, you started to whine about how much I've changed, and how you wish I would act like I used to. You are right about that, I've changed. I've left the foolishness of youth behind me and turned into a man with responsibilities. Right now, I'm taking a great risk, leaping into darkness. If I don't succeed with the store, I'll drag Ling Mo and Jinsong down with me. I can't spare time to worry about your behavior with other men."

Meichen took a deep breath as she suppressed her anger. "I swear to you, there is no reason to think Mr. Hall is in love with me, or I with him. Please put that worry out of your mind."

Chung sighed. "I want you to change your work hours at Mrs. Hall's house. Don't arrive until her grandson has left. And come home before he returns in the afternoon. You'll make less money, but my mind will be at ease."

He put his ledger away and followed her out of the office. She was struck by the musty odor of mildew as they climbed upstairs. Water stains streaked the walls beside the steps, and there were holes where rodents had chewed through rotten boards. The partners had repaired the most visible damage, but there was much more work to do in the living area.

As they went up, they met Ling Mo on his way down the stairs. He handed each of them a letter. "These were delivered to your uncle's house. Your aunt dropped them off. I asked her to stay, but she was in a hurry."

Meichen ripped her letter open and squealed in surprise. "It's from Biyu. I wonder why she's taken so long to write." Her eyes swept over the opening lines. "Ha, she had to move so many times she misplaced my address." She read further and laughed, bouncing on her toes. "The mission board has sent Biyu on a tour of southeastern states to raise money for Chinese missions. She'll be in Columbia, South Carolina, tomorrow, and that's less than one hundred miles from here. She hopes we can ride the train to Columbia for a short visit!"

She clasped the letter to her chest with one hand while she gripped Chung's arm with the other. "I wish we'd gotten this sooner. I know the store opens tomorrow, but I want to see her again, and it's the only day to go."

His arm was stiff beneath her hand. She looked up at his face, fearing he'd insist she stay home. His features were still as he clutched his envelope and stared straight ahead, looking at a distant place visible only to him.

His brow wrinkled. "Ling Mo, take your sister upstairs."

She glanced at Chung and Ling Mo. Chung's lips pressed into a straight line as he held his letter tight in his fist. "I'll be upstairs when I finish reading this."

Meichen's stomach clenched painfully tight. "Is it bad news?"

"How can I know until I read it? I'll come up and talk to you in a while."

Meichen grabbed Ling Mo's arm as Chung trudged down the stairs to return to his office. "I know it must be bad news. Who sent the letter?"

Ling Mo shook his head. "It came from China."

CHAPTER 30

"Anger between a husband and wife should not last the night."

—CHINESE PROVERB

MEICHEN SAT IN A WOODEN CHAIR her brother had rescued from a pile of refuse. Some of the spindles were missing from its back, but it gave her a place to sit next to a window in her bedroom. She took stock of the room, something she rarely had time to do. It looked almost bare furnished with just the bed and chair and the old wooden screen. Their clothes were stored in trunks and crates lined up against a wall studded with a few iron hooks.

Biyu's letter lay in her lap. She read the five pages three times to keep her mind occupied while Chung was downstairs.

She closed her eyes and slowed her breathing to quell her anxious thoughts. But her brain raced on. *What does the letter tell him? Has his mother or father died? Why else would his family contact him after cutting him off?* She imagined all the calamities they might suffer.

Meichen jerked to attention when she heard her husband's voice in the kitchen as he talked to Ling Mo and Jinsong. The bedroom door opened and Chung entered, bringing a kitchen chair with him. She swallowed as he set the chair close to hers. They would have to talk quietly to keep their words inside the room.

"The letter is from my father." His eyes fastened on hers. She clenched her hands together tightly.

"Is everyone well?"

"He didn't say. He's offered me a way to reconcile with my family."

Meichen sighed. "Does this plan include me?"

Chung glanced at his father's calligraphy. "Yes, they've accepted that you will be part of my life. What they ask of me is a simple matter, and it won't really change our lives much. It's a small sacrifice."

"So, what must you do?" Her brow wrinkled. The word "sacrifice" had not reassured her.

"I'll go back to China for a year. My parents already have a bride picked out, and I'll marry her immediately and hope she conceives a son. Whether that happens or not, at the end of the year I'll leave her in China and come back here to you."

"And you think this is a good plan?" Her hands curled into fists.

"Meichen, it will be so easy. We will spend twelve months apart, and then I come back to you and forget about her. If she has a son, I'll never have to see her again."

A chill crept through her body. Could her husband really mean what he said? She felt like some other man had possessed him. "Are you the kind of man like your uncle, who could leave your child behind in China and never see him as he grows and becomes a man? You'd condemn some young woman to a lifetime tied to you with no hope of love and no satisfaction for her body, like Aunt Jiao? Have you become that hard-hearted?"

Chung stared at his letter. "Many Chinese men spend years in America and never see their wives and children. It's a sacrifice they make to provide a comfortable life for their families." He tapped the letter against his palm.

Meichen felt sick to her stomach. "It doesn't matter to me what other men do, or what women in China accept. You think I should agree for you to sleep with another woman for a year, on the other side of the world. I've been here less than half a year, after living five years without you. Don't you care that my heart will break if you leave me?"

"I'm not trying to break your heart or punish you. I'm trying to mend the rift between us and the family." He sighed deeply.

"But what they ask you to do is a way to punish me. Don't you see that?"

"Meichen, my father and my uncles expect some sign of remorse from you. You haven't even written to apologize for offending them."

"I will say I'm sorry my actions offended them, but I won't admit to doing something wrong. You keep saying Chinese people need to adopt modern ideas and knowledge to compete with other nations. On our wedding night, you said women would be important in a reformed China. Then you let your parents treat me as an appendage of you, not a person with rights and ideas of her own. Why don't you lecture your family for their old-fashioned ideas?"

Chung left his chair and paced the room. He stopped to glare at her. "You're still angry because I scolded you this afternoon."

"You spoke like a man from the Ming Dynasty." She thrust her chin up. "It's easy to spout modern ideas with your mouth, but much harder to put them in your heart. A man can't live in two centuries at the same time."

"This is ridiculous. I'm talking about the way we must live, not about political theory." He plopped down in his chair, slapping his hands against his thighs.

Before he could speak, she attacked again. "What if the Americans won't let you back into this country and you have to stay in China?"

"I have merchant status, so they have no way to keep me out. And if for some reason I couldn't leave, you can come back to China. This won't be a permanent separation."

"In China, I'll be forced to live with your new wife. What will my position be? Will your family accept me as your first wife, or will I remain repudiated?"

"I can't answer questions about what might happen in the future, and I see no point in worrying over unlikely events." His mouth twisted, and his voice grew louder. "I told you, they agree that we can live together."

"But am I still your wife, or have I been demoted to the rank of concubine? I won't agree to that." She crossed her arms and each hand clasped the opposite arm.

"Meichen, I need you to accept this plan. If I make this gesture, my parents will be satisfied." He pressed his hands over his eyes and suppressed a sob. "I want to be part of my family. I want my father to send me letters again. I want to know what happens to my brothers and sister." His voice broke. "I was never meant to be a man with no roots."

"And I'm not suited to be part of a harem. Your father's request is an insult to me. If your family accepts me as your wife, there's no need for you to marry again. This second wife is a means to drive a wedge between us, and that's what will happen."

"It won't happen if you trust me to forget her as soon as I leave China. You will make it happen with your complaints and suspicion." He rested his elbows on his knees and leaned toward her. "You're letting your emotions control your thinking."

"Am I? Let's make a legal contract, then. Promise me you'll sleep beside her without touching her, like you did with me for two years."

His mouth hung open. "What about my son?"

"I'll bear your son. You can't run off to China right away. If we try, I could be pregnant before you leave. That's the only way I'll agree. You must promise to be chaste as a monk, and you must write to me twice a month to swear you're keeping your vow."

"What will you do while I'm away all that time?" He stared hard, and she deliberately took her time composing an answer.

"I suppose what I do now. Work for Mrs. Hall, help in the store, keep our home clean, cook for my brother and Jinsong. And visit friends. I'll have plenty of time to help Jim Hall with his book."

Chung's whole body tensed. "I asked you to stay away from him."

"Don't you trust me to be chaste? I'll be just as faithful as you will."

He sputtered. "Just remember, I won't support a faithless wife or another man's child."

"And I won't support a second wife or her children. I'll keep my money for my own future."

Chung ground his teeth. "So, have we worked out terms you can accept? I need to tell my father if I'll be coming home."

"I need to think longer to be sure I haven't forgotten anything important." She swallowed past a painful lump in her throat. "I'll answer you soon."

She went to the bed and sprawled across it, leaving no room for him to join her. He lifted his chair and returned it to the kitchen, closing the door. Her brain whirled as she tried to convince herself she'd imagined the argument with Chung, that it couldn't have been real. He was not cruel or foolish, he would never do what his parents asked because the whole idea of polygamy would disgust a man like Chung with his principles and Western education.

Yet, now he was willing to take a second wife, incredible as it seemed. Meichen's perception of her husband's nature had been terribly flawed, and she floundered in a world turned upside down, tied to a man she couldn't love or respect.

She reclined on the bed, staring out the window as the outside world went dark. Eventually, she heard the three men in the kitchen assembling a meal from the afternoon banquet. She ignored their resentful grumbling and tentative knocks on the bedroom door.

Who cares if they eat? What's the point of eating, anyhow? Just to keep alive and suffer more despair and disappointment?

The commotion outside her door ceased thirty minutes later. She got up to prepare for bed before Chung came back. She would pretend to sleep when he took his place beside her. She didn't imagine he would want to touch her after she'd driven him into a rage. And she felt cold and stiff. She rolled on her side so her back would be turned to him.

She cringed when he joined her two hours later. His hand slid across her shoulder. He hesitated only a moment before his fingers brushed her breast. She scrunched herself into a tight ball to restrict access to her chest.

"Meichen, I know you're awake." The husband she knew would have laughed and tickled her sides and nipped and kissed until she surrendered. The stranger who'd emerged this afternoon had a stern, biting voice. When she remained silent and motionless, he snorted and flipped her on her back. He launched himself on top of her, using his hands and legs to flatten her limbs. He pinned her hands over her head.

"Would you like me to tie your hands and feet to the bedposts, Wife? I hear that's popular in the brothels."

Meichen squirmed and bucked beneath him. "Let me go." She opened her mouth to scream, but he silenced her by pressing his mouth over hers.

He lifted his head to smile, but there was no real happiness on his face. "Go ahead and fight me. It increases my desire."

"Why are you doing this?" She gasped. "I can't breathe with your body crushing my chest."

He balanced his upper body on his elbows. "You are spoiled, Meichen. You came to me a virgin, and I've been gentle with you while I taught you how to make love. Now that you've learned about the clouds and rain, it's your turn to do what pleases me."

"And it pleases you to force yourself on me when I have no desire to do what you want?"

"Force should not be necessary. It's your duty as my wife to give me pleasure and release when I ask for it. I feel restless tonight and tense from my worries about the store. I need you to bring me comfort."

"I don't have the energy to pleasure you tonight." She sweetened her voice. "Too bad your second wife isn't available to help you."

He glared at her mocking smile. With an angry grunt, he shoved her thighs wide apart with his knees and plunged inside her. She stared into his eyes, overcome by shock. He withdrew and thrust again, slamming against her entrance with each penetration. Her mind told her she should struggle, wail, scream, even bite to protest their violent coupling.

But her body responded with eager excitement. Each stroke caused ripples of pleasure that spread through her in concentric circles. As the pace of his thrusts increased, she drew closer to the blissful peak her body craved. His final push produced a sensory explosion unlike any she'd ever experienced. Her arms wrapped around Chung's neck and her legs girdled his waist as his body convulsed.

She clung to him, awed by her powerful response to his forceful possession of her body. This was not at all like the civilized clouds and rain. It was a typhoon with fierce winds that swept everything before it.

His body collapsed on top of her. His mouth blew hot air against her neck, his heart pounded into her chest as he gulped air into his lungs. Her body quivered beneath him and her arm and leg muscles relaxed. With a groan, he slid off her and rested on his stomach. Her right hand struggled under his shoulder, and her foot was trapped beneath his thigh.

Meichen waited for Chung to comment about her astounding climax. He must have noticed her response, which far exceeded any she'd shown before. She frowned when she heard steady breathing and lifted her head to look at him. His mouth was partially open, and his eyes were shut.

How can he be asleep after what he did to me? She balled her hand and punched his sarm. He moaned, rolled onto his back, turned another ninety degrees, and settled on his right side. Meichen glared at his naked back as he burrowed into the feather bed. She plopped back on her pillow, clenching her jaw. While she had shattered in unbelievable pleasure, he had used her as a sleeping draught.

Her opinion was confirmed. Somehow her beloved husband had turned into a selfish pig. She seized the quilt and cocooned herself in it, leaving his body uncovered. It would serve him right to wake up with a frost-bitten stalk. She fumed through the night, wanting Chung to wake so she could confront him. But eventually she fell asleep.

She woke in an empty bed, clenching her eyes against the morning sun. She had taken a week off from her job at Mrs. Hall's house because Chung had insisted she'd be needed for the opening of the store. He must have changed his mind since he hadn't bothered to wake her.

She dressed and hurried to the kitchen. It was empty except for the soiled pots piled in a large enamel bowl. The men may have meant to finish cleaning up before the store opened, but their first customers must have been lined up, waiting at the front door before the sun rose. She heaved a sigh as she tackled the mess.

With a clean kitchen behind her, she glided down the stairs. She wanted to enter the store without attracting attention to herself. There were a few latecomers searching the aisles as the three owners stood around the counter.

"Where are the customers?" Meichen whispered in her brother's ear.

"They have come and gone. Though most were lookers, not customers. Our Chinese friends came early so they wouldn't be late for work."

"There were others, as well. People who live in this neighborhood." Jinsong smiled and nodded at the women still shopping. He walked toward them with the proud manner of a Chinese mandarin. "May I help you ladies find something? Is there a product you'd like to see in the future?" He smirked at his partners. He had spoken the phrase just as Jim had taught him.

Two of the women joined Jinsong, asking about creams and lotions and special teas produced by Chinese doctors. They'd read about these mysterious products in the back of their ladies' magazines. Jinsong took out a notebook and pencil to record their suggestions.

Ling Mo copied his friend's example, kneeling beside a black woman who examined prices. He had no difficulty getting her to talk. She pointed at bins of flour and cornmeal and argued about the price of each one. Seeing her brother flounder in the torrent of words, Meichen joined him.

"She says your prices are high."

"I figured that out already."

"Find me paper and a pencil," Meichen said. "I'm going to write down her suggestions."

"What for? We can't let people wander in here and pay the price they choose."

"You have to get people in the store first. Shave a few cents here and there, and tshe'll tell her friends she saved money here."

When the women were gone, the three men and Meichen discussed their observations. Jinsong was already planning a private alcove to offer special items for ladies, not just beauty products but also delicate handkerchiefs and painted fans. Ling Mo was bickering with Chung over how much prices should be reduced on cornmeal and flour. Meichen had let her mind wander, waiting until she could have a private conversation with Chung.

They stopped talking when Jim Hall pushed the door open and brought a large package over to the counter. He smacked down a box of red wrapping paper as well.

"What is this for?" Chung studied the unmarked box and sniffed. "It smells like tobacco."

"It is. We'll be giving out free plugs of tobacco to each new customer." Jim cut open the package to reveal a long brown rope of compressed fibers. He snipped an inch off the rope, then tore a strip of red paper and twisted the plug inside.

"What about the women customers?" Meichen asked.

"Their husbands will appreciate the tobacco." He grinned. "And some women use it themselves."

Chung frowned at Jim. "You really think this will attract customers? They might come just once to get a free twist."

Jinsong pulled on Chung's elbow. "Then it's our job to lure them back. Every week we can offer some small deal. We act friendly, happy to see them, remember their names, listen to their comments, make them feel important. Everyone will want to come here."

Chung shook his head. "I don't see how we can make money when we give things away. The goal of a merchant is to sell things at a higher price than they cost him."

"Just give it a try," Jim said. "It will look better if people come here often than if the store looks like a ghost town."

Chung left his stool at the counter. "I will leave you to prepare your little gifts for the invisible customers. I need to breathe fresh air."

He opened the front door and Meichen followed him. He crossed the street and walked down the wooden sidewalk to a spot across from his store. Propping his back against a brick wall, he slid his arms across his chest and studied the façade of his building. Meichen slipped beside him.

"The sign draws the eye, Husband. The scarlett words seem to jump from the yellow background. I'm glad you wrote the name in Chinese as well as English."

Chung jerked when he heard her voice next to his ear. He pressed his lips into a flat line as he looked to his left. "I didn't realize you joined me."

"I want to talk to you."

He took several steps away from her. "Must we talk now, when I need to concentrate on business?"

"We must talk before we go to bed." Her voice was calm, but resentment showed in her eyes. She waited, wondering if he would apologize for the violence of last night's coupling. She wanted to tell him if he'd meant to punish her, his plan had failed.

"All right, if I'm not too tired."

"It concerns your second wife."

He waved his arm toward her. Meichen had no trouble interpreting his movement. He wanted to push her and her problems away.

Chung looked away from her face. Across the street, two Chinese men had stopped to read the words on the sign. They chuckled, then went inside. Chung sprang into action, crossing the street with long strides, barely slowing down to open the door.

Meichen watched him while cold humiliation froze her. She looked around to see if anyone was staring at her. She couldn't bear to be an object of pity or scorn, the embodiment of an oppressed Chinese wife. She lifted her head high and kept her spine straight as she returned to the store.

She stomped up the stairs to her room. On the floor behind the storage boxes she found her battered carpet bag. She stuffed the few clothes she owned inside. At the bottom of a cracked wooden box she saw the faded black dress she had worn when she left Colorado. The black bonnet was crushed, but its mesh veil was still attached. The black lace gloves and stockings were stuffed inside the bonnet.

Meichen hesitated, then threw the widow disguise on the bed. She hoped to leave without attracting attention, and that was impossible if people saw her face. She composed a note for Chung, writing in English

with a dull pencil. There was no time to mix ink and struggle with calligraphy.

Husband, my heart will not allow me to share you. If you marry
another woman, consider the bonds you have with me to be severed.
I'll leave you alone while you decide what you must do, since my
presence annoys you. I will send you my address when I have settled
somewhere.

She left the folded sheet on Chung's pillow. Her hand hovered there
as she squeezed her eyes tight. Sorrow twisted inside her, clawing her lungs
with iron-tipped talons that forced her to gasp desperately for air. She
endured the agony without crying out until the spasm wringing her body
subsided.

She changed clothes swiftly. The pain would come again, and she
wanted to be too far away to turn back. She focused her mind on getting
out the back door, walking several blocks to the train depot, and buying a
ticket.

"Where to, ma'am?" The clerk eyed the pile of coins she poured from
a drawstring purse.

"Columbia." Meichen watched as he slid enough coins across the
counter to pay the fare.

"You can sit on the bench right outside the door." The clerk waved
her toward a wooden platform beside the tracks. "Train should be here in
twenty minutes or so."

Meichen followed his advice as she planned to be the first passenger
to board. She balanced her bag on her thighs and drew a deep breath. Soon
she would be safe again with someone whose love and support she could
rely on.

CHAPTER 31

"Friends are the siblings
God never gave us."

—CHINESE SAYING

Columbia, South Carolina, January, 1887

MEICHEN WENT TO THE CHURCH where Biyu would speak that evening. The pastor of the church provided the address of Biyu's hostess. A short cab ride brought Meichen to a house that had once been a showplace. Like the other houses on the street, it needed repairs and a new coat of paint.

Biyu was delighted when her hostess led Meichen to the parlor. "Little sister, I'm so glad you came before I have to leave."

She struggled to her feet and enclosed Meichen in her arms. Biyu introduced Mrs. Fairfax, the widow who was sharing her home, and the lady went off at once to prepare food for Meichen despite her protests that she was not hungry.

Meichen noticed the white shirtwaist and straight black skirt that had always been Biyu's uniform ever since Meichen had met her. Her long hair was braided and wrapped around her head. Most amazing, she wore ordinary shoes.

"Biyu, you unbound your feet!"

Biyu's face wrinkled. "I am able to walk with a cane, but it's painful. Many of the bones were fractured and deformed. I'm too old to heal." Biyu led Meichen to a chair. "I was determined to avoid ridicule when people saw my ridiculous tiny shoes. It also discourages rude people from asking to see my naked feet."

Meichen gasped. "Surely, nobody would be so insulting."

"I could display my feet at a carnival and become famous like Tom Thumb."

She smiled at Meichen's woebegone expression. "It's all right. I get sympathy from the congregations when I explain my disability. It spurs their interest in helping the women of China."

"How long have you been traveling with the missionaries?"

"Pastor Cartwright wrote to the missionary board the day after we left San Francisco. Right after we reached his house I got a message from the chairman, and twos month later they asked me to join this tour to raise money for missions. I'm sorry I didn't write you. I lost your address with all my traveling. When I realized we would be this close to Augusta, I wanted to see you."

"But how did you find my address?"

"The tour director wrote to the pastor of the First Baptist Church in Augusta, and he found your address at the post office. Chinese people must be well known there."

"There are only fifty of us, and we're a novelty. We have a new address now. I'll write it down for you."

"How is your husband? I bet he was surprised to see you."

Meichen hung her head. "Things are not going well between us. In fact, almost everything has gone wrong since I came to America."

Biyu squeezed her hand. "What happened?"

It took a long time for Meichen to finish her story. While she was talking, Biyu's hostess returned with sandwiches and tea. She sat down next to Biyu, and Meichen had to switch from Cantonese into English. When she reached the point where she arrived in Augusta and reunited with Chung she stopped talking.

Meichen poured herself another cup of tea. Biyu waited for Meichen to continue, but she didn't speak. She stared into Biyu's eyes and shook her head. Biyu frowned for a moment, then nodded at Meichen. She set her cup on the serving tray and thanked Mrs. Fairfax for the food, and Meichen followed suit.

"Mrs. Fairfax, would you excuse me if I go upstairs and lie down? I'd like to put my feet up for a while. Meichen will sit with me and fetch anything I need."

"Of course you should rest before you speak tonight. I don't know how you can get any rest riding the train to a different city every day and speaking every night."

"God gives me energy," Biyu said. She took the cane resting against her chair.

Meichen swallowed the lump in her throat as she watched her friend struggle up the stairs. When she reached her room, she hobbled to her bed and collapsed. Meichen put two pillows under Biyu's feet.

"Do you want me to remove your shoes?"

"I can't. It's so painful getting them on, I leave them on all day. I have two hours before I go to the church. Putting my feet up reduces some of the swelling."

Meichen blinked away tears. "Oh, Biyu, why do you go through this torture? Wear Chinese shoes."

"I wold look silly wearing them with my skirt and shirtwaist."

"Then wear Chinese clothes. After all, you are Chinese."

"I see you are wearing American clothes." Biyu frowned. "That's the ugliest dress I've ever seen. Your hat looks like a buffalo sat on it."

"It makes a good disguise. With the veil and gloves, no one can tell I'm Chinese."

Biyu laughed. "I understand. It's annoying when everybody gawks at us."

"It was more than that. When Chung goes to the depot to ask if I bought a train ticket, the clerk will say he didn't see a Chinese woman boarding a train."

Biyu sat up, supporting herself with her arms. "You are running away from Chao Chung? Why? What happened?"

Biyu's arms collapsed and she flopped back on the bed. "Get me a pillow for my head. And drag that stool over here and sit where I can see your face."

Meichen settled beside the bed. "Chung was happy to have me again, at first. But his uncle in San Francisco was furious with me for coming to America without permission. He ordered Chung to divorce me."

"Surely Chung didn't."

"He refused, but then everyone in his family got angry, and his father disowned him."

"He should have expected that."

"He did, but he hoped his father would forgive him. When his father's letter came telling him he was out of the family, it broke his heart. He kept me with him, but his feelings for me changed. He started finding fault with me and he scolded me and scorned my ideas. He said I came to America so I could do whatever I wanted. He even accused me of desiring my employer's grandson."

"Why would he think that?"

"Jim lives with his grandmother. He talks to me about interesting things. And I'm helping him write a book about China. He helped Chung and my brother and a friend to open a grocery store. We're lucky to have so much help from a white man."

"Um." Biyu pressed her lips together. "Have you been alone with this man?"

"Only when I am cleaning or cooking at his grandmother's house. And she's often in a nearby room."

"And you call him by his first name. Do you talk about him often and urge Chung to be more like him?"

Meichen lowered her head. "Not very often."

"Meichen, are you deliberately trying to make your husband jealous?" Biyu sighed and shook her head. "If you are, you're doing all the right things."

"No, of course not. But Chung is so distant from me. I need a friend whose company I enjoy." Meichen studied the flowered curtains to avoid Biyu's stern eyes.

"There are no women you can befriend?" Biyu's tone bordered on sarcasm.

"None who share my interests." Heat flamed in Meichen's cheeks as she spoke the words. She sounded like a petulant child.

Biyu frowned. "I suggest you try harder to find female friends. Imagine how you would feel if your husband had a female friend that he saw often. Wouldn't you be jealous? Go home and apologize to him."

Meichen sniffled. "You don't know the worst. My husband's family is willing to take him back if he does one easy thing."

"Not divorce again!"

Meichen trembled as anger and shame washed over her. "I can stay with him, but he must return to China for one year and marry a second wife because they think I am barren."

Biyu's mouth fell open. "That's ridiculous," she said when her composure returned. "Chao Chung is too modern to do that. Just before he graduated, he sent a petition to the Empress asking her to outlaw foot binding, polygamy, and the marriage of girls below the age of sixteen."

"That's what I thought, too. And then he asked me to let him take a second wife so his family will forgive him. I felt like I'd fallen into a nightmare where nothing made sense. He kept trying to convince me that it would mean nothing to him, and he would come back and forget about her. That confused me even more, that he could be such a callous person. He is nothing like the man I married. Demons must have taken control of him."

"Meichen, there are no demons."

"I heard you read a story from the Bible where Jesus cast demons out of people. If you believe your Bible is true, then you must believe there are demons."

"We can talk about demons later. Right now, I want to hear what you said to Chung. Did you agree to the second wife?"

"Not really. We didn't finish discussing it. I tried to talk to him twice this morning, but he ignored me. I just can't do what he asks. So I packed my things and left."

Biyu kicked the pillows away and swung her legs to the floor as she sat up. "What do you mean you left? Aren't you going home tomorrow?"

"I was hoping I could stay with you."

"But I don't have a home of my own. I depend on the charity of church members who invite me to their homes when I come to their city to speak. The Mission Board can't afford to rent hotel rooms for me."

"Maybe I could help you with your work," Meichen suggested, her eyes brightening. "I can tell all the good things the mission schools do for Chinese women. I spent almost five years in one. Tell the Mission people about me."

Biyu's eyes grew solemn. "To do what I do, you must be a Christian."

"I can be baptized."

"Forgive me, dear friend, but I don't think you understand what Christianity is about. You don't have a fire for Jesus in your belly." She sighed. "I hoped that Chung, and you, too, might become Christians after you both spent several years living at the mission and saw how the missionaries demonstrated what God's love is like. You saw daily evidence of the way they accept and care for those in need, just as Jesus and his disciples did. Both of you even helped the Lesters take care of the orphans and teach them while you lived at the school. But you couldn't take that final step of faith."

"Chung's family would have been horrified if he abandoned their beliefs and took up a new religion. It would be a supreme act of disrespect. And as his wife, I had to follow his lead."

"I understand, Meichen. That's why it's hard to convert most Chinese. Only those with no families who are poor and hopeless like I was are likely to respond to the offer of salvation that Jesus offers them."

Meichen grasped Biyu's hands. "I am alone now, and my husband's family has cast me out. Now you can help me to understand and believe. Maybe one day we could go home and start our own school deep inside China where the white missionaries can't go."

"All right, I'll see what I can do," Biyu promised. "Maybe tonight you can stay here with me."

Biyu spoke to Mrs. Fairfax to ask if Meichen could share her room. Since Meichen was dressed in black, the lady assumed she was an impoverished widow and readily agreed.

Meichen went with Biyu to the church where she would speak. She met the other speakers and the mission director who were touring with Biyu. They also accepted Meichen as Biyu's widowed friend. Biyu spoke with the director, reminding him that unprotected Chinese women were often kidnapped and sold to brothels. The director reluctantly agreed to allow Meichen to stay with Biyu until she could find a place to live and work.

Meichen sat in a pew near the back of the sanctuary to hear what Biyu would say. A women's missions committee sponsored the program, so females greatly outnumbered the men. Young women sat together in large groups, their backs straight and their hands neatly folded on their laps. In contrast, the boys slumped against the pews with sullen faces. Meichen was sure they were there under duress.

An energetic young man opened the meeting by leading several rousing hymns. The audience sang with enthusiasm. One song in particular, about Christian soldiers marching behind the cross of Jesus, rang with militant fervor. Even those who couldn't sing shouted it out. Meichen was deafened and a bit frightened.

As soon as the song ended, two men displaced the song director. They were dressed alike in dark suits and white shirts. The first man, who was tall and narrow, read from the Bible. His companion, who resembled a ball, began a prayer. Meichen shifted in her seat as the prayer went on. She had considered Christianity a religion that required impossible tasks of its followers. As the minister directed God's attention to numerous problems and people who needed help, she concluded Christians expected their god to grant them many favors in return for their devotion.

At last Biyu stood at the podium, quiet dignity radiating from her face. "Many of you are familiar with Lottie Moon, the famous missionary to North China. My name is Li Biyu, and I come to tell you about my home in Southern China, near the city of Canton. My province has suffered from rebellions and war for fifty years. The land is poor, and many people go hungry. What little the people have is often taken away by bandits."

Biyu paused to look around the room, meeting the eyes of as many people as possible. "I know that South Carolina has also suffered from war, and many people here were left poor and hungry. But you have something my people don't. You have your faith in God, and the comfort and blessings of His love. I come here today to ask you to share that love with the people of China."

Meichen watched in fascination as Biyu continued to talk. Her words riveted the people's attention as she told the story of her own life and conversion. Many of the ladies were wiping their eyes with handkerchiefs by the time she finished. At the conclusion, the audience rose and clapped enthusiastically.

Biyu came to sit beside Meichen as the mission director concluded the program. He spoke about the vast number of unsaved people in China and the money needed to support the work of converting and educating the population. The audience became restless as he quoted numbers, and he wisely concluded his speech and sent collection plates into the pews.

After a quiet hymn, much friendlier than the first set, and a blessedly brief benediction, a crowd converged around Biyu to offer praise and support. One young lady with shining eyes took Biyu's hand in hers.

"You've inspired me, Miss Li," she cried. "I want to go to China and help your people."

The mission director, who stood next to Biyu, basking in her glory, eagerly noted the young lady's name and address and promised to correspond with her soon. Meichen pushed herself back behind the crowd, feeling out of place in Biyu's throng of admirers. She stood beside a column near two ladies talking together.

"What a stirring testimony," the older one said. "She made my heart ache for those poor heathen people."

The second lady nodded emphatically, tossing the feathers that topped her hat. "Miss Li is absolutely right. The answer lies in educating the women. Everyone knows women are the guiding light in a home. Men just don't possess the moral strength that we ladies do. Their natures incline them to sin."

"I've always thought so. Won't it be wonderful when the millions in China are brought out of darkness and learn to live as civilized people?"

The ladies walked away, and Meichen stared after them, her face suffused with anger. How dare those women talk as though the Chinese were savages! She simmered as she waited for Biyu to finish accepting praise and questions. The crowd drifted away at last, and Mrs. Fairfax led them to her carriage. They rode in silence.

Meichen helped Biyu up the stairs to their room. Biyu sank onto the mattress with a groan. She allowed Meichen to unlace her shoes.

"It's not necessary to jerk the laces," she said.

"I'm sorry."

Biyu studied Meichen's grim expression. "Is something wrong?"

"I overheard two women talking while I was waiting for you. They said the Chinese are uncivilized."

Biyu shrugged. "I know many of them consider their way of life, their customs and traditions as the only way for Christians to live."

"How can you work with them?" Meichen asked, frowning. "How do they expect to convert people they don't respect?"

Biyu sighed. "Luckily, most of these people will never interact with a Chinese person. But we need their money to support our work. The missionaries who go to China learn better. And think, Meichen, how important our schools are. The Manchus won't rule China forever. When they fall, our schools will provide educated men and women to lead modern China."

"So you think it's all right for people to do the right thing for the wrong reason?"

"I pray their minds will change and God will show them their error. Now," Biyu said firmly, "there's something I want to discuss with you. The mission director has agreed you can travel with me and assist with our work. That means they'll pay your expenses."

Meichen clasped her hands together. "What will I do?"

"You're an excellent example of the good job our schools do. You can tell everyone how we taught you English and how to write in two languages. I'll help you prepare a speech to give."

Meichen shook her head. "I don't want to speak to all those strangers. You can talk about the school. You were the teacher."

"Yes, but you are my star pupil. I'm very proud of you."

"I wanted to learn so I could write my husband, the man who doesn't want me anymore. What good did it do me?"

"Now, Meichen, you know you loved learning just for the sake of it. I've never seen anyone devour information like you. Do you really wish you'd stayed illiterate?"

"No," she confessed. "If it will help you make money, I'll speak at your rallies. I can't expect you to support me."

"There's one other thing you must do. You have to become a Christian and be baptized."

"But I don't believe! It would be a lie."

Biyu gasped. "Just this morning you agreed to do it. You were quite enthusiastic, as I remember."

"That was before I heard those women talking. Christianity isn't such a good religion if the members of a church look down on other people. Aren't we supposed to be their sisters and brothers?"

"You can't judge everyone by the actions of a few. Everyone sins, you know, even after they're converted."

"If Jesus died for the sins of everybody, how can they continue to sin if he took it away? What good does it do them to become Christians if they still sin? It makes no sense."

"But God also works to make people do good things. How can you not believe after what I said tonight? I was only a moment from death when God sent a Christian man to save my life."

"A Chinese man saved you. And maybe Kuan Yin sent him. She's the goddess of mercy."

"You don't believe in Kuan Yin," Biyu scoffed. "I never saw you pray to her. You never kept a statue of her. When the typhoon hit our ship, didn't we both pray to Jesus to save us? And He did."

"I prayed to Kuan Yin, too," Meichen confessed. "I just didn't say it aloud."

Biyu sighed in frustration. "We need you to give a testimony. After all, the people we're asking for money want to make converts as much as they want to educate the Chinese. It will look bad if you spent all that time in a mission school and didn't convert."

"We will compromise," Meichen suggested. "I'll say you told me all about Jesus in the mission school, because that's true. I just won't say I believe in him as a god."

"He's not a god, Meichen, He's *the* God. What can I do to convince you of the truth?"

Meichen pressed her lips together. "You and I will ask Jesus to change my husband's mind about the second wife and make him love only me. When Chung tells me that, I'll believe."

Biyu was dismayed. "It's not wise to test God that way. Sometimes He doesn't give us the answer we want if something is wrong for us."

Meichen's eyes flashed. "Are you saying that your God doesn't support love and marriage? If he can't change Chung's heart and save my marriage, he has no power."

"Maybe Chung's heart is not the only one that needs to change," Biyu said tartly. Then her voice softened. "Forgiveness can go both ways."

Meichen said nothing more, and Biyu gave up the battle for the time being.

CHAPTER 32

"Great acts are made up
of small deeds."

—LAO TZU

MEICHEN STOOD AT THE PULPIT in a large church in Savannah. Her knees were shaking, and she clutched the notes Biyu had made for her as they travelled from Charleston that afternoon. It was her fourth day on the tour, and she had to do her part to stay with Biyu. She was going to speak to a room full of strangers for the first time in her life. Although she'd eaten very little of her dinner, her stomach felt queasy. A sea of faces looked up at her.

Taking a deep breath, she began her speech. "My father was a sojourner. He went overseas to Hawaii to work. He sent support for my brother and me while we stayed with our aunt and uncle. My brother was sent to a school to learn to read and write, but no one thought I needed an education because I was a girl.

"But I was lucky. The man chosen to be my husband was a scholar, well-educated by his father and at a mission school in Canton. He wanted me to know the things he had learned, so when he went overseas he sent me to the school he'd attended. I learned many things there besides just reading and writing. I studied the literature of China and the West, as well as geography, history, and many other subjects. I learned about the Bible and Jesus from Miss Li. I can speak English because she taught me. Many girls in China have no way to learn as I have. They need your help."

The crowd appeared spellbound by her blue silk tunic edged with orange bands and embroidered with butterflies and flowers. Encouraged by their eager smiles and polite attention, she relaxed and spoke her own thoughts. She bowed when the audience clapped and murmured approval at the end of her speech.

As soon as the final prayer was over, she and Biyu were surrounded by excited ladies and girls. Later, the mission director, who counted the money, said they'd received more donations than usual.

For the first time in her life, Meichen felt she had done something that might affect the lives of many other people. She wished Chung had been there to hear and see her. But Chung wouldn't be proud of her. He would be angry she was making a spectacle of herself in front of a crowd. She wasn't living modestly, devoting herself to her home and husband. He would think she only wanted attention and glory.

It took half an hour for the two Chinese women to escape their admirers and find the right carriage. Biyu hurried to sit down, her teeth clenched together. Meichen squeezed her hand as the adrenaline fuelling her elation succumbed to pity for her friend.

"Biyu, I beg you, give up those American high heels. Let me make you some flat cloth shoes that cushion your feet. Or wear this beautiful jacket and skirt you lent me and the lotus slippers shaped to your feet."

Biyu gave a deep, shaky sigh. "I'm a simple teacher. I have to look modest and humble."

"What does that have to do with torturing yourself? The church members accept your cane. Why wouldn't they understand you need special shoes?"

"I don't want to draw attention to my clothing. Jesus triumphed over suffering. So can I."

"Jesus suffered one day. I don't think he wants you to endure agony every day until you die."

Biyu leaned her head against the back of the seat and closed her eyes. Meichen regretted nagging her, but frustration drove her to speak her mind.

"If you must look humble, why am I allowed to flaunt myself in silk?"

"The mission director thinks Chinese clothes are suited to your message. You illustrate the talent of Chinese women and the elegance of our culture. You wanted Americans to understand not all Chinese women are mud-covered peasants."

"I hope they understand that no woman in China wears these clothes every day."

"The director understands that my skirts are too short for you, and the only dress you own is that black horror."

"Your Chinese skirt is also too short for me."

"American ladies don't know how long a Chinese skirt should be."

Meichen and Biyu had been whispering in Cantonese, and they both jumped when Mrs. Fishbourne, their hostess for the evening, interrupted. "Ladies, your tour director asked me to take Mrs. Chow out early tomorrow and find some silk cloth that matches Miss Li's beautiful outfit, to lengthen the skirt. I'm sure she feels uncomfortable with her ankles displayed. And we need the seamstress to take her measurements." She smiled eagerly and leaned forward to pat Meichen's hand. "We'll wire them to the lady who heads the mission committee in Montgomery and ask her to buy two skirts and a black jacket."

Meichen covered her open mouth with her hand. "I can't let the director use the mission money to buy me clothes. I have some money of my own, and I know how to sew."

"Our women's missionary leader collected donations to buy new clothes for you after she met you at the train depot." She held up a hand to stop Meichen's protests. "We are happy to do this for you, and the Montgomery ladies will feel the same. Many of us are widows, and we understand how difficult life is for women without a husband or relatives to support us. Wearing new um...more fashionable clothes will lift your spirits."

Mrs. Fishbourne beamed at them as she leaned back against the seat, and Meichen and Biyu raised their eyebrows as they looked at each other. Once they were alone in Mrs. Fishbourne's guest room, and Biyu's swollen feet were soaking in cold water, Meichen returned to the conversation in the carriage.

"How did she know we were talking about my clothes? I know she doesn't understand Cantonese."

Biyu, who rested in a wing chair with her eyes closed while her pain eased, smirked. Meichen's eyes narrowed. "Did you mention it to the ladies?"

"I didn't have to say a thing. When they met us at the depot, I saw the looks on their faces. I knew they would find a way to get you out of that black dress."

"Why do they care what I wear on the train?"

"As part of this tour, you represent the churches who organized it. It shames them if Presbyterian and Methodist ladies think Southern Baptists don't care about your poverty and won't help you dress decently."

Meichen's face burned. "I don't want their money to be spent on me. It should go to girls in China."

"That's why they took up money privately among themselves. It was meant just for you."

"But I'm not a poor widow."

"You will be a poor divorced woman if you don't reconcile with your husband. Save your money and let the ladies save face."

"Isn't pride a sin?"

"Meichen, these ladies deserve to be proud. Since Miss Lottie Moon asked Southern Baptist women to help raise money for Chinese missionaries and schools, women all over the south are organizing mission committees to answer Miss Moon's call for action. You see what happens when thousands of women work together? They aren't perfect, but they try to help when many others won't."

"All right," Meichen muttered. "I'll take the new clothes. And while I'm out with Mrs. Fishbourne tomorrow, I want you to stay here and rest your feet. I'll draw up more cold water from the well before I go. Take advantage of it while we're here."

"I'll stay here if you promise to take a donation from me and buy yourself a decent hat!"

"How long will it take to reach Montgomery?"

Biyu's eyes rolled up to the ceiling as she counted on her fingers. "We have two more towns in Georgia, so that's four days. After the rally in Columbus, we cross into Alabama, and Montgomery is the third city. So I'd say about two weeks." She laced her fingers together and relaxed her facial muscles into a serene smile. "I have plenty of time to devise a suitable end for the widow's dress."

"The doctor's wife said nearly every lady in her family had used it. It makes me pity all those poor grieving women."

"I'm sure it has given admirable service since the War Between the States. But now it's time to send it to its final resting place. I'll find it an honorable tomb."

CHAPTER 33

"Great souls have wills. Feeble ones have only wishes."

—CHINESE PROVERB

MEICHEN TOOK A SEAT ACROSS from Biyu as their train pulled away from Montgomery. She smoothed her black skirt and adjusted the velvet trim on the collar of her jacket. She removed her small hat sporting a short net veil and set it on the seat beside her, waiting to hear Biyu's opinion.

"You look splendid." Biyu's eyes twinkled. "Are you wearing a corset, or did the seamstress create a way to make you look sway-backed like American women?"

Meichen sniffed. "I refused to wear a corset. The seamstress used boning to get the shape right, and she used thick cotton cloth for the lining. If I remove this jacket, it can stand up by itself."

Meichen lifted a leg to display her flat, blunt-toed shoes. "I also declined to accept their high-heeled, pointed-toe shoes."

"Don't speak of shoes," Biyu said, wincing. "I wish I could wear the slippers you made me all the time."

Meichen glanced at the cane Biyu was clutching. "I know you're in agony."

"And to add to my misery, it's my monthly time as well. I have terrible cramps. Thank goodness we'll be on the train most of the day." She drew in a deep breath and her eyelids sank down to her cheeks. "I took a little dose of laudanum, hoping I might sleep through some of the pain. Will you be offended if I don't keep you company?"

Meichen squeezed her hand. "Sleep as much as you like."

Meichen watched as slumber smoothed Biyu's face. Her own eyes closed as well. She'd risen early to collect an extra skirt and blouse the seamstress had finished late the previous night. A short nap would restore her energy.

She let her mind drift, traveling wherever it pleased. But a new thought brought her awake, slashing into her brain like a lightning bolt. How long had it been since the old red aunt visited her? She had worn the white nightgown three weeks before the store opened. The red aunt should have come while she was in Charleston or Savannah.

She clapped a hand to her mouth to suppress the cry of amazement that hovered behind her lips. How could she have overlooked the message her body had sent her? But it was too early to be sure. She wouldn't tell anyone about her suspicion. Not even Biyu. Especially not Biyu.

A nap now was impossible. Meichen surged to her feet and walked down the corridor between the train's seats. She rubbed the spot on her abdomen where she imagined a tiny boy grew deep inside. She scolded herself and tried not to rejoice so early in case she was wrong. But a quiet hum settled in her heart and wouldn't go away.

...

Meichen's fervor grew as the mission tour went north through Alabama, and then Chattanooga. She imagined the hundreds of schools that would lead China's women into a new century. They would change from mere ornaments or drudges into lights for their daughters to follow. They would stand beside their brothers, husbands, and fathers to create the new China soon to come. While her missionary companions imagined a giant Christian nation, Meichen saw an era when women would have the same rights as men.

She no longer feared the audience, and her impassioned appeals for donations and workers made her almost as powerful a speaker as Biyu. She embroidered flowers on the extension added to Biyu's Chinese skirt in bold red with gold embroidery like the wedding dress she'd worn. She wanted to catch the imagination of her audience, to make them see China as it was, an ancient culture waiting to be revived to greatness with the help of American Christians. If the mission directors wondered sometimes at the tone of her message, they kept it to themselves.

...

As the women dressed for the journey from Chattanooga to Atlanta, Meichen slid her finger around the waistband of her black skirt. It was too snug for comfort.

Meichen felt sure she'd conceived. Joy and fear mingled in her mind. She tried to imagine how Chung would take the news. She knew she should write to him at once.

At the same time, she hated to leave the tour. She enjoyed whipping up the crowd to her own level of commitment and bringing in dollars for her mission. She'd lived all her life in the background waiting for someone else to call the steps she must dance. But while she was with the mission tour she could choreograph her own actions and express her own views. There were just five more cities to visit. It wouldn't hurt to keep her pregnancy secret for three more weeks.

"Meichen," Biyu called. "It's time to go. Hurry up or we'll be late."

Meichen leaned over to pick up her traveling bag and her skirt button popped loose. Biyu stepped behind Meichen to help. She frowned at the gap between the button and the slit in the waistband.

"How have you gotten so fat? This skirt fit well two weeks ago."

"It's nothing," Meichen said, shrugging. "I eat too much."

Biyu pinched the skin on Meichen's arm. "Only your stomach is gaining weight. The rest of you looks just the same." She grabbed Meichen's arms and looked her in the eye. "Meichen, you're expecting a baby, aren't you?"

"Yes," Meichen confessed, knowing it was useless to deny the obvious. "But that shouldn't affect my work. I feel fine. I haven't even been sick to my stomach."

"You will have to stop speaking. A woman can't get up in public in your condition. The congregations would be appalled."

Meichen looked at Biyu in alarm. "Don't make me give up my work. Let me stay with you until the tour is over."

"What about your husband? Do you intend to keep his child a secret from him?"

"I'll write to him today." Meichen avoided Biyu's stern gaze. "But I won't go crawling home. He must promise there will *never* be a second wife."

Biyu smiled. "After listening to your speeches lately, I can't imagine you crawling. But don't go with an attitude of arrogance or self-righteousness, either. Go in a spirit of peace. Do the right thing for your child's sake."

"What if Chung doesn't believe the child is his? I've been gone a long time."

"Give him a chance. He'll know you're telling the truth when the child is born nine months after you left, and it looks Chinese. But you must go soon. The longer you wait, the more doubtful he'll become."

...

Three days passed as Meichen struggled to find the right words for her letter. Chung was probably still angry. And the memory of their last two days together still rankled in her memory. Her first inclination was to write one two-word sentence. *I'm pregnant.*

Maybe he wouldn't even be there. He might be on his way to China to give his parents what they wanted. He might be glad to be rid of her.

It would be much easier to write Chung if she knew his frame of mind. She wrote her brother instead. Ling Mo's answer should be waiting in Biyu's post office box when the tour was over, and she would know if Chung wanted her to come back. When Biyu asked if she'd sent the letter, she was able to assure her friend that a letter was on its way to Augusta.

The tour director had scheduled four days in Atlanta. The city was growing at a tremendous pace, he told his team, and they had been invited to speak at several churches. He expected much bigger attendance than they'd attracted in the smaller cities. Word had spread that two Chinese women were featured in the presentation, and people would come just to see them.

Biyu frowned and muttered in Meichen's ear. "Now you'll find out what it's like to be the main attraction in a freak show. We might as well be two-headed monkeys."

"Some of the gawkers may hear what we say and make a contribution."

Biyu's frown deepened. "I hope Mr. Benton will enjoy counting bags of pennies and nickels they give."

The director continued his speech, repeating instructions he gave before every stop. Meichen ignored him as she watched Biyu brood with her eyes focused on the empty wall behind his head. When he finished, the presenters headed for the sanctuary to practice their movements on and off the platform and learn where they would stand.

After Meichen had joined the group, the mission director had put both Chinese women on the stage at the same time, Biyu on the right side and Meichen on the left. With Meichen dressed in Chinese attire, she wondered if Biyu's message was diminished as people studied the magnificent silk robe she wore. Now she had the opportunity to give her opinion.

She raised her hand, and everyone looked at her, which almost wiped her words out of her head. But she rallied her inner strength to see that justice was done.

"Mr. Benton, I think I should not be visible when Miss Li speaks. I am a distraction to the audience."

"Why don't they both wear Chinese costumes?" called the director's assistant, who was seated in a back pew to judge the effect of the director's staging. "Then they will have double impact."

Biyu straightened her spine and glared at the man. "We have only one costume, and even if there were more, I would not wear one. I did not come from China to take part in a fashion exhibition. I am a modern woman, and I speak about the needs of modern China. I'm here to change people's hearts, not to titillate their senses."

"And you do an excellent job, Miss Li. No one wants to change your presentation against your wishes." Mr. Benton smiled at Biyu and rubbed a handkerchief across his moist, balding head.

Biyu ignored his smile and left the podium. She walked to a pew halfway to the back entrance, moving with cool dignity despite her cane. Meichen stood beside the platform steps waiting for the director to dismiss her.

Sir," the assistant asked Mr. Benton, "Do you think we could find a folding screen?"

"What do we need one for?"

"We could hide Mrs. Chao behind a decorated screen and pull it away when it's time for her part."

Meichen pressed her hands over her forehead as her eyes enlarged in dismay. "No! That would make things worse. When Miss Li speaks, the audience will stare at the screen wondering what's behind it." She stamped her foot. "I won't do it."

Biyu's cane bumped against the wooden pew as she struggled to her feet. "I'm not feeling well today. Please allow me to rest this evening. I feel certain Mrs. Chao can combine my speech with hers."

The director and his assistant watched Biyu's slow progress toward the door, then turned to Meichen. Before they could say a word, she pushed the two men aside and hurried down the steps. "I must also be excused tonight," she called over her shoulder. "I'm the only person who knows how to treat Miss Li's sickness."

The director pulled the sparse hair combed across his scalp. "You must come tonight. The congregation expects to meet two Chinese women."

Meichen pushed the heavy wooden doors open as the director's voice pleaded behind her. She heard one last word as she slipped outside.

"Please!"

She walked around the church until she found Biyu sitting on a wrought iron bench near the entrance. "I told the director I had to stay with you tonight." She sat next to her friend and reached for her hand. "I'm sorry I caused trouble for you. I should have kept my mouth shut."

Biyu clenched her hands into fists. "What you said was sensible. The problem is that assistant Mr. Benton hired. He's a puffed-up noodle head who thinks he knows everything. He won't be satisfied until he turns our program into a carnival. All that matters to him is how many attend. What does it matter if thousands come to see us, if no one accepts our message or cares about helping us in our work?"

They sat in silence, protected from the sun by the large oak tree behind the bench while the fragrance of flowering bushes and the chirps and chatter of birds and squirrels soothed their turmoil. Eventually other team members assembled on the church steps and several carriages drew up. The pastor of the church joined the director to introduce the hosts and hostesses who'd volunteered to house and feed the speakers during their stay in Atlanta.

Meichen left Biyu on the bench while she collected their baggage. The carpet bags were stuffed to the point of bursting, and Meichen staggered under their weight. The man who drove their hostess's carriage jumped down from his perch and took all the bags from Meichen. He carried them easily and loaded them on the carriage.

Biyu struggled to her feet and leaned on her cane. The driver came to their rescue again. He put his arm under Biyu's elbow, supporting most of her weight. The carriage steps were already down, and he lifted her up the steps. After Meichen sat next to Biyu she turned her attention to the two ladies sitting across from her to introduce herself and Biyu.

The two ladies were very different in appearance, one delicate and soft-spoken, the other tall and solidly built. Meichen learned that they lived together, and both were widowed sisters-in-law having married twin brothers.

Meichen kept up her side of the conversation. Biyu was propped in a corner with her eyes closed, suffering too much pain to chatter. The ladies were horrified when Meichen told them why Biyu was crippled.

"How can parents torture their daughters that way?" the small lady asked.

"They do it to help their daughters get a prosperous husband. The smaller the feet, the more desirable the girl is," Biyu said.

"Chinese men certainly have strange ideas of feminine beauty." The large woman huffed.

When they were settled in a large bedroom, Meichen forced Biyu to swallow a small dose of laudanum and removed her shoes. Meichen helped Biyu out of her outer garments and led her over to the bed. Biyu drifted off to sleep. Meichen removed her white blouse and the black skirt that cut into her expanding waist and put on a flowered dressing gown. She laid down beside Biyu and closed her eyes.

A tap on the door startled her awake. Meichen rose from the bed and let the visitor in. Their small, wispy hostess stood in the hall twisting a handkerchief with both hands.

"I do hate to disturb you, my dear, but there's a man downstairs who insists on talking to Miss Li. He says he's the director of the mission tour and refuses to leave, even though my sister-in-law ordered him out of the house."

"I'll go down and speak to him. I just need a moment to put my clothes back on." Meichen pulled her skirt over her petticoat and retrieved her slippers that were pushed under the bed.

Biyu sat up, resting her weight on her elbows. "Tell Mr. Benton to come to this room. We won't talk long, and I refuse to put my shoes on." Her eyes focused on Meichen. "Please cover me with the quilt on the chair."

The petite widow gasped. "Miss Li, you can't have a man unrelated to you come into your bedroom." Her small hands fluttered like butterfly wings.

"Meichen will be with me, and you and your sister-in-law can come as well. I will say nothing that requires privacy."

Five minutes later they heard Mr. Benton puffing as he reached the second floor. His face was red from exertion and embarrassment. He held out his hands toward Biyu.

"Please, Miss Li, reconsider your decision about tonight. It will be extremely embarrassing not only to me, but your absence will reflect badly on the ladies' mission committee and the pastor who have kindly invited us to visit this church."

"Are you saying I can never take time off? What if I suddenly needed an operation? Would you drag me out of the hospital and prop me up on the platform?"

"Everyone would understand if you had a serious illness, but I don't want to tell our audience you didn't appear because your feet are sore."

Biyu's eyes flashed. "My feet are not 'sore,' Mr. Benton. They are agonizingly painful, and the pain never goes away. I wish someone would break the bones in your feet and press your toes against your heels and bind them in bandages that are constantly tightened. Then you would know what real pain feels like."

Mr. Benton shrivelled as the three women ranged around Biyu's bed glared at him. His shoulders slumped and he sighed deeply. "From now on we will have you sit in a chair, and I'll assign a man to carry you to your seat. You can wear slippers."

"I don't need all those concessions, especially being carried onto the platform."

"Biyu, accept the chair and slippers," Meichen urged.

Biyu nodded her head. "And don't let your assistant order a bridal palanquin to bring me to the platform, or a sedan chair, or a rickshaw, or any other silly idea that catches his imagination."

"Don't worry about him, Miss Li. I think I will limit his duties to counting money and choosing hymns for the programs. And lending his arm when your feet are bothering you."

CHAPTER 34

*"Knowing how to yield
is a strength."*

—CHINESE PROVERB

EVERY PEW IN THE CHURCH was packed by the time the program began. There was only one pastor, so the Bible reading and prayers were brief. A lady with a piercing soprano voice led the congregation through several hymns, followed by Mr. Benton welcoming the crowd. The audience was quiet for the first ten minutes, but after that a restive stir travelled across the pews. Mr. Benton condensed his remarks and introduced Biyu.

Every eye was glued to her as she hobbled across the stage to the chair Mr. Benton had provided. Frowning, she nudged the chair to the very edge of the platform so her words would be audible to everyone. Meichen had heard Biyu's message many times and could almost say it from memory. Tonight something was different. The events of the day had stirred Biyu to make her listeners understand the frustration and hopelessness women felt when they had no power over their own lives.

Many women in the audience nodded, and some of the men shifted uneasily in their seats when their wives glared at them. American women were not allowed to vote and they were barred from many colleges that prepared students to enter professions. The fight for equal rights was a frequent topic of debate in American newspapers.

Biyu left the stage surrounded by enthusiastic applause. Meichen, who sat in a chair behind the piano, emerged on the platform. The clapping subsided, replaced by dozens of "oohs" and "ahs" as the audience absorbed the splendor of her silk robes. She waited for silence as her brain hastily revised her speech. She couldn't imagine how she would come close to Biyu's eloquence.

Biyu had omitted much of her dramatic life story because she was too fatigued to speak long. Meichen wanted to make up for the change She began as usual describing her background and family, adding a few embellishments to fix the attention of the audience. Her father changed from a sojourner to a captured Tai Ping rebel who was beheaded in a mass execution. Her mother became a desperate beggar forced into a life of crime. Her brother became a vicious gang member, so when Meichen was twelve, her mother sold her to a wealthy family to keep her out of the clutches of the gang's leader.

The wife of her wealthy owner demanded she work from dawn to midnight and made her sleep on the kitchen floor. One day, by some miracle, the oldest son of her owners saw her and insisted on marrying her and she lived in luxury for a year. Then a terrible sickness struck her husband down. Chinese tradition discouraged widows from taking another husband, and she had no son to support her.

Her mother-in-law made her leave her home. In despair she wandered around the city and decided to kill herself. But God would not let her die. He sent a Christian man to save her from the river and take her to a mission. At that point Meichen's story reverted to fact as she described her years at the school and the kindness of the missionaries.

Many ladies in the pews held handkerchiefs to their eyes. Meichen could have left the platform at that point. But she wasn't satisfied to leave her listeners awash in pity. Her job was to inspire them to join the cause and supply regular donations. She transitioned to the militant end of her speech which left the crowd on their feet, clapping and cheering. Mr.

Benton wisely passed the offering plates as soon as she stepped down from the platform.

After the final prayer and a jubilant hymn, Biyu and Meichen stepped in front of the platform and were mobbed by women of all ages along with a few men. Forty-five minutes later, the church was almost empty except for the men on the mission team who were restoring the chairs and podium to their original places.

Meichen looked down the central aisle, searching for the director's assistant who had been appointed to support Biyu as she walked from the church to the carriage. He was nowhere in sight. Instead, she saw a slender man in a wrinkled tan suit approaching her. Black hair peeked from the bottom of his hat, and his hands and face were definitely not white.

Meichen gripped Biyu's arm to keep herself upright. "It's Chung," she choked out.

The assistant director bumped through a side door and hurried over to Biyu. She directed him to her cane and he offered his arm as she shuffled forward.

"Let's go out the side door. There are no steps to get down, " he suggested.

Biyu changed direction. She leaned most of her weight on the assistant's arm and walked at the speed of a water buffalo stuck in a muddy field. The assistant fidgeted and frowned but he could not force her to move faster. As they reached the door Biyu looked back at Meichen and winked.

Chung had stopped halfway down the aisle, waiting for Biyu and her escort to leave. He moved closer to the platform and opened his arms wide.

"Look, Widow Chao, your husband has come back from the dead."

Meichen's cheeks burned. She studied his eyes, looking for evidence of scorn and sarcasm. "How did you find me?"

He pressed his lips together. "It was easy when Miss Li sent me a telegram detailing your itinerary this week.

Meichen was struck dumb by Biyu's perfidy. She struggled to collect her thoughts. "Do you intend to take me home?"

"I'd like to, if you agree to come." He'd removed his hat and absently bent the brim up and down.

"Will our marriage be the same as it was before I left?"

"I hope not. I am a fool to say this, but we need to tell each other the truth about our feelings. I will go first." He cleared his throat. "Since you came to America to live with me, my mind has been in chaos. I learned the rules for a husband's behaviour from the writings of Confucius and other wise men. I observed the actions of my father and mother, and many other couples. I broke some of the rules for your sake, and I hated myself for concealing facts from my parents."

"I'm sorry I created so much trouble for you, starting with our wedding night."

"That's true. You've done some things Confucius could never have imagined." Chung tried to maintain a serious bearing, but his twitching lips gave away his urge to laugh.

"Have I been such a bad wife?" She moved closer, enticing him to touch her, hoping he had not lost his desire for her.

He backed up a few steps. "That's what keeps my mind in turmoil. My relatives think you are a terrible wife, and I am lucky you left me. But I hear different opinions from Ling Mo and Aunt Mildred and Mrs. Hall, who assume you left because I was cruel to you. They say I should apologize for my actions and beg you to return. I would be willing to do that, but I'm not sure what I did to drive you away."

"You really can't think of *anything?*" Meichen narrowed her eyes and crossed her arms across her chest.

"I'm sorry for the way I acted the last time we ...uh, slept together. I shouldn't have treated you that way."

"There are many reasons why I left." She avoided his eyes by looking down at her stiff skirt and smoothed the wrinkles out. "It was the next day that caused me to leave, when you refused to speak to me and say what you'd decided about a second wife. My heart was breaking and you ignored me."

He touched her hand with his fingers. "I was mortified about the way I'd treated you the night before, and afraid you'd demand an apology.

It was cowardly of me, but I didn't want to admit I'd acted like a barbarian. Instead, I avoided you. I never thought you'd leave me."

Meichen snatched her hand away from him. "Our physical relations are not the problem. Until you tell me there will be no second wife, we cannot reconcile!"

"When I woke up that next morning, I knew I couldn't do what my parents asked. For a few minutes I hoped it was something I had dreamed."

"Then why didn't you wake me and tell me that?"

"I just told you, I was afraid to talk to you just then, when I expected you to condemn me, and possibly cry or even scream. I didn't have time for another fight. I needed to help get things ready for the store's opening day."

"And even though you can write perfectly in two languages you could not leave a note?"

"Meichen, it isn't easy for a man to admit to his wife he's behaved very badly." He paced a few steps down the aisle. "I should never have told you what my father wrote in that letter. If I'd put it away and given myself time to think it over, I'd have told him I couldn't do it and never mentioned it to you."

"Then why did you tell me what your parents wrote? You made me think you wanted to take another wife."

"I never said I wanted a second wife. I said I wanted to regain my family." He stopped pacing and glared at her. "And that is true."

"You acted like it was nothing I should worry about, though I made it plain what I thought."

"I got caught up in the idea of making you jealous. I wanted you to know what it feels like when the person you love turns to someone else. Remember, you'd just finished deriding my jealousy of Jim Hall."

Meichen sank onto the pew next to the aisle where he stood. "Biyu was right. She said I'd hurt your feelings when I spent so much time with Jim. It never occurred to me you'd think I had romantic feelings for him." She looked up at his face and watched the lines of anger fade away.

"I want you to know I apologized to Mr. Hall for my rudeness, and I thanked him for all his help. I mean I did that after I figured out you hadn't run away with him. Ling Mo says I've started to treat him as a friend."

Meichen smiled. "I'm glad."

"He comes by the store often to ask if I've heard from you. You know you hurt his grandmother by running off without saying good-bye to her."

"I was too embarrassed to explain why I was leaving. I should have written her a letter."

He sat beside her. After a brief hesitation, his arm slipped around her and guided her head to rest on his shoulder.

"I watched you speak tonight. When I was at school I went to many meetings and heard some stimulating speakers, but they weren't nearly as inspiring as you. Your talent amazes me."

She wanted to cling to him, but she pulled away. There were still barriers between them.

"It doesn't embarrass you to have a wife who stands before a crowd and speaks her mind? Chinese wives should be meek and accept their lot in life. I can't go back to that kind of life."

"No man I know, of any color, has ever had a wife like you. When the gods send a man a blessing, he shouldn't complain that it doesn't suit him. He should reform himself to accept his gift."

"What if I want to travel with Biyu again?"

"What if I want to visit my family in China and you don't want to come? Or what if we decide to move our business to another city and I must find us another place to live? There may be occasions when we have to trust each other. I believe our marriage is strong enough to bear whatever happens."

Meichen abandoned her doubts as she leaned against him. "Tell me I won't have to wait five years again."

"Not if I can prevent it." Chung wrapped his arm around her. "I have missed you – no, I have *ached* for you every minute you've been gone."

He turned to face her and their lips met. He pulled her tightly to him until she struggled loose so she could catch her breath.

Meichen and Chung stood up and stepped apart as a man's voice rang in the stone entrance to the sanctuary. Mr. Benton stared at them, his eyes bugging out as he struggled to take in what he saw.

He cleared his throat and struggled for words. "I've been looking for you, Mrs. Chao. Your hostesses are ready to leave."

Meichen searched Chung's eyes. "Can you find a place to stay tonight?"

He nodded and answered her in Cantonese. "I'll meet you here at ten o'clock tomorrow."

CHAPTER 35

"One joy scatters a hundred griefs."

—CHINESE PROVERB

AS THEY RODE TO THE DEPOT the next morning, Meichen gazed into Chung's eyes. He grinned, but her expression remained serious. His eyebrows lifted.

"Is something the matter, Wife?"

"Before we board the train, I must tell you something. I made an important decision when I talked to Biyu last night. I hope you will understand."

He clutched her hand. "Tell me."

"When I first joined Biyu, she wanted me to accept baptism to be part of the tour staff, but I said no. Then we prayed together to ask God to repair the problem in our marriage. I didn't think it would help, but Biyu said I should ask anyway. And it seems amazing to me that we are together again, and you've forgiven me and want me back, and all my anger with you has gone away."

"I was the one who needed forgiveness," he said.

"No, I was in the wrong, too. That's the most amazing thing, I think. I don't know what made me change my heart, but I came to understand that I didn't show you real love. I only thought about what I wanted you to do to make me happy. I never considered what you might need from me. And I didn't think about the pain I caused for other people. Like Ling Mo's wife, for instance. Because of me, her husband left her much sooner than he should have. And Ling Mo won't be in China to see his son born."

"There's nothing you can do about that now," Chung said., "no matter what decision you make."

"I've decided to become a Christian and trust God to help me make better decisions. Biyu says He will do that if I ask." She studied Chung's face. "Can you accept my decision?"

"If you really want to do it," he said, "I won't say no. But don't get baptized just to please Biyu."

"I want to have God's help to do what's best. Not just for our sakes, but for another reason." She inhaled deeply." In seven and a half months we'll have a son. You can tell your mother and father you won't need a second wife after all."

He froze and just stared at her in wonder. "Why didn't you tell me? You must have known for some time."

"I was so confused. I didn't know if you wanted me back after I left without telling you where I was going. And I was afraid you'd take my baby away from me. That's your right as the child's father."

He put his arms around her and pressed his lips against her forehead. "How could you imagine such a thing? Was I so cruel to you when we lived together?"

"You scolded me and rejected my ideas. And you distrusted me because of Jim Hall."

Chung shifted her hand to his lips. "I forgot the lessons my father taught me: 'Harsh words and poor reasoning never settle anything. Wisdom is attained by learning when to hold one's tongue.' And this one, of course: 'The more a wife loves her husband, the more she corrects his faults.'"

Meichen laughed. "Confucius truly was very wise."

...

The train jerked as it increased speed. Meichen bounced along with it, and Chung grasped her arm. He pulled her against his body, shoving her hat awry. She would have liked to cuddle against him, but she contented herself with a smile. It was unseemly to show affection in public.

"Were your missionary friends angry when you resigned your part in the tour?" he asked.

"Only Mr. Benton's assistant. He felt two Chinese women increased people's interest in our programs."

"He could increase interest even more if he went to San Francisco and bought a few girls who are trained to dance. I'm sure their stories would bring the audience to tears."

Meichen shook her head. "If he even suggested such a thing, Biyu would tear him apart. She despises him."

"As a Christian she should not hate or harm others."

"She's been praying for her heart to change, but he makes it very hard." Meichen tried to straighten her hat but found it difficult without a mirror.

Chung took it out of her hands and set it atop his own, which rested on his thighs. "When you described your life last night, I noticed you altered it quite a bit. Perhaps the assistant is not the only person who likes sensationalism."

"I didn't actually lie. Many Chinese women have suffered all the griefs I described. Besides, my past is boring."

Chung gaped at her. "A woman who travelled ten thousand miles all by herself through dangers that could have taken her life is not boring. Meichen, you are an incredible woman. Our son will be very proud of his mother."

Meichen rested her hand in his. Under the folds of her skirt he stroked her fingers.

"That's the greatest praise you have ever given me." Her eyes were focussed on her lap so he wouldn't see the moisture in her eyes.

He swallowed nervously. "Does it mean more to you than when I say I love you?"

"Nothing means more than that." She leaned her head back as their eyes met.

Her hand moved to caress his cheek. Their eyes locked, his shining with satisfaction, hers touched with apprehension.

"Chung, please tell me this: You have no doubts that the baby is yours?" Meichen closed her eyes, fearing what his answer might be.

"None at all." He grinned. "Now I understand the last sentence on Miss Li's telegraph. She said you'd been chaste as a nun since you left."

"Do you think your family will forgive me? I've ruined their plans to lure you away from me, but I'm producing a grandson for them."

"I'm sure they'll be happy when I tell them. But the real problem is Eldest Uncle, and he will never yield."

Meichen pressed against her husband's body. She remembered how he kindled an inferno in her hidden places with just a touch of his fingers. She fought a wrenching desire to slide her palm down his thigh. She sighed as she clenched her hands to control them. She couldn't behave that way on a train. It would be hours until she and Chung would be alone.

She wondered if he'd guessed her thoughts and entertained similar notions himself. She shifted herself, seeking a more comfortable position. He lifted his arm off her shoulder, giving her more space. She imagined he was cooler now that she was no longer plastered against him.

Eventually the rocking train induced her to sleep. She woke when Chung gently nudged her. The train had stopped to take on water and wood. A black child entered the car balancing a box loaded with sack lunches. Chung bought two, and Meichen took hers eagerly. It had been hours since she had eaten her breakfast.

As they ate hot fried chicken, biscuits, and sweet potatoes baked with butter and molasses, they returned to the unyielding nature of Eldest Uncle and how to change his mind.

"What does your uncle love the most—his power as head of the family or money?" Meichen asked.

"Oh, money without a doubt. He's already very rich, but he never feels he has enough. It comes from his childhood when the family barely made enough money to eat."

Meichen tapped her fingers together as she thought. "Are you still sending money to your parents?"

"I didn't have much to send them after the store opened. We're still buying products that customers ask for. And Jinsong has taken one corner to cater just to ladies. He's ordering all kinds of perfumes and lotions and painted fans, and I don't know what all, from San Francisco."

"I can help him," Meichen said. "I can embroider slippers and purses."

"Right now, none of us gets much salary."

"Who is supporting your family?" she asked.

"Second Uncle sends money to his son and Aunt Jiao. He may provide a little to my father."

"Then Eldest Uncle must make up the deficit." Meichen smiled. "I bet he really hates that."

"He'll send for my younger brother and make him send money home." Chung sighed.

"When I lived with your family, I noticed your younger brother avoided work if he could. I doubt Eldest Uncle will tolerate a lazy employee."

Chung laughed. "I expect Younger Brother will get a few beatings."

"We must write Eldest Uncle when we get home. We must convince him we can save him money." She bounced to the edge of her seat, her eyes bright. She grabbed Chung's arm and forced him to look at her. "We should follow Aunt Mildred's strategy. Tell Eldest Uncle since he has forced you out of the family, you no longer have filial obligations to send them money. Say you're sorry he must support your family, but you can see no other way."

"You don't really want me to do that, do you? That's not a Christian action."

"No, of course we wouldn't really do it. But Eldest Uncle doesn't have to know that."

"I'll tell him I can't live without you." He glared at her. "And after I humiliate myself by exposing my personal feelings he'll probably laugh and say I'm a lovesick fool. And you are going to write on my letter, too."

"What can I say that would please him? He hates me."

"Apologize for your disobedience. Tell him it would tear out your heart to leave me. Most important, tell him about the baby."

"Why do I have to apologize to him? I don't think I did anything to hurt *him*. Other people did the suffering."

Chung hissed through closed lips. "If you did nothing wrong, why did you sneak out of China without telling my father goodbye?"

"He would have forbidden me to go!"

"How do you know that? My father doesn't always do the conventional thing. Otherwise you would never have gone to school." He shook his head. "This is what Miss Li was trying to teach you. You should have done the right thing to start with and trusted God to work everything out in everyone's best interest."

Meichen pursed her lips as she reflected on his words. At last she bowed her head. "All right, I'll apologize."

He squeezed her hand. "Thank you."

They stopped talking. Meichen snuggled against him and he stroked the inside of her wrist. She closed her eyes and unleashed her imagination as she thought about what might happen that night.

...

Eldest Uncle must have struggled to accept Meichen's apology. His reply to their letter came a month after he'd received it. Meichen and Chung took the unopened envelope to their bedroom to read in private. Chung unfolded the sheet of paper and held it up so Meichen could read it over his shoulder.

They began to smile as they read, and Chung threw the paper in the air when they finished. He pulled her close and kissed her. "We're back in the family. Both of us!"

Meichen kissed him with a fervor equal to his. She crawled onto the bed and sat beside him. "We need to celebrate, just as soon as I give thanks."

"I need to give thanks, too," Chung told her." Mr. Lester liked to say God works in a mysterious way His wonders to perform."

"He performed a miracle to change Eldest Uncle's mind," Meichen agreed.

CHAPTER 34

"A child's life is like a piece of paper on which every person leaves a mark."

—CHINESE PROVERB

Six Months Later

THE INSISTENT WAIL OF AN INFANT informed the people in Celestial Sons' Grocery that Augusta's first Chinese baby had entered the world. Chung untied his apron with trembling hands and turned his customer over to Ling Mo. He tried to maintain his dignity as he left the room but could not resist racing up the stairs to the bedroom where Meichen had been laboring all afternoon.

The doctor was inspecting the child while Mildred comforted Meichen, whose face was turned toward the wall. Tears drifted down her cheeks, and Chung's eyes widened in alarm.

"What's wrong?" he asked, biting his lip.

"It's a girl," Mildred explained as she patted Meichen's shoulder.

"A girl," Meichen wailed, putting her arm over her eyes. "I've failed you, Chao Chung."

"A perfectly normal girl," the doctor announced, giving Chung a stern glance. "See, she's a little beauty." He wrapped the squalling baby in a flannel blanket and handed her to her father.

Chung studied the open mouth and flailing arms, the damp black hair, the tightly clenched eyes, and tiny nose, and a new kind of love he'd never experienced before seized him. He nestled the baby close to his chest, cradling her with one arm while he reached over to stroke Meichen's hair.

"It's all right," he soothed her, laughing over the lump in his throat. "Look at our daughter, Meichen."

Meichen shook her head. "My duty is to bear sons."

"And you will, one day. But it's good to have daughters, too. Just think, she'll have all the suitors she wants. America is full of lonely Chinese men, and some of them don't have wives in China."

Meichen's tears stopped and she looked at her baby for the first time. "You're not disappointed?" She searched his face.

"I'm very happy. And you should be, too." He kissed her cheek and tucked the infant in her arms. Then squaring his shoulders and grinning with pride, he went downstairs to announce the birth of his beautiful American daughter.

The End

AUTHOR'S NOTE

Most historians who describe the Chinese who lived in Augusta, Georgia, in the latter years of the nineteenth century never mention any women or children. Then I read "The Chinese in Augusta: A Historical Sketch," a paper written by Professor Thomas Ganschow, who taught history at the University of Georgia. He found written evidence that a Chinese woman and child were living in Augusta in 1894.

The Geary Act was passed by Congress in 1892. It required Chinese laborers in the United States to be photographed for identity papers. The Chinese people in Augusta were merchants, and thus exempted from the requirements of the law. Just to be safe, they all decided to register and be photographed. In 1894, Mr. Cobb (no first name given) arrived in Augusta. He had been hired by the state of Georgia to take the photographs. Fifty men showed up and one woman and her child.

I know nothing about this woman. What was her name? Was she married to one of the Chinese merchants? Why did she come to the United States when most wives were left behind in China? Did she have any education? How long did she live in Augusta? Was the baby born there? The mystery woman became my inspiration for Wu Meichen.

The registration forms collected by Mr. Cobb were filed in an Augusta government building. A fire destroyed the building and all the records it contained a few years later. Without Mr. Cobb's notes, the existence of the Chinese woman and child would never have been known.

Linda Harvill Strother
January 27, 2020

ACKNOWLEDGEMENTS

A thousand, thousand blessings on my fellow authors in CSRA Writers and my Beta Readers, Sue Rule and Ian Rule, who helped me in numerous ways and cheered me on as I wrote this book.

Thank you, Georgia Romance Writers, for my First Place Maggie Award. I really needed that stamp of approval.

For those readers who like to learn about the historical background of a novel, I recommend:

The Chinese in America by Iris Chang

God's Chinese Son: The Taiping Heavenly Kingdom of Hong Xiuqua by Jonathan Spence

The Great Chinese Revolution 1800-1985 by John King Fairbank

Chinese Proverbs and Popular Sayings with Observations on Culture and Language by Qin Xue Herzberg and Larry Herzberg

General Sherman's Girlfriend And Other Stories About Augusta by Edward J. Cashin has a chapter about Augusta's first Chinese residents.

Coming in August, 2020

The Story of Biyu